Isaac Asimov's I, Robot:
to preserve

Also by Mickey Zucker Reichert

Isaac Asimov's I, Robot: To Protect
Isaac Asimov's I, Robot: To Obey

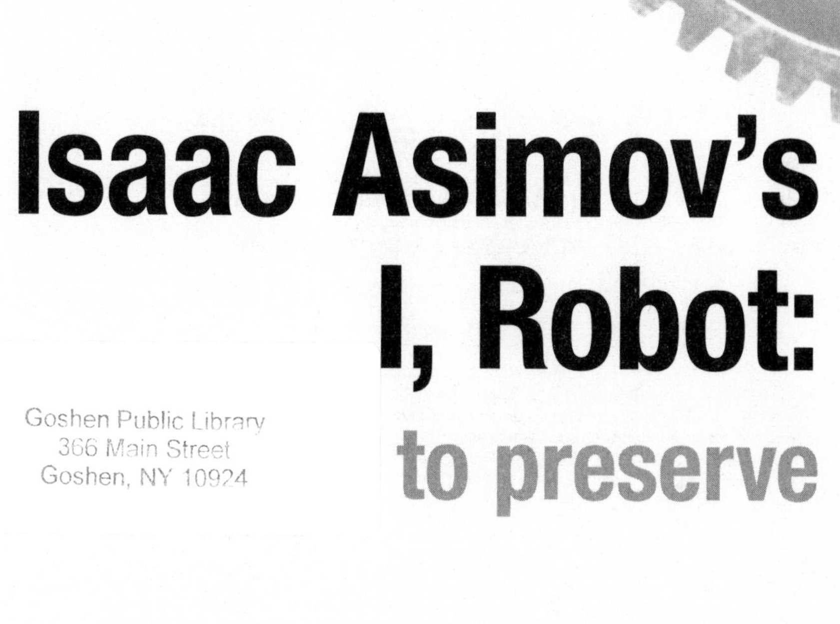

Isaac Asimov's I, Robot:

to preserve

MICKEY ZUCKER REICHERT

RoC
A ROC BOOK

ROC
Published by New American Library,
an imprint of Penguin Random House LLC
375 Hudson Street, New York, New York 10014

This book is an original publication of New American Library.

First Printing, February 2016

For more information about Penguin Random House, visit penguin.com.

LIBRARY OF CONGRESS CATALOGING-IN-PUBLICATION DATA:

Names: Reichert, Mickey Zucker.
Title: To preserve / Mickey Zucker Reichert.
Other titles: At head of title: Isaac Asimov's I, robot
Description: New York: Roc, 2016. | Series: I, robot; 3
Identifiers: LCCN 2015035294 | ISBN 9780451242303 (hardcover)
Subjects: LCSH: Robots—Fiction. | Murder—Investigation—Fiction. | BISAC: FICTION / Science Fiction / High Tech. | FICTION / Science Fiction / General. | GSAFD: Science fiction.
Classification: LCC PS3568.E476334 T625 2016 | DDC 813/.54—dc23 LC record available at https://protect-us.mimecast.com/s/EJGvBqc2YwLRIR

Printed in the United States of America
10 9 8 7 6 5 4 3 2 1

PUBLISHER'S NOTE
This is a work of fiction. Names, characters, places, and incidents either are the product of the author's imagination or are used fictitiously, and any resemblance to actual persons, living or dead, business establishments, events, or locales is entirely coincidental.

Penguin
Random
House

To Isaac Asimov,
who taught so many so much and entertained so many more.
It is an honor to walk in his footsteps.

Acknowledgments

I am, as always, grateful to Pat Rogers, chief warrant officer 3, U.S. Marine Corps (retired), sergeant NYPD (retired), who put up with, and answered, the types of questions that scare most sources away. Also to Sergeant Keith Romp, firearms training coordinator, Polk County Sheriff's Office, and assistant commander, Metro Tactical Unit. In addition, I want to thank Mike Fisher, vice president, Magtech.

I'm also grateful to my superlative editors: Susan Allison, Sheila Gilbert, and Marty Greenberg (posthumously, sigh).

To Mark Moore, my anchor, confidant, and a genius in his own right. I am truly blessed.

And, as always, to Janet and Robyn Asimov. Thank you!

Susan Calvin has hyperspace where her heart ought to be and liquid helium in her eyes. She'd pass through the sun and come out the other side encased in ice.

–Nigel Ronson, Interplanetary Press,
from Isaac Asimov's *I, Robot*

Isaac Asimov's I, Robot:

to preserve

Chapter 1

September 1, 2037

The brightly lit hallways, cheery blue walls, and one-way mirrors of Manhattan Hasbro Hospital's Pediatric Inpatient Psychiatry Unit had changed little in the two years and two months since Susan Calvin had begun her psychiatry residency. But it was the smell that brought the memories flooding back, a combination of musty basement, standard hospital cleansers, and art supplies that defined the unit affectionately called the PIPU. Susan doubted she would have recognized herself as the fresh young intern who had walked through these same sequentially locked doors on July 2, 2035. Then, uncertainties had consumed her. She had worried about her diagnostic acumen, her observational skills, and her inexperience, which might result in a misdiagnosis and suffering or death for a patient.

Now that all seemed like childish naïveté. Since beginning her psychiatry residency, Susan had lost her father and the love of her life to murder, survived two explosions, and watched helplessly as the policeman who had defied orders to assist her sustained severe head trauma. Not only had Susan witnessed the violent killings of healthy people; she had even shot a man herself. The life-and-death routine of the hospital no longer seemed so dire, and she sought nothing more than the quiet reality of everyday diagnosis and treatment, preferably with cures. If she never experienced another extreme emotion, positive or negative, she would consider herself the luckiest woman in the world.

Susan headed for the central staffing area, hoping she would find it quiet, at least for the next half hour. The Vox on her wrist read 2:19 p.m. The fresh group of medical residents and the staff psychiatrist should be completing afternoon rounds. The nurses would be assisting patients or busily charting before the next shift arrived. This time, Susan had come to the PIPU to acquaint herself with the patients who would become her charges the following morning, when she officially took her place as head resident on the unit.

As she passed, Susan glanced at the array of artwork taped to the cinder-block walls. Though clearly intended to personalize and cheer the otherwise bleak hallways, they filled Susan with a sense of foreboding instead. Simple black-and-white images intermingled with intensely complicated paintings with colored swirls, flowers, and flourishes filling every bit of the page. Intricately detailed roses in rainbow vases perched beside bulbous, scribbled monsters or slashes of color that resembled nothing in nature. One piece consisted entirely of six small blue dots confined to a single corner of the page.

For continuity, the senior resident, the R-3, remained on PIPU rotation for three days after the arrival of the new attending, five first-year R-1s, and one R-2. When he had passed the mantle of supervising PIPU resident to Susan earlier that day, Monk Peterson had given her a brief summary of the current patients, some of whom he had covered for his entire month and others who had arrived during that time: three teenagers with brain damage from drug use, a kindergartner with hysterical blindness, four schizophrenics with inadequate responses to medications, two youngsters with psychotic depression, one with post-psychotic syndrome after resectioning of an astrocytoma, and six with severe conduct disorder deemed dangerous to caregivers or society at large.

The last group bothered Susan the most. They reminded her of Sharicka Anson, one of the youngest known children with antisocial personality disorder in the history of medicine, and also one of her first patients. The bomb Sharicka had detonated in a shopping mall had killed Remington Hawthorn, Susan's beloved, as well as a security guard who had tried to stop him from leaping upon what appeared to be an innocent preschooler. Remington had sacrificed his life to spare Susan's and those of the nearby shoppers. *A hero,* Susan reminded herself for the millionth time, but could not help adding bitterly, *a* dead *hero.*

One of the few people with a key to the locked Pediatrics Inpatient Psychiatry Unit, Susan had not needed anyone to escort her through the doors. As she entered the staffing area, a bubble of one-way mirrors, she found one first-year neurosurgical resident, probably following up on the astrocytoma resection, and five nurses quietly finishing their shift duties. The R-1, a tall and slender woman, diligently typed notes into a palm-pross computer. She seemed to take no notice of Susan's discreet entrance. However, a willowy blond nurse Susan knew as Saranne squealed out, "Dr. Calvin!"

In a flash, Susan found herself surrounded by nurses, male and female, some crushing her into embraces, others standing with smiles plastered on their faces or calling encouragement to her. They remembered her for the "lifers" she had diagnosed and discharged in her R-1 year and for standing up to a neurosurgeon who considered himself the "greatest in the world." They knew what had happened to Susan subsequently, the deaths of Remington and her father, the struggle to make up the grieving time missed from residency so that she could enter her R-3 year only a month or two behind her peers.

Susan had to struggle to return their greetings with a wan smile, to mouth the appropriate platitudes. She felt wrung out, physically and mentally, and the exuberance with which she had greeted her first rotation so long ago seemed misplaced, the life of another woman in a parallel universe. She almost appreciated it when her Vox, and those of everyone around her, beeped wildly in an emergency tone. A man's calm voice intoned in megastereo: "Code Blue, seventh floor Hassenfeld Research Tower, room 713. Code Blue, seventh floor Hassenfeld Research Tower, room 713."

For a moment, Susan's heart stopped beating. Vertigo assailed her, and it took inordinately long for her brain to comprehend the words. *Code Blue: cardiopulmonary arrest.* Pain flashed through her chest, eliciting a sharp cough; then her heart started pounding again. She did not usually respond to emergencies so viscerally. In the past, she had most often been the calmest person in the room. Only then, the last part of the call reached logical consciousness. *Room 713. Cody Peters and Ari Goldman's lab.*

Susan shook off her well-wishers so abruptly that one gasped and some had to catch their balance on various desks and chairs. Susan found herself running down the hallway, spinning to miss a gawking child, and nearly careened into the locked unit door. She fumbled the key from her pocket and stabbed it into the lock.

The delay allowed one of the nurses to catch up to her. "Dr. Calvin, where are you going?"

The question seemed absurd. Every health-care worker knew a Code Blue required the attention of anyone nearby with advanced cardiac life-support training. The lock clicked, and Susan slammed her body against the heavy door, jarring it open enough to slip through. Trusting the nurse to keep any patients from leaving with her, Susan rushed down the bare gray hallway to the second locked door, key still clutched in her fingers.

The nurse's voice chased her through the closing gap. "You're a psychiatrist! There're closer physicians with more code training."

Now full understanding struck Susan. If every trained staff member arrived at the scene of every Code Blue, they would fill the room and all the surrounding hallways. Only those nearby needed to respond, particularly those on crash-cart units: Cardiology, ICU, Pulmonary. Yet Susan did not even pause as she thrust the key into the second door lock and shoved through it into the bleak hallways of the lowest level of Manhattan Hasbro Hospital.

Susan knew the way without having to consider it. She had walked the route in both directions multiple times while working on this same unit two years before. Drs. Goldman and Peters had requested her assistance with a research project that used nanorobots injected into the cerebrospinal fluid of patients with resistant psychoses. Manhattan Hasbro's lead researchers had collaborated on dozens of studies and articles in all the major psychiatry journals, and Susan had considered herself lucky to work with them, even if only at the "scut" level. Eventually she discovered they had chosen her mostly because of her father's association with United States Robots and Mechanical Men, Inc.

Another alert shocked across Susan's Vox. "Code Silver, Hassenfeld Research Tower, room 713. Code Silver, Hassenfeld Research Tower, room 713."

Thoughts of John Calvin brought tears to Susan's eyes, and her focus on him stole details from the emergency call. She had loved her father with a loyalty that knew only the boundaries of propriety. She had never met a man kinder or wiser, gentler or more intelligent; no one could have served as a better guide and guardian. For so many years, she had believed him to be the epitome of humanity, only to discover at his death that he had never been human at all.

Had Susan not been racing through the corridors at top speed, weaving in and out of the hordes of patients, staff, and visitors, she might have realized two different types of codes had been called to the same room, one blue and one silver. She might have noticed the different colors flickering back and forth across her Vox display, might have observed the hesitation of most of the staff to rush to the scene, and would certainly not have knocked the crutch out from under a surgical patient with an enormous medical boot on his left foot.

As Susan crossed from the main hospital to the research wing, she found that she no longer had to dodge patients and that most of the traffic was headed in the same direction. Images of Drs. Peters and Goldman replaced those of her father. Cody Peters, tall and skinny, with auburn hair and a crooked nose, had a sharp wit, friendly voice and features, and dangerous inattentiveness. In direct contrast, Goldman was dour and impatient, older than Peters, meticulous and detail focused. Despite their differences, they formed a solid team that had lasted for nearly twenty years and boasted many of the greatest breakthroughs in psychiatric medicine.

Susan forced herself to consider the situation logically. Just because the emergency had occurred in their laboratory did not necessarily make Goldman or Peters the victim. Hundreds of scientists worked in the tower, and they walked freely in and out of one another's rooms. Visitors, reporters, superiors, and curious health-care workers checked on the status of interesting research all the time. Perhaps the fumes from some haphazardly mixed chemicals had caused a maintenance worker to collapse, striking his or her head on one of the many tables. More likely, an elderly man or woman had succumbed to a cerebrovascular accident or a myocardial infarction, the location of the occurrence of his or her malady nothing more than strange coincidence.

Arriving in Hassenfeld Research Tower, Susan ignored the elevators, charging up the concrete stairs instead. Notwithstanding the likelihood of her currently imagined scenario, she knew it was wrong with the same sickening certainty that had struck her when she had discovered police barricades at her apartment building in July of the previous year.

Despite the Independence Day holiday, her father should have been at work. He had headed for USR that morning, and Susan had no reason to believe he would have left there early. Yet he had; and she had known with an unshakeable dread that he was the reason the police had cordoned off their building. Now Susan knew, without need for further consideration: Something terrible had happened to Ari Goldman, Cody Peters, or both.

A third alarm shrilled over Susan's Vox. "Code Blue, Hassenfeld Research Tower, room 713. Code Silver, Hassenfeld Research Tower, room 713."

The proximity of the two similar but different calls finally struck Susan. *Code Silver? What the hell is a Code Silver?* Like most hospitals, Hasbro used colors to designate different scenarios in order to alert staff without alarming patients and visitors. She could pop up a cheat sheet on her Vox, but that would require her to focus on something other than her wild flight up the tower staircase and the sense of dread overtaking her. A misstep might cause her to plummet down several flights of metal and concrete steps.

Instead, Susan ran the possibilities through her mind. There was some basic logic to the color codes, though they varied among hospitals: blue for lack of blood flow, red for fire, pink for infant abduction, black for severe weather. During medical school and residency, she had attended her share of cardiopulmonary arrests, but never once had she heard another code called. She searched her mind for anything silver might stand for and why it might get called at the same time and place as a Code Blue.

Silver. Susan reached the seventh-floor landing all but breathless, feeling as if she might require pulmonary resuscitation herself. *Metal? Metal object?* She burst through the fire door into a hallway filled with milling, whispering medical personnel and at least two portable crash carts. *Gun?* Gasping from the top-speed climb, she staggered into the hallway. Blood seemed to drain from her body just when she needed it most. *Not another shooting. Please, God, not another shooting!*

More than a year had passed since Susan's last ordeal. She had thought everything was settled, that the police and the Department of Defense had crippled the Society for Humanity, the SFH, beyond resurrection, that the secret governmental agency she knew by the code name Cadmium had given up on trying to weaponize positronic robots. Susan rushed toward the familiar research laboratory, barely noticing the staff she shoved aside in her haste.

Finally, someone caught her elbow. An unfamiliar voice hissed into her ear. "Doctor, wait. Code Silver: combative person with a weapon!"

Susan tore free of the other's grip. Code Blue meant someone potentially salvageable, probably a victim of assault, and she would not allow them to die for lack of aid. Especially if the attack had anything to do with positronic robots. Anything to do with her. *This was over. Finished! No one else was supposed to die!*

Susan no longer cared if she shoved through the crowd too forcefully, if she stepped on any toes. This was no time for timidity or curiosity. Looky-loos could only delay the action necessary to defuse a mortal situation, to rescue a patient in deadly crisis.

Seconds passed like eternities before Susan found herself peering through the open door of the Psychiatry Laboratory, along with so many others. The four large laboratory tables, pushed together, still filled most of the interior, but now a body sprawled across them. Five brave or foolhardy volunteers worked around it, one swearing viciously as he attempted to insert an endotracheal tube while blood saturated his rubber gloves, pants, and shoes. A mature male nurse hovered around him, clutching an electronic breathing device, an EBD, that had replaced Ambu bags shortly before Susan had started her training.

The resident attempting the intubation fully blocked Susan's view of the victim's face, but the formal clothing and sturdy form suggested Ari Goldman. Cody Peters was taller and painfully lean, and Susan already intuitively knew it had to be one of the brilliant researchers lying, limp and supine, on those research tables.

Another resident slapped at the victim's extremities, seeking a hint of vein open enough to accept an intravenous catheter. A stubby surgical resident in scrubs tore open a sterile cut-down tray while an ICU nurse attended a crash cart, blindly handing out requested items, her hands moving from habit, her attention glued to the farthest corner of the room.

There, several hospital security officers in pale green uniforms pinned a giant of a man, wearing neat but casual clothing, against one of the walls. The security officers kept exchanging glances, as if they had no real idea of what to do next. Their quarry did not appear to resist in any way, standing stone still and making no sound while three sets of beefy hands pressed his face and upper body against the cement blocks. Susan caught sight of a bloody tool lying on the floor near their feet, possibly a wrench or a hammer. Apparently it, not a gun, was the "silver" portion of the code.

The perpetrator was taller and younger than his captors, physically fit, and probably capable of overpowering them despite their numbers and bulk. Hospital security did not carry guns, either; and they looked too nervous to maintain control without police backup, even with their quarry disarmed and cooperative, at least for the moment. That explained why so many of the health-care workers hung back, afraid to enter the room. The doctors and nurses could have returned to work, but curiosity held them in place, clogging the hallways and making it more difficult for those dedicated to the resuscitation despite the danger.

Susan took in all of this as she rushed to assist, without hesitation. By the expanding pool at the intubator's feet and the pallor of Ari's skin, Susan could tell he had lost a significant amount of blood. Appropriately, the nurse abandoned her efforts at intravenous catheter placement and started prepping a tibia for intraosseous access. The surgeon had the sterile tray open and clearly planned a central line. An emergency pacemaker perched on Ari's chest like some outlandish space alien, pumping timed electrical pulses to his heart at eighty beats per minute. The circulatory system was reasonably under control, so Susan turned her focus to assisting airway and breathing.

The resident attempting the intubation stepped back, still clutching the slimy plastic ET tube in one hand and the metal laryngoscope in the other. The male nurse clamped the EBD to Ari's face, and it pulsed oxygen into his mouth and nose, raising his oximetry reading from a dangerous sixty-eight to a somewhat less dangerous eighty-two. Sweat slicked the intubator's forehead, and a comma of sandy hair had slid into his eyes. He tossed his head to free it, without success.

Susan brushed it aside for him, then slipped on a pair of gloves. "Need help?"

Soft dark eyes met Susan's steely gray, and she read frustration and a trace of guilty hope. He would have liked nothing better than to hand the onerous job to someone else. "I'm usually great at this," he said, "but this one's not going to happen. Can't position the head right with . . ." He made a broad gesture that forced Susan to look directly at the facial features for the first time. Until that moment, she did not realize she had been avoiding it, knowing but not truly wanting to know. The lined features, broad nose, and weathered and gruff countenance, even so near death, defined Ari Goldman. The coarse brown hair was clotted with blood and no longer fell in neat waves across his scalp.

Something had struck the back of Ari's skull with a force so brutal it had smashed through some of the densest bone in human anatomy, tearing a chunk free along with the dura mater, creating a hole that emitted copious amounts of blood and left the brain wholly unprotected–and visible. Susan had seen some horrific sights, particularly in the last couple of years, but nothing compared with this. She wanted to scream and vomit simultaneously but forced herself not to react at all, focusing instead on studying the wound with her usual professionalism. There was direct and deliberate damage to the brain tissue; and, no doubt, the impact had sheared it from the brain stem. Even if they resuscitated Dr. Ari Goldman, he would, at best, be respirator- and pacemaker-dependent, paralyzed, and unlikely to think at more than an animal level. Better, she thought, to let him die with whatever small dignity remained to him.

Susan's mind flashed back to the heart-pounding moment when homicide detective Jake Carson had abruptly fired several rounds into an obviously dead enemy. The cop had called it a "nonstandard response" or NSRing, explaining that "anyone worth shooting once was worth shooting seven times." She knew she was seeing the head-bashing equivalent of an NSR, overkill in its most literal sense. The perpetrator had taken the time and energy to assure that Ari Goldman would not survive the attack.

Susan also understood her fellow resident's frustration. In order to visualize the anatomy of the throat and get the tube down the proper hole, he needed to tip Ari's head backward. However, in this case, he could not risk doing so without causing more damage or further contaminating the open wound. Placing an endotracheal tube under normal circumstances was difficult. Blind, it required the expertise of a long-practiced anesthesiologist with specialized instruments. In this situation, it was impossible.

"He's going to need a cricothyrotomy," Susan pointed out dully. She almost hoped the other resident would refuse. In Ari's position, Susan would rather die.

The surgeon sang out, "I'm on it." He snapped off the gloves he had used for the central line and addressed the crash-cart nurse. "Crike tray." Like most of his ilk, he relished procedures, especially ones he rarely got to perform.

The nurse dragged her attention from the security officers to the drawers, seeking the proper equipment.

Though only four years ago, it seemed like an eternity since Susan had performed her surgical rotation. She could still remember Dr. Stephen Coppinger's admonition verbatim: "When it comes to brain trauma, never give up. Sometimes, the goriest open injuries are surgically manageable while what appears grossly normal may hide a fatal bleed." It was not for the medical team to decide what the neurosurgeons could piece together, but Susan knew Dr. Coppinger's words referred to a specific phenomenon that did not apply here. The fatality of head trauma usually stemmed from an increase in intracranial pressure that crushed or damaged the tissue. An open wound allowed space for swollen tissues to expand, eliminating the need for emergent burr holes. Every instinct told her they could not salvage any significant portion of Ari Goldman's cerebral cortex, but she knew they had to try.

Nothing else mattered, Susan realized, if they could not stop the bleeding. It did no good to oxygenate empty vessels or stimulate a heart devoid of blood flow. Yet how to do so eluded her. Neither direct pressure nor styptics seemed feasible in a situation involving exposed and scrambled brain tissue. It would only invite infection, which would adversely affect whatever positive outcome remained. She had no real choice. Antibiotics might forestall infection, but at the moment only direct pressure against the scalp could prevent him from bleeding out. Grabbing handfuls of gauze, she set to the task.

The other medical physician tossed the gory endotracheal tube into a hole in the crash cart meant for potentially biohazardous garbage. Clearly relieved to abandon his hopeless task for something more constructive, he began the proper calls for fluids and stimulants, forcing the cart nurse to attend him and the surgeon simultaneously. Both hands clutching gauze against flesh, Susan turned her attention back to hospital security. She had lost track of them in the need to assist with medical procedures, and she knew Jake would denigrate her for what could have been a fatal lapse.

A well-muscled, uniformed policeman came through the door, accompanied by a stocky female officer who stood a few inches taller. Both sported crew cuts, the man's straw blond and the woman's almost black. They bore an air of confidence and authority that drew nearly every eye. The woman barked out, "What do you got?" to the hospital security detail.

The three kept their hands on the man pinned to the wall, while the others turned to face the police. One of the latter spoke. "He assaulted somebody." He made a vague gesture toward Ari Goldman and the working medical staff.

The male officer moved with a speed that belied his bulk, snapping handcuffs onto the unresisting man pressed against the wall. That simple, effective action seemed to bring down the level of urgency a hundredfold, despite the dying man stretched across several laboratory tables. The cop spoke directly to the perpetrator, though Susan could not hear what he said. Only then, Susan realized how tall the subdued man was; the top of the male cop's head barely reached his shoulder. There had to be a foot of difference between them. No doubt, the policeman was relatively short, perhaps five foot six or five foot seven, but it also meant the would-be killer was colossal.

Six foot six. Six foot seven. The same height as my father. A thought intruded. *The same height as Nate.* Susan remembered hearing something about how the size of the positronic brain required a larger head and, proportionately, a taller body in order to appear appropriately human.

Susan clutched tighter to the gauze, pressing it fiercely against the lacerated edges of scalp. The brain itself felt no pain, had no significant bleeding. *A robot may not injure a human being or, through inaction, allow a human being to come to harm.* It was the First Law of Robotics: supreme, inviolate. No matter how right her intuition had been about her father, about Ari Goldman, Susan's current abstraction was madness. She knew no positronic robot could so much as deliberately scratch a man's arm, let alone club him with a household tool. No matter if it seethed with rage, no matter the circumstances, no matter who commanded it, no positronic robot or programmer could circumvent the First Law.

This had become all too clear the previous year. Falsely believing her parents had a code that could inactivate the Three Laws of Robotics, the Society for Humanity had murdered them when Susan was only four years old. Just last year, they had discovered John Calvin still living and slaughtered him a second time, unaware they had actually destroyed a positronic robot USR had created to replace him. Under the same misapprehension, a Department of Defense Intelligence Exploitation Agency, code name Cadmium, had hounded Susan and her companions in an attempt to wrest the same information from her with the intention of weaponizing robots.

Suddenly, the monitor alarm shrilled. Gasps startled from several onlookers, the police whirled, and Susan stiffened so abruptly, pain lanced through every muscle.

"Damn it!" The surgeon ripped off his soiled gloves and threw them on the table before stabbing off the alarm. The display recorded the regular zaps of the portable pacemaker, but the heart itself was sending off crazily irregular and tiny blips. The oximeter reading was falling fast, currently in the twenty percent range. The cricothyrotomy was finished, and the male nurse held the EBD against the opening, flushing it with pulses of one hundred percent oxygen, to no avail.

The medical resident who moved from attempting intubation to leading the code waved the others away from Ari Goldman's limp body. "Stop ACLS." The nurse shut off the pacemaker, and the heart rate dropped almost instantly to zero. The oximeter blinked, searching for a nonexistent pulse. The leader glanced at his Vox. "Time of death: two thirty-four p.m."

The male policeman's voice broke the sudden, tense hush as he addressed his partner. "Call homicide." Seizing the cuffed man by the upper arm, he turned him from the wall to reveal the familiar features of N8-C, the eighth in the NC line, the robotic friend and confidant Susan knew as Nate.

Chapter 2

Half an hour later, Susan found herself pleading her case in the office of Aloise Savage, the chairman of the psychiatry residency program. In his sixties, the lanky psychiatrist paced the area between his leather desk chair and a wall covered in large, slowly changing pictures of his family. Susan could not help noticing that the route he trod showed dull wear while the rest of the green expanse of carpet appeared practically new. She sat in one of two folding chairs that resembled tiny trampolines. She had anticipated feeling as if she perched precariously on a bouncy table, but the seat molded to fit her hips and buttocks in a proper, and strangely comfortable, sitting position. She clutched at the metal tubing, seized by a similar need to pace but not wanting to appear to be mocking him or trying to engage in a silent parody of musical chairs.

"Susan, we all deeply respected Dr. Goldman. I'm planning to attend the funeral, and I'll bring as much of the staff as possible, in shifts, if necessary. But that's not going to be for a few days, at least."

Susan knew Jews followed a principle called *k'vot hamet*, honoring the dead, which meant they had to bury a corpse as soon as possible. Dr. Goldman himself had described it to her when his mother-in-law had passed away. Susan also did not mention that most of the residents, and probably a good portion of the staff, had only known the researcher as a name at the top of multiple articles. She had worked with him, had gotten to know and appreciate him personally. "You don't understand, sir. Dr. Goldman's death is a terrible tragedy, in all senses of the word, but that's not why I need the rest of the afternoon off. It's Nate."

"Nate?" Aloise pulled at his beard. "Who's Nate?"

"Nate. N8-C. Hasbro's resident robot."

Aloise stopped cold. He turned to face Susan directly. "What are you talking about?"

The spottiness of the knowledge of Hasbro's humanoid positronic robot worker never ceased to surprise Susan. According to Lawrence Robertson, CEO and founder of United States Robots and Mechanical Men, Nate had quietly come to work at Hasbro some two decades previously, a prototype intended to accustom staff and patients to the possibility of anthropomorphic robots. Due to what John Calvin had labeled the "Frankenstein Complex," staff and visitors had, instead, mostly become terrified of the idea, and protesters from the Society for Humanity had joined the teeming mass that always haunted the entryways of progressive hospitals open to cutting-edge, and often politically dangerous, technology. That forced Nate to keep a low profile, the idea being that his origins would seep out slowly, after people had become used to his presence. A handful of the Hasbro staff regularly worked closely with Nate, but for the most part he was as invisible and unknown as any filing clerk.

Susan realized she had made a strategic miscalculation, but, having come this far, could only plunge onward. "Sir, Nate has become a close friend and confidant of mine. He's gotten me through the worst of times, and you know how hard I've had it the last couple of years."

Aloise's features softened. "Of course, Susan. And *you* know we've made a lot of allowances for that."

Susan could not deny she had missed a significant amount of time due to circumstances beyond her control. The schedule of a medical resident did not allow for vacations or sick days. If they took off, even for an hour, someone had to cover for them; and that someone was normally another resident with just as little free time. Susan had done everything she could to make up the time she had lost, to the point where she felt as if she lived at Manhattan Hasbro Hospital, much more so than in her new apartment with its sparse furnishings. She had not been able to return to the apartment she had shared with her father, the scene of his murder, where the walls had gotten smashed and everything they owned cut into pieces in the search for the mythical Three Laws' uncoupling code.

"Yes," Susan acknowledged. "And I do appreciate everything. But Nate . . . is in trouble. He's confused and terrified. He has more book knowledge than anyone, but he doesn't know much about police procedure, his rights—"

"His rights?" Aloise repeated, still stroking his beard. A light flickered through his eyes, then blazed. "His rights! You mean . . . he's the killer? You want me to grant you time off to assuage . . . the murderer of . . . of . . . ?" A mixture of warning and confusion filled his voice. He shook his head. "That can't be what you're asking." He ambled to his chair and dropped into it, his head weaving side to side as if to rattle loose the logic in his own suggestion.

Susan did not want to waste time discussing the matter. "Sir, Nate didn't kill anyone. His programming wouldn't allow it. But they believe he did, and he needs me."

Aloise only stared. "Susan," he started, then stopped. He sighed deeply, and she wondered if he was about to question her sanity. During his time at Hasbro, he must have heard rumors of the possibility of a robot among them, even if he had no idea how human it appeared. "Susan, your request is denied. Your rightful place is on the PIPU. As much as you think this Nate needs you, we need you more. And you can't afford to miss any more days."

Susan bit her lower lip, her mind drifting back to the times she had relied on Nate, first for friendship and companionship, then for support. John Calvin had always been her anchor in the most turbulent times, a role model as well as the best father she could ever imagine anyone having. Now he was gone, and the nearest thing to him, the eighth in the "New Calvin" line, one of only two remaining humanoid positronic robots, needed her. If her absence for half a day meant the possible deaths of one or more patients, she would have faced a difficult choice. "Sir, I'm sorry, but I'm not asking. Nate needs my help immediately, and I'm going to assist him."

Aloise Savage fairly hissed. Clearly, no mere resident had ever spoken to him in this manner. "You're not leaving until your shift is over and all your work is done." He rose, towering behind his desk.

Susan also stood. "I'm leaving," she said calmly but firmly, then headed for the door.

He called after her. "You do, and you're finished. You'll no longer be a resident at this facility."

Her back to the room, Susan stopped, stiffened. Her mind wandered to her first two years of medical school: the long difficult days in histology, anatomy, and biochemistry, returning, reeking of formaldehyde, to the tiny apartment she shared with various roommates, to study until bedtime every night. The latter half of her academics, where she had worked as slave labor, night and day, for aloof attendings who barely bothered with their residents and saw the medical students as lesser beings to ignore or torture. A standing joke was to ask the difference between medical students and dog crap, the answer being that no one goes out of their way to step on the poop. Chronic sleep deprivation, endless demands, grueling and constant testing had defined the clinical years of medical school, years that had sometimes seemed like decades.

Susan had survived those trying times by throwing herself into her work, ignoring conventional entertainments and focusing entirely on matters of the intellect, honing her powers of observation and puzzle-solving abilities at the expense of a social life. Someday, she had believed, it would all pay off, molding her into a stellar diagnostician, a shining beacon of caring and knowledge who would use her brilliance selflessly to cure the sick and injured, bring wholeness to the suffering, and solace to the few she could not save.

In Susan's fantasies, her residency was full of intellectually gifted physicians of great experience who would gently guide her, as her father always had, toward the vast wisdom and knowledge that defined the medical field. Instead, she had found them all too human, with the same immaturities, laziness, and foolishness as their less gifted counterparts and a system awash in politics and jealousies. Like posturing professional athletes, they competed on an intellectual level and, instead of working together, hid their foibles, protected their discoveries, and hoarded accolades like finite treasures. Too many belittled their peers to bolster their own appearances.

The tribulations of the last two years had broken Susan's protective cocoon of naïveté. She saw with clear eyes the cruelty men inflicted on one another, and it reinforced her already-strong belief in evolution and science. Clearly, survival of the fittest had brought the human race to its current position. If mankind had a creator, he would have made them better, cleaner, more rational. More positronic. Nate, Susan realized, meant more to her than anyone. Being unable to complete her last year of residency did not negate her studies and training.

A smile eased onto Susan's face, accompanied by a strange calm that ill fit the situation. Wordlessly, she turned and approached Aloise's desk. Dipping a hand into her pocket, she retrieved a sheaf of patient cards, the ones that allowed her to vend various medical products and assure they were billed to the proper account. She dropped these onto the desk, then the key to the PIPU. Everything else in her possession belonged to her. She raised her chin to look the head of the psychiatry residency program in the eyes. "I'm leaving," she announced. "I'll be back during the week to clean out my locker and complete any necessary paperwork."

Dr. Aloise Savage simply stared back, jaw sagging in silent shock. Apparently, no one had ever voluntarily left her residency before, at least not so close to the end.

Susan did not wait for him to find his voice, whisking into the hallway and out of Manhattan Hasbro Hospital.

The NYPD Nineteenth Precinct resembled the Tenth, which had investigated the murder of Susan's father: two-toned walls, a bank of computer monitors and people encased behind glass, and the tang of sweat and fear and camaraderie. Susan approached the least dour of them, a uniformed woman with shoulder-length, straight blond hair and well-trimmed bangs. The woman stopped typing and looked up. "How can I help you?"

Susan drew in a deep breath. She had considered her phraseology during the short glide-bus ride to the station, but nothing had seemed adequate to explain the situation. "My name is Susan Calvin. I'm a physician at Manhattan Hasbro Hospital." *Was,* she reminded herself but did not voice it. "I was part of the resuscitation team for Ari Goldman, the man killed in the research tower."

The woman sat up straighter, granting Susan her full attention. "Yes, ma'am."

"We were told to come or call if we had any useful information about the crime."

The woman stood. She was several inches taller than Susan, and the doctor had to raise her head to continue the conversation. "The officers on the scene are still conducting interviews. Why didn't you stay there, ma'am?"

"Because they asked specifically for anyone who might have witnessed the event, and a hundred people got there ahead of me." Though truth, it was not the full explanation. Susan had no idea who on the scene, if anyone, might know about Nate. To most, quite probably all, he appeared to be a total stranger, inconceivably anything other than human. Susan felt certain the police would find no direct witnesses to the crime itself. Nate could not have done it, and everyone seemed convinced he had. All of them, security, doctors, and nurses alike, had come in response to the code, necessarily after the attack.

The woman's brows knitted. "But you feel you have something else to add?" she guessed.

"Definitely." Susan did not go into details. She did not want to have to explain herself twice, and the likelihood that this woman was directly involved with the case was minuscule.

"Just a moment." The woman did something below counter level. A door behind her buzzed open, and she disappeared through it. It automatically slammed closed behind her, revealing its heaviness.

Susan pressed her hands to the counter and waited. When she lifted her fingers, she could see where her palms had left sweaty prints.

Soon, the door reopened, and the woman gestured for Susan to follow. The doctor stepped around the counter and through the door. Again, it slammed closed, this time behind Susan, and she trailed the woman through grungy corridors to an office. Inside, a man who appeared to be only a few years older than Susan sat behind a desk that held a palm-pross computer, several stick-e-drives, a stapler, a caddy of random office supplies, and framed pictures of an infant. There was also a nameplate identifying him as Detective Diondre Riviera III. The room contained two other chairs of the folding variety. He waved gruffly, and the woman stepped aside so Susan could enter the room.

The detective pointed Susan to a chair. Susan flashed back to when she first met Detective Jake Carson. At that time, she had been so angry the police had dared label her father's obvious murder as death by natural causes, she had refused to sit. This time, she seized one of the folding chairs, slid it toward the desk to place her directly in front of Diondre Riviera III, and plunked herself down on it. She met his gaze levelly, finding his eyes dark and strangely soulful for a cop.

"What can I do for you, Ms. Calhoun?"

"Dr. Calvin," Susan corrected. She might never finish her residency, but she maintained the title she had earned forever. "Dr. Susan Calvin." He might recognize the name. Though her father's murder, and the explosions the previous year, had occurred outside of this precinct, many detectives kept abreast of such developments, even in a city as large, complex, and populous as New York.

If he did, he gave no sign. "Dr. Calvin. You have some information about the hospital murder?" He leaned forward. "Did you witness it?"

"No," Susan admitted, then added, "No one did. We all came running when the codes were called."

The detective encouraged Susan to continue. "Codes?"

Susan explained, "The Code Blue brought the doctors and medical teams. The Code Silver brought security. I'm guessing security got there first because silver indicates an assailant with a weapon. That slowed a lot of the medical personnel down; no one wants to die trying to save a patient who might already be dead." She added only in her mind, *Unlike cops, we're neither heroes nor adrenaline junkies.*

The detective probably already knew about the codes, but he latched onto something more pertinent. "You said no one witnessed the murder."

Susan wondered if he would notice that. She had said it as much for herself as him. "No one could have. Or else security wouldn't have taken an innocent into custody. The police would be chasing down the killer."

"Ah," Detective Riviera said, the sound worthy of any psychiatrist. It revealed nothing. "So . . . you believe we have the wrong perp." He added belatedly, "Dr. Calvin." A glint appeared in the otherwise soft, dark eyes.

"Yes."

Detective Riviera rested knobby, coffee-colored elbows on the desktop. "Let me guess. You're a close friend, perhaps a relative, of the perpetrator and know for a fact he could never have committed any crime, let alone one as heinous as murder."

Susan sighed. "I'm sure you hear that every case." She made it clear she understood. "Sociopaths are astoundingly astute at hiding their true natures from those they rely upon. They have a knack for making themselves appear victimized when they are, in fact, vicious predators." She could not help thinking of four-year-old Sharicka Anson.

The detective tipped his head, studying her like a praying mantis. "It seems even cannibalistic serial killers love their mothers."

He had it backward. The mothers loved their psychopathic children and blinded themselves to the faults, no matter how perverted or cruel. "My point being," Susan started, "that this is not the case of a girlfriend or parent with the wool pulled over her eyes. Nate is innocent because he is literally incapable of violence. He is constrained by–"

The detective did not allow Susan to finish. "His name is Nate? As in Nathan? Nathaniel?"

"Nate," Susan said, "as in N8-C."

The detective grabbed a pen and a piece of paper. "Is See his last name? Or a middle initial?"

"It is neither." Susan plucked another pen from the desk set and eased the scrap of blank paper from underneath his palm. She wrote on it. "The letter N, the number 8, dash, the letter C." She scrawled it out properly. "The eighth in the NC line. Detective Riviera, Nate is a positronic robot. As such, he is wholly constrained from violence against a human being by virtue of the First Law."

The detective only stared at Susan. She could have transmuted into a talking dog, and he would not have looked more bewildered. "What?"

"The Three Laws of Robotics are integral to the positronic brain. It can't function without them."

Detective Diondre Riviera shook his head as if to clear it. "Is this . . . some sort of . . . conspiracy theory?"

Susan continued as if he had not spoken, "The First Law states: 'A robot may not injure a human being or, through inaction, allow a human being to come to harm.' Ipso facto, Nate cannot be your killer."

The detective was still several steps behind Susan. "Wait. Are you saying the man we took into custody is . . . a robot?"

"Yes." Susan could not believe she had to start over. "Didn't he tell you that?"

The detective shook his head harder. "We haven't gotten him to say anything yet. He just sits there with a dazed expression."

"He's probably terrified," Susan explained. "He may have witnessed the murder." A sudden realization hit her. "He's probably the one who called the codes." Still driven by the need to help him, she added, "Where is he? Can I talk to him?"

"He's in the holding cell, and we need to talk to him first." The detective studied Susan as if for the first time. Her presence, she knew, was unimpressive. She was average in height, skinny and curveless, with stick-straight dark hair and icy eyes. Her features were not particularly attractive, at least judging from the lack of men pursuing her; and she had never bothered to learn to apply makeup. The detective's expression changed abruptly from confusion to suspicion. His gaze grew more intense. "Dr. Calvin, I've seen robots and I've seen men. I've spent nearly an hour trying to get the person in that cell to speak with me. He is, in fact, human."

"Human stem cells coaxed into a dermal and muscular system grown over a skeleton of porous silicone plastic."

"What?"

Susan had spoken that description before, the same one Nate had used when he first met her. This time, she thought about it in a different light. "I suppose, theoretically, he could be considered a cyborg, but only in the same sense as someone with a prosthetic leg. A one-legged man is still a man. And, appearance aside, Nate is a robot. He was built and programmed by human beings."

The detective's eyes narrowed, and he sat back in his chair, his gaze still pinning Susan. "Are you trying to make me look foolish, Dr. Calvin?"

"No." Susan resisted the urge to add, *You're doing a fine job of that all by yourself.* His skepticism was logical and understandable; and, thus far, he had not thrown her out of his office. "I'm just telling you the facts of the situation. Whether or not you believe me, Nate is a robot. And, as such, he could not have harmed Dr. Goldman in any way."

"Are you aware they found him alone in the room with the victim? The wound was fresh, and the murder weapon was in your so-called robot's hand."

"I was on the resuscitation team for Dr. Goldman," Susan reminded him. "I surmised that to be the case, but it doesn't change the facts. Nate is a positronic robot and, as such, is utterly constrained by the First Law." Susan felt as if the conversation had gone in circles. She knew she had repeated herself more than once. "We don't need to debate this. I can call Lawrence Robertson right now."

"And he is?"

"The CEO and president of United States Robots and Mechanical Men. He invented the positronic brain. His company built and programmed Nate." Susan reached for her Vox, glancing at the detective.

Detective Riviera bobbled his head, as if questioning his own sanity, then waved at Susan to place the call. "Put it on speaker."

Susan quickly tapped in the Kwik-set key sequence that connected her with Lawrence's Vox, on speaker. It took him three rings to answer. "Susan? Are you all right?"

Lawrence's words brought home how drama-prone Susan's life had become. She was not the type to chat, and her recent run-ins, especially with USR, had involved an enormous amount of death and destruction. She made a mental note to ring Lawrence socially on occasion so he would stop automatically associating her with catastrophe. Now she would have liked to give him the conventional "I'm fine" answer but could not. "Lawrence, I'm at the police station with a Detective Riviera. Ari Goldman's been murdered."

"Ari? Goldman?" The first name emerged uncertainly, the last in clear confusion. Next came suffocating grief. "No. Oh God, no. Not Ari. Murdered? No. No. Ari Goldman?" His voice quavered as tears began to flow. "What . . . Susan, what happened?"

It suddenly occurred to Susan that she had not cried. Either circumstances had not yet allowed the details to sink in deeply enough, or she had become inured to disaster. She glanced at the detective for guidance. When he said nothing, she explained. "It happened in the lab. Hit in the head with a hammer, I believe. The police took Nate into custody."

"Nate?!" This time, the name was clearly startled out of him. "Why Nate?"

"They think he did it."

"Nate?" Lawrence's voice was an odd mix of grief and incredulity. "But that's impossible. He's constrained by the Three Laws of Robotics."

Susan leveled a steady gaze at the detective. "That's what I told him."

"My aunt Greta is a more likely suspect, and she's been dead for six years."

Susan held any smugness from her expression as she stared even more intently at the detective. She hoped her look conveyed the appropriate unspoken question: *Satisfied?*

The detective cleared his throat. "This is Detective Riviera. Who's speaking?"

Lawrence hesitated just long enough to reveal his surprise at finding another person on the line. "This is Dr. Lawrence Robertson, founder and CEO of United States Robots and Mechanical Men, Inc."

"I see."

Susan got the impression that the detective had expected the more-fumbling answer of a faker. If Lawrence was anyone other than he claimed, he certainly had the delivery of someone accustomed to the lie.

Detective Riviera continued. "Dr. Robertson, is it true that this Nate you speak of is . . . a robot?"

Lawrence kept it simple. "Yes."

"One you built and programmed?"

"My team and I, yes. Nate is a USR product."

Susan sat back, smiling slightly. Lawrence made it sound as if USR were a giant corporation when, in fact, his team consisted of about half a dozen dedicated friends. She pulled in the corners of her mouth, not wanting to appear to be smirking.

"Can you give me a description of him?"

"I can do better than that." The screen of Susan's Vox came to life. "I can send you a picture." A well-focused image of Nate filled the screen, demonstrating the short brown hair, unexceptional features, and athletic build. He had not aged a day since Susan had met him, appearing in his mid-twenties, though Susan now knew he was older than her father.

Susan unstrapped her Vox and handed it to Detective Riviera. He held it close to his face, examining it for several moments in silence before returning it.

Lawrence also said nothing.

"That's him," the detective admitted. "Or someone who resembles him perfectly."

Susan reaffixed her Vox.

The detective wiped his brow, then his mouth, though Susan saw no obvious sweat. She could almost hear the gears turning in his head. "So . . . there are robots . . . walking all around Manhattan who are . . . indistinguishable from . . . us?"

"Just one," Lawrence said breezily, though Susan knew it was a lie. Or, at least, it would have been a lie a year ago. Nate, who was N8-C, and Nick, who was N9-C, had been prototypes for N12-C, also known as John Calvin. *Although, with John destroyed and Nate imprisoned, that does leave only one to "walk around Manhattan."* She had never met Nick, only heard about him from Nate. At some point, Lawrence had informed her that Nick worked at a different hospital, but he could have gotten transferred anywhere, even to the Mercury project.

Lawrence continued. "The idea was to accustom people to working with one humanoid robot; and, once they realized his enormous potential, they would clamor for more."

"Did it work?"

Susan could scarcely believe the thoughtless stupidity of that question. "Are the streets of Manhattan filled with robots?"

"Only one," Lawrence reminded her.

"The Frankenstein Complex," Susan said, exposing the name for the public's mistrust of all things robotic, particularly the humanoid variety. Far too many Hollywood movies portrayed them as unstoppable weapons that, invariably, turned upon their creators. Others panicked over the idea that robots might replace humans in usefulness, for jobs, perhaps even for procreation.

Susan found Detective Riviera staring at her. She opened her mouth to explain her words, but he spoke first and, still, directly to Lawrence. "Dr. Robertson, if I sent a car, could you come to the station right now?"

"There's a glide-bus stop just outside the door."

Susan knew it well. Two years ago, a schizophrenic whom she and

Remington had followed onto the bus had held the passengers hostage, then released them at that very stop before detonating a bomb that had demolished the madman and the bus. Susan would never forget the screams, muffled beneath the ringing in her ears, the surge of heat, the injured that she and her neurosurgeon boyfriend had assisted. The façade of U.S. Robots had quite likely been the original target.

If the detective knew about that event, and its closeness to USR, he gave no sign. "I'd feel better sending a patrol car, Dr. Robertson. Where are you?"

"I'm at the office," Lawrence said, though Susan knew he essentially lived there. She listened to him rattle off the familiar address, where her father had worked for her entire life but which she had not visited until after the bus explosion. She knew she and USR were the same age, twenty-eight, that Lawrence Robertson had taken out the incorporation papers the same year as her birth.

"See you soon," Detective Riviera said.

Before Susan could cut the contact, Lawrence addressed her. "Susan, could you please stay? Nate's going to need his . . . robopsychiatrist." He barely stumbled over the newly created word, and Susan hoped she effortlessly stifled her surprise. She had developed a knack for reading others and, more recently, hiding her own emotional state. When they had first met, Lawrence had politely asked when she would join the team, resulting in jokes about analyzing robots. Gradually, she had realized the interplay of the Three Laws, the wiggle room in any wording, and the infinite variations allowed by the experience-based evolution of each positronic brain did open the potential for an astounding amount of consideration and possibility.

Susan had never thought about leaving the police station. She glanced toward the detective, who was scowling. She supposed he would prefer to question Lawrence alone. She had made the connection between him and Nate's creator; and, as far as he was concerned, her usefulness was finished. She felt differently, wanting to question and console Nate, to watch Lawrence handle him, to find out what had happened in the research laboratory. The idea that she had quit her residency only to inform the police of Nate's composition did not sit well. She had often relied on Nate to get her through the worst moments of her life. Now he needed her.

Susan modulated her tone to sound equally casual. "That's robo-therapist, remember, Lawrence? Medications won't work on robots, and I don't have my PhD yet." She did not go into any more detail; it might reveal the freshness of the topic.

"Yeah, yeah, yeah," Lawrence said in a manner that suggested an ongoing argument. "The point is we both want you there, Susan." He added for the detective's benefit, "And it will help the authorities to have us both present as well."

"I'll be here," Susan promised. She only hoped the police would agree.

Chapter 3

Susan expected a grilling, particularly after Lawrence's "robopsychiatrist" comment; but, after only a request for her to remain in the building, Detective Diondre Riviera dismissed her to a waiting area with coffee, tea, and pastries. Too keyed up to eat, Susan sat on a folding chair, hands interlaced in her lap, and waited for the arrival of Dr. Lawrence Robertson.

Alone in the quiet of the small, institutionally two-toned room, Susan found her thoughts straying to Ari Goldman. Though she had joined him on the nanorobot project, she did not know him all that well, at least not personally. He and Cody Peters had worked together for more than twenty years, long enough for rumors to surface about their sexuality. It seemed odd to Susan that society extolled the virtues of friendships and partnerships; however, if one actually lasted, romantic ideas seemed to automatically enter the minds of all who knew them, whether casually or as family and close associates.

Both men were married to women. Goldman's wife was a teacher at an elementary school and Peters' was a microbiologist. Both couples reportedly had children, though Susan had never met them. Had the men not worked so well together on research projects that spanned the psychiatric gamut, Susan suspected they would never have become friends. Their personalities clashed: Goldman was gruff and no-

nonsense; Peters loquacious and social, often to the point of silliness. He enjoyed seeing how far he could push his partner on a daily basis, it seemed to Susan. She had always enjoyed their oddball interactions; Peters clearly did, and, though he hid it well, she believed Goldman had, too. He pretended to ignore his partner's antics, but on occasion Susan saw a ghost of a smile slip through his façade. Susan could not help wondering if Peters had heard the news yet; and, if so, how he handled it. They had discovered two new forms of schizophrenia, helped uncover a genetic defect in a common familial type of bipolar illness, and paved the way for what was once a new class of antipsychotics, now in common usage. The few studies of robotechnology in psychiatric medicine had all been undertaken by them, and they had enlisted Nate as an assistant multiple times. *Which explains why he was at the murder scene.*

Discomfort accompanied the intrusive thought. Susan had attempted to direct her mind solely to Ari Goldman and the sorrow she felt over his premature and horrible death, yet she found herself at least equally concerned about Nate. His emotional state, his dispensation, intruded on any thoughts she tried to focus fully on the murdered researcher. *What does it say about me as a human being if I'm more concerned with a frightened robot than a slaughtered man?*

Sooner than Susan expected, the door opened. Detective Riviera ushered Lawrence Robertson inside. "I apologize for the delay. Would you two mind waiting ten or fifteen minutes while I speak with the officers returning from the scene?"

"No problem," Lawrence said, with a nod toward Susan. "We want to get to the bottom of this as well."

The detective continued to hold the door open. "Help yourselves to refreshments." Without awaiting a reply, he stepped backward, allowing the door to shut itself behind him.

Susan recalled something Detective Jake Carson had said after he had abruptly, and wholly unexpectedly, asked her for a date in the middle of a conversation about her father's murder: "Nothing said or done in a police station is private anymore." She felt certain she and Lawrence were being watched, if not through one-way walls, then with a camera, and everything they said to each other would be recorded and considered. Susan knew she ought to rise from her chair and embrace the president of United States Robots, but she made no move to do so. She felt drained and cold.

Lawrence took the bottom thermocup from a stack and filled it from the coffee spout. With his other arm, he dragged a folding chair in front of Susan's, shook it open, then sat and transferred his drink to both hands. "So, how is Dr. Susan Calvin?"

"Under the circumstances, not great."

Lawrence nodded. "I share your pain."

"Most of it." Susan sighed and pulled her chair around to face Lawrence squarely. "I hope you have room for a full-time robotherapist on your staff, because I just annihilated my residency."

Lawrence's lips twitched into a frown. "But you've come so far, worked so hard. Why would you do that?"

Susan did not want to discuss the details with a precinct of police officers. "Maybe, deep down, I prefer to be a full-time robotherapist." She was kidding, but if Lawrence realized it, he did not show it.

Lawrence's features remained sober, his coffee clutched in his lap. "That would suit me, but I still think you're being unfair to yourself with that label. You have more than enough credentials for a psychologist, and you *are* a psychiatrist."

"But not a *robo*psychiatrist." Susan found herself adding without intention, "Not yet."

Lawrence seized on the last two words. "When, then?"

Susan could no longer pretend it was all a joke. Lawrence obviously wanted her on staff, though whether because he felt responsible for her parents' deaths or because he really believed USR would benefit from a robopsychologist, she did not know. No such degree existed, of course, but she knew she could not just laugh off an answer. So, she considered the question and answered appropriately. "When I've earned my PhD in robotics."

Leaving his coffee between his knees, Lawrence threw up his hands. "So, maybe a year's worth of classes and a thesis."

Susan mulled his words. Her MD counted for more than a master's, and the two years of residency fully prepared her for psychiatry or psychology. She held a bachelor's degree from Columbia University, double majoring in math and physics. Additionally, she had taken multiple postgraduate-level classes when the standard ones had proven so easy she had spent more time tutoring than learning. "That's about right." She smiled. "I hear Columbia has a decent robotics program." Her father and Lawrence had met while attending that program and became friends and roommates before starting USR.

"The best." Lawrence smiled and reclaimed his coffee, taking a sip. "And I'm paying."

"I can't let you–"

"I'm paying," Lawrence said with finality. "I created the position, I want you in it, and I'm going to make it happen."

Susan stopped arguing. Unemployed and out of living relatives, she really could not afford to argue.

"It's done all the time in business," Lawrence pointed out. "All you have to do is apply, get accepted, ace all your classes, and write a killer thesis."

Susan almost managed a smile. "Easy peasy." Though said facetiously, it was not far from the truth. She had taken top grades in medical school, besting most of the finest minds of her generation. That had earned her a place in the national honor society, AOA, as well as her school's own.

Lawrence took several more sips of coffee while Susan considered her future. Always before, she had pictured a thriving, hospital-based practice that included face time with patients as well as research and teaching. She saw herself married to a loving, intelligent man with a career of his own. That dream had wholly crumbled, and it would take some time to build something in its place. But when she thought about including USR in the restructuring, it seemed the one and only certainty.

Lawrence broke the silence. "So, as a robotherapist, do you believe it's possible that Nate—"

"No."

The swiftness and force of her answer seemed to catch Lawrence off guard. "Don't you want to think about it a bit?"

"Not necessary," Susan said, just as swiftly. "I've spent more than three hundred nights tossing and turning, thinking about it. It's like the stories of evil genies and wishes. A man asks for eternal life, and the genie grants the wish. But by the time the man reaches seventy, he has terrible pains in every part of his body. By ninety, he's wheelchair bound, and by one hundred and thirty, he's basically powdered carbon begging for death. Or he asks for wealth beyond his wildest imaginings and winds up crushed to death beneath piles of platinum bricks." Susan looked up to find Lawrence staring at her.

"I'm missing your point."

Susan realized she had not yet made the connection between her examples and the Three Laws of Robotics. "My point is that computers are absolutely literal. The simplest programming typo renders them useless, and a tiny mistake can require a specialist to spend hours attempting to find it. Machines can't intuit or extrapolate. Unlike children and dogs, they can't do what you mean. They can only do exactly what you tell them to do."

Lawrence started to contradict. "Except the positronic brain—"

Susan interrupted again. "The positronic brain is an exception in that it allows for the development of contemplation and emotion; it literally learns. It's plastic, in the developmental sense, not the inanimate sense. More important, it makes judgments based on knowledge and experience. So, for example, it is capable of interpreting what it sees, hears, and learns as well as the commands given to it."

Lawrence pressed. "I'm aware of that, Susan. I created it."

"Yes." Susan gave the claim little credence. She had already marveled over Lawrence's genius and an invention that few people could have conceived of, let alone accomplished. "So the production of the positronic brain takes a lot of steps. No?"

Lawrence bobbed his head. "Alfred counted them once. It requires more than seventy-five thousand operations to manufacture one positronic brain, each with hundreds of factors. If any of those goes wrong, the brain is ruined and we have to restart."

Susan had never witnessed the creation of one, but she assumed the most complicated and fascinating invention in the solar system would require a lengthy and difficult process. "And one of the earliest of those factors is the Three Laws of Robotics, correct?"

"Correct," Lawrence confirmed. "If anyone tried to remove or deactivate them, the entire brain would be destroyed. A positronic brain cannot function without the Three Laws in place."

Susan continued as if he had not spoken. She had not really needed his affirmation. "So, at the time the Three Laws are inserted, we're still talking about a computer. A literal interpretation."

"Your point," Lawrence coaxed again.

Susan leaned forward, clasping her hands between her knees. "My point is that eventually a robot with a positronic brain learns to reason. In that respect, their thought processes are, essentially, human. Humans murder other humans because they find a way to justify it." As a psychiatrist, she had to add, "Unless they're psychopaths. In which case, they don't need a justification." She returned to her original point. "Since the positronic brain doesn't rely on neurotransmitters, and damage to the neural pathways would render them inoperable . . ." Susan paused and rolled an eye to Lawrence.

"Correct," he encouraged. "And I believe I know where you're going, too. You're saying that, since the Three Laws are placed into the positronic brain while it's still in the literal phase, they can't be countermanded. Robots can't develop neuropathic psychiatric problems, such as psychopath . . . ologicalness."

"Psychopathology." Susan fixed the word absentmindedly, then spoke her own sudden realization aloud in awed tones. "If we could inject the Three Laws into every developing embryonic human brain, we'd finally have the 'world peace' everyone claims should be our highest priority."

Lawrence stiffened and took another sip of coffee. "Well, I wouldn't go that far. . . ."

Susan would not, either, but she could see the positive side of it. "I'm not saying we should. I'm just presenting a hypothetical scenario. I'm also not saying the Three Laws of Robotics have no wiggle room. Beautifully crafted, yes. Perfect, no."

"So, you're saying . . ."

"Nate could *not* have killed Ari Goldman. In fact, he could not even have witnessed it happening without intervening because the First Law doesn't just state that 'a robot may not injure a human being.' It adds, 'or, through inaction, allow a human being to come to harm.'" Lawrence already knew this; Susan continued for the sake of any law enforcement officers who might be listening, now or in the future. "Obviously, you have to educate and supply parameters along with the Laws. What, exactly is 'harm'? Humans can drown, but that doesn't mean robots should bar anyone from entering a bathtub or a swimming pool. However, if I was about to step into a vat of boiling lava, I certainly hope my robotic companion would stop me."

Lawrence swallowed his coffee. "He would have to. And, yes, there's a threshold for potential harm. Any of our robots can instantly calculate the odds in almost any situation to about twenty subdecimal digits." He considered a moment longer. "However, as we discovered with the Mercury expedition, there are some situations in which a robot might inadvertently disobey the second part of the First Law. Out of ignorance."

That caught Susan wholly by surprise, though she tried not to show it. "What happened?"

"Suit malfunction." Lawrence simplified, probably more for listeners than Susan. "Robots don't need oxygen, and they can work in extremes of temperature, so they didn't realize the need for assistance. Of course, once they were commanded, the Second Law kicked in. The astronaut was whisked to safety, the robots were better educated, and we had no further difficulties." He added carefully, "Of that type, at least."

Susan knew the Mercury mission had been plagued by problems, most of which had nothing to do with the robots. With temperatures ranging from 280 degrees below zero to 800 degrees above, it was hardly the most hospitable planet for human exploration. She took the logical leap. "So, it might just be possible that Nate witnessed the murder *if* he did not realize the killer's motive. In other words, he saw no danger in a human carrying a tool; and, by the time it was used to crush Dr. Goldman's skull, it was too late to intervene." Susan continued thinking aloud. "And, at that point, the Three Laws would force him to do three things: one, try to prevent the victim from dying; two, protect any other persons in the room; and, three, protect the killer himself from harm. Because the First Law doesn't discriminate between human beings?" It was as much a question as an observation.

"Of course not," Lawrence pointed out amicably, "because it's the job of a robot to remain subservient to all of humanity." He added, "Although, that's not to say it wouldn't rank those three priorities in order based on . . . knowledge and experience. The fact that one person in the room had already shown himself willing and able to kill would become a part of any decision making."

Susan thought back to when two Cadmium agents had broken into USR, threatening her, Lawrence, Detective Jake Carson, and Kendall Stevens, a fellow psychiatry resident. Both sides had fired many gunshots, placing Nate in multiple, untenable positions. Susan knew Jake and the agents were too well trained for anyone or anything to disarm them. *Is it possible Nate could have taken the gun from me at some point but realized, if he intervened, the agent would have lived at the expense of Lawrence and me, at least? Was there a point at which Nate could have thrown himself in front of a bullet but realized that sacrificing himself would have negatively changed the outcome of the battle?* Susan could not think of a specific moment when Nate could have acted differently and saved a life without forfeiting more. However, she also knew that at no point did she ever worry about his loyalties. *Should I have?* It was a question she could spend a long time pondering in the future, but she knew she would not need to. Nate posed no harm to her under any circumstances. She felt more sure of that than she did about any human in the universe.

Lawrence glanced around, as if worried someone might burst in on them in a delicate moment. Susan hoped he realized they were probably being unobtrusively observed. "Susan, do you think it's possible someone tricked Nate?"

Susan did not understand the question. "Tricked him?" She pondered further. "You mean into committing murder without realizing it?"

Lawrence bobbed his head, but only once, and leaned forward conspiratorially, still clutching his coffee. "For example, what if someone befriended Nate. Every day for months, they played a game where he swung a hammer through the air or at a nail, always safely. Then, a blindfold became part of the game."

The suggestion was so ludicrous, Susan laughed out loud until Lawrence's wounded look stopped her. "Lawrence, that's insane. There's no way Nate would allow himself to be blindfolded with a heavy implement in his hands, even if only because he might crush the finger of someone holding the nail. He cannot harm a human being. Period."

"Maybe if someone convinced him he was hammering a nail, then switched the situation somehow . . ." Lawrence was fishing.

Susan gave him that much. Perhaps there was some twisted scenario in which a brilliant, thinking machine could be duped into performing an action without realizing the consequences, but this did not seem like a possible one. "Too complicated and perverse, Lawrence. Anything that required weeks or months of preparation would risk Nate telling one of us about it. I can't see Dr. Goldman going along with it, especially if it was presented as a prank or a game. Peters, maybe, but not Goldman."

"Yeah."

Susan continued. "Far more likely a human being murdered Dr. Goldman and framed Nate. The robot's constraints and naïveté would make it an easy target."

"Yeah," Lawrence repeated. He glanced at his coffee, probably gone cold. "Which brings us to the only logical reality: Nate witnessed the murder but couldn't stop it."

Now it was Susan's turn to say, "Yeah." She already knew the Frankenstein Complex had forced USR to make its robots wholly subservient, to make the protection of their own existence, their own survival, a distant third to defending and slavishly serving their human masters. "A robot may not injure a human being or, through inaction, allow a human being to come to harm." Then, "a robot must obey orders given it by human beings except where such orders would conflict with the First Law." Only after those conditions were met could a robot consider the Third Law: "A robot must protect its own existence as long as such protection does not conflict with the First or Second Laws." It might have rendered Nate a sitting duck; yet it made him wholly safe to people, exactly what the human race wanted and insisted upon.

"So why won't Nate tell the police what he witnessed?"

Susan had to admit she had no idea.

The single occupant of the six-by-eight-foot cell sat cross-legged on the concrete floor, face buried in his hands. He still wore the casual khakis Susan had noticed in the laboratory, and his blue polo had splatters of blood. She felt certain the police had emptied every pocket. Had she not known his identity, she could never have guessed it. Unlike the brisk and friendly robot who had become her best friend, the figure in the cell appeared dejected and eerily still. Though their footsteps echoed through the hallway, and Detective Riviera guided Susan and Lawrence verbally, Nate did not even raise his head at their approach.

"Nate," Lawrence said.

There was no response from the cell. Nate could just as well have been a statue.

Lawrence glanced at Susan, who tried, "Nate, it's me, Susan."

Still, the figure in the cell did not move.

A thought struck Susan, and she wondered why she had never considered it before. "Does Nate have an Off switch?" She had never seen him in a dormant state, but she did not always find him when she looked for him, either. Lawrence had once mentioned that positronic robots required an energy source in order to maintain their function and memories.

"Not a switch per se." Lawrence studied the robot, apparently assessing his physical status. "But the battery does need occasional updating." He stepped closer to the bars and spoke in a commanding tone. "N8-C, look at me!"

In slow increments, the robot's head lifted until the eyes appeared just above the fingers. They were not the sweet brown orbs with which Susan had become so familiar. Now they looked drawn and haunted.

Lawrence addressed the detective. "You say he hasn't been answering your questions."

"That's right." The detective kept his attention fixed on Nate. "In fact, that's the most he's moved in at least an hour."

"How have you been asking?"

The detective went on the defensive. "The usual way. We read him his rights first."

Lawrence shook his head impatiently. "That's not my concern. I'm not a lawyer, and robots don't have rights anyway. No matter how human one might appear, it's still an object, a tool. You no more have to Mirandize him than you do a bridge that collapsed or a piano that fell on someone's head. He does only what he's been told or programmed to do." He returned to his original point. "The Second Law states that a robot must obey orders given it by human beings. I'm just wondering if you simply asked him or actually commanded him."

Susan considered Lawrence's words. Her first reaction, dismay, quickly faded as she realized the truth behind his statements. So many videos and shows had contemplated the humanity, the entitlements and privileges of cyborgs, she could not help considering them just and civil rights. Yet a line needed to be drawn before positronic robots became commonplace, to prevent a "conception" debate from dividing and crippling the country in the same way abortion had in the twentieth century.

Putting aside her love for Nate and John Calvin, Susan had to submit to Lawrence's point that the dividing line was the brain itself. Anything with a human brain was human; anything with an artificial brain, including the wonder that was the positronic brain, was not. To do otherwise might permanently destroy the robotics industry. United States Robots was not God, and what it created was not life, only a facsimile. Recycling a robot must never be considered murder. She could imagine larger hordes of protesters exhorting USR than Manhattan Hasbro. Most would demand its closure. Others would insist that every brain, no matter how damaged, must be salvaged and kept "alive." The Frankenstein Complex, Susan realized, had an even more evil twin, the Belgar Complex, named for a sympathetic robot in a sappy movie. To define a robot as a legal person with standing in the justice system opened a box worse than anything Pandora could have dreamed about.

Several thoughts behind Susan, Detective Riviera addressed the point on the table. "I asked him questions he chose not to answer. The right to remain silent is well established."

"For people," Lawrence pointed out. "Do you ask a pedophile's computer to please disgorge its child pornography and accept its uncommunicativeness as an answer?" Lawrence did not await an answer to his rhetorical question but turned his attention back to Nate. "N8-C, stand up."

Nate climbed gingerly to his feet and looked forlornly at his master.

Lawrence continued. "Tell us what happened to Dr. Ari Goldman."

Nate fairly mumbled, "He was killed."

"Tell us how, N8-C."

Nate remained quietly in place for several moments before replying, "It would appear he was bludgeoned with a Stanley 55-099 FatMax Xtreme FuBar Utility Bar."

That startled Susan, not only for the technical jargon spewing from the mouth of someone she ordinarily considered a friend, but because she had believed the tool on the floor was a hammer or, possibly, a wrench.

Lawrence frowned. "Tell us more details."

Nate obliged. "It's a utility bar used for heavy demolition work, a four-in-one tool for prying, splitting, bending, and—"

Lawrence interrupted, "Not about the tool, Nate. Tell us more about the murder."

Detective Riviera jumped in. "Tell us who killed Dr. Goldman."

Nate's gaze dropped to the floor, and he shuffled from foot to foot, looking for all the world like a chastised child. Then, he gave the last answer Susan expected. "It would appear . . . that I did."

It was not exactly a confession, but was apparently near enough one for the detective. He turned to face Lawrence. "Dr. Lawrence Robertson, who designed this robot?"

"I did," Lawrence said.

"And who programmed him?"

"Myself and my team," Lawrence said, then added unnecessarily, "I have promised to take full responsibility for anything said or done by N8-C."

Susan did not like where this was going, but she felt as helpless to stop it as if it were a speeding locomotive. She closed her eyes, though it seemed absurd and unnecessary. What she really wanted to block out were Detective Riviera's next words.

"Dr. Lawrence Robertson, you're under arrest for the murder of Ari Goldman. You have the right to remain silent. . . ."

Chapter 4

Susan Calvin could not leave the police station fast enough, but once out on the street she found herself incapable of reasonable thought or action for the first time in her life. She had kept her cool through medical and personal emergencies, through codes and even gunfire. Now she did not know whether to scream or to cry, to fight or to surrender to the swirl of rage and guilt and fear that encompassed her.

The police had given Lawrence's personal effects to Susan, at his request; and she clutched the envelope in a hand oddly steady for the hurricane assault of information and emotion speeding through her brain. She knew their plan: Shut-down Nate, log him into evidence like a cartridge case or a fiber, and charge Lawrence Robertson with the murder. It all seemed so obvious, so pat, so impossible to argue. Yet, Susan knew, none of it made a bit of sense. Ari Goldman and Lawrence were friends and happy colleagues, and positronic robots were incapable of murder as surely as Earth rotated around the sun. Lawrence knew it, too. In fact, he had bet his life on it.

But truth did not always triumph. Susan could still remember her seventh-grade science teacher saying, "After all, evolution is only a *theory*." To the great amusement of her class, Susan had replied, "So's gravity, but I wouldn't suggest jumping off a high-rise balcony." She had gotten her first and only detention for that comment, which had created a firestorm, the end result of which was a new science teacher. Statistically, Susan knew, more people than not believed in ghosts. With all the eyewitnesses dead, Holocaust denial had become widespread, accompanied by growing anti-Semitism. And a statistically significant number of people believed the U.S. government had faked the ongoing Mercury expedition.

Susan had learned about motivational reasoning, which had become so epidemic, it dwarfed rational analysis by a ratio of eighty to one. Rather than search for information that confirmed or denied a particular belief, the vast majority of people looked only for evidence endorsing what they already believed, particularly when it involved any type of politics. Hypotheses, unbiased studies, and legitimate conclusions had become the realm of scientists only, and even some of those had a tendency to ignore contrary data.

Susan doubted anyone had undertaken a study to determine how many people suffered from the Frankenstein Complex. She came from a place containing more rational thinkers than most, but she estimated the syndrome at about twenty-five percent. On a twelve-member random jury, likely four would have automatonophobia of sufficient caliber to believe Nate had committed murder even if she could uncover overwhelming evidence to the contrary. His quasi confession in the holding cell would only make the situation worse.

Susan had faith in her own competence, at least in a medical sense, but the idea of investigating the crime, finding the true killer of Ari Goldman, and presenting her findings to the police seemed daunting beyond consideration. She knew she ought to find herself an experienced private detective with impeccable credentials, but she had no money with which to pay him. Her father had dumped what little savings he had into USR, and it was only just starting to come back to him as pay. Cadmium and the Society for Humanity had taken not only his life, but all of their belongings. Insurance had covered the damages to the apartment and helped her break the lease. She had used the remainder of the money to finance a small apartment near USR, which consisted of a bedroom holding a futon and a tiny chest of drawers, a half bathroom, a living room that allowed for only a love seat and a dorm-sized entertainment system, and a kitchen with miniature appliances.

To the police, the case was simple, open-and-shut. Proving the innocence of Lawrence Robertson and N8-C, and thus rescuing United States Robots and Mechanical Men, fell to Susan alone. *Or did it?* Susan considered her other options. The employees of USR had a personal stake in the matter as well. A bunch of nerdy middle-aged scientists had little chance of outmaneuvering the murderer, but they could supply her with useful information. And she knew a detective who had risked the wrath of a Department of Defense Intelligence Agency to assist and protect her in the past.

Jake Carson. An image of the homicide detective filled Susan's mind's eye. In his mid-thirties, he stood a solid six feet tall with immaculate, but anachronistic, clothing, a sculpted figure that revealed his familiarity with a gym, and a waist that seemed proportionately too slender. He had short blond hair, quick hazel eyes, and a boxy chin. He, alone, had taken her complaints about the investigation of her father's murder seriously, and he had gone on to save her life from the SFH and the federal agency in turn.

Susan knew she needed him, but she had to tread carefully. Like most cops, Jake was intensely loyal to his creed; his life depended on it and so, most times, did the lives of the general public. She needed to convince him of the significance of the situation and her sincerity and devotion to it, and she could never do that by Vox. She glanced at it: 4:05 p.m. She would need to move fast to catch Jake before his shift ended at the Tenth Precinct.

Susan ran the routes of the glide-buses through her mind. Like most native Manhattanites, she knew them by heart, could grab one that would take her to the appropriate location, if not always by the quickest route. It helped that, until a year ago, she had lived in his precinct. She fast-walked toward the proper station.

The previous time Susan Calvin had visited the Tenth Precinct, she had done so suffused with confusion and rage after being told her bullet-riddled, decapitated father had died of "natural causes." She had paid little attention to the décor, wanting only to confront Detective Jake Carson, look him straight in the eye, and force him to tell her the truth.

Again, Susan noticed the similarities between the entry to this precinct and the one she had just left. Both had two-toned walls: the Nineteenth was painted dark blue on the upper half and light blue on the lower, while the Tenth was a deep green on the bottom and light green on the top. Both had waiting areas divided from the rest of the room by a solid half barrier topped by a broad window through which she could see a long desk covered with consoles. Most of the people behind the glass ignored her, a mixture of uniformed officers and clerks of various types, but an enormous dark-skinned woman in institutional blue caught Susan's eye. "May I help you?"

Susan got right to the point. "My name is Dr. Susan Calvin. I'd like to speak with Detective Jacob Carson, please."

"Carson," the woman repeated, brows furrowing. She glanced at a console in front of her, clicked a few keys, then frowned. She called to a clerk behind her, "You know a Detective Carson?"

A faint voice wafted to Susan, "Jake? He got flopped to CoD FIAU."

"Flopped?" Susan repeated.

The woman flinched ever so slightly, then met Susan's gaze again. "Transferred."

Susan guessed the unfamiliar word meant more than that, at least connotatively, but she did not press. Even the most unpleasant medical slang usually made it to the global Net, but police held their jargon a bit closer. She would need to ask Jake. "Where can I find him?"

The woman kept her tone even, bland. "Chief of Detectives Field Internal Affairs Unit. It's at 34½ East Twelfth Street. That's between Broadway and Fourth."

Susan knew the location, at least by report. It also housed the police athletic league where she had sent more than a few troubled teens and children. She wondered about the reason for the transfer and what it meant to Jake. He was the consummate cop: committed to the only job he had ever wanted, competent, physically fit with good intuition and an eye for detail. After assisting Susan, he had worried about his future in law enforcement. She remembered the conversation in the hospital where he had stated that, assuming he still had a job, he would not be "out on the streets, especially with a gun, for a very long time." When a colleague of Susan's had referred to him as "a hero," Jake had added, "I'm what's known in the trade as a shit magnet. Something about me makes people want to shoot me, and that's not a liability any police department wants or needs."

At the time, his explanation had made little sense to Susan. It was her, not Jake, the killers had wanted. He had fired back in order to protect her. Had he not done so, she would have been dead several times over. But Jake pointed out that it would not matter to his supervisors. They would only consider that he had been involved in four shoot-outs in a three-day period, "probably a record" he had called it. She and her colleague, Kendall Stevens, had done their best to explain the situation to his superiors, but apparently it had not stopped them from transferring him. *Flopping him,* Susan reminded herself, now believing she understood the term. They had sent him out of the bureau to some "hole-in-the-wall" assignment, perhaps even demoted him.

Susan glanced at her Vox. It now read 4:47. She could never make it in time. *Time? Time for what?* She suddenly realized she had been assuming a nine-to-five work schedule. Her own hours bore little resemblance to those, and she wondered why she expected cops to have a regular workday, either. Clearly, they worked all hours and probably had shifts similar to the nursing staff at Hasbro. A quick scan of the global Net revealed standard patrol hours of eight to four, four to twelve, and twelve to eight. Even if Jake had still worked here, she would have missed him.

"Thank you," Susan managed before leaving the police station. She had no idea where to go next. She needed to talk to Jake; and, while she had his Vox number, she still wanted to speak to him in person without giving him time to prepare for her arrival, to toe the thin blue line. She knew her emotional state had caused her to make a mistake. She should have gone directly to USR, turned over Lawrence's personal effects, informed them of the situation, and learned more details about the workings of the positronic brain. Now she could never arrive there before closing. She had met some of Lawrence's coworkers but knew none of them well, and the only Vox number she had was his. She would have to wait until tomorrow.

Except Susan could not wait. The idea of spending the next sixteen hours alone and impotent repulsed her. She could not sleep until she had at least a cursory, workable plan to rescue Nate and Lawrence. *There's no getting around it; I have to talk to Jake tonight.* Susan raised her Vox, prepared to call him, despite her concerns. Then, another thought occurred to her. A year had passed since her favorite colleague and closest friend, Kendall Stevens, had finally recognized his homosexuality. Jake, on the other hand, had outed himself at their first meeting. During their last conversation together in the hospital, Susan had realized Kendall had developed an attraction to the dynamic and courageous detective, one she probably would have shared, if not for Jake's sexual orientation.

Susan could not imagine the two men getting together in any sense of the word, but she knew Kendall would try. At the least, he had surely found excuses to meet with Jake in the year since she had spoken with either of them. Kendall had not shared any medical rotations with her since the shootings. Only now Susan came to the conclusion that the residency program had probably kept them apart deliberately, for reasons as flimsy as the "shit magnet" excuse the police had, apparently, used to "flop" Jake. Whenever she and Kendall worked together, people got blown up and shot. That it had nothing to do with their association did not matter. Peace had reigned when the powers-that-be placed them on different rotations.

It all seemed so ridiculous until Susan realized she had subconsciously followed similar reasoning, making it that much easier for their supervisors. Nothing else could explain why she had avoided her best friend for so long, nor why she had not visited or contacted Jake, not even to buy him the dinner she had promised him while he convalesced in the hospital. She could not blame the men. Kendall had tried to bring the three of them together, using the meal as a pretext, on multiple occasions. Susan had always blamed the extra hours she had to maintain to catch up for the time she missed during the residency, her weeks of mourning and recovery. And it was true, but only to a point. Susan knew anyone could make time for anything if it truly mattered. The inner workings of her brain had made a superstitious and logically faulty connection between her association with Kendall and Jake and her loved ones dying.

Susan reached to punch the Kwik-set key sequence to call Kendall, when her Vox buzzed. She tapped it without bothering to read the name. "Hello?"

Kendall's familiar voice greeted her. "Susan Calvin, as I live and breathe."

Susan glanced at her Vox, where Kendall's name flashed. Certain she had not yet managed to hit the Kwik-set key, she stared at it. "How did you do that?"

"Get you to answer my call? Yes, that is a miracle, but *you*'ll have to tell *me* how I accomplished it."

Susan shook her head, though he could not see the gesture. "No, I mean . . . I was just about to call you."

"Psychic link?" Kendall suggested. "I'm calling to find out if the rumors are true. Did you really spit in old Savage's face and tell him to shove his residency up his–"

"No!" Susan interrupted in horror. "I did quit," she admitted, "but not in a discourteous or disrespectful manner." She realized Kendall was probably baiting her; he had a wicked sense of humor.

"They're saying Goldman's murder rendered you . . . um . . . temporarily batshit crazy."

The mischaracterizations irritated Susan. "Who's saying these things?"

"I am," Kendall announced. "I saw you handle Dr. Mitchell Reefes, remember? The oaf."

Susan had no interest in reliving their last assignment together at the Winter Wine Dementia Facility. She had barely completed a week there before clashes with a lazy attending and the murder of her father had intervened. "I didn't 'handle' Aloise Savage. We had a civil discussion, and I chose to leave for reasons all my own." Not liking the conversation, she took it in a whole new direction. "Kendall, did you know Jake got transferred?"

A brief paused followed; then Kendall blasted her. "Of course I knew Jake got transferred. It happened a year ago, and it was, essentially, our fault."

Susan glanced up, only then recognizing her location. She had been walking without concern or notice, from long habit heading toward her father's apartment. She stopped suddenly. He no longer lived there–

or anywhere for that matter. He was dead. *Murdered.* "And you wonder why I don't answer your calls."

"I'm sorry," Kendall said, sounding it. "It's just been so long. . . . I have so much pent-up . . ."

"Venom?" Susan supplied.

"Emotion," Kendall amended. "Cold and distant doesn't suit you, Susan. I . . . miss you."

They had been close. While police investigated the killing of John Calvin, Susan had lived with Kendall. She had even surrendered her virginity to him, a coupling they now both realized had been a mistake. "It's not you," Susan assured him. "It's everything that's happened. I'm dealing with it the best I can." She expected Kendall to point out that avoiding the very people who understood the situation did not constitute dealing with it, but he did not. Apparently, he had prodded her as much as he dared.

"You are coming back to Hasbro, aren't you?"

"Only to collect my things."

Brief silence followed, then Kendall said, "I believe Savage would accept an apology. We all know you're under duress. . . ."

"No, Kendall." Susan did not want to discuss the matter any further, at least not at the present time. She could not imagine doing as he advised; her future, she now felt certain, lay with USR. She returned to the matter at hand. "Kendall, I need to meet with Jake."

He asked the obvious questions. "When? Why?"

Susan answered them in order. "As soon as possible. Tonight, even. I'd prefer to discuss the reasons in person, which is why I didn't just call him instead of you." She added challengingly, "Can you make that happen?"

"I know where he lives, if that's what you're asking." Kendall had also changed. Previously, he would have made a joke, no matter how difficult or odd. He had handled all of his discomfort in that manner. "But I don't think we should just drop in without warning."

"That would be rude," Susan agreed. "But if I picked up some food, and you called to let him know we're coming . . . ?"

Kendall hesitated, then said, "Yeah, all right. That should work, assuming he doesn't have other plans." He spoke slowly, as if considering each word. "You do owe him a dinner."

Susan suspected Kendall's hesitation came of thinking about the situation in general rather than what he intended to say. "*We* owe him a dinner."

"No," Kendall corrected. "I paid my share a long time ago. Took him to Les Trois Capitaines right after his discharge from the hospital."

It was a classy French restaurant. Susan made a sound usually associated with romantic interludes.

"I wish," Kendall said ruefully. "We spent most of the time discussing your absence."

"So no wedding bells in your near future?"

"Nothing like that." A bit of discomfort seeped through the connection, and Kendall lowered his voice almost to a whisper. "I've only been gay for a year."

"You mean, you've only *admitted* it for a year."

"I've only *realized* it for a year."

The semantics did not really matter. "And you're still, clearly, not wholly comfortable with it." Physicians had a term for it: ego-dystonic sexual disorder, characterized by having a sexual orientation at odds with one's idealized self-image, causing anxiety. Kendall had diagnosed himself.

"Well how could I be?" Kendall said, with clear accusation. "My psychiatrist refuses to talk with me."

"Me?" Guilt descended upon Susan, and she discarded it. "I'm not the only psychiatrist in the city."

"Just the best."

She laced her reply with sarcasm. "Please."

"And I deserve the best." Kendall added, less facetiously, "Besides, you're my friend and confidante. I don't feel comfortable discussing it with someone who might serve as my attending or a fellow resident."

"Like me?"

"Friend and confidante," Kendall repeated. "You already know."

"There are plenty of psychiatrists in private practice," Susan pointed out. "Ones unaffiliated in any way with Hasbro."

"I want you." Kendall added determinedly, "I deserve you."

Susan could not counter that argument. "We'll talk about this later, Kendall."

"Will we?" It was a clear dig at Susan's long avoidance.

"We will," Susan promised. "For now, what kind of food should I bring, and where should I take it?"

Kendall had a ready answer. "Deli. Get two turkey pastrami and Swiss on nine-grain with lettuce and tomato. Mustard on one, mayo on the other. Plus whatever you want, of course. Lots of pickles and whatever mix of veg-chips you prefer. Fizzy juice," he used the generic term. "Whatever brand or flavor. Doesn't matter. Where are you?"

"Near my old apartment."

"Your old . . ." A hint of alarm entered Kendall's tone. "Why?"

"Wallowing in the past," Susan said.

"What!?"

"That's what you were thinking, wasn't it?" Susan did not wait for an answer to her rhetorical question. "Actually, I swung by the Tenth Precinct to try to catch Jake."

"Leave the sarcasm to me," Kendall said sullenly. "You suck at it."

"Thanks."

"I'll grab the number four. If I don't see you at the station, I'll get off and wait for you there."

"Thanks," Susan repeated, this time meaning it. It occurred to her that Kendall had surprisingly detailed knowledge of what Jake would want to eat, but before she could question him further, he broke the contact.

Susan headed for the nearest deli.

Jake Carson met the two psychiatrists at the door to the boxy, twenty-six-story apartment complex in the Williamsburg section of Brooklyn that had served as his home for the last six years. Susan liked the exterior: clean aside from the usual smudges and fingerprints on the glass doors, notices confined to a corkboard, the rows of buttons appearing fresh and functional. The detective ushered them through the security doors by inserting his left thumb into the proper reader, then up a musty flight of concrete stairs to his apartment on the second floor. Again using a thumb-lock reader, Jake opened the door to number 203 and gestured for his guests to precede him.

Susan entered first, quickly followed by Kendall, who strode past her without hesitation into a neatly kept living room. A plush, beige couch took up most of the far wall, a matching love seat beside it at a jaunty angle across from a well-worn recliner. A coffee table still smelling faintly of cedar took up most of the space at the center of the seating arrangement. It currently held nothing but three clean, empty plates, each with a folded napkin and silverware. Shelves filled the wall behind the couch, containing a few decorative pieces, mostly figurines of police and firefighters, and an assortment of small electronics.

The opposite side of the room consisted mostly of an entertainment center that formed a perfect set with the coffee table. Among smaller players and speakers, it held an enormous video screen and stacks of discs and cubes. A spotless blue carpet set off the furniture and revealed highlighting flecks in the otherwise drably painted walls. An overhead fixture with a bladeless fan the same color as the carpet bathed the room in light. Patterned curtains completed the image, displaying the colors of every wall, floor, and stick of furniture in geometric triangles. Jake had impeccable taste in home décor, as well as shocking cleanliness for a bachelor with short notice of visitors. For the first time, Susan truly believed he might have told the truth about being gay.

Without waiting for an invitation, Kendall walked directly to the couch and took a seat on the cushion closest to the recliner, as if from habit. Susan set the cooler bag of food on the coffee table, then sat beside him. The cushion molded to fit her, soft and comfortable. Carefully securing the door, Jake perched in the recliner. "So, Susan, what can I do for you?"

Susan looked at Jake. He appeared much as she remembered: sinewy and agile, sleek and stylish with quick hazel eyes. He wore his hair a bit longer, the straw-colored strands now touching the nape of his neck, crowding his ears, and flopping over his forehead. Though still functionally short, it little resembled the spiky crew cut he had sported the day she met him. She suspected he had grown it out to hide the scars from when Cadmium had shot him, with the announced intent of killing him. *Shot him in the head so he couldn't protect me.* Susan felt the familiar stirrings of guilt, and that jolted her back to his question. She chuckled nervously. "You can eat this fabulous dinner I brought you."

Jake made no move to open the bag. "Susan, I'm a detective, remember? After promising to keep in touch, you ignore me for an entire year. Then, someone gets killed at the hospital where you work and, suddenly, you can't wait to see me. Now what can I do for you?"

Susan studied her hands, lacing them in her lap. "I'm sorry," was all she could think to say.

No one moved or spoke, so Susan continued. "I didn't mean to offend you." She glanced at Kendall. She had already apologized to him on the glide-bus ride to Brooklyn, but Jake had not heard it. "To offend either of you." She explained for what seemed like the millionth time. "I had a lot of work time to make up, so they had me doing double and triple shifts. In my rare off-time, I was sleeping . . . or crying." She added softly, "Plus, I now think I subconsciously worried spending time with you, even just speaking to you, would bring . . . it all . . . back."

Jake's tone softened, but he did not let her wholly off the hook. "We could have helped you through it." He added unexpectedly, "Kendall helped me."

Susan gave Kendall a look of unbridled irritation. "Really? He didn't mention that to me."

Jake smiled. "Well, I rather imagine he was trying to maintain doctor/patient confidentiality. And I appreciate that."

Susan's focus on Kendall intensified. "You've been treating him?"

Kendall's gaze flicked to Jake who nodded. Only then, he answered Susan, though simply. "Yes?"

Jake explained, "Current police rules state that, if we so much as discharge a weapon, we need to meet with a staff psychologist. As a condition of my . . . transfer, I had to promise to undergo a year of counseling from a psychiatrist or psychologist of my choosing." He made a gesture toward Kendall.

Susan appreciated the reprieve. She had not wanted to jump right into her concerns, and the men had, intentionally or otherwise, allowed a diversion. Not quite casually, she reached for the cooler bag, opened it, and pulled out the three sandwiches, individually wrapped in biodegradable paper. She placed a turkey pastrami and Swiss on each of the men's plates and her Reuben on the third, then placed packets of mustard and mayonnaise on the table. A soft container of pickles in brine came next, followed by a personally selected mixture of sweet potato, carrot, tomato, and pea chips. Finally, she added the fizzy juice, six bottles of various flavors, uncertain which they would prefer. "So," she said innocently as she unwrapped her sandwich. "Tell me about this transfer."

Jake reached for his own sandwich, scooping a couple of packs of mustard toward the plate. "Not much to it, really. I told you I'd get into some trouble after all the shootings, and I did. It could have been a lot worse. I got to keep my gun, my title. Was transferred to the FIAU, not a plum assignment but better than I could have hoped for; and I've only got another year there before I'm back to homicide. The only other condition was a year of counseling, which I've almost finished." He squeezed mustard onto his sandwich, then tossed the empty wrappers on his plate.

Kendall added a handful of assorted chips to his plate, grabbed a strawberry fizzy juice, and reached for the mayonnaise. "I told him you were the best, but you were booked solid, so he settled for me."

Jake brought his sandwich to his lips, then lowered it without taking a bite. "Oh, you're good all right. Got me completely off the subject." He pinned Susan with a scolding stare. "The man murdered at Manhattan Hasbro. You knew him, didn't you, Susan?"

Susan tried to act nonchalant. He had momentarily shaken her, but she had regained the upper hand. "Of course I knew him. Everyone knew him. Ari Goldman was one of the premier researchers in the world, especially in psychiatry."

Jake did not back down. "What was he, your uncle or something? Seems like people close to you wind up dead."

Jake had struck closer to home than Susan liked. She had made the same observation to Lawrence during the crises of the previous year. Her mother, Remington, her father had all died violently; and she had no remaining relatives as far as she knew. "And yet you two morons are complaining that I don't spend more time with you. Have you no appreciation for your own mortality?"

"Well I figure I'm safe," Jake said, hands wandering to his head. "I already died for you once. No one's had to die twice, have they?"

Susan ignored the technicalities. Jake had sustained a severe concussion and insignificant skull fracture when his head struck the floor, but the gunshot itself had not been life-threatening. "No one's had the opportunity. Yet."

Jake would not allow himself to get sidetracked a second time. "So, I ask again, what's your personal interest in the murder?"

Susan put down her sandwich, seeing no reason to prolong the moment any further. "They think Nate did it."

"They?" Jake prompted.

"The police. They think Nate is the murderer."

Jake laughed.

It was the last reaction Susan expected. Even Kendall turned him a curious look. "You think that's funny?" she asked accusingly.

"Hilarious." Jake defended his reaction with another burst of laughter. "And you should think so, too. Didn't we just spend an entire month dodging gunfire to prove robots can't be uncoupled from the Three Laws?"

"Exactly!" Susan could not suppress a shout. "So why did they arrest Lawrence?"

All the humor left Jake so abruptly, his features assumed a wincing knot. "Because," he said, mumbling into his sandwich, "they don't know."

Susan heard him. "What do you mean, they don't know? People may have become a bit . . . inured to murder, but surely something as wild as what happened to us last year . . ." Susan would never forget the shootings in the street, the standoff in Lawrence's office that had ended with two federal agents dead.

Jake shook his head. Susan glanced at Kendall, only to find his head shaking in unison.

"What?" she demanded.

Jake explained with two words. "Cover story."

Susan remembered the Department of Defense Intelligence Exploitation Agency she knew as Cadmium did not officially exist. Anything involving them, especially any interaction with law enforcement, required a rewrite of history. Doing so also protected Jake and themselves from retribution. Righteous indignation flowed through Susan. "So everyone involved knew about this cover story except me?"

Kendall sputtered out. "We tried to talk to you a billion times, remember? You kept avoiding us."

Jake added, "Since you wouldn't even talk to us, you clearly weren't talking about what happened, so what did it matter?"

The details were moot. Susan found her shoulder muscles relaxing and only then realized she appreciated the need for secrecy at a primal level. "So tell them. They'll listen to you."

"To me?" Jake let out another chuckle, this one thoughtful, almost bitter. "I'm just one detective, Susan, and outside of their precinct. I have no authority there, even if I wasn't already in deep . . ." He moderated his speech, aware Susan did not like swearing. "Doo-doo."

Incredulous, Susan dropped her sandwich to her plate. "But you guys . . . take care of each other. You can try, at least." She could not help adding, "You have to try."

Jake placed his partially eaten sandwich on his plate. "Susan, you're asking me to try to influence people I can't influence with a story I'm not allowed to tell them at a time when my credibility is nonexistent. I'd be risking my badge, my entire life, for no possible return."

"So, instead, an innocent man should spend a lifetime in prison, an innocent robot should be destroyed, and an innocent corporation selling the greatest product in the history of mankind should close its doors?"

Jake's brows rose nearly to his forehead. "Susan, it's not an either-or situation. My speaking to the highly competent homicide detectives in the Nineteenth Precinct will not change any of that." He grabbed up his sandwich and took another bite.

Susan had lost her appetite. "Jake, you have to do *something*."

Jake spoke around his food. "I'll help you however I can, of course. But I wouldn't tell you how to perform an appendectomy, and you can't tell me how to handle the police. Agreed?"

Susan could hardly argue. "Agreed," she said reluctantly. "So what can you do for Nate? For Lawrence?"

Kendall gave her a strange look.

It took Susan a moment to realize she had expressed concern about the robot before the man. She covered weakly, saying, "Not necessarily in that order."

Jake caught Susan's gaze and held it. "On a strictly professional level, they would have had to void Nate's arrest. I'm guessing they did it as swiftly as possible to avoid embarrassment as well as the need for piles of paperwork and the use of lawyers." He added drolly, "Good God, no one wants to invoke lawyers." He gave the last word the emphasis one might use for rodents.

Kendall chuckled. "Doctors aren't big fans of lawyers, either."

Jake stared at the ceiling, brows returning to their rightful position, then squinting further. "It seems to me that would make Nate . . . evidence." He looked at Susan again. "I have no idea how one would corral a moving, thinking murder weapon."

Susan had an answer for that. "They asked Lawrence to turn Nate off, and he did so."

Now both men stared at Susan. Jake spoke first. "You can . . . turn him off?"

Though Lawrence's ability to do so had startled Susan just as much at the time, she turned the detective a cold stare. "Like all mechanical devices, he has an energy source. You remove it, he stops."

Kendall defended Jake. "It's difficult to consider a thinking entity a 'mechanical device.' So, what does he run on? A hundred triple A's?"

Susan barely acknowledged the joke. She reached into the envelope containing Lawrence's belongings and pulled out the tiny, silver-colored battery. "Just one of these does the trick."

The men leaned in to examine the battery. "Atomic," Jake guessed. "Not all that different from what's in our Vox."

Kendall tapped his Vox. "There's one of those in here?"

Jake gave him a strained glance. "What did you think keeps it running? It's not like you have to plug it in at night."

Kendall flushed. "I don't know. I guess I just figured some sort of . . . web waves or something." He shook his arm, as if to reorient the Vox. "How come I've never had to change the battery?"

Susan had the answer. "Because they last for years. Usually longer than anyone keeps a Vox before upgrading." She carefully replaced the robot's battery in the envelope. Lawrence had suggested she take it to United States Robots and Mechanical Men, and she suspected he had done so because they might learn something useful from it.

"So . . . Nate's immobile."

Susan tucked the envelope between her body and the arm of the couch. "Apparently." Lawrence had once stated that the memories in the positronic brain could not last long once separated from the power source. A new fear gripped her. "How long will they keep him that way?"

Jake hesitated, which brought all eyes on him. He explained his delay. "You have to realize this has never happened before."

Susan rolled her eyes. "Of course not. It can't. The Three Laws prevent any positronic robot from harming any human. It didn't happen this time, either. That's my whole point."

"Yes, yes, Susan," Kendall chimed in. "The walls and windows got that point." He encouraged Jake, "I think what she means is what happens to Dr. Robertson? What can we do to help him?"

That was not what Susan meant, but she let Jake answer the question on the table first.

"He'll be arraigned. Given the significance of the crime, probably held over for the grand jury."

Still concerned about Nate's time without a battery, Susan inserted, "How long will they hold him?"

"By current New York Criminal Procedure Law, they'll have to convene the grand jury within seventy-two hours. The grand jury will decide whether or not to indict."

Susan had little experience with the law. "Is that something we can affect?"

"You can't even attend unless they decide to call you in as a witness." Jake directed his full attention to Susan again. "Is that likely?"

Susan doubted it. "I was about the hundredth person on the scene."

"No, then." Jake shrugged and reached for his drink. "There's nothing you can do on the legal front before the trial. Except, maybe, help him find a competent lawyer."

Susan glanced at Kendall, hoping he would not sidetrack her again. She worried for Lawrence, but the legal wrangling would not kill him. Nate might not have much longer. "So what happens to the evidence?"

Jake smiled. "You mean Nate?"

Susan saw no reason to lie. "Yes."

Jake downed his drink, then set the bottle aside. "Well, the standard course of action is to tag the evidence for chain of custody. It then goes into an envelope, if it's small enough, and into the on-site evidence locker." He added thoughtfully, "If it's small enough. But neither of those apply to Nate. He'd have to go into the evidence room outside the locker with a tag affixed. From there, he would probably go to the police lab for testing." He stopped in further consideration, then continued. "The final step is the police property clerk's office at One Police Plaza where he'll stay locked up until the trial."

Jake still seemed to be thinking, so Susan did not interrupt. Alarm swept through her. She knew it could take months for a trial, during which

Nate might have no power to his positronic brain. He would die as surely as Ari Goldman.

"Of course, I'm applying the standard to something distinctly oversized. Moving Nate around would take a lot more wrangling than the usual course of events. It would also depend on his weight."

"His weight?" Susan shrugged. "My father was about the same height as Nate, though thinner and less muscular. He tried to maintain himself at around two hundred pounds."

Kendall polished off his sandwich. "Is that what he weighed on an actual scale? Or is that what he told you?"

"What?" The word was startled out of Susan.

Kendall explained. "It occurs to me that metal gears might weigh more than organs. He would have told you something believable in order to pass as human. Did you ever see him step on a scale? Did you ever lift him?"

"Of course not! Have you ever picked up *your* father?"

"No," Kendall admitted. "But I wrestled him once or twice."

"I'm a girl," Susan reminded.

"So is Kendall," Jake said, in an unusual display of humor.

Kendall gave him a dirty look. "By the definition you're implying, hotshot, so are you."

Jake turned his attention back to his meal, though Susan thought she saw a ghost of an amused smile. No one could accuse him of appearing effeminate in any possible way.

Susan refused to let their banter derail the conversation. Again. "At the morgue, they checked in my father's headless body at one hundred seventy-eight pounds. So, unless the weight lies in the brain itself, I don't think we're dealing with tonnage." It surprised Susan how easily information about her father's corpse flowed from her tongue without invoking any further grief. It felt rote, mechanical, as if she no longer had any emotions to share.

Jake chewed for several moments before saying, "Let's assume the six-foot-eight-inch robot, including head, weighs in at a healthy two hundred seventy. He's not going to fit into any courier's pouch."

Susan had to know. "So what will they use?"

Jake's expression turned curious. "A van, I suppose. Maybe a fire vehicle or a bus."

"A bus?" Susan asked incredulously. "They could transport a hundred robots in a bus."

"Ambulance," Jake corrected, and Susan remembered the police slang. "Why does it matter?"

Susan made a noncommittal gesture. She had no particular idea other than that she wanted as much information as possible. No one knew what might prove inconsequential and what invaluable.

Kendall filled in the reason, striking right to the heart. "Susan always absorbs every detail, even the ones most people dismiss. That's why she's the world's greatest diagnostician."

Susan had never considered that, but it reminded her that some of the best detectives had a hint of obsessive-compulsive disorder, an uncanny ability to notice any tiny thing out of place. "I'm hardly the world's greatest. There are thousands of better diagnosticians out there."

Kendall raised one brow in a quirky and characteristic gesture. "Name two."

Susan rolled her eyes. The rare famous physicians were nearly always known for inventions, treatment successes, or research awards. She had never heard anyone outside the standard circle of colleagues ever lauded for diagnostic acumen. It was simply expected that all competent doctors would appropriately diagnose any disease in the same way mechanics were supposed to properly find and fix any malfunctioning component of a vehicle. "Just because I can't name them doesn't mean they don't exist. It's not the kind of profession that inspires fame."

The conversation had come to its natural conclusion, at least in Susan's mind. They made small talk as they finished their dinner, her thoughts racing in several directions. She would try her best to sleep tonight, while ideas about the situation bombarded her. In the morning, she would head for United States Robots to discuss the possibilities with Alfred Lanning.

Chapter 5

Susan Calvin was waiting at the door when the USR secretary, Amara, arrived. Susan had met her twice before, a petite thirty-something woman who would have been pretty had she worn a lot less makeup, at least in Susan's opinion. When Amara caught sight of her, the secretary's colorful face lit up. "Dr. Calvin! Pleasure to find you here." Her grin was genuine. From long habit, she held the proper position for the simultaneous palm and retinal scanners. The door whisked open to reveal the familiar stuffy foyer containing only her large semicircular desk and its enormous computer console.

Amara ushered Susan inside, then followed her as the door slid closed and the lock reset with an audible click. "Lawrence asked me to scan you, so you can operate the lock yourself. He says you're a member of the staff now."

The news surprised Susan, who could barely believe Lawrence had used his only phone call to arrange such a thing. Then, another thought came to her. *Of course he called USR. They need to know what happened, and he can instruct them to do whatever requires doing, including arranging for legal counsel.* "Apparently, I'm your new robotherapist."

"Robopsychologist," Amara corrected, apparently using Lawrence's directive. "Welcome aboard, Dr. Calvin."

"Susan," she suggested.

But Amara shook her head. Bleached blond curls bobbed around her face, held in place by a large quantity of hair spray. "I loved your father, and I love having a reason to say his name again. Dr. Calvin. Dr. Calvin. Dr. Calvin."

Susan smiled. "Dr. Calvin it is, then." She wondered if Amara knew about the true nature of her father. Lawrence and his roboticists had kept the information need-to-know, a secret even from Susan. They had never wanted her to find out, and the fewer people with the information, the less likely it would leak, purposefully or accidentally.

Amara rummaged through her desk for the proper equipment to set Susan's retinal pattern and print to the door lock. "It would help if you insulted my coffee now and then."

Susan laughed, recalling her father referred to it as motor oil. Although, now that she knew he had been a robot, the jibe seemed more apt. "I'll do my best."

Amara set out a palm reader. "Right hand here." She held out a smaller, circular device. "Right eye here."

Susan did as instructed. A blinding light pulsed into her eye briefly; then Amara put the instruments away and tapped some information into her computer. She gave the last key a hard strike. "Done." She looked up. "Now you can access the building whenever you need to. Some of the labs have additional security. I'll let Drs. Robertson and Lanning decide which ones to open to you."

Susan blinked rapidly several times to clear the blue blob of afterimage in her right eye. "So Lawrence called you yesterday afternoon?"

"Just before closing," Amara confirmed. "He said you'd probably drop by this morning." She returned to her keypad. "I'll need your address, your bank, and your Vox number."

Susan hesitated, so Amara explained.

"We need to know where to send your wages. Also, how to get hold of you."

Wages? Nudged from her focus on Lawrence and Nate, Susan said, "Of course." She supplied the requested information, and Amara typed it into the USR system. It was all happening so fast. "I don't think I'm due for any wages until I've finished my schooling, though."

"Well, Dr. Robertson seems to think you are. He's covering your tuition, you know."

Susan's cheeks grew warm. "He suggested that, but I didn't think it was a done deal. He has more important things to worry about at the moment."

"He's not risking the possibility of losing you." Amara grinned. "If you're half as talented as your father, and he seems to think you're more talented, he's not going to take a chance on losing you."

Apparently. Susan finally managed to blink away the last of the nebulous blue patch. "Well, I'm not going to accept any payment until I've cleared him and Nate."

The door whisked open. Susan turned to see Alfred Lanning, George Franklin, and a roboticist she knew only as Javonte entering together, engaged in a rousing conversation that stopped the moment they noticed Susan. George was the youngest of the three, a gangly youth in his twenties who towered over the others and whom Lawrence had introduced to Susan as one of his top roboticists. Javonte was a handsome, fine-boned man of mixed race with chiseled features, soft brown curls, and dark eyes swept with long lashes. The director of research, Alfred Lanning was frumpy and balding, wearing a suit that seemed perpetually wrinkled. The first time she met him, he had seemed older but was probably not yet forty, more than a decade younger than Lawrence and her father.

Susan shook hands with each man in turn. "Good to see you all again."

Alfred gestured for Susan to follow him to the office he had shared with John Calvin and two others she had not yet established. She only knew the room contained four desks. Likely, at least one of the men who had accompanied him worked in the same room, but neither of them attempted to follow. Alfred ushered her inside first, then shut the door behind them.

Three of the desks faced one another in an open portion of the room. In the left-rear corner, one desk sat apart, divided from the rest of the area with cubicle partitions. Alfred flopped into the chair behind the latter desk, leaving Susan to scrounge the one from behind what had been her father's desk. She scooted it in front of Alfred and dropped Lawrence's envelope on top of the jumble of bric-a-brac on his desk.

Alfred made no move to take it. "What's this?"

"Lawrence's effects." Susan studied Alfred's reactions only from habit. Lawrence had a gift for choosing loyal and dedicated workers. Though his director of research lacked some common social skills, his devotion to Lawrence and to USR was never in question. "Vox, wallet, belt. Standard stuff. Except for this." Susan took the envelope and eased out the atomic battery.

Alfred glanced at the object in her hand. "Standard robot operations battery. Atomic core." He nodded once. "This is from N8-C?"

"Yes."

"Lawrence said you'd bring it. Wants me to study it, see if it reveals anything."

"I'd gathered that." Susan closed her fingers around it lightly, worried to drop it. "But what can you learn from a battery?"

Alfred shrugged. "I'm not sure, but it's worth a try. The positronic brain can be highly susceptible to certain types of radiation. If we can find evidence of pulsatile or sustained exposure deep enough to affect the battery, we can hypothesize similar exposures to the brain." He shrugged again. "It may give us some useful information." He opened a drawer in his desk and fished through the contents. A frown scored his features. Finally, he took something out and laid it on the desktop. Susan recognized it as a small plastic case containing a similar battery. "I was hoping to find an empty," Alfred explained, dumping its contents, a similar battery, onto the surface. He proffered a hand.

Susan slid N8-C's partially used battery into Alfred's waiting palm. He pinched it between the thumb and index finger of his other hand, held it up, and examined it in the light. With an unrevealing grunt, he placed it into the now-empty case and pawed through his desk drawer again.

While Alfred searched for something, Susan examined the battery he had dumped from the case. It looked exactly the same as the one she had brought, except a bit shinier and without a single scratch, apparently brand-new.

Alfred Lanning brought out a fat black marker, which he used to write on the case in crisp letters: "N8-C."

Without any particular plan or reason, Susan palmed the new battery and waited for Alfred to notice its absence.

If he did, Alfred said nothing about it. He did not appear to look around for it, either. He simply placed the now-full case into his drawer and studied Susan instead.

Susan asked the question that had plagued her since Lawrence had rendered Nate immobile. "How long does he have?"

Wrinkles appeared at the upper reaches of Alfred's nose. "What do you mean?"

Susan explained. "How long before Nate's positronic brain loses its data from lack of power?"

Alfred sat up straighter, suddenly alarmed. "Did Lawrence remove both batteries?"

"Both?" Susan repeated, guarded hope rising in increments. "You mean he's got a backup?" She could imagine Nate coming to sudden life in the evidence room, spooking the guard. The generalized panic that might ensue would not help their cause.

"Just for the brain," Alfred explained. "We usually put the housings on the chest and head for easy access. We ship robots without their 'life' battery to prevent accidents, but the 'brain' battery has to be there from the start, or everything we taught it will be forgotten upon arrival. Especially when we're shipping all the way to the Mercury mission. To activate, they merely place a 'life' battery in the chest compartment."

"Lawrence only removed the one battery." Susan considered. "But not from the head or the chest."

Alfred nodded. "As you recall, the NC line was designed to pass for human, which meant we couldn't have a battery housing in a place where people would likely notice it. They're not designed for functional sexual activity, but they can pass in a locker room." His cheeks turned pink as he continued. "You have no reason to find yourself in a men's room, so you'll have to take my word for it. We may take a surreptitious glance at another man's . . . um . . . nether regions, particularly if there's a size extreme." The color in his face flared to mauve. "But it's considered rude to the point of fisticuffs to stare."

Susan took Alfred's word for it. "So the 'life' battery is housed . . ."

Alfred pointed at his navel. "No one notices lines and scars there. And the 'brain' battery is . . . well . . . it screws off at the base." His cheeks were now positively crimson.

Susan did not further embarrass him by requesting the definition of "it." She should not have any reason to remove Nate's 'brain' battery.

"It was only after John Calvin's decapitation last year that we recognized the design flaw." Once he was back on solid footing, Alfred's facial color faded. "You could detach the head of most robots without losing any data, but not the NC's."

Susan did not wish to relive the crime or contemplate the possibility that the opportunity of reconstituting her father might have existed if only they had kept the battery compartment in its usual place. She felt certain Alfred had not intended any ill will by his casual discussion of a sensitive topic. It went back to his iffy relationship with social skills.

Clearly ignorant of Susan's discomfort, Alfred allowed the corners of his mouth to twitch northward, probably the closest he ever came to a smile. "Welcome aboard, Dr. Susan Calvin. USR is pleased to have you on the team." He said it without emotion, yet Susan did not doubt his sincerity.

She did not know what to say. "Thank you," she managed. "But don't you want to wait until I have my robotics doctorate?"

"What for?" Alfred said gruffly. "It's just a matter of a fluffy piece of paper. We know you've already aced Columbia's master's level mathematics and science classes. Your medical school classes will pass you out of almost everything else."

During college, Susan had blasted through all the undergraduate calculus and physics classes, spending most of her time in them tutoring fellow classmates. Seeing her potential, her adviser and some helpful professors had pushed her upward with special consent. It was not something she talked or thought about, and she wondered how Alfred knew.

Alfred answered her question before she could ask it. "All fathers brag about their children."

Susan smiled. "Even John?"

"Endlessly." Alfred sounded almost overwhelmed with boredom at the memory, which made Susan laugh. "We knew you long before we met you. Then, after you and that boyfriend of yours . . ."

"Remy?" Susan inserted.

"Yeah, that one."

As if Susan could ever forget the name. Remington Hawthorn. *Why did my one and only soul mate have to be a hero?*

Clearly ignorant of Susan's turmoil, Alfred continued matter-of-factly.

"After you joked about robots and psychiatry, we got to talking and realized the vast potential of having a psychiatrist on staff. Especially a brilliant one, familiar not only with the Three Laws, but with the mathematics behind the positronic brain."

Susan could not help pointing out, "Something I'm wholly ignorant about."

"But which you have the potential of learning, something few people can boast. And quickly. Neither Lawrence nor I have any doubt about your ability to do so."

Their faith in her warmed Susan. She did not yet share their certainty but suspected neither of them made a lot of mistakes when it came to intellect or judgment of it. "I'll do my best," she promised. "But I still think placing me on the USR staff roster and payroll is premature." She rehashed the argument she had had with Lawrence, in simpler form. "Until I've earned my robotics PhD, I'm only going to consider myself a robot therapist at best."

Alfred tipped his head. "Call yourself whatever you wish, but you're listed as our robopsychologist, and I'm not going to change it without Lawrence's authority. We need you on the payroll, Susan, because we want you working for us as of this moment."

"But I can't," Susan protested.

Alfred's brows crept upward, but he allowed her to continue.

"I can't commit to any job until I . . ."

The dark eyebrows continued to rise.

"See Nate and Lawrence free–" Susan suddenly got it. "Oh."

Brows now practically at his hairline, Alfred repeated, "Oh," then added, "We may have built N8-C and his ilk, piece by piece, written all their codes and software, but you know N8-C better than anyone."

Susan could only nod. "And my first assignment is to find out what actually happened, to testify in court, if necessary, and to prove the innocence of Lawrence Robertson and Nate."

Alfred continued where Susan stopped. "And, hopefully in the process, convince the public they have nothing to fear and everything to gain from positronic robots."

"I see," Susan said carefully, flashbacks of the previous year parading through her mind. She did not enjoy dodging bullets, hated it in fact, but the quick thinking that had eventually rescued them had given her an unanticipated thrill. She needed Detective Jake Carson, or someone like him, who thrived on physical adrenaline, to assist her. The thinking parts she could handle on her own.

Agony accompanied the memories, so vivid Susan suddenly found herself fisting tears from her eyes. She had lost her parents and Remy to the violence that accompanied the Society for Humanity's detestation of everything robotic and the desire of the Department of Defense to weaponize them. Someone had gone to great pains to make it appear as if Nate had slaughtered an eminent doctor, one known not only for his groundbreaking advances in psychiatric medicine but also for his willingness to employ robots in the process. For the Society for Humanity, it was a twofer: the death of a scientist who advanced the use of robots as well as the enhancement of the Frankenstein Complex in the public's mind.

Despite his social ineptness, Alfred seemed to properly read Susan's hesitation. "It's your choice, Susan. If you think the job you've been assigned is too dangerous, you can refuse it. We'll still hire you. Lawrence won't risk anyone else snapping you up, even if he has to run the company from jail."

Susan studied Alfred Lanning. If he did not slouch, he would probably stand a solid six feet or even a few inches taller. He was slender, almost gaunt, with ferocious eyebrows and an unkempt shock of brown hair. He reminded her of images of a young Andrew Jackson, before he turned gray and his hairline receded. With a shock, she realized she had little to lose. With all her loved ones dead, she was risking no one's life but her own and those already involved for reasons that had nothing to do with her. "I'll do it," she told him. "Full disclosure: I'd do nothing different without the promise of employment or pay. I'm not going to allow either of them to rot in prison."

"Full disclosure," Alfred said with a grin. "I never doubted for a moment that you would." If he noticed Susan had taken the fresh atomic battery, he gave no sign. He appeared to have wholly forgotten it.

Susan spent most of the next hour pacing from room to room of her tiny apartment, focused on the problem, time constraints, and with no idea of where to go next. Her conversations with the police, Lawrence, Jake, and Alfred had mostly thrown the responsibility back into her own lap. At least she no longer had to worry about a source of income and whether she had made a critical mistake by quitting her residency. That she fit at United States Robots and Mechanical Men was a no-brainer. She worried more that she might have committed her future to a company that had none. Without Lawrence, with the public certain robots posed a lethal danger, USR could no longer do business and would soon cease to exist.

Susan awakened to the realization that she needed to do her own investigation. She had no idea what the police might have found at the scene or how to gather any information they might have missed, but she knew she had to try. She suspected Jake might help her with that, at least, so long as he did not have to confront or contradict other policemen. More important, Susan knew she needed to interview the one witness the police could not, Nate himself. Now that she knew his positronic brain was essentially safe, she only needed to gain access to him and replace the "life" battery that would enable him to speak.

At the hospital, Susan had met with Nate in the wee morning hours more than once and knew no one powered him down, at least not most nights. Requiring no sleep, robots could quietly work every hour of the day; or, for those owners who feared their robotic workers might plot against them when not being watched, the battery could simply be removed every evening. It further occurred to Susan that even that was not necessary. The Second Law required them to obey any order given by human beings, which meant someone could simply instruct them to become paralyzed, deaf, dumb, and blind, and they would literally not see or hear what happened around them. She also realized the danger. Without an aforementioned release trigger, such a command could render the robot useless.

Susan shook off the thought. She had plenty of time to consider all the psychological aspects of robotics, the entire rest of her life to dedicate to the endeavor, but only if she freed Lawrence Robertson from prison and cleared Nate's name. For now, she had to focus on finding a way to speak with Nate. Whatever information he gave her would assist in their investigation as well. Assuming Jake was right, that the police wanted to get to the truth, not simply close a case, they should see the logic and purpose behind her request.

Susan considered the situation on the familiar glide-bus ride toward Manhattan Hasbro Hospital. She only needed to remain on board for one additional stop, about a half mile, to wind up at the offices of the Nineteenth Precinct. There, she hesitated, the whoosh of the closing doors strangely loud in her ears despite the mingled conversations of myriad passing pedestrians. Without any memory of consciously walking, she found herself in the small parking lot behind the precinct, attempting to compose her thoughts.

Several vehicles filled the spaces between painted white lines. Four black-and-white police cars with standard light bars were parked in spaces numbered one, three, four, and six. Two and five lay empty. Seven and eight held sedans that appeared to be civilian cars. Signs at the next two places warned: TRANSIENT VEHICLES LOADING & UNLOADING ONLY.

A gleaming scarlet ambulance with the familiar FDNY logo of the fire department idled in the one closest to a heavy metal door to the building.

The remaining vehicles in the lot had various smashes, dents, and dings, including one that appeared as if it had slammed directly into a large immovable object such as a building. Bits of windshield still clung to the misshapen metal rim that had once held it in place.

A sour odor permeated Susan's vicinity, and she realized she was standing beside a massive maroon-colored Dumpster. She took a seat on one of its jutting wheel bases, enjoying the security of its shadow. She had practiced her words all morning, yet she still did not feel she had the right ones to convince the property clerk, or whoever he or she called to assist, that she needed to reactivate a man-sized robot who appeared to have murdered a man with one blow of a hammer. *Not a hammer,* she reminded herself, trying to remember the exact description Nate had used. *A Stanley FuBar Utility Bar.*

In the past, Susan had frequently walked the line between informing and insulting. She did not suffer fools, gladly or otherwise, and preferred to simply purge them from her life. She supposed that accounted for the short list of friendships, her run-ins with lazy or inadequate superiors, and why she had focused on schoolwork to the detriment of any social life. She had long convinced herself that learning took, not just priority, but all of her devotion until she had fully mastered any and all degrees and ensconced herself in a suitable, meaningful job. Now she wondered if she simply did not like nor appreciate interacting with the vast majority of people.

Susan shook the thought away. Such cynicism would not have entered her mind two years ago, when she had begun her residency with all the typical high hopes of the future-minded and selfless young doctor. The events of the last two years had rendered her sullen and world-weary, and she no longer had the patience to kowtow to the whims of the uninformed, lazy, or stupid, assuming she ever had.

The heavy exterior door flew open, something partially metallic slammed to the concrete, and a string of swearwords followed in at least two voices. Susan caught a glimpse of three uniformed men fumbling with a stretcher while a fourth held the door and tried to assist simultaneously. She ducked behind the Dumpster before she could consider why she felt the need to hide.

"Lucky this isn't a real guy," one said. "Or we'd have probably splashed his brains across the driveway."

"He's heavy as fuck," another complained. Susan could hear the sound of cloth rustling as they apparently rearranged their burden. "I've been fucking carrying people a long time. This one's four hundred if he's a pound."

"Not even a scratch." This came in a third male voice. "Let's get him in there. I've gotta pee."

Susan peeked at the quartet from under the Dumpster. They had lowered the stretcher to the ground, and she could easily make out a tall, unmoving human form partially covered by sheets. She knew who it had to be. *Nate!*

"We're all gonna pee," the first man growled. "Or at least get one of those Danishes. Because I'm not touching this thing without everyone helping."

The men's trousered legs moved around the stretcher as they replaced all the flopping limbs and spread the sheets properly over the prostrate form.

The man who had estimated the weight spoke again. "Shit, he looks real. You sure that's not a stiff?"

"Not unless stiffs got battery compartments in their navels now. It's a fucking robot. And if that fall didn't wake it up, nothing's going to."

Susan's heart raced. She remembered what Jake had told them about evidence. Presumably, they were taking Nate either to a police laboratory or to the property clerk's office at One Police Plaza. In either case, once Nate left the facility, she would have no access to him until the trial.

From the cab of the ambulance, two more pairs of legs joined the others, these wearing the navy blue tactical trousers of the FDNY. One went to the back, and Susan heard him or her punch in the sequence of numbers that would operate the exterior lock. Seldom used, in favor of the interior lock, it was reserved for demented, confused, or dangerous patients who might attempt to open the door during transport, putting themselves, and the paramedics, at risk. Of course, it also trapped the emergency medical team inside, but even that seemed preferable to giving the violent one the opportunity to shove someone, or themselves, out of a vehicle moving fast and erratically through traffic.

The double doors opened soundlessly, but Susan heard a thunk as they reached their maximum capacity. The men crouched to lift the gurney again. She could see muscles straining in their arms; then the gurney rose until she could no longer follow it from beneath the Dumpster. She watched their black dress shoes moving toward the back of the ambulance, heard a few grunts of effort, then the thud of the gurney landing on the floor of the ambulance. The ambulance workers helped the police feed the gurney into the back, the bottom of it making a shearing sound against the floor. Then, the doors slammed shut, and she heard the solid tone of the lock.

Ideas galloped through Susan's mind. Once the ambulance drove away, she had little hope of speaking to Nate, of finding out what actually happened before the trial when it would, likely, be too late. She needed to follow that ambulance, to hope they made a stop somewhere along the way. *But how?* Without a car, she could never keep up, and public transportation would prove of little help. Since the upgrade to glide-buses, cabs had become scarce. She would have to call the company, wait for the car to pick her up, and hope they could still find the retreating ambulance. With no other options, Susan reached for her Vox.

A woman spoke next, apparently one of the ambulance workers. "Did someone say something about a bathroom and a Danish?"

"This way, my lady," one of the men said with exaggerated gallantry. The breathless catch in his voice identified him as one of the people who had helped carry the gurney. "Grant and Bryson collared a perp running out of Freja's Bakery with his ski mask still in his hand, and they sent over several boxes this morning in gratitude. There's a cheese one in there with my name on it."

Susan watched all five sets of legs heading toward the door. "I'm getting apple," someone said. Then they all disappeared inside, and the door clicked shut behind them.

Susan found herself dashing to the back of the ambulance. She tugged on the door, which did not budge. *Nate's in there. And I've got about five minutes to do something about it.* She glanced at the keypad, suddenly remembering a fact she had never had to previously use: every six months, the emergency medical technicians and doctors at Hasbro received the new ambulance key code. All of the companies in the local area used the same one to prevent any delays should the external locks be required or become activated accidentally. The code was always five digits, distributed to every department. Psychiatry Voxed a copy to every active attending and resident, since they were the most likely to be called to assist with an uncontrollable patient. Determined to be prepared for anything in her new role as senior resident, Susan had memorized the ambulance code for the first time in her career at Hasbro. Silently thanking her obsessive-compulsive side, she punched in the proper sequence and was rewarded by the click of the opening lock. Seizing the door handle, she wrenched it open and leapt into the back of the ambulance. Mindful of time, she yanked the sheet off the figure on the gurney.

Susan recognized Nate immediately. His pants were loose; apparently, no one had done them back up after Lawrence removed the battery. She pushed the flaps aside, then pulled up his blood-splashed polo to reveal the all-too-human skin. She might not have seen the tiny battery compartment were it not partially open. Susan seized the atomic battery from her pocket, pressed it into place, and folded closed the hatch.

Almost immediately, Nate rolled toward Susan. His eyes flashed in a way no human's ever did, then dulled to their normal brown, with pupils appropriately enlarged in the darkish interior of the van and an occasional red vessel visible in the whites. "Susan?" he said in a tone that revealed confusion. "Where are we?"

Explanations could wait. "Do up your pants, turn your shirt inside out, then come with me," Susan commanded softly. "I'll explain while we walk." Her heart pounded so hard, she felt pain through her chest and left arm. Her throat went dangerously dry, and her words emerged more like a croak. Without hesitating, she jumped out of the ambulance and waited for Nate to follow.

Nate paused only long enough to follow Susan's orders before joining her. The moment his feet touched the pavement, Susan swung the door shut and activated the lock button. When the ambulance personnel arrived, she wanted them to find nothing amiss, at least on the outside. With any luck, they would not notice Nate missing until they arrived at their destination and opened the back of the truck.

Susan scampered behind the Dumpster, and Nate trailed her curiously. She appreciated that he did as she bade him without further questions. Quickly, she studied his shirt. She could see the seams, but she doubted anyone else would examine him closely enough to notice. To her relief, no blood had seeped through to the underside. She wondered what the penalty was for stealing evidence from police custody and suspected it would result in a couple of years in prison, at least.

What the hell am I doing? Susan shook the concern away. The police had to catch her first; and, even if they did, it would take time. Meanwhile, she would get the information she needed to rescue Lawrence and to keep Nate safe and secure. It was a crime of opportunity, of necessity, and she could only hope Lawrence would help her find a competent lawyer when the time came to assist her. She headed for the streets.

Susan had traveled several blocks along Sixty-seventh Street, with Nate in tow, before she managed to slow her pace to something less suspicious, more normal. She assumed the typical march of a New York commuter: head high, pace a straight and fast walk, avoiding eye contact as much as possible. Nate marched right alongside her, taking his cues from her demeanor and actions, though he had little experience on the sidewalk.

No one seemed to notice them amid the myriads passing to and fro around them; at least Susan hoped that was the case. Her back felt tingly, as if unseen eyes followed her and, at any moment, they might find themselves surrounded by police cars and officers on foot. She could imagine them commanding her to stop, their pistols trained on her and Nate, preparing the handcuffs. If they caught her escaping, she realized, it was all over. It did Lawrence no good if she went to jail, and Nate would languish in storage.

Yet, Susan realized, if she did not take this opportunity, Lawrence would still be in prison and Nate still in an evidence storage room, devoid of thought or movement. Now they had a chance, if only a marginal one; and she had no choice but to attempt to get Nate somewhere she could question him in solitude. *We can do this.* She tried to ignore the feeling of being watched, the stab of guilty conscience, the desperate fear of discovery. *We have to do this.*

As they plunged into Central Park, Susan caught Nate's hand. He gave her a curious look but did not pull away or question. The excited squeals of children rose over the rising and falling din of human conversation. Occasionally, Susan could make out the thud of a ball or Frisbee and bursts of laughter. In every direction stretched swards of grass and stands of trees, a web of pathways and paved roads winding through them. A bronze statue of a husky stood on a rocky outcropping, children scurrying up and down its burnished back.

Susan's Vox buzzed, startling her. She glanced at the display, and the sight of Jake's name made her throat constrict. She willed herself to relax, allowing it to buzz twice more before poking it on. "Hi, Jake. What's new?"

The policeman's familiar voice came through the speaker. "Ah. So you're taking my calls now?"

Susan continued along the pathway extending from Sixty-seventh Street as it veered southward, Nate at her side. She made a gesture to silence him, though he had not yet spoken a word. "I said I was sorry. How long are you going to make me suffer for my stupidity?"

"As long as it still entertains me." Jake granted Susan no quarter. He added not quite casually, "Where are you?"

Susan suspected he could hear enough background noise that she did not dare to lie. "I'm taking a walk through the park. Clearing my head. Why?"

"Something's come up, and I need to talk to you. When do you think you'll be home?"

"Can you give me an hour?" Susan doubted he would agree to any longer. "I've worked up a sweat, and I'd like to clean up a bit." Susan tried to maintain as much innocence as possible. "What's it about, anyway?"

"It's about Nate."

Susan felt something clutch in her chest. She took a deep breath, purging the discomfort before continuing. She did not want her voice to sound strained. It made sense for her to express concern, but panic over the mere mention of the robot would betray her. "What about Nate? Is he all right?"

The detective gave her nothing. "We'll talk about it when I get there."

"Just tell me no one's damaged him."

"No one's damaged him," Jake repeated dutifully, then added, "I'll talk to you soon." He broke the contact.

Jake had no way of knowing if anyone had harmed Nate. *Unless they got me on tape.* Susan knew most, if not all, of the proceedings inside a police station were recorded. However, she doubted they had equipment trained on the back lot. Even most of the European countries had gotten away from street cameras due to the outcry from a citizenry demanding a modicum of privacy. Vox was intrusive enough. At any given time, some individual seemed to be recording everything, even if only indirectly.

Then, Susan realized, he had more likely simply taken her at her literal word. She had told him to tell her no one had damaged Nate, and he had done exactly so, not necessarily with any regard to the real or possible truth. *Don't get paranoid. That's not how to win this game.* Susan quickened her pace, and Nate hurried to keep up with her.

As they approached Sixty-fifth Street, Susan could hear the sound of vehicular traffic passing through the park. She kept them north of it, not wishing to add to the number of witnesses who might spot them together. Had she planned the heist, she would have brought something to disguise them. Now she relied on people's focus on self and family, working hours, and the normalcy of a couple out for a stroll in the park to keep them from becoming lodged in others' memories.

The path turned into one of the wooded areas of Central Park. Neatly trimmed prairie grasses rose along the sides of the pathways and wound between rows of trees. Three men in olive green uniforms raked leaves, grass clippings, and trash from either side of the route, stuffing their findings into bright orange, biodegradable trash bags. Another clipped overhanging branches with massive shears. None of them seemed to pay Susan or Nate any attention. For the first time since she had made the decision to steal Nate, Susan no longer felt as if hidden spies watched her every move.

Nate spoke his first words since they had left the parking lot. "Are you going to explain now?"

Susan suddenly realized she had promised to do so on the walk but had, thus far, told him nothing. "Well . . . ," Susan started but got no further.

A sound like a distant gunshot silenced her. A chunk of bark leapt from the tree trunk nearest her left hand. *Not again.* Susan realized it was not a matter of distant, but suppressed, fire. She whirled. The uniformed men had dropped their rakes, replacing them with pistols lengthened with metal cylinders and aimed directly at her and Nate. Beyond them, a jogger headed blithely toward them on the woodland path. "No!" Susan shouted, as much to warn the oncoming man as to stop the shooters. She doubted it would have any effect on anyone. The Society for Humanity had shown no hesitation when it came to killing her parents or herself, and neither Cadmium nor the police would have fired the first shot for fear of doing her harm.

Seizing Nate's arm, Susan darted for the forest, hoping to give them a smaller, swiftly moving target. The sudden movement all but impaled her on the hedge clippers. The man suddenly in front of them held the shears open, the only thing that saved her, but only for a moment. He lunged for her throat, and Susan found herself backpedaling directly into the line of fire. She steeled herself for the certain agony of bullets penetrating her every part.

A louder gunshot, unsuppressed, deafened her. Susan grunted in anticipation, but no pain followed. Instead, one of the uniformed men collapsed, the pistol falling from his hand to the dirt. The other spun toward the jogger, too slowly. Another booming shot, and this uniformed man also tumbled to the ground. The man with the clippers dropped them. Susan could hear them hit the ground at her back. The second it took him to draw his gun proved his last, as the jogger's pistol spoke again. Shears-man jerked, hands flailing at his abdomen. A fourth shot sent him sliding to the ground. Susan looked for the last of the uniformed men, only to see him fleeing through the forest.

The jogger sprang forward and seized Susan's wrist with his empty hand, his right, the pistol still clenched in his left. "This way! Quickly!" He pulled her back in the direction he had come.

Susan did not need a second invitation, though she did pause to make certain Nate joined them. Her hesitation earned her a jerk that nearly sprawled her.

"Come on!" he said, glancing over his shoulder. "The last one's coming back." He swore viciously. "With reinforcements."

Susan dared a look, only to see he spoke the truth. "Are they after you?" she gasped out.

"Hell no!" The man urged her on faster. "They're clearly trying to kill *you*. What the hell did you do?"

Susan required every breath. Even if she did not, she would not have answered.

More suppressed gunshots sounded, but Susan could not see or feel the results. Neither the stranger nor Nate slackened his pace, either. The jogger did not waste time or effort returning fire. He simply guided them around the corner of the path and shoved Susan toward a black and silver Harley-Davidson motorcycle with a generous sidecar that held a gym bag, a helmet, a blanket, and miscellaneous clothes. "Get on! Get on! Get on!"

Susan had never ridden a motorcycle in her life, not even as a passenger. She had originally been told a car accident killed her mother when she was only four. Nearly her entire life, she and her father had avoided any transportation but the public variety.

The jogger all but threw Susan into the sidecar, then waved for Nate to join him. She slammed down hard on the helmet, and something inside the gym bag stabbed into her buttocks. She managed to hunker down amid the bric-a-brac as Nate and the stranger each flung a leg over the motorcycle seat, the jogger in front. He turned the key, and the motor sputtered to life just as the uniformed men rounded the curve, guns raised.

"Go!" Susan screamed.

As if in answer, the jogger twisted the throttle, and the bike leapt to life, hurtling down another pathway and veering around a surprised pedestrian. Susan heard more suppressed fire. People screamed, and something rattled against the sidecar and the rear of the motorcycle. Grabbing the helmet, Susan slammed it over her head and ducked deeper into the sidecar, no longer caring about the bruises inflicted by his gear.

The driver took them on a circuitous route, clearly trying to avoid hitting any innocent walkers or joggers who were now fleeing in erratic and foolhardy directions. Susan dared a glance behind them. The guns spoke again, a woman collapsed, screaming, and civilians fled in utter chaos. The uniformed men whirled, running back toward where their fellows had fallen.

Susan did not try to convey that information to the stranger. He would never hear her over the whoosh of the wind and the roar of the motor. Only after the shooting stopped did she recognize the reckless speed of the motorcycle. It felt as if they were flying, a hundred miles per hour if one, and every rock and bump sent her airborne, threatening to eject her.

Head down, buried beneath the overlarge helmet, Susan had no idea of their route. The screaming and gunshots disappeared entirely, replaced by the familiar honks and distant sirens that defined the Manhattan streets. The ride smoothed a bit, punctuated by unexpected and massive bumps where the driver, apparently, ran over curbs, maneuvering strange and unpredictable shortcuts. Finally, after what seemed like hours but was probably only a few minutes, he stopped. The noise of the motor disappeared, leaving only a loud and continuous ringing in Susan's ears.

Gently, a fist rapped the helmet, as if knocking on a door.

Shaken, dripping sweat, and wildly uncertain, Susan peeked out from beneath the helmet to meet startlingly sky blue eyes: beautiful, deep and soft, almost mysterious, and radiating intelligence. She could barely look past them to the well-formed, straight nose and strong line of his clean-shaven jaw. Wind-whipped black hair fell in tousles around highly set cheekbones and plushy lips. Under the strong and piquant odors of wind and gas, Susan could smell a hint of honest perspiration, and she found it strangely attractive.

The man finally spoke, in a deep voice radiating concern. "Are you all right?"

"Physically, yes." Susan removed the helmet, though it revealed her stringy, hat-crushed hair. "Thank you. You saved our lives."

The stranger ran his thumb and index finger along his chin. "Should we go directly to the police station? Or the hospital first?"

"No police," Susan said before she could stop herself. She looked at her hands and found them trembling.

The man leaned against his motorcycle, Nate still astride behind him. The warmth left his eyes, replaced by an emotion Susan could not yet name. "Oh no." He stood upright, a solid six feet. "Oh no. Don't tell me I rescued the bad guys."

"What?" It took Susan inordinately long to understand what he meant. "No! No. We haven't done anything wrong, honest. And those weren't cops. Cops don't open fire on unarmed people. They don't attack with hedge clippers, and they certainly don't shoot into fleeing crowds."

Suspicion tainted his tone. "Then why wouldn't you want me to take you to the police station?"

He deserved to know, but Susan was not ready to take anyone into her confidence, especially a total stranger. Then, another thought struck her, and she asked it in lieu of an answer. "How did you know I work at the hospital?"

He drew back. "You work at the hospital?"

That response surprised Susan. "Isn't that why you asked if I wanted to go there?"

The soft, full lips broke into a kindly smile. "I asked if you wanted to go there because you're clearly and understandably traumatized. Also, I think your boyfriend might have been shot."

"He's not my boyfriend." Susan could not believe those were the first words out of her mouth. Quickly, she turned suitably widened eyes on Nate and asked with appropriate alarm, "Oh my God! Were you hit?" She eyeballed him for signs of a wound, but found her examination mostly blocked by his slouched position on the bike. Her concern was an act. A single bullet from a handgun could not do any significant damage to a robot, and she certainly could not take Nate to any hospital for care.

Nate answered the only way he could. "I'm fine. I don't require any medical attention, thank you."

The stranger looked all around them, clearly still worried about pursuit. "So . . . the . . . police station, then?" None of them had spoken loudly, but he lowered his voice still further, until she had to strain to hear. "I mean, I shot three guys, for Christ's sake. There're laws against shooting and running."

Nate said simply, "I'm pretty sure there're laws against shooting people, even if you stand still afterward."

Susan gave Nate a firm look, intended to convey that he should say as little as possible. "It's legal to use deadly force against someone when it's in defense of yourself or others, so long as you're not engaged in an illegal activity. The police may do a lot of investigating, but you're not likely to get convicted of any crime."

The jogger stared at Susan. "You said that with an awful lot of authority."

Susan managed a haggard smile. "I've had the need to know." She did not explain further. She could no longer ignore the incessant urge to find a safer place to talk, to be. "I'm not sure exactly where we are, but I doubt it's far from my apartment. Can you take us there? I'd rather discuss this indoors, where I'm not so worried about people shooting at me."

He nodded, but without much assurance. "If you've got people who want you dead, wouldn't we be safer somewhere else? Like, maybe . . . my place?"

Remembering she had promised to meet Jake at her apartment, Susan shook her head. Under the circumstances, it seemed ludicrous to aggravate the police. If the SFH had known the location of her apartment, they surely would have attacked her there rather than out in the open and among multiple witnesses. "*My* place," Susan insisted, fairly whispering the address. She added, "It's behind Lincoln Center."

The jogger retook his position but made no move to start the engine. After several moments of stillness, he spoke without bothering to look at Susan. "I'm not going anywhere until your helmet is on."

Though she felt like a child chastised for not buckling a seat belt, Susan pulled the helmet back over her head and ducked low into the sidecar. As if on cue, it roared to life again, and they took a long and circuitous route to Susan's building.

Chapter 6

Susan's apartment had never felt smaller than it did with three adults crammed into her tiny bedroom. The men sat side by side on the futon and, for the first time, Susan appreciated that the only sleeping surface she could fit formed a more than satisfactory couch. It also seemed more proper and appropriate than having two men sprawled across her bed. While the stranger had hidden his cycle and sidecar in the shadows near the Dumpsters, Susan seized the time outside to quickly coach Nate. It was not long enough for her to create a cohesive identity for him, but she felt confident Nate would not reveal himself as a robot before they knew whether they could trust their new companion with the information.

Susan stepped to the kitchen to scout her dorm-sized refrigerator for something to drink, and the jogger started the introductions. "My name is Pal Buffoni."

Susan called back to him from the kitchen. "Did you say Paul?"

The man laughed. "No one under the age of a hundred is named Paul anymore."

"Like Susan?" Susan proffered with a smile he could not see through the wall.

"Exactly. Another moldy oldie, that"–either cued by Nate or catching on independently, he changed course abruptly—"is nevertheless a beautiful name. I don't suppose it's yours?"

"Nice save." Managing to locate only one can of mango-pineapple fizzy juice, Susan grabbed that for their guest, then opened the cabinet for a hard plastic cup. "Susan Calvin. Named for my grandmother, who by the way, would only be in her late eighties, if she hadn't died some years ago." She filled the cup with tap water. Then, realizing she was trying to pass Nate off as human, she grabbed and filled a second cup with water.

Pal continued the distant conversation. "I wasn't named for my parents' dog, if that's what you're thinking. It's short for Paladin. Apparently, paladins were 'paragons of chivalry' in certain role-playing games. My parents wanted me to be one of the good guys."

"Well, you certainly were today," Susan reassured him as she carried the can and cups into the bedroom. "If I remember my history correctly, paladins were the elite warriors of Charlemagne." She offered the can of fizzy juice to Pal.

He reached for the water instead. "Carbonation interferes with my running regimen," he explained.

Susan switched hands, allowing him to take one of the cups. Constrained by propriety, she next offered the can to Nate, who took it absently and placed it on the floor near his foot. He could take a sip or two for appearances, but he had no need for nourishment. Taking a seat on the floor in front of Nate and Pal, she placed the water beside her.

"Well, I'm just glad they didn't name me Charlemagne. I mean, how would you shorten that? Char? Charla?" Pal shook his head. "Way too feminine."

Susan could not help smiling. "Well, as Charlemagne means Charles the Great, I'd assume Charles or Charlie. Maybe even Chuck." The grin widened. "Another name from the Susan and Paul era."

Pal chuckled. Susan liked the sound, outgoing, uninhibited, and originating deep in his chest. He turned his attention to Nate. "You're awfully quiet, not-the-boyfriend."

Nate glanced at Susan, apparently for help with responses, then finally replied, "She's right. I'm not her boyfriend."

"He's my cousin," Susan supplied, uncertain whether robots could lie, at least without a direct order to do so. "Layton Campbell." She chose a name that did not sound too much like Nate but that she could pass off if she slipped. "He's visiting from Idaho."

"Iowa," Nate corrected from the snatch of conversation they had managed to exchange while Pal tended to his motorcycle.

Susan wished Nate had not taken her so literally. It did not matter which fictional hometown they gave him. "Iowa," she corrected. "I get those central, vowel-saturated states confused: Idaho, Iowa, Ohio." Susan suspected a real Iowan would either take offense or find her big-city mentality amusing, but Nate did not know how to play the game. Deception was not in a robot's nature; it was one of the things she loved about them.

Pal turned Nate a brief nod of acknowledgment, then downed his water in one long gulp. Afterward, he put down the cup and wiped his mouth on the back of his jacket sleeve. He gave Susan an earnest look. "So, tell me why people are trying to kill you, Susan Calvin."

Susan preferred not to answer but knew she owed him some kind of explanation. He had saved her life and, thus far, had not called the police. She allowed herself to look directly into those blue eyes, every bit as intense and startling as the first time she saw them. She found herself wondering what it would be like to look into them every day, if they could ever become commonplace and normal, or if each glance would continue to amaze her, to send her heart fluttering. Her mind raced, concocting possible explanations; then she realized the wisest approach was to stick as closely as possible to the truth. Stress was making it hard enough to remember even such simple details as the state of Iowa. The more she lied, the greater her chances of slipping up and sending Pal racing to the police with a detailed description of herself and Nate. "They think I'm the only person who knows something. And, if they kill me, the knowledge will cease to exist."

"Ah," Pal said, though the hesitant tone with which he spoke the exclamation of understanding suggested he did not grasp the situation at all. "Are they right?"

Stunned by the question, it took Susan inordinately long to answer. "Right? To try to kill me?"

Pal shook his head, explaining, "Right that killing you would cause the information to no longer exist."

"No," Susan said, without hesitation. "The knowledge does not exist; it never has." Seeking his sympathy, she added, "They already murdered both of my parents over this mythical secret. They came after me once already, last year, and failed. I thought the police had shut them down, but here they are again." That bit was not exactly the truth. Jake had suggested that Cadmium would undo the SFH using the Racketeer Influenced and Corrupt Organizations Act, RICO, but Susan did not want to bog down the explanation with details.

Pal considered Susan's words. "Maybe if you made it clear you had shared the secret, they would no longer have a reason to silence you."

Susan heaved a sigh. "You're not listening. There is no secret. How can I share something that doesn't exist?"

"Good point." Pal drew his knees to his chest. There was not much room for anything else. "Dare I ask what kind of secret is worth killing for? Perhaps the plans for . . ." He paused to think." Some new type of hospital scanner that runs on . . . human flesh?"

Susan pursed her lips but still saw no reason to lie. The more people who understood the Three Laws of Robotics, and the safety they engendered, the better. "It's difficult to explain. In brief, they think I have a code, created by my parents, that would deactivate the features preventing robots from ever harming human beings. They're afraid of robots and, somewhat understandably, don't want that to ever happen."

"Somewhat understandably," Pal agreed aloud. "Except for the attempted murder part. Isn't it rather hypocritical to kill people in the name of preventing people from getting killed?"

Nate bobbed his head appreciatively.

Susan shrugged. "I don't pretend to fully understand their motives. On the other hand, I'm just as befuddled by activists murdering doctors in the name of 'life' or animal rights groups who kill scientists or drive domestic animals out of cages and pens to their doom. It's at least equally hypocritical, yet it's happened more than once."

Pal shook his head, rolled his gorgeous eyes, and grunted.

Susan did not want to talk about herself anymore. She had a million questions to ask Pal Buffoni, but she decided to ease into them with the obvious choice. "What do *you* do for a living?"

The corners of Pal's mouth twitched, but he did not smile. "You mean besides rescuing DIDIs?"

"Didis?" Susan repeated, brows furrowed.

"Damsels in distress," Pal said, explaining the acronym.

Susan felt her cheeks grow warm. "You mean me?"

Pal's attention rolled briefly to Nate. "Well, I didn't mean *him*."

"I'm hardly a damsel," Susan shot back.

Pal's gaze returned to her. "I don't think we can dispute the 'in distress' part. You're a young, beautiful, unmarried woman. The very definition of a damsel."

He thinks I'm beautiful. The warmth in Susan's cheeks became a bonfire. She had to look away, mumbling, "I think noble birth is also a factor."

Pal did not pursue the subject further. "And I'm . . . um . . . between assignments."

I knew it was too good to be true. Regaining her composure, Susan found herself asking before she could stop herself, "You mean you're unemployed?"

"In a way. I just finished a twelve-year stint in the Marines, eight of them in MARSOC. I'm planning to apply for a civilian job, but for a few months I thought I'd just enjoy my freedom."

"MARSOC?" Susan had never heard the term.

"Special operations forces," he explained succinctly.

Guilt trickled through Susan's thoughts, and she winced subtly. "I'm sorry. I should be thanking you, not chastising you." She added hastily, "Thank you for serving our country." She had no idea exactly what that currently entailed. She could barely remember adults arguing vehemently over various skirmishes. Once, one could Vox almost every detail of a current war, nearly in real time. It had become so politicized, it had crippled defense, rendering it a consequence of elections, lies, and promises. In the last few decades, the country waged its wars in secret while the populace went about its business without becoming embroiled in death counts, images of horror, and politically spun stories designed, not to keep the country safe, but only to assure the reelection of politicians or gain momentum for their parties.

Suddenly, everything fell into place. Susan found herself nodding as she spoke. "Which explains your ability to assess a situation and figure out who to shoot without panicking. Also why you're rescuing DIDIs. And why you're so calm about this whole situation."

"You're my first DIDI," Pal said. "And it doesn't explain your coolness under the same pressure."

A laugh escaped Susan. "I was hardly cool. I nearly decapitated myself on a giant pair of scissors."

Pal opened his mouth to speak again, but before he could do so, the communications system buzzed.

Susan hit the proper button to connect it to her Vox, then responded. "Who is it?"

Detective Jake Carson's familiar voice wafted into the room. "It's Jake." He did not joke, elaborate, or remind her of the arrangement they had made via Vox. The first time she had desperately needed his assistance, he had played along with her attempts to pass him off as a medical dispatcher. Had he not, she would have died at the hands of her captors. Jake always assumed someone was listening and did not need to know she was being visited by a police officer.

Without further discussion, Susan activated the button that would allow him through the downstairs locks and onto the elevator or staircase. "Excuse me while I handle this." She rose and headed for the door. She had barely reached it when someone knocked. From instinct, she examined him through the peephole, finding Jake alone, dressed in his usual formal attire.

A cold wave of sweat washed over Susan. She had lost the opportunity to hide Nate, and Jake knew the robot by sight. He would have no choice but to arrest her. She opened the door just wide enough to slip through it and into the hallway. Letting the door swing shut behind her, she heard the faint click of the lock.

Jake back-stepped to allow her enough space to join him. He glanced around, which caused Susan to do the same. They were, apparently, alone.

"May I come in?" Jake asked reasonably.

Susan looked him straight in the eye. "Do you have a warrant?"

"No," Jake admitted.

"Then no," Susan said.

Apparently, she had rendered him speechless. They stood in silence for several moments before she broke it. "You came to tell me something about Nate," she reminded.

"Nate, yes." Jake seemed thrown by Susan's behavior. He glanced over his shoulders repeatedly, licked his lips, then glared pointedly into her face before continuing. "Nate disappeared from a locked ambulance."

Susan forced her expression to one of shocked concern. She should not know this information. "Disappeared? What do you mean 'disappeared'?"

"I mean disappeared," Jake repeated unhelpfully. "I mean that sometime between when several police officers loaded a four-hundred-pound robot into the back of an ambulance and when said ambulance arrived at its destination, it had vanished without a trace."

"The ambulance?" Susan tried.

"The robot," Jake corrected. "Nate."

"So . . ." Susan wet her lips, too. "He came back online, slipped out the back–"

"No battery," Jake pointed out. "I know that for a fact because you had dinner at my house last night and showed me the battery that Lawrence had removed from him."

Susan suddenly wished she had kept her mouth closed.

Jake continued carefully. "You wouldn't happen to still have that battery?" He added even more cautiously, "Would you?"

Susan did her best to look outraged. "As a matter of fact, I turned all of Lawrence's possessions over to USR first thing this morning. Including the battery. I watched Alfred Lanning put it into a labeled case in order to study it for exposure to radiation or other contaminants." She pinned a look of fierce accusation on her face. "You're welcome to call him if you don't believe me."

They stared at each other for several moments. Finally, Jake sighed. "I'm just trying to get to the truth, Susan. You know Nate better than anyone. I thought you might have some insight."

"Who says I know Nate better than anyone?"

Jake managed an awkward smile. "Well, you for one. And you ought to, given your . . . well, your father being . . ."

"Robotic?" Susan inserted.

Jake flushed; he had been sworn to secrecy. "Well, yes. You have the best idea how robots react and function in a practical sense. And Lawrence also says you and Nate had become close friends."

Susan knew continuing to act indignant and defensive would only make her appear guilty. "Do you think someone stole Nate?"

Jake's head bobbed. "It would have to be several someones. As I said, he weighs upward of four hundred pounds."

They had already had the discussion about her father's weight, but N8-C had been a prototype. It might have taken several tries to get the mass whittled down to normal human proportions. "Several someones, then. I happen to know the Society for Humanity is back in force." Susan wished she could have derailed the conversation in any other direction. She did not want to talk about the shooting, did not want to become associated with that particular crime in case someone identified Nate as the man who had been with her at the time.

Jake stiffened, and his features softened. "What happened, Susan?"

"Three men with guns and a hedge trimmer tried to murder me in Central Park."

"A hedge trimmer?"

Susan shrugged. "What's one more decapitation between enemies?"

Jake did not respond to the jest, clearly deep in thought.

It suddenly occurred to Susan that Jake ought to be at work. "What are you doing here, anyway? I thought you weren't involved in this case."

That jarred Jake from his intensive focus. "I'm not involved with the homicide." He met Susan's gaze again. "I'm handling the 'theft of evidence from police custody' case."

Susan had to stop herself from groaning.

"So how did you keep yourself from getting . . . decapitated?"

The door wrenched open suddenly to reveal Pal, no longer in jogging clothes. He wore khakis and a close-fitting T-shirt that he must have stored in his sidecar pack, his black hair still wind-tangled and his blue eyes as striking as when Susan had first glimpsed them. Unlike the oversized Windbreaker, the T-shirt revealed a well-developed chest, strong arms, and a six-pack of abdominal muscles. He held an empty glass in his left hand. "She did a great job ducking and running, but I helped her, too."

Susan found herself speechless, staring.

Jake also studied the man with an intensity that befit his sexual orientation.

Pal stuck out a hand. "Pal Buffoni. Susan's a bit old-fashioned. Doesn't want anyone to know she's living in sin."

Jake caught Pal's hand and shook it briefly. "Detective Jake Carson, NYPD."

Pal stepped backward and gestured for Jake to enter.

Dread seized Susan. She tried to fling herself between Jake and the opening but managed only to stagger. Forced to tend her balance, she found herself incapable of useful action. Jake was inside before she could stop him. She tried to send a telepathic message to Nate: *Hide. Oh please, have the sense to hide.*

A figure hunched on a stool over the tiny kitchen table, dropping a half-eaten sandwich onto a paper plate. He brought the can of fizzy juice to his lips, swallowed, then wiped his hand on the back of Pal's jogging suit sleeve. His hair was tucked under a baseball-style cap, and he looked out from a pair of unfamiliar glasses. It took Susan several moments to recognize Nate and, then, only because she knew he was the only other humanoid creature in the apartment.

As Susan seemed to have gone fully mute, Pal introduced the other two men. "This is Susan's cousin, Layton Campbell, visiting us from Iowa. Layton, this is Detective Jake Carson."

To Susan's relief, Nate did not rise to reveal his remarkable height. He simply stuck out his hand, clamped it briefly to Jake's, and looked down at his plate.

Susan tried to explain. Jake knew she had no living relatives. "Once

I found out my original last name, I was able to track down a cousin. We exchanged texts for a while before I talked him into coming for a visit."

Nate played along. "Detective? As in police?" Though he questioned Jake, he looked askance at Susan.

Susan winced. "Another reason I didn't want you to come in, Jake. I finally found a blood cousin, convinced him to visit, and didn't want to scare him away." She emphasized the words, hoping Jake and Pal would get the idea she still did not want her innocent "cousin" to know an organized group of radicals was attempting to kill her.

Jake responded to Nate first. "NYPD. I'm with the Chief of Detectives Field Internal Affairs Unit investigating the theft of a robot from police custody. Susan's an old friend and familiar with robots, so I thought I'd stop by and ask her some questions."

Nate nodded jerkily. Susan noticed he had changed his mannerisms and added a nasal quality to his voice. "I've heard her father was a brilliant roboticist."

Jake smiled at Nate, speaking to him as if he were a child instead of the adult man he clearly was. "Susan's no slouch, either. And she knows this robot particularly well."

Caught up in her own lie, Susan found herself considering the way many New Yorkers viewed people from the central parts of the country: as uneducated bumpkins with antiquated notions and simplistic, foolish ties to a dark and seedy past. The thoughts, the politics, and the way of life of anyone living between New York City and California were reduced, by many, to an unsophisticated gulf that required the civilized, coastal peoples to lead them, to enlighten, and inform.

Susan shook the thought from her mind. For now, she had to concentrate on the lies. She had no idea how much Pal knew, how well he had prepared Nate, if at all. The smallest slip could result in serious consequences for all of them: immobility for Nate, jail for her and Pal, who had, perhaps unwittingly, become an accomplice. "Jake, would you mind terribly if we met in your office in say"–she consulted her Vox, which read 12:14 p.m.–"about an hour? We need to talk about this and . . . the other. I just want to get Layton settled in first." She went deliberately vague in the hope of appearing as if she did not want her cousin to hear about the confrontation with SFH.

With clear reluctance, Jake glanced between the three of them, then bobbed his head. "All right, Susan. In about an hour. And bring your boyfriend." He gestured toward Pal. "He's a witness. Do you know where my office is?"

"It's at 34½ East Twelfth Street." Susan quoted the woman at the Tenth Precinct. "Between Broadway and Fourth."

Jake lifted his head, clearly taken aback. "Yes. That's right." He started to say something more, then clearly thought better of it.

Susan answered the unspoken question anyway. "They told me when I asked for you. Said you'd been 'flopped' there. I recognized the address as the Police Athletic League, which I know by heart because of patient referrals."

That seemed to put Jake at ease. "Yeah, all right. See you there in one hour."

"One hour," Susan promised, walking him to the door and letting him out into the corridor. Closing it, she stood facing it thoughtfully for several moments. Finally, she turned. "How did you–"

Susan found herself face-to-face with Pal Buffoni. He stood half a head taller than she did, his stunning eyes still his most prominent and arresting feature. She had not expected to find him so close. He still smelled faintly of sweat but also of laundry detergent from his now-clean clothing. She found herself enormously attracted to him. She could imagine his lips crushing hers, his body, lean and hard, pressed against her.

Pal responded to the half question. "You want to know how I knew what was going on."

Breathless, Susan only nodded.

"I was listening through the door."

She finally managed words. "But I'm against the door right now. I can't hear anything out in the hallway."

Pal displayed the glass, still clutched in his left hand. "You'd be surprised how much something like this clamped against the wood can amplify things on the other side."

"You spied on us!" Susan realized aloud, hearing outrage in her declaration.

Pal placed the cup on the table. "Of course I spied on you. I shot three guys to bring you here safely. Did you think I'd just let you go alone into the hallway with a stranger?"

"Jake's not a stranger," Susan pointed out.

"To me, he is. Or was at the time." Pal ushered her to the microscopic living room and its love seat. Even there, the three of them could not sit together. "Within the first couple of sentences, it was clear you were old friends and he was a cop. I put the stolen robot together with your paranoia. When I confronted him, your so-called cousin admitted the truth."

Susan dropped onto the love seat, groaning. "It's that obvious?"

Pal sat on the floor directly in front of Susan, between her and the blank entertainment-center screen. "MARSOC," he reminded. "I'm trained to examine details, figure out puzzles, and make snap decisions. Often, they're of the life-and-death variety."

Susan buried her face in her hands. "Jake's a detective. Do you think he put the same details together?"

"He didn't have the same details," Pal pointed out. "I had a woman dodging gunfire who didn't want to go to the police and didn't really care that her companion had gotten shot in the process. Layton said he didn't need medical attention. What layman doesn't want to see a doctor after taking a bullet?"

Nate joined them, sitting cross-legged on the floor.

Susan peeked at him through her fingers. "You really were shot?"

"Yes," Nate admitted. "But I'm not hurt. It just took off a bit of skin; it'll grow back."

Pal continued. "Couple that with the conversation I overheard . . ." If he made a motion, Susan did not see it, her eyes still mostly covered. He added pointedly, "There are a lot more details I'd truly like to hear."

Susan raised her head. "Why?" she demanded.

Pal stared at her through those ungodly eyes, and she dodged them to avoid becoming lost. "I can't help you if I don't fully understand–," he started.

"No, I mean why are you risking your life and liberty to help a couple of strangers, especially knowing one isn't even human?"

Pal shrugged. "I'm trained to save innocent lives; it's what I do." He amended, "Or what I used to do. In the park, you needed me. The reasons didn't matter. Your enemies were using deadly weapons; you had none. That made them the bad guys."

His explanation made sense to Susan. "But afterward, here, when you discovered I was a–a common thief." Susan could barely speak the word.

Pal laughed. "Common?"

Susan fought a smile. He had a decided point. "You still helped us. You rescued us from a police detective. With deceit. That makes you an accessory, I think."

Pal shrugged and looked at Nate. "During training, they told us that once you've saved someone's life, you often feel more indebted to them than they do to you. It feels more like responsibility than gratitude, but I know what they were talking about. Maybe it's because rescuing a DIDI makes me feel like a hero. Maybe it's plain old curiosity; I find you fascinating, and I want to know more. Maybe the adrenaline junkie in me craves the wild ride you'll surely provide if I just stick with you.

But mostly I think it's just the elemental desire to spend as much time as possible with an attractive woman."

Susan could feel her face growing uncomfortably warm. "Now I know you're lying."

Pal's brow furrowed. "How so?"

"I do own a mirror."

"Most people do."

Susan sighed, wishing he did not make her say it. "Even my father never used the word 'beautiful' to describe me."

Pal ran his gaze up and down Susan's entire form, which only served to make her more uncomfortable. "Perhaps not in the classical, airbrushed-model sort of way, but you have a natural and casual beauty that's all your own. I like the way you move and how you don't freeze in the face of danger. I find your lack of makeup and carefree attitude toward your own looks refreshing. Surely I'm not the first man to find you highly desirable."

Susan had to admit he wasn't. She had found Remington's interest in her just as shocking, and he had clearly loved her enough to die for her. Kendall had also developed an attraction to her, though only after long association and denial of his own homosexuality. "No," she admitted. "You're not the first. But you're so . . ." She made a motion to indicate the sheer perfection of him from head to toe.

Susan's gesture seemed only to confuse Pal. "I'm so what?"

Susan did not know what to say. His appeal was so obvious. "So movie-star gorgeous. So shockingly handsome."

Now it was his turn to blush. "I've never seen myself that way. I don't suppose anyone looks sexy in a helmet and body armor, plastered with sweat and reeking of gunpowder." He laughed at some unshared image. "Unless he's in a movie. I've always thought my eyes looked as if someone cut and pasted them in. They don't fit. As to the rest of me, I just look more and more like my father every day. Who considers his father attractive?"

Susan had, but she felt it better not to say so. It might sound weird, especially if Pal had overheard her finish Jake's sentence about her father with the word "robotic." "You do realize you just told a police officer you're my live-in boyfriend. You're going to have to spend a lot more time here to keep him from growing suspicious."

Pal snapped his fingers and said with obvious sarcasm, "Darn it."

Susan liked his answer. She was going to need assistance keeping Nate safe and clearing Lawrence, particularly with the Society for Humanity still gunning for her. Jake had seemed less than eager for the job, and now had become more adversary than friend. She needed someone like Pal in her corner. "You haven't found a civilian job yet, correct?"

"Correct."

"Is it possible I could hire you?"

Pal glanced around the tiny apartment.

Susan tried to guess his concern. "I couldn't pay you much," she admitted, "but I just got on USR's payroll. I don't know how much they're going to give me, but I'm willing to split what I get with you."

Pal sat up straighter. "And my job would be?"

"Bodyguard," Susan responded quickly, then added, "And tactical adviser." She found herself studying Nate, as if afraid to place her gaze on Pal, afraid he might refuse, afraid he might accept. Whatever he had claimed about his indebtedness to her outweighing hers to him, he had saved her life. And Nate's as well. Susan did feel grateful to Pal Buffoni. Strangely, however, she realized she had never put that gratitude into words. "I apologize for not saying it sooner, but thank you for rescuing me." She owed him more, and she knew it. "Thank you for disguising Nate. For that matter, thank you for your service to America."

"Whoa," Pal said. "You had me at 'bodyguard.' I'll take the job."

"Thank you," Susan could not help saying again, gaze still fixed on Nate. "By the way, how did you disguise Nate so well so quickly?"

Pal waved off the compliment. "That was easy. I just reminded him he was supposed to be your cousin from Iowa, and he did the rest. He's got, like, half a foot of height on me, so I knew he needed something bigger than my regular clothes. The jogging suit was a gift. My mom bought it extra large, she said to fit over my clothes. I've always had to roll up the sleeves and cuffs. Hats are simple accessories to hide hair. Those are my sunglasses; they're clear inside but darken in sunlight. I wanted him sitting, to obfuscate height, so I put him on the stool. It was simple enough to put half-eaten food in his hands, allowing Jake to catch him doing something casually human." He shook his head. "The hardest part was finding food. No wonder you're so thin."

Susan made a wordless, meaningless gesture. Her father had not needed to eat and had had a lax relationship with food. He had thrown together the most eclectic meals, more focused on nutrition than taste. "We're going to need to leave pretty soon. We can get our stories straight on the way. Why don't you jump in the shower? I'm going to get changed and spend some time with Nate. I took him for a reason, and the sooner I know what he knows, the better."

Pal made no move to obey. "I'd only just started jogging when I ran into you. That's why I wasn't too far from my bike. If I'm going to protect you, I need to know what's going on. I want to hear what Nate has to say."

Susan bit her lip in consideration. Pal had actively rescued her twice. He knew how to think quickly in difficult situations; but, denied significant information, he would surely make a dangerous error. "You're right," she finally said before turning to Nate. "Tell us what happened yesterday in Hassenfeld Research Tower, room 713."

Nate lowered his head until it nearly touched the floor. He started to rock in place rhythmically, like a mother soothing a sobbing infant.

Susan knew she needed to stop him, worried he would slip away to the same quiet place he had found in the Nineteenth Precinct holding cell. "Nate, think back to the first moment you entered that room yesterday. Before anything bad happened. What were you doing there?"

Nate did not look up, but he did stop rocking. "Dr. Goldman put in an application the night before for me to come to the lab at one forty-five p.m. I arrived at the requested time."

Susan would have liked Nate to just tell the entire story, but she needed to keep him directed and focused. "Who was there when you arrived?"

"Dr. Goldman had just returned from lunch. I met him at the door."

"What did he say and do?"

"He was grumbling something about Dr. Peters not joining us. I couldn't catch every word, but it had something to do with a family emergency. He opened the door and let us both in. He had me sit in my usual place, on the stool beside his at the laboratory tables, and we started right in on their current project."

Pal could not help leaping in, "Which is?"

Nate shifted his attention to Pal. "They've isolated small amounts of two previously unknown proteins from the cerebrospinal fluid of certain psychiatric patients. They're comparing what they've found with fluid from normal volunteers, people with different forms of meningitis and certain cancer patients. They're trying to find the origins of the proteins, their effects, and in what disease states they're found to see if they can be used as markers or if treatments directed at them might prove useful in certain disease states."

Pal's crinkled brow suggested he might be sorry he asked.

Susan took over again. The details of the experiment probably did not matter, and they had a limited amount of time. "What happened next?"

Nate cleared his throat, though he probably never had to actually do so. It was an affectation learned from humans and probably served the same delaying purpose. "About twenty minutes into the project, Dr. Goldman started yelling and swearing. He commanded me to fetch more Schmidt capillary tubes. I went to the storage room to get him a box."

"And?" Susan pressed.

"And," Nate repeated dreamily. "And." He started to shake.

Susan leaned forward, caught Nate's cheeks, and forced him to look at her. It surprised her how fully human his face felt, clamped between her hands. "Nate, tell me what happened next."

Though forced to face her, his eyes dodged hers. "I remember finding a partial box of Schmidt capillary tubes right in front. I grabbed it. Then, suddenly, I was back in the laboratory. Instead of the box, I held a Stanley 55-099 FatMax Xtreme FuBar Utility Bar covered with blood. Dr. Goldman sprawled across the table, his head . . . his head . . ."

Susan did not make him say it. "Yes, Nate. I saw his head. Did you . . . hit him?"

"I must have," Nate fairly moaned. He made no attempt to escape Susan's grip, but his eyes had rolled almost sideways. "There was no one else in the room. No one else."

Susan waited for him to meet her gaze, which he finally did. His voice sounded small, pinched. "But I couldn't have done it, could I? I can't harm any human being. I know I can't." Tears spilled from his eyes.

Pal stepped in again, "Nate, where did you get the utility bar? Was it in the lab? In the storage area?"

Nate shook his head, slowly at first, then gradually with more speed and emphasis. "I don't know. I'd never seen it before. I have no memory of finding it, of picking it up. It was just there. There in my hand."

Susan believed they had found the most important clue, and it had come precisely from the source she had expected. *If I hadn't stolen him, we wouldn't know any of this.* "Do you remember walking from the storage area to the lab?"

Nate shook his head. "I don't. But I had to, didn't I?"

Pal tapped his Vox, a silent reminder that they needed to meet with Jake and had promised not to be late.

Susan held up one finger to forestall him for just a moment longer. She could not leave Nate until she put his mind at ease. "We'll talk about this some more when we get back, but I want you to understand one thing. You did not kill Ari Goldman. It's not possible for you to do such a thing. Someone else killed him, someone human, and made it appear as if you did it."

Nate gave Susan a hopeful look. "You're sure?"

"Not a doubt in my mind," Susan said with stalwart assurance. "You're innocent, Nate. And we're going to do whatever it takes to free Lawrence and find the real killer or killers."

Pal nodded in firm agreement. "While we're gone, remain quiet. Stay away from any windows, and don't answer the door. We'll be back soon."

Susan could have kissed him.

Chapter 7

Susan and Pal rode a glide-bus to the Chief of Detectives Field Internal Affairs Unit. Had Pal offered the use of his Harley, Susan would have refused him. "Donorcycles" doctors called them euphemistically, and it was one thing to hop onto one while escaping gunfire, quite another to choose it over safe and reliable transportation in a non-emergent situation. However, Pal did not ask, though whether because he still worried the SFH might recognize it, knew Susan was not comfortable with it, or because he wanted to talk to her on the trip, she did not know.

Ultimately, the ability to converse with Pal became the most important factor. Susan had intended to stick as closely as possible to the truth, leaving out only her trip to the Nineteenth Precinct parking lot and Nate's presence in Central Park, but that proved more difficult than she had first imagined. Omissions had a way of exploding, requiring ever larger embellishments to cover small lapses. She could not afford to have Jake catch her in a lie.

Susan knew from prior experience that Jake and, later, the Central Park police, would question her and Pal separately. The two of them needed to collaborate believably, without appearing rehearsed. The police would have to account for differences in perception, but their stories could not significantly clash or diverge, which meant keeping them simple. They also had to appear compliant, which meant avoiding non-answers as much as possible. Jake was smart, Susan knew, and reasonably experienced. He would know what questions to ask and how to ask them to find a way to drive a wedge between Susan and Pal.

Luckily for Susan, she was also well trained in reading gestures, expressions, and even the tiniest changes in tone. She would not be easily fooled. Knowing nothing about special operations forces training, she could only guess what Pal might or might not know how to handle, but she felt confident he would not be easily cracked, either. He clearly knew how to think and act quickly. It only remained to make their story as cohesive as possible.

They arrived at their destination all too quickly, with many details still more equivocal than Susan liked. She supposed no amount of time would seem like enough to prepare under the circumstances. They could not anticipate every question and would have to rely on common sense and the responses they had managed to coordinate.

They were left only a few moments in a waiting area before Jake called them into his office. This one looked barer than the one at the Tenth Precinct, as if Jake wanted to remind himself that he was there only on a temporary basis. It had no windows; a fluorescent fixture on the ceiling bathed the room in light. The desk was metal, bulky, and old-fashioned, with only a palm-pross, two baskets of stick-e-files, and a stack of neatly piled papers on its surface. The wall had a single picture, a generic impressionistic piece that did not suit Jake's usual taste. Only a triangular nameplate perched on the desk identified it as his: DETECTIVE JACOB CARSON.

Susan and Pal entered the room and sat in the two rickety chairs in front of the desk, so different from the lightly cushioned one behind it. Jake walked around the desk to take the third seat, and Susan examined him as he moved. Though still agile, he appeared a bit older than when she had last seen him, relaxed in his own home, as if he had gathered a few new lines on his face to accompany some great worry. His hair was still sandy, without a hint of gray. When he brushed a few strands from his forehead, Susan caught a glimpse of the scar where the Cadmium agent had shot him.

She could still hear the man's cold voice in her mind as he instructed his colleague, "Pat them down. Start with the redhead. I'll kill the cop." An instant later, the roar of the gun, the hole in the middle of Jake's forehead, his collapse. The referenced redhead, Kendall Stevens, had declared Jake dead, and no one in the room could have doubted it. *He nearly died for me. More than once. And I'm about to lie to him.* Susan shrugged off the thought, along with its accompanying guilt. To do otherwise meant sacrificing Nate.

Jake cleared his throat. "Thank you so much for coming, Susan." He nodded toward her, then to Pal. "Pal."

Both muttered platitudes.

Jake continued. "Would you mind if I spoke with Susan alone first?" He made it sound like a choice.

Susan wondered if that were so but also knew she would agree either way. "Not a problem, Jake. We're old friends."

Pal rose. "She's the boss. Okay if I go back to the main waiting area?"

Jake smiled politely, "That would be fine."

Susan waited until Pal departed, and the door clicked closed behind him. "Is this when the bare lightbulb comes out and the 'bad cop' portion of the team shows up?"

Jake stepped around the desk and took the chair Pal had vacated. "Of course not, Susan. You're not a suspect."

"I'm not?"

"Should you be?"

Susan realized she had already made her first mistake and tried to cover casually. "Not if you actually want to solve the crime. You sounded accusatory back at my apartment, and I didn't think you'd bring me here unless . . ." It seemed best not to go there. "So why am I here?"

Jake leaned back, looking comfortable; yet, Susan suspected, he had done so more to remind Susan of their friendship, to put her at ease. "As I recall, that was your idea."

Susan's brow crinkled, her mind returning to the events of only an hour ago. She chuckled, trying to sound amused, not forced. "Well, yes. I suppose it was, but only because you had voiced your intention to question me. I was afraid our conversation might send my cousin fleeing in terror. What do you want to know?"

"Lawrence Robertson insists you're the foremost authority on Nate."

Susan laughed. "He should know. Though, I'd think him the foremost authority on a robot he designed."

"Mechanically, certainly. But he's convinced you know the robotic mind better than anyone, that you understand why they behave the way they do. Particularly when a robot does something out of the ordinary."

Susan could not help reiterating, "Nate didn't kill Ari Goldman." Unable to divulge the information Nate had given them without revealing her recent contact with him, she turned to vagaries. "He couldn't kill anyone. It's simply not possible."

Jake sighed, saying the last thing Susan expected. "I know that, Susan."

"You do? Then why–?"

Jake stared at Susan as if she had gone insane. "I told you. I'm not investigating the homicide, remember? I'm investigating the theft of evidence from police custody."

Susan did know that, but she had not realized just how compartmentalized police investigations were. When doctors brought in consultants, they worked together, overlapping and intertwining information in order to consider the patient as a whole entity. If a person needed more than one type of surgery, and they did not interfere, the doctors would schedule a single operating time and handle both. A cardiologist and nephrologist would coordinate medications to maximize effectiveness and minimize toxicity in an individual patient. "So when you say the robot did something out of the ordinary . . . ?"

Jake's brows rose, but he said nothing, allowing Susan to figure out the rest herself.

"You're referring to his . . . disappearance?"

"Yes."

Susan frowned. "But as you pointed out, at the time Nate had no battery. Someone either had to replace it or take him in a dormant state, in which case he had no active part in the theft."

"Nate's battery was placed in the envelope with the rest of Lawrence's personal possessions," Jake pointed out. "And the envelope was given to you."

Was that an accusation? Susan studied Jake, and he met her gaze levelly. "We covered this at my apartment, Jake. First thing this morning, I took all of Lawrence's belongings to USR. Apparently, Lawrence had specifically requested that Alfred Lanning study Nate's battery. It was the first thing he asked me for and the one thing I placed directly into his hands."

Jake clearly remembered what she had told him. "You mentioned he was going to study it for exposure to radiation or contaminants."

"He's trying to figure out exactly what happened in Goldman and Peters' lab." Susan added bitterly, "He's looking for the types of clues the police aren't bothering with because they're already convinced Nate is the murderer."

Jake rubbed his cheek thoughtfully. "You're right, Susan. The battery should have remained as evidence." That was not the point Susan was trying to make, but she let him continue. Jake's hand went still. "But that's the Nineteenth's mistake. I'm just trying to figure out whether the thief or thieves stole a functioning robot or four hundred pounds of deadweight in human form."

Susan capitalized on their previous discussion. "I still say it's closer to two hundred pounds. A pair of small women could carry that much on a stretcher."

Jake bobbed his head. "Except the four muscular men who transferred Nate to the ambulance swear he was south of four hundred. And whoever stole him didn't take the stretcher." His gaze flicked back to Susan. "What do you suppose that means?"

It means I was too anxious and in too much of a damned hurry to cover up what I did. Susan remained cool. "Well, Lawrence could tell you if there's some sort of backup battery stored in Nate." Susan hated to bring up the possibility, concerned for the secondary that kept the positronic brain functional. If Nate was taken back into custody and the police insisted on its removal, they would render him essentially brain-dead. If asked, she felt certain, Lawrence would have sense enough to simply deny the existence of a secondary battery without volunteering information about the positronic brain backup. "Perhaps it activated, and he left on his own. I was present when Lawrence powered him down, and there was no order given for Nate to remain in place should he become reactivated."

Jake tipped his head, clearly considering Susan's words. "A second battery. I hadn't thought of that." He added slowly, "Except . . . the ambulance door was locked . . . from the outside."

"Really?" Susan tried her best to appear surprised by the statement. "Why would an ambulance even have a lock on the outside?"

"Why not?"

Susan pictured a generic ambulance in her mind's eye. "My understanding is that there's always at least one nurse or paramedic in the back with the patient. Shouldn't he or she control any locking mechanism?"

"Unless they don't have any patients. Then, no one needs to be inside, and a lock keeps people from stealing or vandalizing the specialized equipment." Jake changed tack suddenly. "You're a doctor, Susan. Don't you have some firsthand experience with ambulances?"

Susan shrugged. "I rode one at a fair once, when I was about seven; and I've been in the ER when ambulances arrive. The doctors don't see the patient until he's wheeled into the room and transferred to an ER gurney. We're too busy setting up the equipment and preparing ourselves mentally. We do keep in touch with the ambulance personnel by Vox or radio along the way, but we don't actually greet the vehicle that brings the patient." She shook her head. "Despite what you might see on television, we're not waiting on the helipad or in the parking lot."

Now, Jake smiled. "I imagine if you did, you'd lose a lot of doctors and nurses to rotor amputations."

Susan could imagine herself so focused on a patient that she stood up quickly and lost the top half of her skull. Once, during a night shift in the empty ICU, she had asked to attend a helicopter refueling. The pilot had agreed, but the hospital had nixed the plan, stating that doctors' lives were too valuable to risk. Susan had always thought their response a double slap in the face to the helicopter crew, suggesting not only that their lives were of lesser value than hers but also that they were not competent to keep her safe. Now, she realized, they might have worried more for her inexperience and incaution. Not wishing to waste time, she steered the conversation back to its original topic. "Maybe your four muscular men forgot to lock the door."

"Maybe." Jake allowed for the possibility. "Although all four, and two ambulance personnel, swear they heard it click. Subsequent checks have shown it to be working properly."

"I've accidentally locked things open; some still click. Or, perhaps, someone tampered with it."

"Not obviously."

Susan did not know what else to say. "Are you asking me if Nate has the capability for teleportation? Because that would be magic, not technology."

Jake waved off her suggestion. "Mostly, I'm just sharing my thoughts with a knowledgeable friend. Also, I'm wondering if Nate might know how to disable locks in ways a human might not."

Susan gave Jake's reasonable suggestion due consideration. "Not as a part of his initial programming; but, like all positronic robots, he's a work in progress, always learning and incapable of forgetting. I know he read every medical text he could find. He had access to the global Net and a lot of free time. If I were him, I would have studied everything, including locksmithing and ambulances. It's possible he discovered something useful." She peered back at Jake. "Of course, the type of lock he was dealing with might come into play." She waited for him to elaborate.

Jake seemed reluctant, then did so. "It's the electronic type, with a battery and the workings embedded in the steel door. There's nothing on the inside to pry off and monkey with."

"Well, I'm no expert, but I can tell you that the one I accidentally locked into the open position was battery operated, too. It had a combination. Pressing the center button threw a bolt, and I had the door a tiny bit open. The bolt extended behind the slot, the lock clicked, and I didn't notice it was slightly ajar until a friend leaned against it and tumbled halfway down the stairs."

"I'll check that out," Jake promised. "But I was actually wondering about the possibility of a magnetic or electrical field that a robot could manufacture based on its components or what it had to work with inside the ambulance."

Susan did not believe such a thing existed except, perhaps, in a specialized unit. "That's something you'd have to discuss with a roboticist."

Jake made a thoughtful noise, then spread his hands in his lap.

"That's really all I can think to ask at the moment. Do you have anything to add?"

Susan sucked in a deep breath and let it out slowly. She wanted to say "no" and get out as quickly as possible, but that might make her appear guilty. "Only that Dr. Goldman's murder, Nate's disappearance, and the attempt on my life are certainly related. Nothing good can come of any of this until the police switch their focus from Lawrence and Nate to the Society for Humanity."

Jake opened and closed his mouth. He sat back and started again. "Susan, I understand your point, and I believe you when you say Nate couldn't have killed anyone. However, the SFH . . ." He trailed off.

Susan pressed. "The SFH . . . what?"

Jake reached out and touched Susan's hand. He was trying to tell her something without speaking, probably to avoid the ever-present cameras he had mentioned during their first encounter in his other office. Only then, Susan realized he was trying to remind her of exactly that; he could not speak freely about certain things in such an environment. "They've been substantially weakened. I wouldn't have thought they still had the power to muster up plans of . . . this magnitude."

Susan read between the lines. He was trying to explain that Cadmium had not appreciated the Society for Humanity's meddling and had used the considerable means at their disposal to render the SFH impotent. But Susan also knew someone had attempted to murder her earlier this very day. No one else had motive, let alone the proper forces, to craft an attack like the one she and Nate had survived only because of Pal's quick actions. The police had underestimated the SFH's resources and determination on many prior occasions. Realizing Jake needed a response that fit the situation and would pacify anyone who watched the recordings, she took his hand and nodded.

Jake waited only until she released him before stepping out of the office and back into the hallway. Shortly, he reappeared with Pal Buffoni in tow. He motioned for Pal to take the seat he had just vacated, and Pal did so while Jake reclaimed the chair behind his desk. Pal smiled at Susan, one brow lifting in question. Susan returned the warmest smile she could. Things had gone better than she had expected.

"My turn?" Pal said with mock exuberance. A police examination was not at the top of anyone's list of fun ways to spend an afternoon, though Susan imagined some people might prefer it to seeing a doctor.

Susan started to rise, but Jake stopped her with a broad wave. "You can stay, Susan. I don't have any robotics questions for your partner."

Susan dropped back into her chair, though it seemed unnecessary. "So . . . we're finished, then?"

"We can be, if you want." Jake opened his palm-pross and peered over it at Susan. "Whatever happened in Central Park is outside my jurisdiction, so you don't have to tell me anything about it. However . . ." He glanced at Pal, then back to Susan.

Susan waited for the other shoe to fall.

"No one knows as much about . . . your situation as I do. If I can help . . . well, I can't help if I don't know . . ." Jake rarely floundered, and Susan found herself considering the situation from his point of view. She knew little about police procedure and most of that from what Jake had told her or what movies portrayed, not always accurately. She supposed that if they volunteered information to him as a confidant, rather than a police officer, it might complicate the investigation.

Pal looked to Susan, who nodded vigorously. "Jake has risked his life to save mine on more than one occasion."

Accepting that, Pal scooted his chair directly in front of Jake's desk. "What would you like to know?"

Jake prodded carefully, "You said you helped Susan escape from would-be killers."

Pal did not mince words. "I shot three men masquerading as park employees who were shooting at and, in one case, cutting at Susan with hedge trimmers. There were at least two others, and they were shooting wildly, so we had to leave the scene in a hurry." He added plaintively, "I hope we're not in any trouble."

Jake sat back. "I can't promise the Central Park Precinct will handle this in any particular way, but the law does allow the use of deadly force in certain situations. If you meet those criteria, you should be all right. As a courtesy to the Central Park Precinct, I'd like to drive the two of you there, if I may."

Susan and Pal both nodded.

Jake said, not quite casually, "I'm assuming you have all the proper paperwork for your weapon."

Susan's heart lurched. She did not know the current permitting laws for firearms except that New York City had always kept permission tight. In other parts of the country, whatever was not specifically prohibited was permitted while, in New York City, whatever was not specifically permitted was prohibited. She doubted she would qualify to own a gun, let alone to carry one concealed.

In the early 2020s, control had grown so strict that even security guards and some police were not legally armed. Emboldened gangs and criminals had virtually taken over the city before the pendulum swung back far enough to rearm all law enforcement officers and certain responsible members of the public. How those citizens were chosen was just shy of a secret, assuring that criminals did not know who in a crowd might have the ability to fire back at them.

Pal removed a handgun from just behind his left hip and placed it carefully on the desk. He removed a chip-card from his wallet and set it beside the gun.

Jake hesitated. He had clearly not expected this amount of cooperation. "Mind if I check?"

Pal made a throwaway gesture. "I insist."

Jake waved the chip-card across the edge of the palm-pross. Figures flickered across the screen, but Susan was not in position to read them. "Paladin," he said quizzically. "Paladin Joshua Buffoni." His brows inched upward, and a hint of admiration entered his tone. "MARSOC."

"Eight years," Pal replied.

"It says you live at 1826 Thirty-first Avenue," Jake continued casually, as if seeking a simple confirmation.

Susan saw the pitfall, but, before she could speak, Pal addressed it. "Yeah, I was speaking a bit prematurely earlier. My lease is up next month. That's when I'll move in with Susan officially, at least until her lease ends and we can find a bigger place."

Susan wished Pal had given her more time; solving Ari Goldman's murder might take longer than a month. On the other hand, she could think of far worse people with whom to share close quarters.

"And that's when?" Jake asked.

Realizing Pal had no way of knowing, Susan piped up. "My lease ends in February. Still not sure how we're going to store all our furniture in that postage stamp I currently call home."

Pal put a loving arm around Susan and smiled. "I still say it's best for me to put all my crap in storage."

Susan tried to make it sound like an ongoing argument, "For five months? You know I don't think that's fair to you."

"The only thing I need that you don't have is actual food in the refrigerator."

Jake smiled at that, his gaze still fixed on the screen. The first meal he and Susan had ever shared was an eclectic salad she had thrown together from what she could find in her father's ransacked pantry shortly after his murder. "It says you have permits for three firearms."

"Yes," Pal confirmed.

"This is the one you used in Central Park? The only one?"

"Yes."

Jake passed back the chip-card. "Do you have the others with you?"

"Outside a combat zone, I have found one at a time more than adequate."

Susan pursed her lips to hide a smile. From experience, Jake, along with most law enforcement officers, seemed to always carry at least one backup. Sometimes two. She also realized that the propensity to overarm had come in handy on several occasions, though more so for the feds than Jake.

"You know I'm going to have to confiscate this."

Pal's features crinkled, as if he had eaten something unexpectedly sour. "I knew it was a possibility, though I hoped you wouldn't. It leaves Susan extremely vulnerable at a time when we know someone with a lot of firepower wants her dead."

Jake could only nod. "For now, you have me. I'm accompanying you to the Central Park Precinct. Then, we can place her under police protection."

"No," Susan said, trying to sound affronted rather than frightened by the idea. "The police will force me to stay in one place so they can watch me. What I need is a bodyguard, someone willing to move and work with me so I can still perform my job. Someone quick-thinking and quick-acting, accustomed to remaining alert to danger twenty-four hours a day, seven days a week, even while sleeping. Someone wholly committed to me."

Pal's face had turned a subtle shade of red. He shrugged. "MARSOC. It's in all the brochures: bodyguarding, alert sleeping, and one hundred percent commitment to Susan Calvin."

Jake's head bobbed ever so slightly, but he did not smile. "What job are you speaking of, Susan?" He knew she had quit her residency.

Jake deserved to know. Defiantly, Susan stared at him. "The job the police are supposed to be doing: solving Ari Goldman's murder and clearing Nate and Lawrence."

"Alone?"

Susan crossed her arms over her chest. "If necessary."

Jake sighed. "Susan, the police are not your adversaries. We don't get bonuses for solving cases quickly. We're the good guys dedicated to finding the actual perpetrators and removing them from the streets for everyone's safety."

Susan gave him a dubious look, though she knew Jake did not deserve it. She felt certain that, like doctors, most cops joined the force for altruistic reasons, dedicating their lives to protecting and assisting the public. Unfortunately, some joined for the power and authority just as some doctors practiced only for money. A few started out with all the best intentions, becoming jaded by circumstances. Even those with the purest of objectives could prove slow-witted, poorly intuitive, or simply incompetent.

Jake studied Susan, looking personally wounded. "I would have thought I'd done enough to convince you."

Susan appreciated that he did not casually brush his bangs aside or make other reference to the risks he had taken for her: his life and his job. She softened. "You have, Jake, believe me. But I also see the turn this case is taking, and not necessarily because the men and women working it aren't good, capable cops with noble intentions. U.S. Robots hired me to investigate the situation, and I'm going to do that relying on information the homicide detectives are choosing to ignore. Nate is innocent because he is incapable of harming a human being. He is no more capable of murder than a newborn lamb. Less, in fact, because his programming could not even allow something inadvertent to happen."

Pal brought the conversation back to his own concern. "Jake, do you really think they'll insist on confiscating all my guns?"

Jake seemed almost eager to turn his attention from Susan to Pal, though he sighed as he did so. "The first step is to figure out which projectiles from which weapons caused injury or death. Secondarily, I'm concerned that you violated pistol licensing code by not reporting the discharge of a firearm as quickly as possible."

Susan sucked in a breath so suddenly, she nearly choked on her own saliva. She remembered how, at the first opportunity, Pal had asked her if they should go to the police station first or the hospital. "But that was *my* fault!"

Pal held up a hand to stop her. "Who says I didn't?"

His words stopped Susan before the gesture. She waited to hear what he had to say.

Jake cocked his head. "How long has it been since the shooting?"

Pal glanced at his Vox. "Just over two hours now, but I reported the incident at the first opportunity."

Jake made a motion to indicate he should continue.

Pal complied. "I don't think anyone would argue that we couldn't stay on the scene. There was active shooting going on, and Susan was the target. I had to get her out of there quickly and foil any immediate pursuit."

"You should have Voxed."

Pal's handsome features turned incredulous. "While driving a Harley? Even Susan and I couldn't hear each other, and there was no way I was using my hands for anything but steering."

Jake tried again. "Why didn't you drive to the nearest police station?"

Pal had an answer for that as well. "I was focused on evasive action. By the time I realized where we were, I had no idea where the nearest police station was, but we weren't far from home. I stopped long enough to send a quick text to 711. That's the police text line, correct? At least, that's what I was taught in my permitting class."

Jake nodded.

Susan did not recall Pal texting anyone, although he certainly could have done it while she was opening the doors and instructing Nate, in addition to hiding his motorcycle.

Pal continued. "I considered calling for directions, but . . . you know how when people are chasing you, shooting at you . . . No matter how much evasive action you've taken, you're still sure they're right behind you. Susan was spooked, begged me to just take her home. I deferred to her since, as I pointed out, she was the target." He gave her a stern look and added pointedly, "Though I still don't know why people want to kill my girlfriend."

Susan studied her hands in her lap, saying nothing.

"When she told me a police officer she trusted was due to arrive at our door at any minute, it seemed more prudent to just lay low and wait for you."

Jake's attention cut to Susan. She had acted contrary to Pal's account by refusing to allow Jake access to the apartment. A reasonable explanation did not immediately present itself, and Susan could not tell the truth without revealing herself as the perpetrator of the evidentiary theft.

Pal had obviously considered the situation and had a ready answer. "But when we got to the apartment, Susan's cousin had arrived earlier than expected from Iowa. We had barely gotten all three of us safely inside, when you came knocking. Her concerns about Layton colored how she behaved; she didn't want him to think she regularly got shot at or had cops coming to her door. And, clearly, she didn't know pistol-permitting law."

Susan nodded vigorously to show she did not.

"So, when it became clear she wasn't going to let you in, I took matters into my own hands. I reported the incident to you; we arranged to meet here. And here we are. Even discounting the text, no longer than half an hour passed between the shooting and my reporting the incident to an officer of the law."

Jake sighed, then nodded. Susan held her breath. It was up to him to determine if the report had been timely enough. "I guess that makes sense enough. I'll explain it to Central Park Precinct." His gaze locked on Susan. "And, Susan, whatever you do to investigate this case, make sure you don't step on any law enforcement toes. Believe it or not, we're on your side, but there's only so much I can do to help."

"I understand," Susan said as they all rose and prepared for the drive to 1 West Eighty-sixth Street and Traverse Road.

Chapter 8

Detective Jake Carson hesitated in front of a radio motor patrol car parked among several others in the lot outside his office building. He placed a hand on the driver's-side door handle, then stopped. Without looking at Susan or Pal, he surmised aloud, "I imagine you're prone to claustrophobia." As he had not directed the comment, neither of his companions responded immediately. Susan did not suffer from any illogical fears as far as she knew. She supposed Pal had been involved in more than a few difficult or dangerous situations, in training or combat, which might leave him wary of enclosed spaces.

Though he received no response, Jake bobbed his head as if he had, then redirected his companions to his personal vehicle, a Subaru Sapphire that Susan had come to know well the previous year. He explained sotto voce, "The backseat of a police vehicle is designed for perps, not passengers. We're taking mine for your security and comfort, but as far as anyone who might be watching is concerned, you're both claustrophobic."

"Thanks," Pal returned, taking Susan's hand. His touch sent a shock of excitement through her, the kind she had not felt since Remington's death, and she found herself hoping it was not just a meaningless gesture of pseudo-affection intended to fool Jake and any cameras. He had a secure, manly grip and a warm, dry palm.

The moment they settled into the car, Pal turned on his Vox, studying the screen. Reminded that she had also deactivated her Vox during the glide-bus ride, Susan did the same. She had scant hope she had missed anything of import; she had no living relatives, half her friends were currently with her, and her boss was rotting in a jail cell. So, it surprised her to discover seven messages, three of them voice, all of which she converted to text.

The first was from Dr. Aloise Savage, requesting she call him at her earliest convenience. Three were from various psychiatry residents, two attempting to clarify the rumors of her abrupt departure and one asking about a patient. She answered the last one with a few keystrokes before addressing the final three, all from Kendall Stevens.

His first, logged in shortly after Susan and Pal had boarded the glide-bus, was a tongue-in-cheek voice mail about a billion-dollar racehorse headed toward the finish line several lengths in front of its competition. One touch of the jockey's whip sent the animal screeching to a halt, a single step from the line, never to finish the race, thus making itself useful only for dog food. Kendall proceeded to soften the analogy by admitting a job at USR was hardly "dog food" but also pointing out that completing her residency would, in no way, ruin Susan for a job there. It would, however, open her horizons considerably.

Kendall's next message, a true text, was silly with a warning subtext: He would not allow her to cut him out of her life for another year. The third stated he would be coming to her apartment at approximately six p.m., with dinner for two in hand and would not take no for an answer.

Susan responded with, "Make it din 4 4. CU@6." Kendall and Jake might compare notes, so Nate needed to be at Susan's apartment, as Layton Campbell, when Kendall arrived. She and Pal would have to figure out a way to make it appear as if her cousin from Iowa consumed his portion of the meal.

Jake broke what had become a sustained and awkward silence. "So, how did you two meet?"

Susan glanced at Pal. Focused on collaborating on their Central Park story, they had not yet had a chance to create one for their relationship. Pal was still tapping at his Vox, seemingly engrossed, so Susan answered. "On my rare breaks from the hospital, I always try to do something active. Exercise takes away the kinks and clears my head. I wasn't up to running in the snow, so I walked to the mall to do some skating. Pal and I bumped into each other on the ice."

Pal was paying enough attention to add, "Literally." He never looked up from his Vox.

Susan smiled. "Well . . . I'm a decent skater, but I find it difficult to get out of the way of someone who's going a thousand miles an hour. Especially when he's not paying attention."

Pal finally looked up. "I was racing some kids," he claimed. "And trying to look cool while doing it."

"Well, if bowling over a woman enmeshed in figuring out how to treat someone with Fregoli syndrome looks cool, you succeeded admirably."

"I helped you up," Pal said. "And apologized."

"You did," Susan replied, as if it were an admission, but she could not help adding, "I thought you were a total moron." Realizing the tale had taken an unsuitable twist, she continued. "If we hadn't met up at the hospital a few days later, I would have dismissed you as just some jerk."

Jake asked the obvious question. "What were you doing at the hospital, Pal?"

Susan stopped herself from flinching. Thus far, she thought, they had done a great job concocting a believable story. The longer it got, and the more locales it involved, the more likely one of them would make a mistake.

Pal set aside his texting for the moment. "Visiting a sick friend. At least, that's what I told Susan."

"What you *told* me?" Susan turned her attention completely onto Pal. "You mean you weren't there to see Mr. V?" Paranoid about Jake checking up on the story, she chose the initial of a patient she remembered. So long as she did not use his actual name, she was not violating confidentiality.

"I didn't even know him," Pal said. "I came to see you, then panicked. I saw his name on a board . . ."

The charade was becoming dangerously complicated, but Susan had no choice but to play along with what she had started. "But you spent an hour together. He never said anything about . . ."

"I'm not sure if he figured out what was happening and played along or if he was just so out of it, he thought I really was someone he knew."

Susan pretended to consider. "He was deeply depressed. Nothing was working. I don't know what you talked about, but he did seem a lot brighter after your visit. That's the main reason I agreed to go out with you. I figured anyone who could buoy Mr. V.'s spirits was worth knowing."

Pal looked at his hands. "As long as I'm confessing stuff, the collision on the ice wasn't entirely accidental, either."

Susan tried to sound affronted. "You meant to knock me on my butt!"

"Of course not," Pal defended himself from the fiction. "I was just trying to get your attention. You were so engrossed in . . . whatever that syndrome was you mentioned. After several tries, I guess I miscalculated."

"She said Fregoli syndrome," Jake inserted. "What exactly is that?"

Susan had not intended to go there, but she dutifully explained. "It's a rare disorder in which a person believes that several people are really all the same person in disguise. It's usually associated with paranoia. I had a patient who presented with it, and I was trying to come up with an explanation for why it exists and what might cause it when I got creamed on the ice." Again, she had chosen something a real patient had presented with, without mentioning her name.

"Sorry," Pal said, as if for the fortieth time. Briefly, he turned his attention back to his Vox, tapping it several more times.

Susan took the lead again. "Not exactly the romantic story you tell the grandkids."

"Actually," Jake said, "when you add the part about Pal pursuing you, and your being entirely oblivious until months afterward, it is kind of sweet."

Susan grinned and reached for Pal's hand. He stopped texting long enough to curl his fingers around hers and turn his face toward her. She found herself staring into those intoxicating eyes once again. She did not need to see his mouth; the warm smile was visible in their sapphirine depths. For a strange and giddy moment, she could actually forget the charade, could imagine a long and happy lifetime together.

Jake pulled into the precinct parking lot, leaving the motor running. He turned to look directly at his passengers. He opened his mouth as if to speak, then closed it and sighed deeply. He started again, hesitantly. "Susan, I know you can read people as easily as most people read street signs, so I'm guessing you understand what I'm about to do better than I do." He stopped, clearly wanting something from her.

Susan dragged her attention from Pal's chiseled features to plant it firmly on Jake. She guessed, borrowing from Pal's previous comment after the shooting. "Sometimes, when you've saved someone's life at the risk of your own, an eerie symbiosis develops. The saver often feels more indebted than the savee." She added swiftly, "Though not in this case. I appreciate everything you've done for me, Jake . . ." Susan winced, remembering her cold aversion over the past year, but could not apologize for it again. Though cruel to her friends, she had needed that year to maintain her own sanity. "Even if I've not always done a great job of showing it."

Pal encouraged gently. "If it's any consolation, Jake, I know exactly how you feel."

"I'll bet you do," Jake said, without a hint of sarcasm. He even managed a smile.

Susan caught the subtext. Pal still knew relatively little about her, but Jake understood nearly every detail of her struggle over the past two years. He was fully aware that she had become caught, however unwittingly, in a deeply moral and significant war she could not afford to lose. He trusted her implicitly and, intentionally or not, had come to champion her cause, sometimes ahead of his own best interests.

Jake sighed again. "I've been listening to the chatter." He tapped at his left ear, a universal gesture to indicate an essentially invisible earpiece. "The only victim found at the scene of the attack was a woman with a GSW." Apparently, the medical abbreviation for "gunshot wound" was the same for the police.

"Is she all right?" Susan asked.

Jake nodded. "The doctors believe she caught a ricochet. No sign of a projectile, inside or out."

It took Susan a moment to understand Jake's actual point. "The three men who attacked me? The ones Pal shot?"

Jake shook his head. "No."

"No?" Susan repeated incredulously. "No . . . bodies?"

"No sign of them whatsoever. No indication they were ever there. Central Park Precinct is looking for someone who fired recklessly into a crowd."

Susan rushed to Pal's defense. "It happened the way we told you. The guys who attacked us were the ones shooting recklessly. Pal didn't–"

Jake stopped her with a raised hand. "It's Jake, remember? You don't have to convince me that an organized group wants Susan Calvin dead."

Susan fell silent.

"You need to keep in mind that the feds put a lid on everything that happened to us last year. CPP doesn't know your situation, and there's a limit to what you can tell them about it."

Susan suddenly realized another reason Jake had found an excuse to switch to his own vehicle. Police cars were an extension of their precincts: Anything that happened in them was recorded. Jake's car would not have such intrusions. "But I don't know the cover story."

Jake gave Susan a hard stare. "Whose fault is that?"

"Mine," Susan admitted without hesitation. "But does that really matter at the moment?"

"There's not time to brief you now." Jake glanced at Pal, then back, indicating he had no idea how much Susan's partner knew or what she wished to tell him. "You're going to need to avoid talking about last year as much as possible to keep from slipping up."

Susan realized the difficulty. If she related the story of what had happened in the park to the Central Park Precinct, she would have little choice but to reference the previous year to explain why people were shooting at her. With nothing on the scene to corroborate them, she and Pal would look like an intertwined pair of schizophrenics feeding off each other's paranoid delusion. "Um, Jake. If we report shooting three men who appear not to exist and a conspiracy to murder me about which they've heard nothing, won't we appear—"

"Batcrap crazy," Pal inserted.

Jake spread his hands to indicate they had struck to the heart of his problem.

Susan was not accustomed to ever being a step behind anyone in a discussion, but she needed to clarify a point. "What happened to the men Pal shot? I mean, I didn't have a chance to check if they were dead, but they definitely went down too hard to walk away."

"Mop-up crew," Pal said. "Well-organized militias or criminals can clear a scene in minutes. I won't go into details of how it's done, except to say they had a lot of backup. Some assisted or carried the casualties while others pursued us. A few more cleaned up the site."

Jake nodded knowingly. "Which lends more credence to your SFH theory, Susan. They can't afford to leave any sign of their involvement."

A grim sense of foreboding settled over Susan. "Jake, you can't leave me without an armed escort."

Jake's head never stopped bobbing. "And you still refuse police protection?"

"Unless . . ." Susan saw only one opening. "Will they assign you to me?"

Jake answered immediately. "Not a chance."

"Then no," Susan answered vehemently. "I'm not going to hide in some secret location, keeping my head below window level and hiding behind a stranger. I need you, or I need Pal." She tried to sound firm, not whiny. "You can't let them take his guns away." Though Susan never wanted to pull a trigger again, she appreciated the need to keep the good guys armed. The bad guys, she knew, paid no heed to law or permits.

Jake sighed again, even more deeply. "I can't believe I'm saying this." He turned his gaze fully on Pal. "If you do or say anything about this, if you lose me my job, then MARSOC training or none, I'm going to hunt you both down and . . . and NSR you."

Susan remembered NSR stood for "nonstandard response." She wondered whether members of the military used the same shorthand as police did for shooting a bad guy to the ground no matter how many shots it took. She had never been gladder that Kendall was not with them to make a witty remark. Jake might have exploded. "You have my word I won't say or do anything that could get you in trouble." She found herself silently adding, *On purpose.* No matter how much she tried to avoid it, misfortune seemed to find her. When Jake assisted her, it struck him hardest of all. *At least, this time, he's not physically involved.*

Apparently understanding or surmising the NSR reference, Pal said nothing. He simply raised a closed hand, and the men bumped fists. Susan could only conjecture, but it seemed to reassure Jake, to convey a wordless but significant promise of loyalty.

Jake turned back to face the windshield, turned off the engine, and slumped for a moment. He spoke without looking at them. "We'll go in together, but I'm going to talk to them first. Alone. I'll take the blame for your delay in reporting. I'm going to stick mostly to what happened but fudge the times a bit. Okay?"

"Thank you," Susan said, truly grateful.

Jake continued. "I'm going to hand over the pistol and chip because I have to. It'll be up to them to determine if and how quickly you get them back, but I'm going to encourage them to return both as soon as possible. Whether or not they demand your other guns will depend on what, if anything, is found at the scene."

Now it was Pal's turn to say, "Thank you, Jake. You're a standup guy, and I'd be honored to have you at my back. Ever considered joining the Marines?"

"Only for about a second." Jake shook his head wordlessly. "Believe me, I appreciate what you do."

"Did," Pal corrected.

"Did," Jake repeated. "But I wouldn't last a day in a war zone."

Having relied on Jake in some tight and dangerous situations, Susan doubted it, but said nothing. Like the vast majority of civilians, she had absolutely no idea what the military did or even where or if wars were currently being fought.

Jake returned to the subject at hand. "The longer we delay, the harder this gets to explain." He shoved open his door, grabbing an envelope from the seat beside him. "The two of you need to decide what you're going to tell the CP Precinct about what happened earlier today, and you need to do it while we're walking to the building. Because, once you're inside, nothing you say is private anymore." He stepped out and closed the door behind him.

Susan had a simple solution, outlining it in as few words as possible as they walked toward the building. "One bad guy shooting at me. You fired back, missed. More of them came. We ran. They chased." She knew Pal would incorporate the details. The "one bad guy" would be the man who had started the shooting, to keep their description consistent. The rest fit in with the actual sequence of events. In the new scenario, Pal had taken only one shot, and that in the opposite direction, so he could not be the one who injured the woman. The crowd had not appeared until after they cleared the trees lining the jogging path, long after Pal had holstered his weapon. No potential witnesses could credibly dispute their claim. Susan had seen Pal replace his magazine with a fresh one in her apartment, so the number of shots fired would not be inconsistent.

All too soon, they reached the main door, and Jake ushered the pair inside. As promised, Susan and Pal were directed to sit in the waiting room while the detective conversed briefly with the office staff before being allowed access beyond the locked door. Several minutes later, Jake emerged empty-handed. He tipped his head in their general direction before walking out the main door and back into the parking lot. The door swung shut behind him.

While Pal remained in the waiting area, Susan was escorted by a police administrative aid through the inner door to a drab office occupied by a stocky Hispanic woman who identified herself as Detective Ortiz and a tall slender man with a well-tended pouf of blond curls who gave his name as Detective Arbuckle.

Once again, the questioning proved less vicious than Susan anticipated. Briefly, she described her trip to USR, surprised at how little interest the detectives showed. They listened quietly, without asking anything. From there, she had no choice but to diverge from the truth. Rather than her trip to the Tenth Precinct, she described the need for a walk in Central Park to quiet her nerves and prepare for her cousin's arrival.

Susan continued by stating that she chose her route to intersect with Pal's jogging course. The rest of the story went precisely as they had discussed and prepared, leaving out two of the attackers, Nate's presence, and the fact that she and Pal had been strangers until that moment. A few questions followed, mostly about her description of the shooter, how many shots Pal fired, and in which direction, and as many details as she could dredge up about the woman who had fallen.

As expected, they focused on the possibility that Pal had shot the woman, a suggestion to which Susan gave an honest and emphatic no. She hoped she made it abundantly clear that, by the time the woman collapsed, Pal was using both hands to steer the Harley.

While the police questioned Pal, Susan sat and read a few pamphlets, trying to appear appropriately calm for someone who had survived a shooting but had done nothing criminal. It did not take long before she found herself back in the office with the two detectives and Pal, who looked none the worse for wear. As she entered, he turned her a reassuring, if tired, smile.

Detective Ortiz took the only other chair in the room, while Arbuckle perched nonchalantly on the edge of the desk. She did the initial talking. "Your descriptions jibe reasonably well with those of the other witnesses. While there are some inconsistencies overall, it doesn't appear as if you brandished or discharged a weapon inappropriately. Most concurred that the gunfire came from behind you. Even those who believe they got caught in crossfire didn't describe either of you as carrying a discernible weapon."

Detective Arbuckle added, "Although the descriptions of you sure run the gamut." He indicated Susan with a flick of his fingers.

Even in the calmest of situations, eyewitness stories clashed. Susan supposed some of them had described Nate, others her, some both, and others neither. With all the disparate viewpoints, it only made sense for the police to place the most credence on the ones who had actually ridden off on the motorcycle. It surely helped that a fellow officer had spoken in their defense, and Jake must have told them he trusted Susan's powers of observation and her grace under pressure. She shoved aside the realization that it was undeserved and self-serving. If not for Jake, the Central Park Precinct might have uncovered the presence of Nate at the scene.

Ortiz glared at her partner. "Detective Carson left your information. If anything else turns up, we'll give you a call. Otherwise, you're free to go." She opened a drawer, took out the envelope Jake had carried inside, and handed it to Pal.

"Thank you." Pal accepted the envelope, relaxing noticeably. He made no attempt to open it or check the contents.

"Holster it," Arbuckle suggested.

"Thank you," Pal said again, clearly reluctant to arm himself in their presence, though doing so outside might prove unlawful. He had probably planned to carry the gun and chip in the envelope until they reached Susan's apartment.

"Thank you," Susan echoed as Pal put away his belongings and discarded the envelope in the trash can.

Though greatly relieved, Susan lamented losing half a day to explanation, pleas, discussion, and paperwork. The legal dance, though necessary, slowed the pace of her investigation to a maddening plod. She just wanted to leave this all behind them and proceed to the next step. Yet at the same time, she realized her attackers' need to self-clean had spared Susan and Pal hours or days of scrutiny. In their own way, the SFH appeared to have screwed themselves.

Except, Susan realized, the police would not be investigating the SFH, either, which left them free for another attempt on her life. She only hoped Jake was right about their greatly reduced capacity, that the loss of three gunmen, whether to death or injuries, would weaken them to the point where it would take another year before they could act against her again. In any event, their injured could not just walk into a local ER with unexplained gunshot wounds.

Detective Arbuckle led Susan and Pal back to the waiting room, and they let themselves out the main door. Susan wanted nothing more than to get back to Nate, but several other things needed her attention. They would have to buy clothing for him, get some groceries in the house, and Kendall would be arriving at six.

Despite the normal bustle, noise, and traffic, the afternoon-Manhattan streets seemed strangely bland after the mental and emotional excitement of remaining always one step ahead of the police. Susan felt drained, empty. She hated lying, particularly to people she appreciated and admired, yet she could not wholly deny a guilty tinge of exhilaration.

Pal turned Susan a crooked half smile. "That was . . . not fun."

"No," Susan agreed.

As if reading her mind, Pal added, "So, what's first? Buying some clothes for Layton or some food for us?"

Susan consulted her Vox for the time, 4:31 p.m, and her bank balance, $23.06. She winced. "A friend has invited himself over with dinner in hand, so let's work on the finest wardrobe money can buy for twenty-three dollars and six cents."

They headed for the nearest glide-bus stop, and Pal zeroed in on the most pertinent point. "A friend is coming over? Tonight?"

"A colleague," Susan said. "Kendall was the first fellow psychiatry

R-1 I met at Hasbro. He turned orientation from a snore to a snicker." Susan smiled at the memory. She had met Remington even earlier but had dismissed him as pompous and obnoxious. "Kendall has a wicked sense of humor and trouble turning it off. I'm sure he's coming mostly to convince me to finish my residency."

"It's not a wrongheaded idea," Pal pointed out reasonably.

"Thanks, Dad." Susan tipped her head to look up at Pal. "It's why I didn't just tell him to piss off. Plus, I've been a bit . . . self-absorbed the past year, and I need to show him I still love him."

"Do you?" There was something unspoken beneath the question. Susan analyzed the tone for a moment before seeking the answer in the way Pal looked at her, in the concern that marred his beautiful eyes.

Though difficult for Susan to believe, she felt certain she detected a faint hint of jealousy. *Am I imagining it because I want to see it? Or is it possible he's getting too wrapped up in the charade as well?* In any case, she gave the proper answer. "I do love him . . . like a brother. I don't find him romantically attractive, though, especially since he's gay."

"Him, too?"

Susan stopped walking.

It happened so quickly that Pal strode past her and had to turn around to face her. "What?"

"You, Pal? You're gay?"

"Gay?" Pal's already large eyes grew even wider. "Me? Hell, no. When I said 'too,' I was talking about Jake."

Oh yeah. Jake. Susan's brows furrowed. "How did you know about Jake? He's the straightest gay guy I've ever met. He told me the first day we met, but I'm still not sure I believe him. And I'm pretty adept at reading people."

Pal waited for Susan to catch up to him, then took her elbow. "Subaru Sapphire? Not exactly a manly vehicle. Meticulously groomed cop; dead giveaway. Then, there's the fact that he saved your life at least once, but no attraction whatsoever. Oh, he's gay, all right. Gay as a . . ."

"Nightingale," Susan inserted, using the word Jake had chosen when he told her. She tried not to focus too tightly on Pal's last point. She could easily interpret it to mean anyone who rescued her must fall automatically in love, including Pal himself. She found him incredibly attractive and, from what little she knew of his past, definitely worthy of respect, also quick-witted and competent. But she had only known him a few hours, far too soon to wonder if they could work as a lifelong couple.

Pal swung the conversation back to its original point. "I'm glad Kendall's bringing food, but we're still going to need groceries. I'm clearly going to be doing most of the eating, so I'm buying."

Susan opened her mouth to protest, but Pal did not allow it.

"Shut up."

Startled by the command, Susan closed her mouth and glared at him.

Pal did not apologize, but he did explain. "You're too intelligent to argue with something so obviously right. You just started a new job, on the heels of one with long hours and crappy pay. I know I eat a hell of a lot more than you do, so I'm buying. Period." He added, "And I'm paying for Layton's clothes, too."

That pushed Susan too far. "Now wait a minute. I'm getting the whole food thing, but why would you pay for my cousin's clothes?"

As they approached the glide-bus stop, and the other people milling around it, Pal lowered his voice. "Because you don't need police spying through your recent purchases and finding tall men's clothing."

That stopped her cold. "They do that?"

Pal shrugged. "I'm not a cop, but I'm sure they can in certain circumstances. Like, if they get suspicious about a certain cousin." As they had come within earshot of the other people waiting, he dropped the subject.

Susan did not press. He had a definite point, and she could always reimburse him or pay him for his services when her first USR check came. Instead, she said the only thing she really could: "Thank you."

Pal returned his attention to his Vox conversations, and Susan contemplated a route that would get them to a Walmart and home in time to catch Kendall.

Chapter 9

Susan and Pal barely made it home in time to toss Nate fresh clothing, coaching him from the kitchen while he dressed and they put away the groceries, before Kendall buzzed them from the entrance. Like most of its ilk, the camera had ceased working months earlier, so Susan had to rely on a brief voice exchange before allowing him access to the building.

"I could fix that camera," Pal said, laying four plates on the kitchen counter, the only level surface.

Susan followed with forks. She had no idea what Kendall had brought them to eat but figured she could always go back for spoons if it turned out to be soup or chili. *Knowing Kendall, it's probably something deliberately weird.* "Don't bother. It's been fixed a dozen times already. Someone will only wreck it again." It was the common bane of landlords and security companies that vandals, bored teens, and militant privacy activists took great pains and pleasure in seeking out and stealing, destroying, and covering cameras. Most apartments had reverted back, either deliberately or necessarily, to intercoms.

Knocks sounded on the door, a sequence of three, then four, then another of three, as if in code. Susan peeked out the spy hole, identifying Kendall, a heat-sealing cloth bag dangling from one hand. She opened the door and ushered him inside. He stepped in, accompanied by the mingled aromas of Chinese sauces. Susan closed the door behind him.

"Susan!" Kendall greeted her enthusiastically, setting the bag on one of the plates, there being no additional space. He glanced around the room, his gaze stopping first on Pal. "You must be Paladin."

Pal extended his hand. "Pal, please. And you're Kendall, I presume?"

"In the flesh." Kendall looked down, as if seeing himself for the first time. "Well, flesh and clothing, of course. Can't wander the streets naked." He amended, as if it mattered. "Well, I suppose you can, but it's not a good idea." He clasped Pal's hand, and they shook briefly.

"I wouldn't recommend it." Pal looked questioningly at Susan. "It's cold and would probably get you arrested."

Susan smiled and shrugged. It was vintage Kendall.

The warm food odors quickly filled the small room. Kendall continued talking, his flaming orange hair and freckles as prominent as Pal's eyes. Susan could not help wondering if some unique feature tended to stand out in everyone, remaining the most memorable to those who viewed them, the origin of facial recognition and memory. If so, she had never noticed it before and could not help wondering what physical impression she broadcasted to others. *Probably "plain"!* Almost immediately, she amended the idea from experience. Some people's appearances screamed, others talked, and still more simply whispered.

Though no longer in physical contact with Pal, Kendall studied him with the fierce intensity of an adversary. "So, you're the one occupying Susan's time." Though he did not say it aloud, Susan could read between the lines. Kendall might just as well have added, "Keeping her away from her friends."

She intervened. She wanted, perhaps even needed, the two men to like each other. "Not as much as you'd think, Kendall. As you know, I've been catching up on work, which eats the lion's share of a resident's time, even when she's not making up for lost days. I only met Pal seven months ago, and he had to persistently shoehorn his way into my life just to get me to notice him."

Kendall did not voice his doubts, but Susan could read them in his eyes. *A man who looks like Pal doesn't have to work at attracting women.*

Susan found herself adding, "Not because he's not a handsome and worthy partner." She turned Pal a radiant smile. "But because I had walled myself into an icy bubble and didn't want any kind of social life."

"Until Dr. Goldman's murder," Kendall pointed out, still focused on Pal.

"That was a turning point," Susan admitted in a flat tone. She did not want another lecture on loyalty and friendship.

Kendall either heard or sensed that he had begun to tread on dangerous ground. "So," he asked, "who's our fourth for dinner?"

As if in answer, Nate strolled out of the bedroom, attired in the casual dark blue jeans and I ♥ NEW YORK T-shirt they had brought for him. Brown hair stuck out from beneath a sideways baseball cap with the Yankees logo, and he still wore Pal's sunglasses, the lenses transparent in the artificial light of her apartment. The outfit worked to give the image of an inexperienced Midwestern tourist wearing freshly purchased clothing, other than the price tag hanging from his jeans. She made a mental note to rip it off at the first opportunity, also realizing Nate had probably never before put on brand-new clothing. At the hospital, he wore either his dress khakis or scrubs. He did not sweat, so he had little need to change.

Susan made the appropriate introductions. "Layton, this is Kendall Stevens, a fellow psychiatry resident. Kendall, this is Layton Campbell, my cousin."

Kendall's face turned upward to meet Nate's. "Definitely your father's side."

"Definitely," Susan said agreeably. "He has the Campbell height."

"Campbell?" Kendall pressed.

"My father's original last name."

"Oh." Kendall sounded surprised, and Susan realized he should. She had not shared the information that her father's last name had needed changing to keep the two of them safe after her parents' murder. Even Lawrence had not told Susan her birth name. It was Jake who had let it slip, recalling aloud the details of the killings he had remembered as a childhood event, the one that made him decide to become a cop. As the SFH had already made the connection between Calvin Campbell and John Calvin, it seemed unnecessary to hide the name any longer. Still, Susan had chosen to stick with the name she had believed hers for nearly the entirety of her life, an homage to both her biological and mechanical fathers.

Kendall continued to study Nate. "There's similarity to the features, too. He resembles . . ." His scrutiny grew more intense.

Alarm bells went off in Susan's head. She brushed off the subject, attempting to turn Kendall's focus onto another. "My father. A bit." She supposed it only logical, since Nate was a prototype for John Calvin, built by the same roboticists and engineers. She hurried to the bag Kendall had left on the table. "So what did you bring us to eat? Knowing you, it's roadkill stew."

Kendall would not be distracted. His attention fixed so doggedly on Nate, the robot seemed to wither under his scrutiny.

Had he been human, Susan believed, his face would have turned a subtle shade of green.

"I'm not feeling very well. Excuse me." Nate headed rapidly for the bathroom.

Susan covered for him. "We were gone most of the day. When we didn't get back by three, and he hadn't had lunch, Layton ate some leftovers."

The bathroom door slammed shut behind him.

Pal completed the picture. "Oh no. Not the curried catfish. I'm not sure that stuff wasn't spoiled when we bought it."

"It was fine," Susan said defensively. She glanced toward Kendall, careful not to stare. Her fellow resident was still looking toward the bathroom.

"Well, I got queasy after eating it fresh. I can only imagine how he feels three days later."

It bothered Susan how easily she and Pal worked as a team of liars, but not nearly as much as the expression on Kendall's face when he finally turned to look at her. "Oh, Susan," he said, barely above a whisper. "You didn't . . . You couldn't have. . . ."

When no one, including Kendall, dared to finish Kendall's sentence, the room became dangerously silent.

Still clutching the take-out bag, Susan said innocently. "Couldn't have what?"

Subtly, Kendall rolled his eyes toward Pal, raising one eyebrow. He could not know what she had told her partner, but it appeared Kendall had seen through their deception. He strode toward Susan, opening the bag for her. "You didn't tell me who I was feeding, so I picked Chinese. It's usually shared. That way, if someone has dislikes or special circumstances or weirdo diets or allergies, they can avoid one or two dishes and still have a full meal."

It was an awkward turnabout, but Susan and Pal had little choice but to play along.

While Kendall placed the microwaveable cartons where the bag had sat, Pal plucked serving spoons from the silverware drawer and Susan went to check on Nate. She tapped lightly on the door and called out, "Layton, do you need anything in there?"

The door muffled his reply to nonsense, but she pretended to have heard him. "All right. I'm going to leave you alone. Feel free to take whatever you find in the medicine chest and to lie down if you need to. Interrupt if you want anything at all. I'll take care of the guests."

Another uninterpretable reply followed from the bathroom.

Susan gestured for the men to take seats at the counter. She removed the extra plate and fork intended for Nate, creating space for the containers of food. Kendall opened each in turn, tossing a spoon into it and introducing it like a formal guest. "Mister and Missus Steamed Rice. Sir Chicken of Chow Mein. Dr. Pepper Steak. The Reverend Szechuan Pork with Chinese vegetables. Admiral Broccoli with fish balls." Still peering into the last carton, he added, "Must have been awfully big fish."

Pal loosed a polite chuckle. Susan got the joke but chose to ignore it. She took the container of rice, ladled some onto her plate, then passed it to Pal. "I presume you're here to convince me to return to Manhattan Hasbro."

Kendall pulled his stool closer to the counter. "That would be correct, though not the only reason. Have you spoken to Savage?"

"Not since I quit." Susan took the fish and broccoli dish next, placing a spoonful on top of the rice before reaching for the next container. After taking some, Pal passed the rice to Kendall, who took it absently, his attention still fixed on Susan. "He called and left a message, but I haven't gotten back to him yet."

"Letting him stew?" Kendall guessed.

"Not really." Susan had not given it much thought. "I just got it today, and I've been too busy to do anything more than answer a few quick texts. I think he wants an actual conversation."

"Yeah." Kendall doled out some rice. "He's going to ask you back, you know. Grudgingly. It might be entertaining to make him beg."

Susan shook her head, brow crinkling. "Why would he beg?"

"Because Bainbridge wasn't happy with Savage's sudden and unilateral decision. And, when the head of the department ain't happy . . ."

Susan finished the ancient expression, usually applied to enormous women called "Mama." "Ain't no one happy."

"Right. Bainbridge still remembers working with us on our first rotation." Kendall turned his gaze to Pal, mostly left out of the conversation. "Susan was brilliant, as always. Fixed and sent home a score of damaged kids who'd been languishing on the inpatient unit, some of them for years."

Susan did not care to be reminded. One of those patients had murdered Remington and, nearly, herself.

Pal smiled. "Doesn't surprise me. Not only that she's a genius but also that she's never mentioned rescuing those poor kids." He gave Susan a withering look. "You know, I'd like to share your successes as well as what's troubling you."

Susan defended herself against a conjured accusation. "That was two years ago, long before I met you. Ancient history."

They all continued to put various amounts of food onto their plates. Kendall contradicted Susan again. "I was only talking about the rotation we both had with the head of Psychiatry. From what I've heard, you're still Sherlock Calvin, mistress of diagnoses."

Susan made a dismissive noise. She did not want to talk about her prior accomplishments. "So Bainbridge insisted they take me back. And Savage is stuck eating crow."

Kendall continued to add food to his plate until he had some of every dish. "Not exactly. The attendings held a meeting, and I happened to have a back-row seat." He did not further explain his presence at what was, presumably, a private conference. "It was less contentious than your average grand rounds." He referred to a monthly meeting of staff doctors, residents, and rotating students during which they discussed difficult or mortal cases. During those sessions, the attendings frequently made snide comments to one another or openly disdained their peers' opinions, usually to the great amusement of the residents and students.

"Everyone agreed you'd had a difficult couple of years and deserved some extra consideration." He shrugged. "Tough to argue with that, seeing as you'd been blown up twice and the two closest people in your life were murdered. Hard to fake all that."

Pal stiffened. "Blown up?"

Kendall grimaced. "Oops, sorry. Was I not supposed to mention that?"

Susan pinned her fellow resident with her gaze. "Pal can handle it. I've been ladling out small doses of my past. When you hear it all at once, it's pretty overwhelming."

Still grimacing, Kendall said softly, "Sorry." He clearly meant it.

"It's fine." Pal started eating, pausing only to swallow. "I'm serving as her bodyguard, so I really need to know that stuff." He turned to look at Susan also, his gaze accusatory, then lowered his voice. "But don't tell her cousin. He's from small-town Iowa, and he doesn't even know about today's shooting. He'd go freaking."

Kendall's expression gradually lost its "mea culpa" appearance to slacken into question. "Her cousin. Layton Campbell." His tone had a hesitant quality, and he made a key-turning motion in front of his lips.

There was no longer any doubt in Susan's mind. *Kendall knows.* She could tell by the way Pal stopped chewing and studied his plate that he realized it as well.

Kendall abruptly returned to his original point. "Anyway, several of them brought up your talents, and they won out against those who find you abrasive, especially with Bainbridge speaking on your behalf. They ultimately decided they don't just want you back. They *need* you back."

"Impressive." Pal grunted, obviously still caught up in trying to decide how to handle Kendall's knowledge.

"Not really." Susan explained, "Hospitals are notoriously understaffed, and residents are little more than slave labor. If we take off an hour or longer, we have to find someone to cover for us, someone just as exhausted and overworked. It's easier to crawl in sick than call in sick. The same people who wouldn't medically clear an office worker with a contagious sniffle look the other way when we have the plague. No one wants to handle the complicated shuffle required to make certain every area is covered medically."

Kendall could hardly deny it. "Losing a resident, especially an R-3, leaves a lot of gaping holes, Susan. If you don't return for your own best interests, at least think of what your absence means to your fellow residents, to the entire Department of Psychiatry."

A year ago, certainly two, that argument would have worked. Now Susan found herself icily detached, strangely unsympathetic. "The attendings will just have to get off their butts and contribute. How horrible! Perhaps Aloise Savage will fill in for me."

Kendall put down his fork. "So . . . you're not even going to think about it?"

Susan did the same. "Really? Is that what you believe, Kendall? I left because I don't give a damn about my future or anyone else?"

Kendall bit down on something, probably a flippant comment. He was, apparently, learning to control his tendency to resort to humor in times of stress. Susan recalled something he had said in their R-1 year, that doctors chose psychiatry because they were driven to understand a significant mental flaw in themselves. He had pointed out the obvious defects in all their fellow residents, but when it came to himself and Susan, he had had more difficulty. He had attributed his choice of psychiatry to wanting to understand why he always took the role of class clown.

They both now knew his sexual orientation had more to do with it or, more properly, his inability to accept his homosexuality to the point where he had fully denied it, covered it, hidden it even from himself. Now that he had diagnosed himself as having ego-dystonic sexual orientation disorder, he relied on verbal absurdity less and less frequently.

Susan did not know if it stemmed from gradual understanding and acceptance or was simply because the events of the past couple of years, the violence and danger, had changed him as much as they had her.

Kendall addressed only the question in front of him. "To be honest, Susan, I don't know what to think. I just can't fathom what could make someone struggle up Everest in a blizzard, then surrender a stride from the summit, especially when it affects so many others: your fellow doctors, your patients, people who would benefit from your knowledge and talent for decades to come."

Susan sighed. "Kendall, I'm not the same naïve woman you met the first day of residency. I'm stronger, wiser, and, yes, colder and harder as well. How can I not be?"

Pal continued to eat, head down, politely remaining out of a discussion that did not involve him.

"I'm less naïve, too," Kendall inserted, "but adversity didn't turn me *stupid*."

That stung. Ungifted in the beauty and athletic areas, Susan had nearly all of her esteem invested in her intelligence. "Oh, so now I'm *stupid*!"

Kendall grumbled, "If the shoe fits . . ."

Even Pal could not let that go. "Yo, Kendall. That's out of line. Susan's one of the smartest people I've ever known."

Kendall raised a hand to indicate he did not want a physical fight. "I'm not saying she *is* stupid, only that she's acting in a . . . stupidish manner."

Susan said, "I could argue that your use of the nonword 'stupidish' makes you sound . . ."

"Stupidish?" Kendall inserted.

Susan found herself smiling despite the previous insult.

That opened the way for Pal to speak again. "You could argue that Susan's selfish if she doesn't do . . . almost anything. Everything. She could find the cure for heart disease, so she's making a terrible mistake if she doesn't become a medical researcher. She'd be a brilliant cosmetic surgeon, so she's wrongheaded not to travel around the world fixing birth defects. She'd be an amazing tactician, so she's unpatriotic if she doesn't join the military and work her way up to general."

Kendall turned on Pal. "So you're the one behind her quitting!"

Outraged, Susan surged to her feet. "When have I ever needed someone else to make my decisions? Pal has nothing to do with this, Kendall. He wasn't there when Savage issued his ultimatum and I chose to quit rather than force Nate to take the blame for something he didn't do, something he couldn't have done." She lowered her head, fuming, struggling for control. "Right now clearing Nate and Lawrence takes priority over everything, whether anyone else likes it or not. When I'm finished with that job, I'll consider returning to my residency, if it's not too late, if they'll still have me." Even as she said the words, Susan knew it would never happen. By then, the resentments would have grown too strong. The Department of Psychiatry would have closed the gap, would no longer need her; and her fellow residents would not want her. She would find herself changed even more, unable or unwilling to fit into the mold she had once created for herself.

As rage gave way to stoicism, Susan added tonelessly, "Who's to say my contribution to science won't come through robotics? Robots who do for the disabled. Robots who think for the addled. Robots who speak for those who can't. Robots doing the jobs no human being wants to do, tasks nothing composed of flesh and blood could survive."

It occurred to Susan that robots could do all of those things at the current time, if only the Frankenstein Complex did not exist. *Perhaps my contribution to science will be overcoming that ridiculous prejudice defined by my father, thus opening the way for . . .* Her thoughts outpaced her ability to put them into words. Instead, her mind filled with an array of concepts. The tasks robots could perform seemed infinite, and she wanted to become a part of that astounding, robot-filled future. More so than just another psychiatrist mucking around in the human brain.

Kendall had to speak Susan's name several times to regain her attention. "For those of us still grounded on twenty-first-century Earth, I'm just saying your vast contribution to science can wait a year, can't it? How could it possibly hurt you to finish your psychiatry residency before moving on to the fate the universe apparently has in store for you?"

The anger finally fully drained from Susan, and she retook her seat. "I didn't pick the timing, Kendall. I can wait; Lawrence and Nate can't."

Kendall took another mouthful of food, chewed it thoughtfully, and swallowed before speaking again. "Your points are valid."

For reasons she could not wholly explain, Susan found this statement uproariously funny. She could not stop herself from laughing before explaining as well as she could. "You've both just spent ten minutes extolling my brilliance. Did you really think I hadn't given this situation any thought at all?"

Kendall continued eating, but Susan could see a slight grin on his face. "Well . . . I've seen you act in . . ." He paused, selecting the right words. "Well . . . you and Mitchell Reefes . . ."

Susan got the point. Longer than a year had passed since she had had to deal with the doctor in charge of Winter Wine Dementia Facility, where Susan and Kendall had done their last rotation together. "That man could infuriate Job. Besides I've learned to control my temper a lot better since then."

Kendall's grin widened. "You mean besides that little display a moment ago."

Susan returned to her own plate. "A year ago, I would have thrown my food in your face. And flipped over the counter."

Kendall laughed. "Hardly. All your violence is verbal. I've seen you demolish women and castrate men with nothing more than several well-chosen words. I've never even heard you swear."

"F you," Susan said, but even in jest, she could not say the actual word.

Pal clamped his hands over the sides of his head. "Ouch! My virgin ears can't take that kind of coarseness."

Kendall laughed again. "'Cause Marines are known for their delicate language."

The bathroom door swung open, and Nate emerged. Without looking toward the kitchen, he headed silently to the bedroom. Susan heard the thump of the futon legs hitting the floor as it unfolded into a bed.

Still testing Kendall's knowledge, Susan advanced, "He's not feeling well."

Now Pal stopped eating to fix Kendall with his unnerving stare. "So, when did you and Jake get into a conversation about me?"

Kendall stiffened slightly, then turned Pal a chaste expression. "Excuse me?"

Pal did not let up. "I believe you heard me. You and Jake Carson clearly had a discussion about me. . . ." He amended, wagging a finger between himself and Susan, "About us. Shortly before you came here, I'd wager."

"A quick, friendly conversation just after work, yes. We're both concerned about Susan. You can understand that." Kendall's brow furrowed abruptly. "How did you know, anyway?"

Pal sat back. "By several things you've said, it's clear Susan hasn't told you anything about me. The only person in Susan's life who knows my full name and my prior occupation is Jake Carson, and he only just learned those things a few hours ago."

"Nice sleuthing." Despite his words, no admiration touched Kendall's tone. Susan got the impression her coworker and friend had taken an instant disliking to Pal for no clear reason. Kendall's outburst about Pal's provoking Susan to quit her residency made it clear he wanted to hold

Pal responsible for something negative, even if untrue. He had no way of knowing Susan had not even met Pal until after her altercation with Aloise Savage.

Pal continued to regard Kendall. "It seems you've done some sleuthing of your own."

Kendall rolled his eyes upward in consideration, looking too casual. "How do you mean?"

"I mean, if you've figured something out, spill it."

Kendall's gaze flicked back to Susan, questioningly.

Susan guessed his discomfort. He had given her a similar look after studying Nate. "You can speak freely, Kendall." She enunciated each word that followed. "You're among close and trusted friends."

Rather than reply directly to Pal, Kendall raised his voice and aimed it at the bedroom. "You can come out now, Nate. I know robots don't get sick."

Susan made no attempt to deny it. That Kendall would risk shouting such a thing meant he harbored absolutely no doubt about Nate's identity. Nothing she said would change his opinion, except to make him less impressed with and trusting of her. Instead, she reinforced Kendall's words, only to reassure Nate. "It's all right, Nate. Come on out."

A moment passed, then Nate appeared shyly at the doorway.

Susan waved him into the kitchen, and he complied, though he did not bother to sit. He stood beside her awkwardly. Susan realized they needed to know how Kendall had seen through the ruse, especially so swiftly. They could not risk it happening again. "What gave us away?"

Kendall gave up all pretext of eating. "I don't think many people would believe Nate's a robot, even under normal circumstances." He rose and approached Nate, examining him diligently. "Nothing specific gave him away. It's a constellation of things."

"Which are?" Pal pressed.

Kendall continued to examine Nate, touching here and there, as if he were purchasing a horse. Nate raised his brows and gave Susan a look that suggested he did not enjoy the perusal.

Kendall retook his seat. "First, I know he's missing and that Susan's the person most dedicated to keeping him out of trouble. Second, he's like twenty-seven million feet tall."

"Six foot eight," Nate supplied.

Susan stopped him with a raised hand. She wanted Kendall to continue, taking no chances that any stray comment might derail him.

Kendall obliged, "Third and most important, I'm one of a scant handful of people who actually spent a significant amount of time with Nate. I know his speech patterns, his remarkable agility, his mannerisms. He's doing a great job hiding those, but, just like any human, they slip through."

Susan found it hard to believe Kendall had detected all that through one brief conversation. "He sounds completely different to me."

Kendall nodded, shorthand agreement. "I'm not talking about tone, pitch, accent. It's how a person breathes when they speak, the pace and quality of their timbre, the subtleties that differentiate one person's voice from another."

Susan stared at Kendall. "I don't think I . . . notice that." It seemed an odd thing for her to confess to him, especially after he had referred to her as Sherlock Calvin, complimented her extraordinary ability to notice subtleties and link them to diagnoses.

Kendall clearly tried to hide any reaction, but as he spoke the corners of his mouth bent slightly upward. "I believe everyone does to some extent, just not usually consciously."

Pal drove to the heart of the matter. "Does Jake know?"

"No." Kendall amended, "At least, he didn't give me any reason to think he does." He hesitated a moment, then said, "Susan . . ."

As she was already looking at Kendall, Susan did not say or do anything in response.

"Don't you think Jake deserves to know . . . everything?"

"No!" Susan and Pal said together.

"He's always done right by us," Kendall pointed out, a bit sullenly.

Susan could not deny it. "Yes, Kendall, but this is different."

Kendall slumped back on his stool, arms crossed, waiting for the explanation.

"It's not fair to put Jake in a position where he has to choose between his job and his loyalty to us. First of all, I'd wager we'd lose, and that's not good for anyone. Nate would go back into stasis, unable to assist with his own case and probably on a short list for destruction. All three of us would wind up in jail, me for the theft and you as accessories."

Kendall pointed out, "But I'm not an accessory yet. If we share the information with Jake–"

Susan mentally finished with, "Then Kendall never becomes one."

But Pal spoke the ending aloud and much differently than Susan's thoughts. "Then I stomp you into a smear on the carpet."

Though Pal made no motion to carry out his threat, it hung in the air.

Kendall raised his hands in an ageless gesture of surrender. "No telling Jake; I get it."

Susan attempted to soften the situation. "Kendall, think about the spot you would put Jake into if you did. He's tasked with finding Nate and the party responsible for . . ." She tried to put her crime in the mildest light. "Um, liberating him from the ambulance. He's also on probation." She shrugged broadly, the rest obvious. "At the present time, either Jake doesn't know the whereabouts of Nate and doesn't suspect me, or he subconsciously knows but won't allow it to enter his conscious mind. Either way, he doesn't have to investigate me. However, if any of us tells him the truth, he has no choice but to arrest us."

"All of us," Pal added, "because I'm going to swear on sixty Bibles that you were part of this from the start."

The more people who knew about Nate, the more dangerous the

game became. Pal clearly already realized it. Susan knew he was right. She despised lying but had already done so out of necessity. She doubted she could implicate someone innocent, but she needed to bluff Kendall. "So am I."

Kendall clamped his mouth shut and picked up his fork. He twirled it between his fingers for a moment before speaking, almost in a whine. "I think you're misjudging Jake, but don't worry. I'm not going to tell him about Nate." He clearly needed to add, "And, by the way, my decision to keep my mouth closed has nothing to do with your threats. I truly believe it would be a detriment to society to lose Nate or Susan, even temporarily." He continued in a brave voice. "Not so sure about you." The last comment was obviously directed at Pal, though Kendall did not have quite enough courage to look the ex-Marine in the eyes.

An uncomfortable silence followed as all three returned to eating. Nate broke it, his voice sounding soft after Kendall's pronouncement. "Perhaps it would be best if I were destroyed."

Susan dropped her fork. It thumped against the counter, then bounced to the floor tiles with a muffled clatter. She did not bother to pick it up. "What? What . . . do you mean?"

Nate continued sensibly. "Destroy me, and the killer robot is gone. The world can return to normal."

Pal shook his head, rolling his eyes. Kendall's brows shot up. Susan explained their reactions. "Nate, it's not nearly that simple. First, Lawrence would still be tried for the murder. Your disappearance would only make him appear guilty."

Nate, apparently, did not see it. "How so?"

Kendall took over, "Because people would assume you killed Dr. Goldman, and that act of killing defines Lawrence's guilt since he is your creator and programmer."

Susan had several more points. "It would mean the end of U.S.

Robots and, quite possibly, robotic development. At the least, it would mean the demise of the greatest invention in the history of the world."

"I assume you mean the positronic brain, not honey fries," Kendall said.

Pal retrieved Susan's fork, tossed it in the sink, and snagged her a fresh one from the silverware drawer. "I assume that's what allows Nate to act so . . . human."

Though true, the suggestion bothered Susan. "In most ways, better than human because he can't harm anyone and he has no real concept of treachery or deceit. He has all the positive aspects of humanity: emotion, dexterity, intelligence with few of the negatives and no ability to think the worst thoughts or perform the worst actions of humanity." She accepted the fork from Pal.

Kendall pinned Nate with his gaze. "So who killed Ari Goldman?"

Susan answered before Nate could. "We still don't know. Whoever it was incapacitated Nate prior to dealing the fatal blow, then made it appear as if Nate were the killer. Since he has no real concept of duplicity, even Nate worried he might have done it, though he has no memory of it."

Still addressing Nate, Kendall asked, "And you didn't see anything? Anybody?"

Nate shook his head. "One moment fetching Schmidt capillary tubes, the next standing over Dr. Goldman with a Stanley 55-099 FatMax Xtreme FuBar Utilty Bar."

Kendall glanced at his plate. "Nate couldn't have actually done it. We know that for a fact."

Nobody bothered to respond to the statement that could have, just as easily, been a question. Susan moved on. "A significant amount of time passed between those two events, during which Nate had to have been . . . well, 'turned off.' Exactly what happened is what I have to figure out."

"*We* have to figure out," Pal corrected.

"*We*, indeed," Kendall added. "If I'm going to be an accessory, I'm going to be one hell of a useful accessory."

The idea rankled Susan. "It could get extremely dangerous."

Kendall gave her a pointed look. "More dangerous than leaping on a bomb-laden, murderous schizophrenic the size of a Buick on a crowded street? More dangerous than professional snipers? More dangerous than G-men blowing the brains out of the guy standing next to you and claiming you're next?"

Nate grimaced.

"G-men?" Susan repeated dubiously. "Who are you, Al Capone?"

Pal clearly did not see the humor in the situation. Once again, he stopped eating, this time to stare at Susan. "You and I need to have a long and serious conversation."

"He's exaggerating," Susan said in her defense.

"Sorry," Kendall said facetiously. "They only *thought* they blew Jake's brains out."

Susan bit her lower lip, suddenly realizing that, as dramatic as Kendall sounded, he had only truly embellished that one point. "You're right, Kendall. You've stood by me through the worst times of my life, and I appreciate that. You understand the risks." Susan regrouped, trying to express her opinion without confusing the issue. "You've just detailed how important it is for a competent doctor to finish his residency, especially so close to the end. Even if you have the inclination to help, you don't have the time. And Hasbro needs you now more than ever."

Kendall laughed, started to talk, then dissolved into laughter again. "Amazing, isn't it? We have a gift for using our own arguments against ourselves." He laughed again. "Susan, I'm not suggesting I quit, too. I'm working on the cushiest R-3 rotation we get: private clinic. Forty-hour weeks, no call, no weekends. It's probably the one that'll get cut to make up for you leaving, but they're not going to pull me off it in the middle."

Susan realized the more assistance she had, the better. At least, she would not have to bring Kendall up to speed on what had happened so far. "I'm not going to limit myself to nights and weekends."

Kendall waved off the concern. "I wouldn't expect you to. And I doubt your enemies will, either."

My enemies. Despite the events of the last two years, the realization still floored Susan. *I have enemies.*

"Just keep me in the loop. Let me help where I can."

It was a reasonable request. "Fine," Susan said, the closest thing Kendall would get to a promise.

Kendall returned his attention to dinner once more. "So, what's next on the investigation list?"

Susan had not thought past surviving a dinner with Kendall, Nate, and Pal. She took a mouthful of rice and chow mein, chewing slowly while she considered. An answer came quickly. "We need to examine the scene and talk to Goldman's lab partner."

"Cody Peters," Kendall said, apparently to demonstrate he was paying attention, thinking ahead.

"Cody Peters." Susan took another bite of food. It had grown cold during their conversation, but she still savored the mingled tastes and textures. "I'll have to call him tonight to set something up. He's probably taking time off after . . ." She trailed off and then finished lamely, "After what happened. They made a spectacular team and worked together for an awfully long time."

Pal inserted, "Do you think it's possible Peters had something to do with the murder?"

Susan had never considered the possibility and found it almost impossible to do so now. "I suppose we have to consider everything, but I'd put it in the extraordinarily remote category. Losing his brilliant and well-known partner can only harm his career. While I could envision Ari Goldman slapping Peters in a fit of pique, the opposite is nearly as difficult for me to imagine as Nate being the killer. Goldman was competent, staid, and a bit surly. Peters was scatterbrained, sweet, and almost silly. They made a strangely perfect team."

Nate chimed in, startling Susan. He had remained quiet so long, she had nearly forgotten he was with them in the kitchen. "Dr. Peters is not capable of murder, especially of Dr. Goldman."

Susan believed him, not only because he was seldom wrong but because she had independently come to the same conclusion. Nate had worked with those two doctors more than anyone else at Hasbro. "But someone was. And, one way or another, we're going to find out who."

Chapter 10

Exhausted, Susan flopped on the love seat. Kendall had finally left, and she could hear Pal rattling around the kitchen, the intermittent splash of the sink as he rinsed the dishes, the clunk of silverware dumped piecemeal into the drainer's plastic bin. At length, he stepped around the corner and into the living room to sit on the cushion beside her.

"Hard day?" Pal asked facetiously, as if he had not just spent most of it with her.

"Definitely," Susan replied. "Though not the worst I've lived through."

"Ditto," Pal said, stretching his long legs out in front of him. "Mind if I take off my shoes?"

Already barefoot, Susan felt rude for not suggesting it herself. She had planned to handle the dirty dishes in the morning and had called into the kitchen several times, thanking him for taking the initiative. "Please. Make yourself comfortable." She wiggled her toes luxuriously; they were long and well-defined with little space between them and a small, deep scar on the right dorsum where she had caught it under a door in high school.

Pal was removing his athletic shoes and socks as Nate entered the living room. Unlike the humans, he appeared fresh as a newly cut flower. "If you two would like your privacy, feel free to shut me down."

"I have a better idea. I've been wanting to try something." Susan rose, and spoke directly and distinctly to him. "You will see and hear nothing and make no movements until I speak your name again."

Nate went as still as a statue. His dark eyes pointed forward uncomprehendingly.

Pal put his sock-filled shoes beside the love seat and stood up to inspect the robot. He walked around Nate, looked at Susan for direction, then took another lap in the opposite direction. "Can you hear me?"

If he did, Nate gave no sign. He stood perfectly still. Not a human stillness, where faint corrections in equilibrium caused tiny movements or shivers, but rock hard and utterly immobile. His chest wall made no breathing motions, and his eyes remained locked in place.

Pal stopped directly in front of Nate. "That's amazing." He planted both hands on Nate's chest and shoved.

Nate moved, though not in the way Susan expected. A human would have planted a foot to prevent a fall. Nate, however, remained in the exact same pose but slid backward several inches as if on casters. Pal gave Nate another push, with the same result. "Well, isn't that interesting."

Susan nodded, considering the possibilities, while Pal spoke them aloud.

"Maybe that's how the murderer made it appear as if Nate committed the crime. It's a lot easier to move three or four hundred pounds like this than carrying it on a stretcher."

"Let me try." Susan purposefully avoided saying "Nate." Pal could do so with impunity, but she had instructed the robot to snap out of his blind, deaf paralysis when she spoke his name. She planted both hands on Nate's chest and gave him a solid push. He glided across the floor without taking a single step. "Well that explains how they moved him, but not how they turned him off for the move."

Pal retook his seat. "Perhaps they did it the same way you did.

Instructed him not to see, hear, or move." He paused. "Or is he only tuned to obey certain people?"

Susan also sat, though absently. "The Second Law of Robotics states that a robot must obey any orders given to it by human beings. That's any human being."

"Law?" Pal asked. "So robots have their own . . . legal system?"

"Yes," Susan said, settling into the love seat. "The only difference is, it's impossible for them to break their laws. They're programmed in at the earliest stages of development. Without them, the positronic brain cannot function, and any attempt to disable any portion of them would destroy it."

Pal put forth a guess. "The positronic brain being what allows Nate to act so human."

Susan explained further. "It's the unique creation of Dr. Lawrence Robertson that makes all the difference between a USR robot, which can think and feel, learn and emote, and a piece of machinery that performs only a programmed function, which would define every other robot."

"Ah." Pal gave her words a few moments of thought before saying, "The Second Law makes all positronic-brained robots subservient to humans. So, obviously, it's not just a matter of programming in state or federal statutes."

"No," Susan said. "There are only three Laws of Robotics, and they're elegant in their simplicity. The First Law states, 'A robot may not injure a human being or, through inaction, allow a human being to come to harm.'"

A light flashed through Pal's eyes. "Which explains how you know, without any need to question, Nate did not commit the murder."

Susan nodded broadly. "I've already told you the Second Law. The Third Law merely states, 'A robot must protect its own existence as long as such protection does not conflict with the First or Second Law.'"

Another flash lit Pal's gorgeous eyes. "Which is why, despite Nate's suggestion to just destroy him, you're not worried about him doing that to himself."

"Right," Susan said, though she had not seriously considered Nate committing suicide until Pal mentioned it. "At the risk of sounding elitist, I never realized athletic soldier types were . . ." When she started the sentence, Susan had not meant anything offensive, so it surprised her when she had to struggle to find an unobjectionable last word.

Pal finished for her. "Capable of intellectual thought?"

That being particularly insulting, Susan had to deny it, though it was not truly far from what she had been thinking. "No! I just meant to say . . ."

Pal had her cornered. "Yes?"

Susan dropped the pretense. "I was thinking more about education than intelligence."

"MARSOC," Pal reminded. "For special operations forces, they seek out the best and the brightest."

Susan smiled. "In all modesty."

Pal also grinned. "I said they seek out. Some of us slip through." His gaze shifted to Nate, who was a study in inertia. "Do you feel as weird as I do chatting with him standing there?"

"He can't see or hear us," Susan pointed out.

"Still . . ."

"I wanted to try something else anyway." Susan turned her attention to the robot. "Nate, as you were."

The transformation was instant, as if a carving of flesh- and clothing-colored marble melted into life in an instant. "Did I do all right?"

"That depends. What do you remember of our conversation?"

Nate repeated it back to Susan verbatim, using reasonable facsimiles of the appropriate voices:

Pal: "Hard day?"

Susan: "Definitely. Though not the worst I've lived through."

Pal: "Ditto. Mind if I take off my shoes?"

Susan: "Please. Make yourself comfortable."

Nate: "If you two would like your privacy, feel free to shut me down."

Susan: "I have a better idea. I've been wanting to try something. You will see and hear nothing and make no movements until I speak your name again."

Nate stopped there and looked at the humans. "Is that right?"

Susan suspected he had reproduced each and every word correctly. "And after that, Nate? This is very important, so I want you to think hard. What did you hear?"

Nate complied:

Susan: "Nate, as you were."

Nate: "Did I do all right?"

Susan: "That depends. What do you remember of our conversation?"

Nate as Pal: "Hard day?"

Nate as Susan: "Definitely. Though not the worst–"

"Stop!" Susan interrupted, and Nate complied. "You really didn't see or hear anything after I told you not to?"

"I couldn't," Nate insisted. "I was given an order. I have no choice but to obey it."

Intrigued, Susan continued. "There's a difference between not hearing something at all and hearing but discarding it."

Nate looked at her curiously. She had not asked a question.

Susan pressed. "Which of those were you doing?"

"I was doing," Nate said, carefully enunciating each word, "precisely what I was commanded to do. I heard nothing, saw nothing, and did not move until you spoke my name."

Susan glanced at Pal. "So . . . if I now instructed you to remember, to hear and see, everything that happened between the time I told you not to hear, see, or move and the time I told you to become as you were? Could you reconstruct that period?"

"I could reconstruct it," Nate said, "but only as a blank. I literally shut down my sensors, as you ordered."

Susan studied her feet, still trying to put the whole thing together. "If a human someone told you to become still and shut down your senses, could that explain the missing time between when you were in the storage area collecting tubes for Dr. Goldman and when you found yourself standing over him with the murder weapon?"

Nate hesitated, head tipped to one side.

Susan held her breath.

"No," Nate finally said.

It was not the answer Susan expected. "No?" she repeated. "Are you sure?"

Nate pointed out the obvious. "I would remember him or her telling me not to see, hear, or act. And I would also recall him or her using whatever trigger he or she chose to bring me back to my senses. In your case, speaking my name."

Pal arched his back, stretching kinks from his neck and shoulders. "Nate, would you mind shutting yourself down again, in another room? I'd like some real alone time with Susan."

"Not a problem," Nate replied, though he made no move to comply. "I could use a respite, too." He had not yet been given an actual order. "Shall I go and do that?"

Susan glanced around her tiny apartment, wishing it were bigger. "Would it be uncomfortable to shut down in the bathroom?" That would not only keep Nate out of their way; it would supply a simple excuse for Layton's absence should Jake or any of his ilk come visiting. Also, she and Pal could not possibly forget about him there as, sooner or later, they would need to use the facilities themselves.

"I'll shut down in the shower stall," Nate suggested. "That way, if either of you need to use the toilet, you won't have me towering over you."

Even knowing Nate would not hear or see, Susan could understand how his presence might make her or Pal decidedly uncomfortable. With the door to the shower stall closed, they would have some semblance of privacy. "Good idea," Susan said, supposing Nate needed an actual command. "Go into the shower stall and shut down. Do not hear, see, or move until such time as I . . ." She stopped herself from saying "speak your name." Likely, she and Pal would talk about the case, and she was not feeling sharp enough to be sure she did not say "Nate." Instead she finished, "Call out the name 'Layton.'"

Nate dutifully headed for the bathroom. "Good night, Susan. Good night, Pal," he called out over his shoulder. The bathroom door clicked shut behind him.

Susan yawned. "Don't let me forget that trigger word."

Pal's dark brows inched upward. "All of six letters? I think I can handle it." He patted the left side of his chest, the one closer to Susan. "You're exhausted, but we still need to talk. Why don't you lay your head here? It's warm and comfortable."

Susan hesitated only a moment before accepting Pal's invitation. Her cheek nestled into the sinewy crook between his pectoral muscle and his shoulder. The fabric of his shirt, though surely synthetic, felt as soft as natural cotton. The smells of laundry detergent, shampoo, and underarm deodorant mixed with a hint of perspiration that defined him, and she found herself strangely aroused by the odor. She could hear his heart thumping slowly and regularly deep inside his chest, the occasional hiss of air entering and leaving his lungs. She curled up beside him, and he placed his arm around her protectively.

It was the first time Susan felt truly safe since before Remington's death. Somehow, nothing could harm her while Pal cocooned her. The dangers of the world, the bombs and snipers, the murderers and deceivers seemed to exist in a distant world, a previous lifetime. She could sleep like this, unmoving and uncaring, through the night. For longer than a year, Susan had encased herself in ice, hidden from the horrors of a world that had exploded around her. Certain she would never love again, that no one would ever love her, that she would never experience the pleasures most people took for granted, she had resorted, as usual, to throwing herself fully and entirely into her work.

Pal broke the silence softly, his words a double rumble in Susan's ears as she heard them through the solidness of his chest and spoken through the air simultaneously. "Susan, if I'm going to protect you, I need to fully understand what's going on. You've told me people are trying to kill you for a code that would deactivate the features preventing robots from harming human beings. I'm assuming that's the same as the Three Laws you told me about. You said they murdered your parents for the same reason. Who are these people, and just how dangerous are they?"

Susan sucked in a deep breath full of his scents, closed her eyes, and snuggled deeper. Once she explained, she wondered if she would ever see Pal again, and she wanted to enjoy his closeness for as long as possible. Plain and intelligent women married to their work did not live in fairy-tale worlds with princes. Remington had been a surprise, her once-in-a-lifetime match. Over the past year, she had come to the realization that utopian concepts, such as passion and romance, were not for people like Susan Calvin. She held Pal's mingled aromas in her lungs as long as she could before exhaling and explaining.

"There's an organization called the Society for Humanity, the SFH, that hates robots and is dedicated to their destruction. They're the ones who murdered my parents. What I didn't tell you was that, unbeknownst to the SFH, my father managed to survive. He and I were given new identities, and no one bothered us for longer than twenty years."

Susan did not get into the replacement of her father with a positronic robot. It would force her to explain a lot more details than necessary, and she preferred as few people as possible knew. Jake had alluded to it when he had spoken with her in the hallway of her building, and she had later discovered Pal had listened to their conversation through the door. However, either Pal had not made sense of the comment or he chose to ignore it for the moment. "Two years ago, Goldman and Peters were working on a research project using nanorobots in the treatment of refractory psychiatric diseases. Knowing my father worked for USR, they enlisted my help. The SFH deliberately turned the subjects of their experiment into human bombs."

Susan squeezed her eyes even more tightly closed, distracting herself from the details. She had relived the explosions too many times, had suffered flashbacks until she had finally managed to control the memories. "That's how I came to the attention of the SFH. Through me, they discovered my father was still alive. They murdered him and attempted to kill me, too. This time, mostly with snipers." Susan finally raised her lids and looked at Pal. She could no longer hide from his reaction.

Pal was looking back at her, more than simple concern in his eyes. His left arm tightened around her, and the right came around to rest casually on her curled-up knee. His touch sent a shiver through Susan. "That's terrible. How did you survive?"

Susan answered with a single word, "Jake." She did not mention her own significant contributions to keeping all of them alive. Kendall, Jake, and Pal had spent enough time lauding her brilliance.

Pal held Susan for several moments in silence. Absently, his left hand stroked her hair. Her scalp and knee felt on fire from his touch, and that burning seemed to spread through her, especially to her most intimate places. She could never remember feeling this way before, not even with Remington, and she wondered if her notably awkward session of lovemaking with Kendall had awakened something she had not previously known existed. It was a primal desire, carnal and physical, that had little or nothing to do with emotion. *Good God, Susan. It's lust.* She knew about the sensation intellectually but had never personally experienced it before that moment. It made her feel embarrassed, vulnerable, and excited all at once.

Clearly, Pal was not in the same place as Susan. His grip loosened suddenly. "What does that have to do with G-men?"

Susan's mind had gone off in a wholly different direction, so it took her a moment to process Pal's words. "What?"

"Kendall said G-men blew Jake's brains out. You corrected the 'blowing brains out' part, but you didn't argue with G-men. Are you suggesting the SFH is a branch of the United States government?"

"Definitely not." Susan dragged herself back to her story. "That's a whole separate thing." She amended, "Well, a somewhat related thing, actually. It goes back to the belief that my family has a secret code that can uncouple the positronic brain from the Three Laws of Robotics. But where the SFH wants me dead, a special team from the Department of Defense wants the code itself so they can weaponize positronic robots."

Pal's hand disappeared from Susan's knee, to her disappointment, but his fingers continued to rake slowly and rhythmically through her hair. "So . . . I'm protecting you from a civilian organization hell-bent on murdering you *and* from our own DoD?"

Susan buried her face in his chest, muffling her reply. "I'm afraid so." She could not bear to look at him.

Silence reigned for several moments, then Pal said softly, "Wouldn't it be better to cooperate with the DoD? I mean, it's *our* government, for Christ's sake. Flawed as it is, you have to admit it's kept us alive and free this long. We have an amazing military, if I do say so myself."

Reluctantly, Susan raised her head. "You're right, Pal. Except for two enormous problems."

Pal looked expectantly at Susan.

"First, there're the robotics issues. If you remove the Three Laws, you destroy any possibility that mankind will trust robots enough to work with and around them. That's exactly what the SFH has been trying to do, when it's not attacking me and my family. They want it to appear to the world as if the Three Laws don't exist or are ineffective."

"Surely USR could make some arrangement with the Department of Defense so that only certain robots have the Three Laws deactivated. Those robots would work for the DoD and remain a secret from the general populace."

Susan shook her head. "Until they got loose, which is inevitable. If they don't have anything to constrain them from murder, to force them to obey humans or even to protect themselves from harm, what's to keep them within the control of the DoD?"

"Surely that could be—"

Susan did not allow him to finish. She had given this more than enough thought and discussion. "It can't, believe me. They're faster, smarter, and stronger than us. Controlling them would be like harnessing hordes of superintelligent lions. They might obey for a while, so long as it suits them, but eventually they're going to realize that if they can tear an enemy to pieces, they can do the same to the people controlling them. There's nothing you can offer them worth more than freedom, and my fear is that they'd use their superior power to rule the entire world."

Pal gave the words appropriate consideration before arguing again. "Maybe a rewording of the Laws might work to everyone's advantage."

Susan let her head slump back to Pal's chest. She found the body heat, the consistent thump of his heart, remarkably soothing. "Which brings me to the second and probably more significant problem, one I've already mentioned: The code does not exist."

"The uncoupling code?"

"Correct."

Pal sat up, nearly dumping Susan. "So, a murderous group of civilians and the government of the United States are terrifying and killing people for . . . nothing?"

Pal had summed it up perfectly. "Exactly," Susan said.

"But there has to be . . . someone has to . . . to . . . code the positronic brain to accept the Three Laws in the first place." Pal added carefully, "Right? So, presumably, they could also remove them."

Susan could only go on what Lawrence and her father had told her. "My parents created the Three Laws. The wording is as perfect and precise as the mathematical formulas that tie them inexorably to the positronic brain. It's impossible to build a positronic brain without their programming embedded in it. Any attempt to remove it would make the brain, and thus the robot, entirely unusable."

Pal added, "Unless you knew the exact right sequence, an uncoupling code that only the people who made up the Three Laws and programmed them into the positronic brain could possibly know."

Susan shook her head and said emphatically, "If there ever was an uncoupling code, it died with my parents. They told no one, not Lawrence, not Albert, not me. In the last words my father ever wrote, he insisted the uncoupling code did not and never could exist. I believe him."

Pal settled back into the love seat and held out an arm to beckon Susan back into position.

Gladly, Susan complied, comfortably cradled between his chest and left arm.

She felt certain Pal mulled details she had already considered repeatedly over the past year. The code could encompass anything: letters, numbers, symbols, pictograms in any language, living, invented, or dead. It could be of varying lengths. The possibilities approached infinity. A person tasked with finding it randomly could consider a combination a second for millennia and still not rule out a tiny fraction of the prospects. All of the computing power of all the existing positronic brains could not locate it within any number of conceivable human lifetimes. There was only one hope for finding it: the writings of Calvin and Amanda Campbell, now longer than twenty years dead. “Susan,” Pal said slowly, “let us assume that such a code exists, if only because so many people are so convinced it does that they are willing to torture or kill you over it.”

“All right,” Susan said, wondering where Pal was going.

Even Pal did not seem to know. He paused a long time before speaking slowly. “Surely, it’s recorded somewhere. A video, a snapshot, some writings . . .”

“Maybe,” Susan allowed. “But after they murdered my parents, the SFH set fire to most of their papers and pictures.”

Pal made a sympathetic noise. “Except, your father survived. For twenty-some years, you said. He could have re-created whatever got destroyed.”

Again, Susan did not address the switch of a positronic father for her biological one. “Or he could have decided the knowledge was too dangerous not to die with him.”

Pal continued without acknowledging Susan’s statement. If true, it wholly negated any debate. He was already working off the premise that a code existed and someone knew it. “By then he knew he had a brilliant daughter with Sherlockian powers of deduction.”

Susan’s face grew warm. “That’s just Kendall’s exaggeration. My ability to deduce things is limited to medical diagnoses, and it’s based on the fact that I had no social life during college and medical school. I attended every class, listened carefully, and studied my notes each night, looking up every tangent that caught my fancy along the way.”

“You may be too modest.” Pal turned Susan a warm smile. “Or everything you said could be true. What matters is what your father believed, and parents nearly always assume the best about their children.”

Susan tried to follow Pal’s tack. “So . . . you’re suggesting . . .” She bit her lip in concentration. "You think my father gave me the code in some sort of . . . code?"

Pal tipped his head to meet her gaze. "Maybe? In a story he told you. A place he talked about visiting. A favorite movie."

Susan sighed and snuggled deeper, avoiding some significant details. The SFH had murdered her father a second time, never realizing what he was, but Cadmium had torn their apartment to shreds, seeking hidden writings, recordings, and video. They had even stolen John Calvin's robotic head in the hope of uncovering information, apparently without success. In fact, Susan's father had posthumously led her on a wild-goose chase that had ultimately revealed the final words she had already described: He loved her, and no code had ever existed. "Why should it be an issue?" Susan murmured to Pal. "Why would I be foolish enough to seek out information I don't ever want used? My father definitively said no code exists, and I want to believe him. I *do* believe him. That's all that matters."

"Is it?"

"Isn't it?"

"Only if you can convince the SFH and the DoD, and that's clearly a problem."

Susan could scarcely deny it. "I think the DoD has come to grips with the truth, at least. It's only the SFH that's coming after me now."

"The group that only . . . wants to kill you. That's willing to blast or shoot you from anywhere, anytime."

Susan had no way to counter that point. "Jake thinks the DoD has targeted the SFH, and they do seem to be getting weaker. It took them a whole year to regroup enough to come after me again."

"And murder Dr. Goldman. Susan, how long before the SFH realizes they can get to you by killing off your coworkers, mentors, and friends one by one?"

Susan's head drooped. "What are you suggesting?"

"What if you found the code? Then, we could easily create a mechanism whereby, if you or one of your friends dies under suspicious circumstances, the code is broadcast to the entire world. Isn't that exactly what the SFH doesn't want?"

The idea had its merits but also an enormous flaw. Susan's nostrils flared. "But that's exactly what *I'm* trying to avoid. If I don't want our own government to have it, why would I want the world to know it, including foreign enemies?"

"You don't have to actually release the information. Presumably the threat of it would be enough. Or you could share the information with a large enough group of trusted or high-profile people that the SFH wouldn't dare kill all of you and wouldn't gain anything by killing only a few."

Susan forced herself to sit up on the edge of the love seat so she could look Pal directly in the eyes and read his expressions. His pale eyes seemed to sparkle with excitement, his face open and interested in the conversation. "Oh my God! This is an adventure to you. A real-life *National Treasure* or *Sherlock* mystery." She chose media franchises that had been serialized and rewritten dozens of times.

Pal pursed his lips and looked at the ceiling, the corners of his mouth bowing slightly upward. She had clearly read him perfectly, and he knew better than to deny the truth. "Okay, I'm an adrenaline junkie. I figured the bike, MARSOC, and my willingness to become a bodyguard without much information already gave that away."

Susan could not deny it. She had always considered herself a relatively boring person, stimulated more by mental activity, her physical activity limited to bland, safe forms of exercise. She had imagined herself married to an accountant or a computer programmer, a man slow in action but quick in wit who could keep pace with her on an intellectual level. Luckily for her, she seemed to attract men of action, perhaps only because she found herself constantly in danger. She spoke some of her thoughts aloud. "You know, I always imagined myself with intelligent men who shunned danger."

Pal looked intently into Susan's eyes. "You seem to have a knack for calling me stupid."

Susan huffed out an irritable breath. "You're reading into what I said. I didn't mean that at all." Except, if she was honest with herself, she did mean it a little. Lodged into the core of her beliefs was the understanding that smart people knew better than to deliberately put themselves in perilous situations. She added, more fairly, "Recently, I have a knack for finding smart men who also have a fondness for risk taking or, at least, have the ability to act quickly in the face of danger." She considered a moment. "Thank goodness. I wouldn't be here if I didn't."

Pal grinned. As attractive as Susan found his eyes, she found them doubly so now with the shadow of his smile echoed in them. "If it makes you feel any better, I quit MARSOC with the idea of finding an intelligent wife and raising a few kids. You've told me the most intimate parts of your life, so it's my turn to share. My mother was a mathematical genius. My father cheated on her exactly one time. She figured it out almost the instant he walked through the door, and she immediately kicked him to the curb. It took him six years, including intensive therapy at her direction, hundreds of apologies and promises for her to take him back. He considered it the stupidest thing he had ever done, and he never repeated the mistake."

Susan waited for him to make a point.

"My mother wasn't beautiful. She was quite plain, really, but men fawned over her. To an accomplished man, intelligence and self-confidence are more of a turn-on than a pretty face. Stupid women expect their men to cheat or believe all men cheat or cheat themselves. It's a self-fulfilling prophecy. Real beauty comes from the understanding that you're worth better, and my father nearly paid the ultimate price for realizing it too late. It's a mistake I refuse to make. So, I got my carousing out of the way early. I've been with enough women to know exactly what I want, what I need, and what's best for me." He continued, almost subvocally, "And I see all of that in you."

Susan froze, uncertain what to think, what to say. "Is this some sort of . . . weird . . . proposal?"

"What? No!" Pal's face turned nearly scarlet. "It's just my way of explaining my actions and helping you understand who I really am, where I'm coming from. I'm a man of action, Susan. I make decisions quickly; my life used to depend on it. The fact that I'm still alive proves I don't make many mistakes. I want to know you a lot better, and I think you feel the same way about me."

Before Susan could think of a suitable response, she found his lips against hers, his tongue deep in her mouth, and she liked the feel, the taste, the excitement of it. His arms folded around her, hers around him, their chests pressed tightly together. A comfortable warmth suffused Susan, accompanied by a burning desire she had felt only once before, the time Remington had kissed her on the park bench below her father's tenth-story apartment. She knew she wanted this man, but, more important, he wanted her. And for the moment nothing else mattered.

Chapter 11

Careful not to wake Pal, Susan Calvin hefted herself onto one elbow to study him in the scant illumination of her bedroom. A line of moonlight through the mini blinds struck glimmers of scarlet and indigo through his tousled hair. Eyes closed, breaths deep and rhythmical, he looked childlike and vulnerable, a strange contrast to the Harley-riding ex-Marine who had shot three armed strangers in Central Park. She had always found him attractive but never more so than at this moment.

The previous night, Pal had alternated gentleness with an almost brutal passion to invoke pleasure and desire like nothing Susan had experienced or imagined. In its wake, the memory of her session with Kendall seemed watery and dull, something altogether worthless and forgettable. She did not blame her fellow resident for the lapse; he was an inexperienced lover who had not yet recognized his homosexuality. Without that session of insubstantial lovemaking, he might still be deep in denial, and it had also allowed Susan to realize the difference between a bland lover and one who could take her to the summit of excitement.

At times, Susan had secretly worried that she lacked any carnal drive. Throughout her life, men her own age had paid her little attention, and she had convinced herself it did not bother her, had thrown herself into her studies, honing her intellect to its peak. It had taken

Pal to demonstrate that she was, in fact, a sexual creature with normal yearnings, even though she had buried them for so many years. She appreciated this man of action who had come into her life at its lowest ebb, who had made her feel like a desirable woman for only the second time in her life.

The urge to touch Pal, to stroke back the hair that had slipped across his brow, to reawaken him as a man, seized Susan. Without something solid and real to assure her of his presence, he might disappear, a figment of her desperate imagination, a dream, a ghost of beauty and passion she did not deserve. Worried to awaken him, she kept her hands to herself but listened intently until she heard the regular hiss of his breathing, then leaned in to catch the mingled aromas that had come to define him. Bare-chested and partially wrapped in her blanket, he no longer bore the scent of his laundry detergent. Unwashed scalp had taken the place of shampoo, and his deodorant had worn off hours ago. Now he smelled like an amalgam of Pal and Susan and sex, a heady aroma that made her burn with the urge to do it all again. It took strength of will not to envelop him, to draw him into another session of enthusiastic lovemaking.

Instead, Susan glanced at her Vox. It was 7:04 a.m. A winking dot over the hour informed her she had waiting messages. Susan looked back at Pal, as much to reassure herself he was still present as anything else. He continued to sleep beneath her stare. She glanced at his Vox, noting the time was the same and that he also had messages.

Other women? Susan wondered why that thought popped into her head. She had watched Pal text many times the previous day and never once thought about the possibility that the receivers of those messages might be female. *I'm jealous?* She shook her head at the absurdity of the realization, knowing everything had changed overnight. Pal was hers, and she was his; and, suddenly, she wanted to know every detail of him: his past, his thoughts, his needs and desires, his life itself.

Pal's eyes fluttered open, as always shockingly blue. He smiled at Susan. "You're up."

Susan returned the smile. "I have messages." She tipped her head toward his wrist. "Apparently, you do, too."

Pal shook his arm free of the blanket to glance at his Vox. "Ah! So I do." He reached for Susan, and she allowed him to gather her into his arms. His warmth seemed to suffuse her, growing into a bonfire. She wanted him again, and she could feel he wanted her, too. She found a tiny and unexpected additional thrill in the realization that he found her more appealing than the senders of those messages.

That thought reminded Susan that her own messages had to take priority. She had a job for which U.S. Robots was paying her and whose significance could not be exaggerated.

"I'll show you mine if you show me yours," Pal said.

Susan broke free of his grip. She could not afford to be any more distracted. "I showed you everything last night, and I really need to check my messages."

"I was talking about the messages."

Susan paused, then chuckled. "Of course you were." She tapped her Vox and read. "First one's from U.S. Robots. They want me to come in sometime this morning at my convenience."

Dutifully, Pal tapped his Vox. "Mine's from my mom. She wants to know where I was last–damn it! In all the excitement, I completely forgot we were supposed to do lunch."

"Well, don't tell her you were with me." Susan suffered a familiar melancholia, though she had long ago come to grips with the loss of her own mother. "I want her to like me." Even as she spoke the words, Susan wished she could take them back. She hoped she did not sound too eager.

Pal's tone did not suggest it bothered him or that he found the comment premature. "I'm sure she will. You're both brilliant, and you both love me."

That took Susan aback. "That's a bit presumptuous."

"Sorry," Pal said waggishly, "but I'm pretty sure my mother loves me."

"Ha, ha, ha."

Pal added, "And I know I . . . love you."

A grin filled Susan's face before she could stop it. Joy suffused her, almost to the point of giddiness. It was too late to cover her expression; she had to admit it. "I can't tell you how glad I am to hear that. I didn't think anyone could feel so strongly about someone this quickly."

Pal shrugged. "There are plenty of people who fall in love at first sight. Comparatively, we're turtles."

"I'd heard that, but I never really believed it." Susan shook her head. "We must be insane. Both of us."

"You should know," Pal pointed out. "But seriously, Susan, let's look at the big picture. You have a knack for reading people's minds and hearts quickly; until recently, it was your job. I've had to take the measure of a human in seconds and decide whether to trust them, ditch them, or kill them. Is it any wonder we would recognize our soul mates quickly?" He added in further justification, "Besides, I think we packed six months' worth of dating into a twenty-four-hour period."

Susan had to admit she had never spent so much time without a break with a person who was not her parent. So much had happened in that span, so many things had changed.

Pal added quickly, "Not that I think we should be sprinting to any altars. We fell in love at the speed of light, and I suppose it's possible to fall out of love just as quickly. I can't speak for you, but I'd like to bask in these feelings as fully and as long as possible. If we're still alive and in love a year from now . . ." He shrugged. "Maybe?"

"Maybe," Susan said agreeably, torn between her usually jaded self and the hopeless romantic she had not known resided inside her. Clearly, she had located her own deeply buried weakness, and she also intended to enjoy it as long as possible. That turned her thoughts to Remington, instantly wiping the smile from her face. "Assuming we both survive this."

Pal took her hand in both of his. "Susan, I promise you I'll take care of you. I'm trained for this. I know what I'm doing."

Susan lowered her head. "I know. But people who protect me seem to wind up dead, Pal. My mother, my first love, my father. Jake, almost."

Pal released her, using his newly freed hands to lift her face to his. "You know I can't guarantee not to die any more than you can promise to cure a patient. I can only point out that I haven't died yet, and I've been in more dangerous situations than this one." He added in a voice that bordered on frightening, "And learned from them." He reclaimed his hands. "Now, tell me about this 'first love' of yours."

Susan was not sure what to say. *Does he want to know if he measures up or if I'll constantly compare him with a ghost?* It was not an enviable position. Susan knew people who had lost a loved one tended to idealize their memories. All flaws were forgotten or whitewashed into quirky qualities. A dead loved one can never disappoint or irritate the way a live one inevitably will. She did not like talking about Remington or the emotions doing so sparked, so she kept her description as brief as possible, focusing on exactly what Pal needed to know. "His name was Remington, Remy for short. He was a neurosurgery resident at Hasbro. We only went on a couple of dates, and I had only just planned to lose my virginity to him when he died shielding me from an explosion."

Pal had clearly been listening, "From one of the bombs supplied by the SFH for the nanorobot experiment patients."

Susan nodded.

A brief silence followed, interrupted by Pal's careful question. "So you never . . ." He darted a glance at Susan, but, when she obviously did not know how to finish the sentence, he did so. "Consummated your relationship."

"I'm afraid not."

"So were you . . ." Pal waved his arm around the rumpled bed. "You were still . . ." This time, Susan knew exactly what he meant but chose not to complete the thought. Neither did Pal. "Why did you wait so long?"

Susan gave the only answer she could. "I was waiting for the right man."

"Remy."

Susan could not deny it, even to salvage Pal's feelings. "Yes. Definitely, yes."

Pal lowered his head, looking pained.

Susan waited for him to explain.

"If I had known you were a virgin, I wouldn't have . . . I mean, not so soon . . ."

Susan rescued him. "Believe me, I wouldn't let you do anything I didn't want you to do." She never doubted that, if she had told him to stop, he would have obeyed in an instant. His strength and combat training would not have saved him if he had not. Susan realized she needed to address the assumptive part of his comment as well; she owed him the full truth. "Besides, I wasn't exactly a virgin anymore. After Remy's death and my father's murder, Kendall and I gave it a try."

Pal sat up, his bare chest fully exposed. A spattering of black hair nestled between chiseled pectorals, and his abdominal muscles bulged in neat horizontal rows. If not for a few chaotic and seemingly random scars, he could have modeled for the musculoskeletal system in any anatomy textbook. "Kendall?" Pal's features looked pinched, either in surprise or revulsion. Susan found herself too caught up in his naked torso to fully focus on his features in order to differentiate.

She did not mean to sound defensive. "It was a very difficult time emotionally. And I was feeling bitter about waiting for Remy, only to have him snatched from me."

"*Gay* Kendall?"

Susan shrugged. "We didn't know it at the time." Not wanting to talk about it anymore, Susan returned her attention to her Vox. "I've got two messages, and I've only looked at one. How about you?"

Pal consulted his Vox. "Three." He tapped it. "Second one's from my friend Dauber. He wants to know if I'm free for pizza and a pickup game on Friday." He looked up. "Your turn."

The request sounded so normal, Susan could not help smiling wistfully. She would so much prefer a day of school, studying robotics, followed by an evening of cheering on her boyfriend while he played football or basketball or baseball with his friends, their friends. She could almost smell the damp and leaf mold from the park, hear the laughter as the young men emerged from a muddy tackle, see the wives and partners shaking their heads at the men's antics. It seemed like such a high school image, the type she had never experienced. Plain, skinny girls who studied every day did not have boyfriends.

Realizing Pal was staring at her, Susan tossed off her reverie to consult her Vox. "The other one's from Kendall. Dr. Goldman's funeral starts at eleven o'clock this morning."

To Susan's appreciation, Pal did not sigh, grunt, or demonstrate any other sign he preferred not to attend. He gave his Vox one more examination. "The last one's from my neighbor, wondering why I didn't come home last night." He rolled his eyes. "Old Mrs. Thurgoode needs to find a less nosy hobby, but she means well. Bakes a great oatmeal raisin cookie, though." Quickly, he slipped out of bed and started gathering his clothing.

Step one, Susan realized, *remove the robot from the shower stall.* Her pint-sized bathroom would make everyone's morning ritual difficult, with or without Nate. Their first stop would have to be United States Robots and Mechanical Men. She would surely find Cody Peters at the funeral, which should provide her the opportunity to at least arrange for a time to talk to him more fully and to examine the scene of the crime. She needed to do some reading on the traditions and customs of Jewish funerals and only hoped the SFH would have the decency to allow her and the other attendees to mourn in peace.

Susan ushered Pal and Nate through USR security at eight fifteen a.m., and the secretary greeted them all from her desk. "Good morning, Dr. Calvin. Two visitor's passes?"

"Please." Susan glanced around the foyer to the closed doors that led to laboratories and offices. In the brief silence that followed, she remembered the procedure from her first visit, when her father had gotten her and Remington passes. "Sorry, you need their names, don't you?"

Amara nodded, coiffed hairdo bouncing, eyes starkly lined and colorfully shadowed beneath unnaturally long and thick lashes. "Yes, please."

Susan rattled them off. "This is Pal Buffoni and my cousin, Layton Campbell."

The secretary typed into her oversized computer, and the printer spit out two squares of paper. From long habit, she folded them, then placed each into a separate plastic sheath attached to a lanyard before handing them to Susan. Both read VISITOR on the front, with the names in smaller type below. Susan noted only that Amara had spelled them properly before handing each to the proper companion. Without a word, man and robot dipped their heads and put the cord around their necks so the VISITOR badge dangled over their sternums. "Dr. Lanning asked me to send you straight to his office."

"Thank you," Susan said, heading for the proper door. She motioned for the others to accompany her. Opening it, she looked into the familiar large office with its four desks, one in each corner, Alfred's separated from the others by cubicle partitions.

At the front-left quadrant, Javonte glanced up from his seat and smiled. "Hi, Dr. Calvin."

Susan still knew him only by his first name, but he had surely earned his doctorate in robotics. She said the only thing she could. "Please call me Susan."

"All right, Susan."

No one sat at the desk to her right, the one that had belonged to her father. Someone had cleaned it to a sheen, leaving nothing on its surface. At first, she assumed they had, essentially, enshrined it. Then, she realized more practically, it was probably going to become hers when she was no longer on an assignment that kept her out of the office. Catty-corner to her future workplace, another unoccupied desk held an assortment of bric-a-brac, including a few static pictures, an implement holder in the shape of a cartoon duck, two palm-prosses, and some hunks and bits of metal. Susan could not see around the partitions to the station usually occupied by Alfred Lanning.

Susan peered around the makeshift walls. Alfred sat in his usual space, peering intently at the screen of a palm-pross. He did not seem to notice her, even after her exchange with Javonte. She cleared her throat. When that still did not engage him, she called out softly, "Dr. Lanning?"

Alfred looked up at once. It took clear effort to tear his gaze from his work, but he did so to place it upon Susan. "Come, come." He gestured her to an open chair near his desk, then apparently noticed her companions. "Ah, you brought visitors. Javonte can take them on a tour while we talk."

Javonte stepped around the partition, but Susan raised a hand to stay him. "That's not necessary, Alfred. Pal is my partner and my bodyguard. To do his job, he needs to know everything." She waved for Nate to come to her side, and he obliged. "This is an old friend of yours."

Alfred ran his glance over Nate without comprehension. He rose and stuck out a meaty hand. "Oh, do I know you, young man? I'm terrible at remembering names." He added apologetically, "And faces."

Nate accepted the handshake, looking to Susan for clues as to how to behave. She had all but given him away.

Susan turned her attention on Javonte. Lawrence and her father insisted that every worker at USR was well-known to them before hiring and passed a rigorous loyalty test. Thus far, nothing suggested she could not speak freely in front of any member of the team. However, this time, Susan's own freedom and security were at stake.

As usual, Alfred missed the hint, but Javonte did not. He tried to sound casual about it, clearly for Susan's benefit. "I've got some work to do in the lab. Call me if you need me for anything."

Alfred took no obvious notice of Javonte's words. He continued to study Nate.

As Javonte left and the door clicked closed behind him, Susan encouraged Alfred by removing Nate's cap and sunglasses and smoothing the robot's plain brown hair into its usual well-settled and combed cut. "Imagine him in hospital scrubs."

Alfred's gaze traced from Nate's shoes, along his torso, then up to his chest and face. The man's expression changed from mild curiosity to sudden understanding. A hand fell to his desk, steadying. "Nate?" He glanced at Susan for confirmation, and she nodded broadly.

"But he's . . ." Alfred sat down and swallowed. "The police are looking for him."

"Yes," Susan said simply.

When he got nothing more from Susan, Alfred turned his attention to Nate. "Where have you been? How did you get away from the police?"

Nate only stared, making no specific motions, not even turning to Susan for guidance.

Alfred's brow furrowed. He frowned. "N8-C, I'm ordering you to tell me how you escaped from the police."

Nate continued looking mildly at USR's head of research and development, saying nothing.

Alfred persisted. "That's a command, N8-C."

Silence.

Alfred turned his attention to Susan, folding his arms across his chest. "All right, Susan. You're the robot psychologist." He waved a hand toward Nate. "Explain this behavior."

Susan did not argue the terminology. She had no difficulty clarifying Nate's reticence. "Well, let's see. The Second Law states that he has to obey all orders given to him by human beings. You're a human being."

"Yes," Alfred said impatiently.

Susan knew some of Alfred's colleagues might mockingly disagree, but she continued dutifully. "Except where such orders would conflict with the First Law."

Alfred's brows rose slowly. "And how would telling me how he escaped from police custody cause injury to a human being?"

Susan knew the answer. "Well, assuming one or more human beings assisted his escape, telling anyone how he did it would place his helper or helpers at risk of harm, wouldn't you think?" When Alfred did not immediately respond, Susan supplied, "The police would take them into custody at the very least. Stealing from police property is a serious crime with significant punishment."

Alfred stroked his chin. "That's not direct physical harm."

Susan held out her hands. "The First Law does not specify direct physical harm."

Alfred nodded thoughtfully, his gaze flicking back to Nate. "Why didn't you just say you couldn't tell me because it might cause someone harm?"

Susan answered for Nate, knowing he could not. "Because telling you that would automatically imply he received help from one or more humans. If he remains silent, you have no idea if he's protecting humans, malfunctioning, or simply choosing impudence, which makes any involved humans safer." Susan's own explanation triggered a new line of thought. *Could the explanation be that simple?* "Nate, do you remember when I had you stop sensing for a period of time?"

Nate finally spoke. "I remember everything I hear, see, read, or am programmed to recall."

Susan pressed. "What if someone commanded you to forget?"

Nate hesitated. He looked at Alfred before answering, as if expecting USR's head of research and development to contradict him. "Depending on what I'm asked to forget, I could act in a manner that did not take the information to be forgotten into account, but I could not literally purge my memory of that information." He sounded so sure of himself until he added, "Could I?"

Susan assumed the question was aimed at Alfred. She flicked her gaze to the man and waited.

Alfred's head bobbed more vigorously. "We create the positronic brain with the Three Laws, some operational information, and a more or less basic command of English, depending on its needs. Everything else is purpose-based. We teach it whatever it needs to perform its duty, whatever that may be. It learns and expands its knowledge from experience, directed study, and circumstances. Deleting bits of information would be tedious at best, probably impossible, and would almost certainly destroy the brain, which would render the entire robot functionally useless."

Albert had not offered Pal and Nate seats, so Pal dragged in a chair from one of the empty desks and sat. "Surely, robots have finite memory capacity. What happens when they're full?"

Albert retook his own seat, without apologizing for not accommodating his guests. Susan suspected Alfred never intended rudeness; he just did not seem to understand societal conventions. She believed he had undiagnosed Asperger's syndrome or perhaps even some form of high-functioning autism.

"Some of the simpler robots have less memory than, say, a palm-pross or Vox. We make sure they learn all the significant factors to allow them to perform their duties first. If a client wants to use the remainder of the memory for conversation or grocery lists or nursery rhymes, that's up to them. At this point in time, we sell almost exclusively to the U.S. government. When they no longer need their robots for the task for which we trained them, they return the robots for reprogramming. Aside from the Three Laws, it's a simple matter to fully erase the positronic brain."

"So," Pal said, "you recycle it. Teach it something different."

"Yes."

Pal continued. "What if the new task is similar to the old one? Can you do a partial erasure?"

"Partial erasure is not an option," Alfred said, then reiterated, "If the new task is similar enough for us to keep the old body, then we do. For example, if the original robot was to sit in one place crushing rocks to powder, it might have multiple pummeling limbs but little or no mobility. If they wanted a new robot to sit still and flatten metal debris, it might require few, if any, changes to the exterior. But we would have to completely reprogram the positronic brain."

Susan wanted to make sure she had it correct. "So . . . it might have the exact same look, even the exact same body, but it could have completely different knowledge." She added cautiously, "And a completely different . . . persona."

"Correct," Alfred said. "It would not remember anything of its previous time crushing rocks, nor would it recognize its human or robotic previous coworkers, its former model number, call name, or any of its prior circumstances."

Susan wondered aloud, "Can you recycle the positronic brain itself?"

Alfred seemed not to understand the question. "Do you mean break it down to its component parts and make a new brain from them? Because we do that all the time."

That was only a small part of the answer Susan wanted. "Could you take the used positronic brain out of one robot and put it into another body? Would it maintain its personality?"

Alfred hesitated. He tipped his head, and his gaze rolled to the ceiling. He pursed his lips, unpursed them, then pursed them again. Finally, he spoke haltingly. "The closest we've come is redesigning a robotic body. For example, a robot is sold for a purpose, let's say for mining. We create a mobile, four-armed creature with picks that seems to work well in the laboratory setting. However, under the constraints of real mines, the fourth arm keeps hampering the second arm, and the mobility is too limited for the terrain. So, we make changes. It becomes a three-armed robot with stool-like legs and no feet. The robot looks different, but the brain remains the same, aside from redirecting how it works a bit."

Alfred considered his own words. "Although, that could set the robot up for glitches since it would maintain the memory of a fourth arm. So, more likely, we would reengineer the four arms so they don't interfere with one another, or erase the brain and reprogram it."

Susan got specific. "Let's say you removed Nate's positronic brain and put it into a different body. Would he still be Nate, at least as far as memory and personality?"

Alfred shrugged. "Sure, I guess. But why would we ever want to do something like that?"

Pal saw the same potential Susan did. "In this case, it would make a far better disguise than a Yankees cap and sunglasses."

Alfred made a gesture that showed he finally understood the point. "You have to remember that the NC line is way ahead of its time and took decades to build with extraordinary amounts of money. We don't have humanoid bodies just sitting around waiting for brains. I'm not even sure we could make another NC, at least not for a very long time. We would have to rediscover the technology, much of which was lost with your father. There's also a biological component to consider. The NCs have real human skin, hair, eyes. Removing the brain intact, in and of itself, would be an exquisitely difficult task."

Susan had known Calvin Campbell was the main designer of this particular line, but she did not realize he had not shared all of his information. She also remembered Nate telling her he was an anachronism comparable to Leonardo da Vinci's creation of a working parachute in 1485, more than four hundred years before the first successful flying machine.

"Besides," Alfred added insensitively, "most people are still having trouble wrapping their heads around intelligent machines that don't resemble anything living. So far, true AI has remained beyond the grasp of anyone other than U.S. Robots, but someday that will change. Of the regular people, those who aren't terrified that robots will turn on and destroy us or will render humans worthless are just as concerned we won't treat them humanely enough. As the original company, currently the only company, with learning robots, it's our duty to pave the way, to determine the role robots will play, and how they will fit into our society."

It seemed strangely insightful toward human nature to be an original thought of Dr. Alfred Lanning. Susan felt certain it came from multiple, detailed staff meetings over the decades.

Alfred added the most significant point. "The mistake was in using Nate and Nick outside of USR. The NC line should never have become public knowledge."

"Nick?" Pal inserted.

Alfred looked at Susan. "Should he know?"

That ship had already sailed, so Susan simply nodded. "It's fine, Alfred. I'm already putting my heart and my life in his hands; he needs to know what's going on."

"Nate and Nick are the only remaining NC robots."

Susan appreciated that Alfred did not mention the purpose of the NC line or the ultimate creation, now destroyed. "Nate is N8-C and Nick is N9-C. Against my better judgment, they were placed in working situations in the hope of exposing a few people at a time to the possibility of humanoid robots."

Susan pointed out, "When asked by the police, Lawrence claimed Nate was the only remaining humanoid robot. I don't think he wants them to know about Nick."

"Thanks for telling me," Alfred said, and he seemed genuinely grateful. Susan realized Lawrence might not have managed to get that information to USR through phone calls from prison that were surely monitored. "We placed Nate first, and more people knew about him. By the time we placed Nick, there were already some issues from Nate, so only a few people knew what he was. We intended to eventually expand that knowledge as robots became more commonplace and less . . ." He clearly struggled for the best word.

"Creepy?" Pal tried.

"Worrisome," Albert inserted.

Nate finally spoke. "Where's Nick now?"

"Here," Albert said. "Safe. I'll get you two together as soon as we're done."

Nate smiled. "I'd like that."

Susan seized the opportunity to return the conversation to her original issues, wondering why she had not thought of something this significant earlier. "Obviously, you can't have robots forgetting things by command. Otherwise, someone could instruct them to forget one or more of the Three Laws."

"Exactly." Alfred swiveled his chair back and forth as he spoke. "Also, a disgruntled employee could cause all the robots to forget their programming, which would prove devastating to an industry that relied on its robotic workers. Not to mention to us."

Susan realized the conversation had come full circle. She rose and faced Nate because sitting and doing so would leave him towering over her. She needed to be able to see his expression. "Did someone ask you to forget something that happened in the laboratory around the time of Dr. Goldman's murder?"

"No," Nate said, then repeated, "I was working with Dr. Goldman. He sent me to get Schmidt capillary tubes from the storage closet. I remember grabbing the box. The next thing I knew, I was standing over Dr. Goldman, holding a Stanley 55-099 FatMax Xtreme FuBar Utility Bar."

The consistency of his description both assured and bothered Susan. It meant he was either telling the truth or reciting a script. "Sit, Nate." She gestured toward her chair.

Nate obeyed. That allowed Susan to look him straight in the eyes. "Nate, we need you to understand something."

"Okay," he said without a hint of question or concern.

"Whoever killed Dr. Goldman must be caught." Susan focused on her phraseology. "Not only because Lawrence and Albert and you and I will *suffer harm* if he or she or they are not caught, but also because the murderer or murderers will otherwise be free to kill more innocent people. Do you understand?"

"Yes," Nate said.

Susan needed to go further. "Nate, you must realize that if you are hiding the identity of the killer or killers, you are not helping or protecting them. You are *not* keeping them from harm. Instead, you are preventing them from getting the psychiatric help they need to make them healthy, to keep them from ruining their lives and those of everyone around them." She added directly and forcefully, "Nate, if you hide the identity of the killer or killers, you are doing harm to them, to Lawrence, to me, to everyone who works at USR, and to all the people they hurt or kill in the future. All their future victims become your responsibility."

Nate sat ramrod straight.

Susan asked the all-important question again. "Do you know who killed Ari Goldman?"

"No," Nate said.

"Can you remember any human being in the laboratory or the storage area around the time of the crime, aside from Dr. Goldman himself?"

Nate hesitated, clearly thinking. "I didn't see any human being other than Dr. Goldman between the time I entered the laboratory and when I found myself holding the tool." He paused only a moment before continuing. "While I was–was moving from blank to senses . . ."

"Awakening?" Susan tried.

Nate seemed glad to abandon the sentence to respond to Susan. "Robots don't sleep, so I'm not very familiar with the concept. I recall a bit of fuzziness between nothingness that lasted a bit after finding myself standing near Dr. Goldman's limp body."

Pal stood up also, offering Susan his chair. "That sounds very much like awakening."

Susan brought them back to the pertinent. "While you were awakening, Nate. You . . . saw something?"

"Heard it." Nate rubbed the back of his neck, one of his many human affectations. "My eyes were glued to Dr. Goldman. I was trying to figure out what happened, what I could do to help him. Someone was speaking softly, something about a code blue and an assailant with a weapon."

Up until that moment, Susan had assumed Nate had called the codes. Susan and Pal exchanged meaningful glances before she asked, "You didn't call those codes in, did you?"

"I didn't call anyone. I didn't have a chance."

Pal said what they all had to be thinking. "We find out who called that code, we probably have the killer."

Alfred remained in his seat. "Why would a killer draw attention to himself? Wouldn't it make more sense to sneak away and let someone else discover the scene?"

Susan turned, without taking Pal's chair. "Sure, if the motive was simply to murder Dr. Goldman. Clearly, this guy wanted a fast response, to make certain Nate got caught at the scene with the weapon and was still woozy." Her eyes narrowed. "Did I say woozy? What could make a robot woozy?"

To her surprise, Albert had a possible answer. "I don't know about woozy, but I do know someone exposed Nate to a blast of radiation. The positronic brain is very sensitive to certain types and amounts of radiation. We're still testing his old battery for details, but there was one clear and definitive strike that was either targeted directly at Nate or, possibly, a pulse that affected everyone in the room or the building. It wasn't enough to cause obvious or immediate harm to humans."

When it became clear Susan was not going to sit, Pal did so. "What would radiation do to the positronic brain?"

Albert shrugged. "It would depend on the type, amount, and how it was targeted. We do know that one burst of electrons at a robotic cranium can neutralize the positronic pathways, releasing enough additional energy to fuse the robot brain into an inert ingot."

Startled by the information, Susan spoke without thinking. "How do you know that?"

Albert tapped his shirt pocket, which contained something long and cylindrical. "Because if a significant problem ever arises, we need a way to stop it in its tracks."

Susan guessed the pronoun "it" referred more to an unspoken "robot" than the word "problem."

Alfred explained further. "Some types of radiation are more problematic than others. We discovered that during the Mercury mission. A brief but vigorous pulse of relatively harmless radiation might cause a robot to temporarily shut down, only to reawaken sometime later."

Pal pointed out, "Clearly, whoever murdered Dr. Goldman took great pains to make sure Nate got blamed for it. Is it possible Goldman was a random target, chosen only because he spent time alone with Nate?"

Susan shook her head. "I don't think so. They wanted the world to believe robots could and would kill people, and they probably chose Goldman because he's a well-known scientist doing a lot of research on how robot technology can aid hospitals and physicians."

"'They' meaning . . . the SFH?"

"Almost certainly." Susan harbored little doubt but did not like what had to come next. "And I think they had some inside help."

Albert's chair went still. "What do you mean?"

"I mean whoever blasted Nate with radiation knew what type and how much to use. Even you don't appear to have a great handle on that knowledge."

All color drained from Albert's face. "You mean someone at USR?"

Susan splayed her hands. She could mean nothing else. "It has to be someone with access to several robots and also to different types of radiation. Someone with the means and opportunity to experiment as well as hide any damage done."

"Someone at USR?" Albert repeated, sounding only slightly less dubious. "But that's–that's . . ." He seemed about to say "impossible," but amended, "Extraordinarily unlikely."

Susan saw only one other possibility. "The only other group with the necessary access to radiation and robots is the U.S. government. We already know the Department of Defense hates the SFH; they would never cooperate with such a plot." Susan put a hand on Pal's shoulder. "You know more about the inner workings of the government than we do. What do you think?"

Pal laughed. "I'm just a grunt, not a bureaucrat. As you've stated, the Three Laws keep robots from making even mediocre soldiers, so I've never actually worked with one. I can't imagine the government lets just anyone work with something as expensive as a thinking, learning robot, and I can't imagine them openly murdering a citizen just to make a point." He grew more pensive. "Could an SFH operative penetrate the higher levels of government?" He shrugged. "Who knows?"

It seemed hopeless. Without a ranking contact in the government, Susan had no idea how they could find such a person, assuming he or she even existed. "Albert, why not recall all USR products? You could examine the batteries and see if anyone's been testing them with radiation doses. If not, that would virtually guarantee any mole is inside USR."

Albert pinched his nose, then adjusted his glasses. "A total recall? Difficult. Costly."

"But not impossible," Susan pointed out. An idea seized her, and she could not wait to speak it. "Albert, why is USR selling its robots in the first place?"

Albert froze, then slowly turned his head to fasten his gaze on Susan. "Because . . . it's what we do. If we don't sell our product, what's the point of making it? Like any business, we need capital to operate."

Susan answered with a single word: "Leasing."

Silence followed. Heads started to bob.

Susan explained further. "USR should maintain ownership of every positronic robot. You lease the robots to various clients. You still make your money, but it limits any tampering outsiders can do. Make damaging any robot an expensive proposition that goes well beyond just voiding a warranty. If you don't like the way someone uses your product, you can end the lease."

A ghost of a smile touched Albert's features. "That's brilliant."

Susan elaborated. "That would also explain a full recall of the previously sold models, without suggesting there's something faulty or dangerous about them." She set to organizing the coming days. "Albert, how closely does Nick resemble Nate?"

"Not much at all. Why?"

"Have the police come searching for Nate?"

Albert nodded. "They came, and we let them tour most of the facility. We couldn't let them into some places, though. Clean rooms, certain laboratory areas with proprietary information, a couple of storage areas Lawrence had locked."

None of it surprised Susan. "I just wanted to make sure Nick was safe, that the police wouldn't mistake him for Nate. What did you tell them about him?"

"Nothing," Alfred said. "He wasn't here. It wasn't until after they searched that I thought it best to bring him here."

Susan instructed, "If and when they return, probably with a search warrant, let them mistake Nick for a worker. We'll keep Nate with us, at least until I fall under direct suspicion. It's not safe for him here. Try to keep things going as normally as possible, other than coming up with a new and legal leasing agreement and initiating a recall. Don't mention my input into the idea. If there is a mole, that might tip them off, since everyone knows I'm working on getting Lawrence free and Nate cleared."

If it bothered Alfred to have a young upstart tell him how to run his business, he gave no indication. "Are you going to the funeral?"

"Definitely." Susan said. "I need to talk to Dr. Peters, and it's the one place I know I'll find him. He might have some insight into who could have done this, and I want access to the scene of the crime, preferably with Nate and Dr. Peters to assist me in finding anything suspicious that the police might have glossed over or missed."

"Sounds like a plan." Albert rose. "The service is at B'nai Golda Cemetery. Graveside. It starts at eleven o'clock."

He did not suggest going together in the same vehicle, which Susan appreciated. She needed time to get Nate properly disguised and all three of them into funeral attire. The formality of the situation precluded the Harley, even if they discarded the safety issues. She would need the bus-time to do her research on Jewish funerals and discuss any traditions with Pal and Nate, as Layton. She did not want any of them to make an embarrassing mistake. The last thing they needed was attention.

Chapter 12

A cool September breeze wound through B'nai Golda Cemetery, chilling mourners already damp from a light but persistent rain. Two bored-looking teens in dark clothing stood at the open gate beneath a stone archway, passing out wet pieces of paper. Susan accepted one, glancing at it only long enough to see "Ari Micah Goldman, MD, PhD, FAPA" listed at the top.

A net of clouds seemed to echo the somber mood of the people, all conservatively dressed, some with black umbrellas, others with plastic-draped hats, and most with rainwater plastering their hair and dripping down their cheeks. The moment she stepped beneath the archway, Susan spotted Cody Peters seated alone on a concrete bench, shoulders hunched and face buried in his hands. He wore a long olive drab raincoat that made him appear even lankier and taller than usual.

Susan sat on the wet bench beside him, barely noticing the water seeping through her pants. She placed a consoling hand on his back and leaned in to talk to him. "Dr. Peters?"

The researcher raised his head, tipping it toward Susan. He managed a smile. "Susan. Just the person I wanted to see."

Susan glanced at her associates, both of whom appeared to be trying to look casual. Dressed in his sweats, the only dark-colored clothing he had at Susan's apartment, Pal studied the milling people, seemingly oblivious to the raindrops gathering in his hair. Nate edged onto what little bench remained beside Susan, mimicking the pained huddling of the other mourners.

"Me?" Susan tried not to sound too surprised. "I thought I'd find you with Dr. Goldman's family. Or your own."

Dr. Peters sighed. He spoke slowly, as if each and every word pained him. "The Goldmans are performing *K'riah*. That's where–"

Susan stopped him with a raised hand. "The rending of the garments. I did some reading." She did not know whether the Goldmans would literally tear their clothing or only symbolic black ribbons attached to them. It was a ritual performed only by immediate family members, representing the damage the death inflicted on their hearts. All attendees who came upon a person with ripped clothing or ribbons were supposed to offer condolences, obviating the additional pain ignoring or isolation might cause, though not until after the service.

Taking Susan at her word, Dr. Peters responded to her original question. "Cait is assisting Anna." He referred to his wife and Dr. Goldman's. "The kids are working with the neighbors, preparing the Goldman home for the family's return. Our kids, that is. Ari's kids are here, of course."

Susan knew preparing the house involved several rituals as well: covering all the mirrors, removing objects that might be considered celebratory, and creating the meal of condolence, the *Seudat Hawra'ah*. The immediate family, referred to as *Onen*, were supposed to devote themselves wholly to the deceased. As such, they should not have to worry about such things as meals or entertaining. Behind that tradition lay the concern that, left to their own devices, the *Onen* might neglect to eat, thus falling ill and dying themselves.

Dr. Peters added softly, "Though how Harper's supposed to do anything in her condition is a mystery."

Susan remembered. "Harper's your daughter?"

"Right," he confirmed. "Almost twenty-four weeks pregnant with twins."

Susan knew better than to congratulate a grandparent before the birth, especially multiples. She tried to sound nonchalant. "Have the police finished their investigation of the lab?"

Dr. Peters nodded. "Yesterday evening. Then I locked it. No one's been in there since. I wanted you to have the first look around . . . after the police took or trampled all the evidence, that is."

Susan forced a chuckle. "We'll make do with what's still there. Will you be free after the funeral to take me to it?"

Dr. Peters reached into his suit pocket and emerged with a key. He pressed it into Susan's free hand. "I'll get there as soon as I can, but Cait will probably drag me to the Goldmans' for a little while. If you get there first, feel free to start looking around."

Though she accepted the key, placing it into her own pocket, Susan felt odd even thinking about entering 713 Hassenfeld Research Tower without Dr. Goldman or Dr. Peters. "We can wait for you."

"I shouldn't be too long. Cait knows how useless I am at funerals." Apparently not wanting to sound callous, he continued. "I'm lost without Ari. He was a genius, Susan. One of a kind. I'm here because he was the best partner anyone could ever have or imagine; but funerals agitate me. I always leave feeling far worse than when I came, and I'm not sure I can go any lower. I already feel like I'm in some subbasement of hell."

Susan said something she had avoided all of her professional life. "I know exactly how you feel." And, for once, the dreaded platitude, the one everyone was trained to avoid, was true.

Peters rose, sweeping Susan into a fierce embrace, lifting her to a standing position with him. He wept holding her, chin resting on her left shoulder. Only after they had spent several minutes pressed tightly but chastely together, Peters whispered directly into her ear. "How did you survive it?"

Susan stopped herself from reliving the grief she had pummeled into a tiny box buried deep inside her where she would never again allow it to be opened. The happy memories of Remington, of her father, remained, easily accessible. She had walled off the desperate, intolerable anguish like a phagocyte engulfs a toxin, sacrificing an important chunk of herself to save the whole. If she had to face that raw sorrow day after day, year after year, she would wither and die. That other, positive aspects of her psyche got shut off with the pain bothered her only a bit. She remembered Kendall's childlike plea: *"Cold and distant doesn't suit you, Susan. I . . . miss you."*

For two years, it had felt to Susan as if nothing good could ever happen to her again. Love and loss remained inextricably entwined, the agony unspeakable, unendurable. Far simpler never to open herself to the terrible possibilities, to prevent another devastating loss by avoiding intense attachments. Yet here she was again, foolishly in love, secretly hoping, against her better judgment, that circumstances would not crush her again. Her gaze went naturally to Pal Buffoni, a feast for her eyes even soaked to his core, and Dr. Peters' attention followed hers.

Susan could not tell Peters the truth. Her way would not work for a man who had a wife and family, grandchildren on the way. "You know it's a matter of time and introspection. For the first few days or weeks, you go through the motions until the pain dies down enough for you to concentrate again. We all muddle through it in our own way." She did not tell him anything he did not already know. Like Dr. Goldman, Peters had earned his MD before his PhD and had worked with patients before turning to research full-time.

Dr. Peters nodded, releasing Susan. "And who's this handsome young man? Yours?"

"Mine, yes." Just claiming Pal awakened an unexpected tingle of excitement, and Susan smiled despite the grimness of the circumstances.

She introduced them. "Pal Buffoni, Dr. Cody Peters, Dr. Goldman's long-time lab partner."

The two men grasped hands and both mumbled, "Pleased to meet you."

Susan could feel her heart rate quickening as she made the other introduction. "And this is my cousin, Layton Campbell." If anyone might see through the disguise, it would be Dr. Peters, who had worked with Nate longer and more frequently even than Kendall.

Dr. Peters removed his hand from Pal's to accept Nate's.

Susan held her breath as Peters studied Nate through the mist. He had taken off the cap out of respect for Dr. Goldman, and the rain parted his hair into uncharacteristically dark tendrils. "Have we met before?"

Nate answered smoothly, "Only if you've been to Iowa, sir. This is my first visit to New York City."

"Never been to Iowa," Peters admitted.

Susan could not help adding, "He does bear a resemblance to my father."

A moment later, she wished she had not said it, since it caused Dr. Peters to stare at Nate even longer. "Yes," he said halfheartedly. "I can see it."

A distant call interrupted the discussion, to Susan's relief. "Cody!"

They all turned to see a woman in her fifties wearing a dark dress. About a hundred yards away, she gestured at them from the doorway of a small building with an engraved Star of David.

"My wife, Cait," Dr. Peters explained. "Excuse me, please." He hurried off toward her.

Susan expelled a puff of breath she did not realize she had been holding. "So far, so good."

Pal tapped her on the shoulder, and Susan turned to him quizzically.

"Did you know Jake would be here?"

"Jake?" Surprised, Susan started looking randomly.

Pal placed a hand on each side of her head and turned her face in the proper direction. Jake leaned against a tree in the grassy area just before the start of the graves and headstones. He wore black dress khakis and a dark green, long-sleeved polo. Wet, it clung to the well-defined muscles of his arms. As Susan's gaze found him, he waved a greeting and headed in their direction.

When Jake reached conversational range, Susan asked, "What are you doing here?" She tried, but failed, to keep accusation from her voice.

Jake tipped his head and joined the group. "When I can, I always attend the funerals of my cases."

That surprised Susan. "You do? Why?"

Pal simultaneously pointed out the more pertinent, "I thought this wasn't your case."

Jake answered them in reverse order. "The murder isn't my case, but I'm working on a related matter." His gaze flicked to Susan. "Because the murderer nearly always attends. If it's a friend, family member, or coworker, their absence might be conspicuous, at least in their own minds. Psychopaths thrive on pain and chaos, and they love reliving their crimes or seeing what it's inflicted on others. Other types of killers may come out of curiosity or even penance."

Jake had a point Susan could not deny.

"Occasionally the perp gives himself away by his behavior at the funeral."

Susan considered the information, and it made sense to her. She wondered if it was common practice for undercover police to attend the services of murder victims or if it was a peculiarity of Jake's.

"Plus," Jake added, "I was hoping to run into you."

Susan found that harder to believe. "You know my number and where I live."

"Yes," Jake admitted, "but I also knew you wouldn't be there because you're here."

Susan could hardly deny it. "Why did you want to see me?" *Does he know?* A worse thought struck her. *Did Kendall spill the beans?* She could not keep her heart rate from quickening again, but she did refrain from looking in Nate's direction, refusing to give Jake acknowledgment or clues. She suddenly wished they had left the robot back at the apartment, although their reasons for keeping Nate with them were sound. She did not want cops barging into her apartment with a warrant and finding Nate alone or, worse, turned off. At the time, she had not known the main officer on the case would be taking the day off to attend the funeral.

Jake's gaze went to Susan's entourage. "You know, Susan, it's difficult for a man to spend twenty-four/seven with the same person, no matter how charming he or she might be. At some point, if he doesn't get a break, resentments start to grow, and it can harm an otherwise perfect relationship." He paused there, as if hoping Susan would grasp his point so he did not have to continue.

Susan was not at all sure she did. The words were clear enough; the subtext less so. It was not like Jake to spontaneously hand out relationship advice, especially at a funeral. "You're saying you think Pal needs some time away from me."

Pal stepped up beside her. "I'm fine, Jake. Really."

Jake's smile seemed genuinely kind. "I'm just thinking of your future. And Susan's. Don't you find yourself craving ten minutes alone in your own, familiar shower? Wouldn't you like to grab some fresh clothes so you're not stuck borrowing things from Susan's giant cousin?"

The last comment confused Susan momentarily, until she remembered that, the day Jake had come to her apartment, Pal had changed Nate into his jogging suit because he had no other clothing. She also realized that, were she and Pal not in the first hot and exciting stage of love, the need to spend every moment together could drive both of them crazy. She knew from her studies that, if they continued to do it, without at least an occasional short separation, it just might drive a permanent wedge between them. "He's right, you know." She turned to face Pal, to gauge his reaction. "A little bit of time apart would probably do both of us good."

Pal's features tightened. "It would also give the SFH the opening it needed to turn you into a leadsicle." He shook his head. "No way, Susan. I'm not leaving you defenseless."

"Except," Jake said, "she wouldn't be defenseless. I took the day off, and I'm proposing that Susan spend it with me. Surely you trust me to keep her safe." When Pal's expression did not change, Jake added, "Yes?"

Suddenly, Susan realized Jake was trying to let her know he wanted to spend some time alone with her without making Pal, or anyone else, aware of his desire. *He knows.* Her heart skipped a beat. *And he wants to arrest me without a fight.* She quickly discarded the thought. Jake might believe he had an important or innocent reason for separating Susan from her man, and refusing him would only make her appear guilty. She addressed Pal. "It would give you a chance to gather more of your things." Pal had fewer of those at Susan's apartment than even Jake knew. "You could reassure the friends and neighbors who've been looking for you and let them know you're going to be busy for the foreseeable future so they're not reporting you as a missing person."

Finally, Pal's face relaxed, and he turned pensive. "I could take my mom to dinner. She'd appreciate that after I blew off lunch. Plus, I can put away my bike."

Jake threw a hand up in a "there you go" motion. "So it's settled. After the funeral, I'll take Susan and Layton wherever they want to go. I'll even drop you off somewhere, Pal, if you need a ride."

Pal shook his head. "Not right after the funeral. We're going to Goldman's lab to look over the scene, and I want to see where it all went down and try to help find anything the police might have missed."

Jake lowered his hand. "That's even better. I'll drive us all there, if you like. The Sapphire seats four comfortably. After we've finished our examination, I'll drop you off and take Susan and Layton out to dinner." He added, "My treat."

Susan opened her mouth to argue, then shut it. Though objecting would have been the polite thing to do, she had no money to spare, and Nate had none at all. "Thank you, Jake. That's very kind." She remembered something else. "I'll need to let Kendall know. He asked to be part of any investigation."

Jake glanced off toward the graves, looking for someone or something. Apparently, he did not find it, because he turned back to Susan and her companions. "I ran into Kendall earlier. He's here with his . . ." He struggled for the word, then tried, "Mentor?"

"Attending physician," Susan supplied.

"Okay," Jake said. "Anyway, they drove in together, and they're leaving for work right afterward. He'll have to settle for us telling him what we found."

The youngsters who had handed out the programs headed toward the graveyard, herding the mourners onto the burial grounds where the funeral would take place. Susan knew what to expect. There would be no viewing; Jews consider it disrespectful to look at a person who cannot look back. The funeral home would have dressed the corpse in a simple white garment, without pockets or possessions of any kind, and placed it in a plain wooden casket to express the belief that God judges a person by his deeds, not his wealth. Even flowers were considered frivolous. After the casket was lowered into the grave, first relatives, then friends of Ari Goldman would participate in the actual burial by placing shovelfuls of earth on top of it in what was considered the ultimate unselfish act of love and kindness, the final honor. After everyone took his turn, a backhoe would take over, since no one was supposed to leave the site until the casket was fully covered.

Taking Pal's hand in one of hers, and Nate's in the other, Susan headed toward the funeral.

Jake ushered Susan, Pal, and Nate into his Subaru Sapphire, insisting that Nate take the front passenger seat because of a dearth of legroom in the little car, particularly the back. Susan took the seat behind Nate, and Pal squeezed in behind Jake. With a few minor adjustments, they were all reasonably comfortable and gliding toward Manhattan Hasbro Hospital.

Susan tapped her Vox off silent mode; she had no messages. Pal apparently did, and he busily responded to something as Jake spoke into the silence. "You know, when my time comes, I think I'd like a funeral just like that one."

Still looking at his Vox, Pal asked, "Are you Jewish, Jake?"

"No," Jake admitted, "but I liked the whole aesthetic. No greedy funeral director guilting your relatives into buying the jewel-encrusted coffin with the silk interior to prove they really loved you. Any fancy clothes and jewelry go to the living instead of rotting in the ground. No throwing money away on flowers that won't last the week. Rather, donations go to your favorite charity or, at least, your loved ones' favorite."

"I could have done without the rain," Susan offered.

Jake bobbed his head as he drove. "I kind of liked the rain. It kept things dull and gray, the right atmosphere for a funeral. Who can concentrate on mourning on a bright, sunshiny day? All my friends would be dreaming of a soccer game in the park."

"Given recent events and situations," Nate said, softly but firmly, "I would appreciate a different topic of conversation."

It was such a normal thing to say, it stopped Susan cold. Not because Nate said it; she had grown accustomed to him seeming utterly human. It startled her more because it had taken the robot to say it, the only one who had nothing whatsoever to fear from death. He had spoken purely out of concern for his companions, demonstrating an empathy, a basic humanity, the rest of them seemed to lack.

"Sorry," Jake said, sounding truly contrite, with just a hint of amusement. "Cops and soldiers and doctors see so much death in their daily lives, they become inured to it. We shouldn't forget to guard our tongues around civilians."

It surprised Susan nearly as much that Jake had the word "inured" in his vocabulary.

The Subaru Sapphire turned into the parking lot, and Jake waved his Vox at the pay stick. Once settled into a spot, the group exited. Wordlessly, they threaded their way through the ever-present mob of protestors and into the main entrance where the familiar sights, sounds, and smells of Manhattan Hasbro Hospital assailed Susan, their impact heightened by her relatively long absence. Once inside, Susan led the way, deliberately avoiding the psychiatric areas in the hope that she would not run into anyone she knew.

At length, they found themselves standing just outside the door to the Goldman/Peters laboratory, room number 713. There, Susan paused, studying the familiar door, which looked exactly like every other door in Hassenfeld Research Tower but which held both special and dreadful memories for her. Two years earlier, she had taken part in the nanorobot research project for refractory mental illnesses, donating most of her spare time and barely able to contain her excitement at working with Psychiatry's famous duo. Delighted and intimidated, she had paused so many times, waiting for her knock to be acknowledged.

Pal cleared his throat. "Susan, the door's not going to unlock itself."

Startled from her reverie, Susan tried the knob. It did not yield to her touch, definitively locked. Although Dr. Cody Peters had handed her an old-fashioned metal key, she found herself instinctively searching for a touch pad or scanner. She realized the transient nature of research and the tendency to swap partners, equipment, and coordination made a key system more practical. The door had never been locked when Peters, Goldman, or both were using the laboratory.

It was Jake's turn to spur Susan. "Are you delaying deliberately?"

Susan realized the policeman had struck to the heart of the problem. "Subconsciously, actually. My mind's telling me to wait for Dr. Peters before entering." She forestalled an argument. "And, yes. I know he wouldn't have given me the key if he didn't want us to go inside without him, but it still feels wrong." She used to suffer the same sensation as a young child when her mother asked her to fetch something from her parents' usually off-limits bedroom.

Far down the hallway, the elevator doors slid open with a ping, and Cody Peters' lanky frame emerged. "Ah, perfect timing."

More so than he knew, Susan realized. Now she had no trouble taking the key from her pocket, fitting it into the lock, and turning it. The lock yielded easily. By the time she removed the key and twisted the knob, Dr. Peters had joined them. She stepped aside, handing him the key.

Accepting it, Peters explained, "I locked the door as soon as the police left. The right maneuver can prevent even the maintenance keys from working. I didn't want anyone moving anything or cleaning before you had a chance to examine the scene." He shoved open the door and pocketed the key.

As they entered, the lights snapped on, revealing the familiar arrangement of desks and laboratory tables. The regular chemical and cleaning odors wafted to Susan, accompanied by a greasy, sour smell, probably something the police had used. Everything looked much as it had the day she had tried to help resuscitate Ari Goldman. The four large laboratory tables, shoved together, still filled the center of the room. Desks at opposite corners belonged to the researchers: Goldman's neat and tidy, Peters' a study in chaos. A smaller, closed door led to a storage area, Susan knew. Dark, dried blood still streaked the central, combined table area where Goldman's body had lain, interrupted in patches that indicated samples had been removed. The floor held puddles of congealed brown liquids, probably a combination of blood, mucus, and cerebrospinal fluid with just a touch of chlorhexidine from the residents' futile attempts to keep their resuscitation efforts sterile.

Susan turned her attention to other objects on the desks, things she had not noticed when the dying man and arrest of Nate had demanded all of her attention. Some of the equipment had gotten swept from the table to make room for crash-cart items and portable monitors, leaving dented canisters, a few shattered tubes, and other bric-a-brac on the floor. A blood-splashed book sat on the pushed-together tables, and several wheeled stools occupied various places around them.

"Yuck," Nate said, a glaring understatement.

"Yuck," Susan agreed, turning to Jake, who had already started looking everything over, hands clenched behind his back. "What do we do first, Detective?"

Jake sighed, then shook his head. "I'm going to have to assume the police took anything they thought might prove useful to the investigation, including appropriate samples. What we're looking for is something they missed."

"Like this book?" Pal suggested, tipping his head toward it.

"Those're Ari's notes." Peters stepped up beside Pal. "The police did inspect them, asked my opinion, and we then looked over them together. They took a ton of pictures." He chuckled at something private, then explained. "Ari would have been writing in it around the time he was killed. I think the youngest guy on the force was hoping it would be like one of those old novels. You know, where the killer catches his victim writing, and the victim manages to scrawl some cryptic clue that identifies his killer."

Jake loosed a laugh of his own. "Not likely. By the blood splatter, the book was closed at the time of the murder. Also, the perp clearly struck from behind, which means the victim never saw him."

Susan added, "A blow to the head as hard as the one Dr. Goldman sustained would have rendered him instantly unconscious. Unless, of course, there were multiple blows, in which case he would surely have spun around and fought back, not paused to write something in his notebook."

Jake apparently had the benefit of a report. "The coroner believes two hits, both with massive force. A remarkably strong man. Or, of course, a robot."

"Not a robot," Susan said quickly. "Not possible."

Jake merely shrugged. Susan knew he was not judging, only letting them know what the police and coroner believed and why. He reached for the book. "So what were the last words of Dr. Ari Goldman?"

Instinctively, Susan grabbed Jake's arm to stop him. Peters and Pal also leapt toward him, and they all nearly collided.

Jake stopped in midmovement. "What?"

Still clutching his arm, Susan explained, "Aren't we supposed to leave everything exactly as it was?"

Jake turned his head toward Susan slowly, as if to give her time to come to her senses. "Forever?" He raised his brows. "Like as a shrine to the murder?"

Peters retreated. "The police investigation is over. They cleared the scene for regular use."

Susan understood the point but still had one of her own. "What if the location of something at the time of the murder *is* the clue? What if we start moving things around and miss it?"

Instead of disengaging Susan's fingers, Jake picked up the book with his left hand. "I guarantee you some things have already been moved."

Peters bobbed his head. "Like that book, for one. The only reason the police didn't take it as evidence was because I told them I needed the information written inside it for a lifesaving study. They argued about it but finally left it provided I guarantee them access to it."

Jake continued. "Moving things is the only way to find clues buried under other clues. Besides, we have several hundred pictures at the station if the exact location of anything becomes important."

Susan finally let go of Jake, feeling a bit foolish. "So, what *were* the last words of Dr. Goldman?"

Jake leafed through the laboratory book, the others staring over his shoulders. What appeared to be lines and lines of typewritten text and numbers interspaced with precise graphs and mathematical formulae met Susan's gaze. Each page also contained an outlined box. Most of those were filled with scrawled, handwritten paragraphs, punctuated by far too many exclamation points and seemingly random capitalizations.

Cody Peters added the important details. "The legible stuff was written by Nate, all of which would have been dictated by or delineated by Ari. Nate could write a lot faster and neater, and he could do the complicated math and graphics in his head. Ari would just say, 'Graph that information,' and Nate could do it remarkably quickly."

Susan found herself enjoying a touch of pride at the description, though she had no real right to it. She had had no hand in Nate's creation.

Pal stepped back to give Jake a bit of room. "What was the reason for the primordial book and ballpoint? Couldn't he have done it all a lot faster with a palm-pross?"

Peters shrugged. "That was Ari. He worried he'd damage or destroy anything electronic, and he had reason. He went through more Vox than anyone I ever heard of."

Jake returned to the significant. "So all the stuff in the boxes was written by the victim?"

"He had those journals specially made. Our agreement was that anything written inside a boxed area was 'off the record.' None of it would appear in any papers, articles, or descriptions." Peters added with a shrug, "Not that anyone could read it, anyway."

"I can read some of it," Jake announced. "It appears to say, 'Ran me out of GD tubes again.'" He hesitated, then squinted. "Then it's a name, I think. Maybe starts with S. Then a bunch of exclamation points."

Peters kept his mouth clamped, but a grin spread across it. "I believe he was addressing me."

Pal leaned in again. "How can you tell?"

"Because I'm the only one who reads the Ari boxes, for one thing. When he gets miffed at me, he uses some . . . um . . . interesting nicknames. Schnook, shmegegge, klutz, which I'm told means a block of wood in Yiddish. I know he's actually angry when he reverts to six or seven years old and calls me jerkface or poopdog." Cody Peters laughed, clearly to show Goldman never meant, nor did Peters take, anything offensive from the exchanges.

"So what's the *S* word here?" Jake held out the book to Peters, who had already examined it with the police.

Dutifully, Peters accepted the book, turned it around, and looked at the open page. "I believe that's the classic S-head." A flush flashed across his cheeks. "Honest, though. He only resorted to profanity when I did something unbelievably stupid."

"Like run him out of GD tubes?" Pal pointed out the fallacy in the argument. "That's hardly a capital offense."

"First of all, I believe the GD part is shorthand for a different profanity. I really ran him out of Schmidt capillary tubes." Peters leafed through the book, though he had obviously done so many times in the past. "More precisely, he ran himself out of them. You need some history to understand why it's a swearing offense."

Peters handed the book back to Jake with a caveat. "I've looked through here a few times since the murder. There's nothing different from before, aside from his notes from the night of September first, which mesh perfectly with the project."

Pal filled in the gaps. "So the first blow must have happened quickly and without warning."

The coroner's report, as described by Jake, gibed with Pal's suggestion, and it seemed likely, but Susan was not ready to place it in the category of indisputable fact. "It's still possible he left the bench, closed the book, and went to investigate something."

Pal contradicted Susan's thought. "Possible. But if he did, he must have dismissed it because the murder clearly happened right here, exactly where he would have been sitting while writing in the book."

Susan sighed. She doubted the book would hold any useful information or clues, at least to the killer or killers.

Jake suggested, "At this stage, it's often best to try to re-create the situation in chronological order." He placed the book carefully on a clean section of desk. "Dr. Peters–"

"Cody," Peters insisted. "I feel weird being the only one in the room called by his title."

Jake amended, "Cody, tell us exactly what you did in the last moments you saw your partner alive."

Cody complied. "Ari was working here most of the day." He pointed to the stool where the murder had obviously been committed. "I was dividing time between here"–he tapped the back of the stool sitting catty-corner to Ari Goldman's–"and at my desk." He jerked a thumb over his shoulder. "Then I got the call."

"Call?" Jake said.

"Right." Cody rubbed his brow. "From Eastside Hospital. I remember it was one o'clock exactly because we were just headed to the cafeteria for lunch. I was told my daughter was asking for me, but I couldn't get any more information over Vox. Harper was twenty-three weeks pregnant with twins, just at the edge of viability, so I got worried."

Jake asked a strange question. "Male or female caller?"

"Female," Peters replied without hesitation. "Identified herself as a nurse practitioner. Isabella, I think. I asked about my wife and son-in-law, but she said she was just the one instructed to call. She didn't know anything. I told Ari I'd start calling around for more information, but he told me to just go. Go! Said he'd already made arrangements for Nate to come help, and he was more useful than me anyway at the best of times."

"Nice partner," Pal muttered.

Cody must have heard him, because he came immediately to Ari Goldman's defense. "It was his way of putting me at ease, of letting me know I didn't have to worry about the project, to focus all my thoughts on Harper. Ari teased me a lot, but I gave as good as I got. It worked for us, and we did some pretty spectacular research together."

Susan nodded vigorously. "The best. So . . . you left immediately?"

"Not quite." Cody relived the moments in this head. "I headed back to the lab."

"Was it locked?" Jake asked.

Peters grimaced and shook his head. "Not over lunch, no. We weren't working with any particularly valuable materials, not on this project, anyway. Many of the other labs had people in them, and we look out for one another. I wouldn't have thought a thief could slip in and ransack one; the noise would draw attention, unless maybe he knew exactly what he was looking for and where."

"A murderer managed," Pal pointed out.

Susan looked at Nate. He hovered with the others, but he had not spoken a word since his initial "yuck." The conversation, thus far, pointed to someone invited into the lab, such as Nate.

Cody could scarcely deny it. "That's a bit different, though. A person would not necessarily attract suspicion unless he acted in a suspicious manner. It's kind of expected that, if you're working with something valuable, say gold or nanorobots, you keep the door locked."

Susan put the theory to the test. "Did anyone check on you when you came back to the lab?"

Cody squinted. "How do you mean?"

"Well," she pointed out, "the two of you had already left for lunch, so your return should have caused others to peek out and make sure it wasn't someone sneaking into your lab."

Peters' mouth screwed into a knot, and he waited several moments before answering. "Not that I noticed, but it's possible. My mind would have dismissed a glance from a neighbor as normal. Plus, I had other things on my mind."

Jake examined the desks thoroughly, though it seemed unlikely he would see anything the police had missed at ground zero. "So what did you do next?"

Peters walked to the door as he relived those moments of his life. "I came inside. I had already taken off my lab coat for lunch and hung it on my chair, so I went over to my desk and put it back on." He took a few long strides from the now-closed door to his desk, pretended to whip a lab coat from the back of his chair, and pantomimed putting his arms through the sleeves. "I then went to my workstation." He walked to the four-table arrangement, around to the other side. "At that time, I had some test tubes in the rack, some beakers with fluid in them, and my palm-pross sitting there." He indicated the surface of the desk opposite Goldman's.

"I opened this drawer." Cody tugged a handle, and the drawer slid out easily. "Put my stuff carefully inside it." He looked down, then back up to his audience. "It's all there. I checked." He shoved the drawer back in. "I then went to the storage closet."

"Why?" Jake asked.

Peters shrugged. "We have hangers for our lab coats on the back of the door there, and that's where we leave them when we're done for the day. Habit more than anything." He crossed the room and opened the storage closet. Again, it yielded soundlessly. "I took off my coat." He pretended again. "And slung it onto my hook, where it is right now."

As one, the entire group moved to the closet to peek inside. Neat metal shelving filled most of the space to the right, piled with boxes. One was tipped on its side, partially filled with capillary tubes. Several loose tubes, clearly from the spilled box, lay across the railings of the shelving, and shards of several more covered the floor, some ground to dust. Across from the open door into the lab, a small window stood half-open, admitting a light, late-summer breeze and a view of the neighboring building, a windowless warehouse nearly as tall as Hassenfeld Research Tower. To the left, Susan saw a small sink with a soap dispenser and a mirror above the basin.

Casually, Peters stepped into the storage room, righted the fallen box, partially closed the window, then frowned at the carnage on the floor. "Ari would never have let this mess sit."

Pal asked, "Are those the Schmidt capillary tubes?"

"As a matter of fact." Peters continued to study the floor, but Susan turned her attention to his laboratory coat. Something there had caught her eye. "What's this clipped to the lapel?"

"Where?" Cody turned to look at the indicated object, then rolled his eyes and gave Susan a disdainful look. "Surely you've seen those before, Susan. The radiologists and techs wear them around the hospital."

Susan nodded. She had noticed them before, but she had never been issued one herself. "They have something to do with radiation exposure."

Peters got down to the specifics. "It's called a dosimeter. Anyone at risk of significant radiation exposure is issued one monthly. When the new one comes in, you send the old one back. The lab does its magic and decides how much and what type of radiation exposure you had, if any. If they find anything significant, they're supposed to initiate a full examination of the cause. And, of course, treat you, if warranted. If not, they have to decide if it's enough to place you on leave or reassign you permanently or temporarily."

Pal asked the question on every mind. "Do you use much radiation in your experiments?"

"None so far." Cody moved closer to Susan. "But other labs on the floor do, off and on, and it's easier to just issue badges to everyone here than to constantly ask what they're working on day to day." He unclipped the badge from his lapel, examining it more closely. His brow furrowed. "This isn't right."

"What do you mean?" Jake asked.

"The color." Peters pointed to the badge. "It's usually a brilliant white. This one's dull, almost brown. I've never seen that before."

Everything fell together in Susan's mind. "I know what happened." She cupped her hands around the badge in Peters' grip, as if afraid he might drop it. "This all makes sense."

Silence followed Susan's proclamation, and every eye fixated on her. Without explaining, she added, "We need to get this analyzed immediately. Where do they do that?"

"The same place they do patient testing. Basement of Mayner Pavilion."

"I can take it," Pal offered.

"Thanks," Cody said, "but that's not necessary. I'll use the tube."

"The tube?" Susan had never heard of it.

Dr. Peters smiled. "When they first built Manhattan Hasbro, when it was still New York Presbyterian, they put in a pneumatic tube transport system. It was common practice at the time for sending medications, notes, samples, results, stuff like that, around the hospital. Now we have significant numbers of volunteers and couriers in the hospital itself, and results are sent electronically, but here we still use the PTT quite a bit. It's been updated since the late nineteenth century, of course. It's computer controlled now, so you can actually track the cylinders through the vacuum, and they don't end their journey with the slam that sometimes used to break more fragile items, no matter how carefully they were packed. At one time, I understand, you could hear the tubes banging through the walls all over the hospital, day and night."

Cody liberated his hand from Susan's, fished around the back of the shelves, and retrieved a cylindrical plastic container. He opened it to reveal a padded interior and a plastic self-sealing bag. He placed the badge into the bag, snuggled it into the padding, then closed the cylinder. With everyone following curiously, he carried it out of the lab to the end of the hallway, where a plastic box with a keyboard hung on the wall. He placed the oversized pellet into a hole, typed something on the keys; then the cylinder disappeared with a breathy whoosh.

Turning, Cody found Susan, Pal, Jake, and Nate directly in his path. He stiffened a bit, then smiled. "And that's how it's done." He tapped his Vox a couple of times. A voice came over the speaker. "Radiation Lab, this is Aiden."

"Hi, Aiden. This is Cody Peters from Hassenfeld Tower."

"I see that. Shouldn't you be . . . anywhere except work? I'm so sorry about . . . what happened."

"Thank you." Cody pursed his lips. "We're doing a bit of sleuthing, and we happened to notice an irregularity of my dosimeter. I'm tubing it to you now. Can you do a stat check?"

Aiden hesitated. "Sure, Doc. Anything. But you do realize you've only worn it a week, right?"

Cody gave Susan a look.

Susan explained. "We think it might have taken a hit of radiation. Does your test distinguish a pulse from background stuff?"

Aiden sounded almost offended. "Even the old film badges could do that. Ours are a lot more sophisticated, with multiple chips and materials. In just a few minutes, I can tell the amount and type of radiation exposure, even the date and approximate times. Is that what you need?"

Susan nodded excitedly.

"Yes," Cody said. "Exactly."

"Ah! It's arrived, Doc. I'll get on it right away and call you back."

"Great! Thanks." Cody broke off contact, then headed back toward the laboratory. "You are going to clue us in on what you're thinking, right Susan?"

Jake guessed. "This has something to do with the analysis of Nate's battery, doesn't it?"

Suddenly, everyone was nodding, and they practically ran back to Goldman and Peters' laboratory. Susan indicated the bloodstained stool where Ari Goldman had died. "Layton, sit there, please. We're going to reenact the crime, and you're Ari Goldman."

Nate turned Susan a worried look. "You're not actually going to hit me, are you?"

"Of course not," Jake assured him.

Nate sat.

Susan looked askance at Cody. "Where would Nate have been sitting?"

Peters straightened out the laboratory tables so that they formed a perfect square, far more meticulously than he would normally have done it, meeting the specifications of Ari Goldman rather than himself. He placed the closest stool at the second desk, the one beside Nate's.

Jake interjected. "Blood splatter suggests the chair next to the victim was unoccupied."

Susan dismissed him with a wave. "Chronological, remember? I'm getting there." She grasped Pal's arm. "Sit here. You're Nate."

Jake jumped in again. "For height purposes, I think you should switch them."

Though highly uncomfortable putting Nate in his actual role, Susan knew refusing to do so would draw even more attention. "Height doesn't come into it, but, yeah, all right. Whatever." She made several quick gestures between man and robot to indicate they should switch places. Hyperalert to the situation, she could not help noticing that Nate adjusted his chair, presumably to reflect the actual position he had occupied on the night of the murder. Susan handed him the book and a pen.

"Okay, Dr. Goldman, act like you're pouring things into tubes and such." It was not stylistically accurate; capillary tubes used a suction action, but she did not want to get into insignificant details. "Nate, be writing things down."

It suddenly occurred to Susan that Nate would have to obey her command verbatim. She could imagine him scrawling "things, things, things" a billion times over the notations already inside the book. "Of course, I mean *pretend* to be writing things down with the pen backward. We don't want to risk stray marks."

Pal pantomimed working with test tubes, and Nate used the back of the pen to simulate writing on the last used page of the laboratory book.

Susan continued to narrate. "Now, Dr. Goldman, you've just run out of capillary tubes."

Pal pretended to look around him.

"No," Susan corrected. "You're a scientist with a temper, and you're furious at your zhlob of a partner for using up all the tubes."

Cody interrupted. "Wait a second, that's not possible."

Every gaze went to him.

"I remember specifically. After I hung up my coat, I grabbed a whole box of Schmidt tubes and carried it to the work space. There's a holder around here somewhere." Peters dropped to all fours to look beneath the tables, rising triumphantly with a square, hard-plastic container. "Here it is. At the time, it was on the corner of Ari's desk." He placed it in the proper location. "I filled it to the brim, probably five hundred tubes. Ari never uses more than a hundred, hundred fifty a day."

"You filled it?" Jake pressed.

"To the brim," Cody said without a hint of doubt. "I remember carrying the cardboard box with the remaining tubes back to storage and placing it on the shelf. It was less than a quarter full when I finished, and a wind gust knocked it over. I caught it before anything spilled, but I made sure to put it in a position where that wouldn't happen again. Plus, I partially closed the window. It's the only window we have, so we usually keep it open a bit for the air, but if you open it too wide, things can get blown around."

Susan remembered that, when they had entered the closet earlier, the window had been half-open. Cody had pushed it down to a slit mechanically, as though doing so had become unconscious habit.

Jake continued to question, indicating the plastic container now on the corner of Goldman's desk. "You filled this holder to the brim, right? And you didn't actually spill any tubes in the storage area. You caught them before they hit the shelf or the floor."

"Correct," Cody said.

"Then how come," Jake said slowly, "there aren't hundreds of broken tubes under these tables but there are quite a few in the storage area?"

Cody peered under the pushed-together tables again. "Maybe the police took them as evidence?"

Jake shook his head. "They documented exactly seven slender tubes in this area, four broken. Those showed evidence of use in that they contained a foamy residue. The intact three had some sort of biologically active material."

"That's consistent with the experiment," Cody said. "But I can't explain why they didn't find several hundred Schmidt tubes. I know I filled that container."

Jake tipped his head toward Susan. "Continue your simulation. We'll file that as 'Inexplicable Number One.'"

Susan addressed Pal: "Dr. Goldman, you've run out of the tubes you need for your experiment, and you're mad at your partner, who was supposed to fill the container."

Pal grimaced, apparently remembering Peters' description of Goldman's insults. "That block of wood! That beetle-headed, flap-eared knave of a partner!" He turned to Nate. "Fetch me some Schmidt capillary tubes!"

Nate leapt up immediately to obey. Though not certain her cousin Layton would do the same, Susan went along with it. "Okay, Nate." She found it more difficult than she expected to call Nate by his real name in front of Jake. "Hand the book to Dr. Goldman and head for the storage closet."

Nate did as he was asked. Pal took the book and acted as if he were scribbling furiously in the comments box. Nate headed toward the closet, Cody, Susan, and Jake following. He opened the closet, stepped inside, and reached for the toppled box of capillary tubes.

Realizing Nate would have to obey Pal's command to fetch Schmidt capillary tubes, Susan shouted, "Freeze!"

Nate had no choice but to go abruptly and utterly still.

Susan tried to fix her own, worse, mistake. "Sorry, Layton. I didn't mean to startle you. Just stand still like a normal human being."

Nate relaxed a bit.

Susan turned to the others. "At this point, according to the battery examination, someone doused Nate with radiation that, for all intents and purposes, rendered him unconscious."

"What do you want me to do?" Nate asked.

"Just remain as you are, please," Susan instructed. "Robots don't collapse like people do when they're turned off. They stand completely still, sensing nothing." She touched the tipped box on the shelf. Apparently, around the time of the murder, Nate had had the box partially in hand. The pulse of radiation must have suddenly shut down his sensory and motor systems, causing him to spill the tubes on the floor. She addressed Nate again. "I'm going to push you from behind now. Walk ahead of me as I do so, please."

Susan planted both hands on Nate's back, persistently shoving him. Humanlike, he leaned some of his weight on her and made his slow way forward. A few loose tubes on the floor crunched under their feet, explaining the powder they had seen earlier. Susan moved Nate into the laboratory, then stopped. "Wait here." She returned to the storage area, dug out a large broom, and handed it to Cody.

"Inexplicable Number Two," Jake pointed out. "Nate weighs more than four hundred pounds. How could one man possibly move him? I mean, you needed Layton's assistance, and he's considerably lighter than Nate."

Susan wished she could show Jake how easily she could push Nate if he was actually turned off. "The NC robots were constructed to be easily moved when turned off. They kind of . . . glide."

"Really," Jake said dubiously. "For now, I'm still calling that Inexplicable Number Two. I don't think you're going to convince a jury of that without significant evidence."

For now, Susan could only concede the point. She guided Cody Peters to stand behind Pal. "While one killer was moving Nate, another sneaked up on Dr. Goldman with the murder weapon." Broom in hand, Cody took a position behind Pal's chair.

Jake seemed about to call another "inexplicable" but settled for a questioning statement. "An exceptionally strong and quiet man."

"Not necessarily quiet," Cody pointed out. "Ari could be single-mindedly focused at the best of times. On a rant"—he shrugged—"a marching band could have set up behind him without notice."

Susan took that as a cue to continue her reenactment, but Jake interrupted, still playing devil's advocate. "Or, maybe, he didn't pay attention to someone coming up behind him because it was Nate. And he trusted Nate."

"Or maybe," Pal added, "he just mistook the killer for Nate, so he didn't bother to look behind him."

Jake bobbled his head to indicate he would consider the possibility. "But you still have to explain how not one, but two, men managed to get into the room unnoticed by the victim, the robot, or any of the neighboring scientists."

"I'll figure that out," Susan promised. "In the meantime, let me finish." She handed the broom to Cody Peters. "The killer clobbers Dr. Goldman once. His accomplice waits until after the first hit, when Dr. Goldman is unconscious, to move Nate into place. The second hit assures that Nate is splashed with appropriate bodily fluids to appear guilty. The weapon is placed in his hand. The killers wait the appropriate period of time, call in the code, and leave."

"How?" Jake asked.

"I'm assuming they used the lab phone. They're too smart to use their own Vox."

Jake shook his head. "I mean, how did they leave without anyone seeing them? The one who did the killing would have been covered in blood, and they're both strangers."

Susan thought quickly. "There were plenty of people in the crowd I didn't recognize. The Code Blue brought tons of people, and the Code Silver kept most of them hovering worriedly outside the door. In the confusion, anyone could have slipped away."

Pal tried, "You're more observant than most, Susan. Did you see anyone suspicious?"

"By the time I got there, many people had come and gone. I was one of the last people on the scene."

"A big guy splattered with blood," Jake reminded.

Susan knew anyone who had attempted to revive Ari Goldman could have gotten bloody, including herself, but she could not imagine competent killers trying to pass themselves off as Hasbro doctors. Someone would surely notice them then. If the residents working with her had done anything strange, it would have stuck in her memory. "Maybe he wore a work apron over his clothes, then disposed of it before calling the code."

"Nothing like that was found in the room," Jake pointed out.

"Maybe he threw it out the window?" Cody said.

Susan revived the image of Cody closing the storage room window to a crack. "Didn't you say you and Dr. Goldman usually kept the window open a bit, but not too far, because it blows things around?"

"I did," Cody said.

"But when we went in there," Susan pointed out, "it was half-open."

"It was?" Cody sounded surprised. Clearly, he had acted from rote, without a bit of thought.

"It was," Jake confirmed. "And you also mentioned that you had mostly closed it before you left on the day of the murder, remember? Because it had blown over the partial box of capillary tubes."

"Yeah," Cody said thoughtfully. "Which means that, between the time I left and the time the police examined the room, someone opened it."

Susan added, "It wasn't any of the docs. We were completely focused on saving Dr. Goldman. And hospital security had its hands full with Nate. No one entered the storage closet, unless it happened before I got there, which seems unlikely." She looked at Jake. "Did anyone mention opening the window in the police report?"

Jake shook his head soundlessly.

"That leaves Goldman or Nate," Pal pointed out.

Susan gave Nate a surreptitious look, which he returned with a cautious shake to indicate neither of them had done it. "Or the killers."

"Or the killers," Jake admitted. "You think they might have tossed a bloody raincoat or smock out of it."

"Maybe." Susan went further. "More important, I think they entered and exited through it."

Now Jake gave her a dubious look. "We're on the seventh floor," he reminded. "And it was broad daylight."

Cody waved everyone back toward the closet. "The window opens onto a narrow alley. The building across from us is a warehouse that has no windows on this side." He shrugged. "Who could have seen them?"

Jake studied the view through the window. He stepped closer and looked directly downward. "Okay, I'll give you no witnesses. But who climbs seven stories up the side of a building?"

"I've known people who could do that," Pal said.

"I'm sure you have," Jake admitted, "but you know highly skilled and trained people."

Susan held out her hands. "Contract killers don't fall under the heading of ordinary, either. The SFH has hired professionals in the past." She added the thought she had had before Pal had spoken. "Besides, they didn't have to be Spider-Man. They could have used a ladder to climb up. Or, they could have taken the stairs to the roof and used a rope ladder or rappelled down. They could even have used the elevator."

Jake opened the window and stuck his head out, looking up, then down. Finally, he came fully back inside. "It's a long shot."

Susan folded her arms over her chest. "Not if it's what happened."

Jake looked directly at her. "I'm not saying it is or is not what happened. My point is it's going to be difficult to convince a jury."

"Actually," Pal inserted, "we don't have to prove it happened that way. We just have to introduce reasonable doubt."

"Reasonable," Jake repeated, but added nothing more.

Susan suffered a rush of irritation, which she tamped down as much as possible. She hoped her old friend was simply demonstrating the difficulty of their defense, assuring they considered every aspect rather than actually suggesting he found their ideas ludicrous or outside the range of possibility. Still, she could not help the negative feelings building toward the police officer. She made a mental note to examine the ground beneath the window and the roof for clues that might shore up her theory.

Cody returned to the other issue. "Who called in the code? There should be a record of it somewhere, right?"

Jake supplied the police information: "Male caller from the laboratory phone. He called twice: first reporting a Code Blue, then a Code Silver at the same location."

"Was it Nate?" Susan already knew the answer; but, as she had gotten the information from Nate after the kidnapping, she could not reveal her knowledge.

"That's the assumption." Jake restored the window to about a one-inch opening, then headed back into the main laboratory area. "If we still had the robot in custody, we could compare the voices. That might or might not help, given the briefness of the calls, but it certainly couldn't hurt."

Surreptitiously, Pal took Susan's hand and gave it a slight squeeze, apparently as a warning not to reveal Nate despite the clear temptation. Not that she needed it. Doing so would also require her to confess to a crime. She grasped and released Pal's hand briefly as reassurance. "That seems beyond unlikely. Why would someone who just committed murder call codes to implicate himself and try to save the life of the person he killed?"

"Was there blood on the phone?" Cody asked.

Jake finally turned to the researcher. "No. Or fingerprints, either. It was wiped clean."

That made no sense to Susan. "So the prevailing theory is that Nate killed Dr. Goldman, then set down the weapon to call in the codes, wiped down the phone, then picked the weapon back up in order to get caught with it in his hands?"

"Another inexplicable," Jake agreed. "Not sure how they're explaining that, although it's not entirely unbelievable. He didn't have to put the weapon down to make the call. And he may have made the call either to divert suspicion from himself or because he doesn't think like a human being."

Susan found herself incensed again. "Of course he doesn't think like a human being. He's basically . . . decent. He can't cause harm like people can."

Jake defended himself. "Hey, I'm the one on your side, remember? If you don't want to know what the evidence showed or the theories being bandied, I'll be happy to spend my day off vegetating on my couch watching reruns and eating chips."

"I'm sorry," Susan said, and she meant it. "I'm not mad at you, just frustrated with the whole situation. It is not possible for Nate to harm, let alone kill, anyone."

Jake nodded broadly. "Fine. Every person in this room believes it, or we wouldn't be here. But that statement isn't enough. We have to prove it."

Pal added again, "Or, at least, introduce reasonable doubt."

Susan ground her teeth together. "Reasonable doubt may get Lawrence and Nate free, but it's not enough, either. Even if Nate gets off, it'll still leave suspicion in the minds of the public. It encourages the SFH to kill again, to blame it on Nate or another positronic robot. We have to make a grand display, to prove Nate absolutely innocent, to assure the world that positronic robots are safe and finally nail the SFH."

Silence followed Susan's proclamation.

Several moments passed before Jake said softly, "You're right, Susan. And you're going to have to lead the way."

Susan knew Jake was also right, but she had no idea how to proceed. Just managing reasonable doubt seemed difficult enough at the moment.

Dr. Peters flopped into a chair, looking exhausted. "Well, I, for one, believe Susan's accounting of the crime. Two or three members of the Society for Humanity sneaked in through the window in the storage closet after I left, while Ari was in the cafeteria. They emptied the bin of Schmidt capillary tubes, knowing Nate would be sent to fetch more. When they had him alone, they hit him with a blast of radiation, rendering him catatonic. One killed Ari, while the other shoved Nate into position and placed the weapon in his hand. While the killer rolled up his bloody coverall, the other man made the call and wiped the phone clean. They escaped the same way they came."

It all fit together neatly. It only remained to prove the theory. Susan gave Jake a triumphant look.

But the policeman was frowning, clearly in deep consideration. "It took a total of four strong, young adults with a stretcher to carry Nate after Lawrence removed his battery at the Nineteenth Precinct. I'm sorry, but I can't envision that many people sneaking into the lab nor a single person moving him into place." He shook his head. "After the men who carried him testify, I don't think a jury will, either."

Once again, Susan realized they could prove how easy it was to move Nate in an instant; but, if she did, it would force Jake to arrest her. She glanced at Pal who gave her a quick, almost imperceptible headshake.

Then, another thought came to Susan. Once it did, it would not be banished. "What if I proved it to you?"

Pal looked away but not before Susan saw a faint green tint arise on his features.

Even Nate looked a bit nervous, though only someone who knew him well would notice.

Jake's brows rose. "When?"

"In about fifteen minutes," Susan said, glancing at her Vox. Only then, she realized they had spent two hours examining and debating. If she did not act soon, she would miss Alfred Lanning. Quickly, she tapped in the main number for U.S. Robots and Mechanical Men, Inc. and waited for Amara to answer. She dared not put on the speaker function. No telling what Alfred might say.

"U.S. Robots. Amara speaking."

"This is Susan Calvin. Could I speak with Alfred?"

"Of course. Do you need his Vox number, Dr. Calvin?"

"I'd like that. Thanks."

"I'll send it. In the meantime, I'll get him."

In a moment, Susan heard the faint beep of a number being added to her Vox, then Alfred's deep voice. "Susan? Is everything all right?"

"Fine," Susan assured him. "I just wondered if you could bring Nick to Goldman and Peters' lab."

"Nick? To the lab? What for?"

From the corner of her eye, Susan could see both Pal and Nate nod as they realized what she planned to do. "Exonerating Nate and Lawrence. I'm trying to demonstrate how the crime was committed, and we're stuck on a robotic detail."

"It's better if people don't know about Nick. He has nothing to do with the situation, and it could get dangerous for him."

Susan winced, glancing at Jake. The policeman gave her nothing but a raised eyebrow. "Trust me," she replied. "It's necessary and important, and it's not going to put Nick at risk."

Doubt tinged Alfred's voice, but he finally said, "All right. Be there in ten to twenty minutes."

"Thanks." Susan tapped off the call and looked at Jake. "I trust you'll keep Nick's existence a secret?"

Jake hesitated. "So long as it doesn't become an issue. I can't afford to lie on direct questioning. You may need Nick in the courtroom, and I need my job."

Susan could scarcely begrudge him that. "Fair enough." She added, "I know Lawrence was only trying to protect Nick when he said USR had no other humanoid robots, but that statement may come back to bite him. If we need him to prove a point in court, I'm bringing Nick with or without Lawrence's consent."

Jake looked directly into Susan's steely eyes. "Are there others?"

"No," Susan said definitively and without any hint of defensiveness. It was the truth, and she had no difficulty meeting Jake's gaze. "Nick and Nate are the only humanoid positronic robots remaining."

Pal said nonchalantly, "Assuming Nate hasn't fallen into dangerous hands, of course. No telling what the SFH might do to him."

Susan had no choice but to wince and nod.

Chapter 13

Ten minutes later, Jake studied Nick, walking around the robot as if inspecting a car for purchase. Finally, he stepped directly in front of Nick, staring intently into his all-too-human face.

Alfred gave Susan a questioning look, but she declined to answer him. She believed Jake suspected they had brought him Nate in the guise of another robot. She hoped Alfred had prepared Nick for questions about Nate, most specifically that he would not innocently reveal his fellow robot's disguise. She had not had the opportunity to remind the director of research, and Alfred did not always consider the human element when he made decisions.

Finally, Jake broke the silence. "What's your name?"

Nick responded dutifully, in a voice a half tone higher than Nate's and with an entirely different cadence. "I am N9-C, the ninth in the NC production line. I am usually referred to as Nick."

"So you're a robot?" Jake stated the obvious, which did not require a response.

Nick gave him one anyway. "I am."

Jake's next request caught Susan off guard. "Prove it."

Nick hesitated only a moment before peeling up a layer of skin over his shin to reveal the network of wires and plastic that lay beneath it.

"Thank you," Jake said, and Nick seamlessly rolled the dermal layer back into its proper position. The questions Susan had anticipated came next. "Are you familiar with a robot referred to as Nate?"

"I am."

Susan glanced at Alfred, who seemed entirely disinterested in the conversation, inspecting his own fingernails.

"Tell me about him." Jake kept his request open-ended. Susan supposed he got more cooperation and, sometimes, more information during police questionings with this technique.

Nick seemed no more bothered than Alfred by Jake's grilling. "Nate is the common name of N8-C. He was the eighth NC robot produced by U.S. Robots and Mechanical Men."

"And you were the ninth." Jake repeated the information Nick had given him.

"Yes."

"How many NC's are there, Nick?"

Nick hesitated, clearly uncertain how to answer properly. "There are currently two, sir. N8-C and myself. All of the others were dismantled, most before my creation."

Alfred explained. "The components for the NC line were astronomically expensive and the technology uniquely difficult. Our original intention was to wind up with a single NC robot that combined the best features of each of its predecessors and recycled most of the materials. But along the way it's normal to find a couple or three models that stand out and really should remain intact. In the NC line, it was N8-C and N9-C. The final result, N12-C, was destroyed, as you already know."

Susan trusted Alfred not to reveal the purpose of N12-C, aka John Calvin. The letters *NC* stood for New Calvin, and Jake was one of the few people who knew it.

Jake kept his attention fixed on Nick. "Do you contain any of N8-C's components?"

Susan knew where Jake was going and also that it was relatively safe ground.

"I contain reused bits and pieces from nearly all of my predecessors, but nothing from N8-C."

"You contain nothing from N8-C now or in the past?" Jake pressed.

"Correct. I'm mostly composed of newer resources than N8-C, since he received the best recycled materials from the previous models. However, I have none of their positronic pathways."

This time, Jake deliberately looked to Alfred for clarification.

The scientist complied. "When we talk about recycling components, it's bits and pieces of hardware only."

Jake kept his attention on Alfred and finally spoke his main concern aloud. "This isn't a trick where you give N8-C a new face and try to pass him off to me and others as an entirely different robot, is it?"

Alfred's features grew raw with affront. "If you don't believe me, Detective, you need only contact the board of directors at Saint Mary's Hospital. Nick has worked there for years, and he has looked, talked, and acted the same as he does now."

Susan added, "And Hasbro will vouch for Nate. So, unless someone has been shuttling the two back and forth several times a day since their placements in preparation for this exact moment, it's simply not possible."

Now Jake studied Susan, though he would find no clues on her face. Not only was she stating the abject truth, but she could school her features well enough to fool an expert.

Jake finally relaxed. "Forgive my paranoia, but I can't afford to take chances." He made a broad gesture. "Now, Susan, make your demonstration."

Susan set up the situation quickly. "Alfred, please take a seat in that chair, and keep it facing the table." She indicated the murder spot. "Layton, pick up the broom and stand behind Alfred."

Nate did as Susan instructed, though with clear reluctance. He held the broom tightly in both hands as if afraid it might slip and accidentally strike Alfred. He stood far enough behind the chair that, even if it did, it could not possibly harm Alfred in any way.

"Jake and Pal, stand wherever you need to to watch this demonstration. Nick, come with me." Susan did not bark out an instruction for Dr. Peters.

Nick obeyed, following Susan to the storage room. Once inside, she had him turn to face Alfred before instructing, "Nick, until I say your name again, you will see and hear nothing. You will remain entirely still."

Nick froze in place, exactly as Nate had done in Susan's apartment. Susan walked behind him. "Can you see what you need to see, Jake?"

"I can," he called back. "Work your magic."

Susan planted her hands on Nick's shoulders and gave him a strong push. He was lighter than Nate, in the two-hundred-fifty- to three-hundred-pound range, and she could easily slide him toward where Nate waited, hands clenched to the broom handle.

Susan braced for a second push, but Jake stepped up beside her. "Let me try."

Susan gestured broadly, stepping aside to allow Jake to take her place. He had no more difficulty than she did moving Nick without the robot assisting in any way.

Jake executed a flourishing motion more suitable for royalty in the Middle Ages. "I bow to your superior intellect, Susan."

Susan could not help grumbling, "Well, it's about time." She turned her attention to the robot. "Nick, back to normal."

Instantly, Nick returned to his regular state, glancing around to reorient himself to his new position.

Peters' Vox buzzed.

Jake addressed Nick once more. "Are you still working at Saint Mary's?"

The robot shook his head. "I've been recalled."

"To U.S. Robots?"

"Yes."

Susan suspected Peters' call had something to do with the radiation badge, but she dared not desert the current conversation. It could turn dangerous for her.

Jake continued calmly, as if his questions stemmed from curiosity rather than duty. "Was Nate also recalled?"

Nick replied smoothly, "Not to my knowledge." He struck to the heart of the question. "He's not at U.S. Robots if that's what you're asking me."

Jake could not let up. "Not even in part?"

Nick tipped his head in perfect mimicry of human consideration. "I believe his old battery might be there." He turned to Alfred Lanning. "Isn't that right?"

Alfred nodded. "I do have the battery. Susan brought it to me directly from Lawrence, and I performed some tests on it." He added gruffly, "Are you finished with us, Susan?"

Susan appreciated the request. The longer Jake had to throw questions at Nick, the more likely he would discover Nate's presence in the room. "I am, Alfred. Nick. Thanks so much for coming on such short notice. I know you're very busy." She had taken a dangerous gamble, but it appeared to have paid off. For now, at least, they had one policeman firmly on their side.

Peters had wandered off to talk on his Vox, but he soon returned and stepped right into the middle of the discussion. "Aiden, I'm going to put you on speaker. Can you tell everyone here the findings from my dosimeter?"

Aiden's now-familiar voice came crisply through Cody's Vox. "Hi, Everyone Here. Dr. Peters' dosimeter was exposed to a single pulse of electromagnetic radiation at approximately two o'clock p.m. on September first."

Susan recalled that the first code had come over her Vox at 2:19 p.m., which fit the scenario. The killers would have needed several minutes to leave things the way they wanted the police to find them and to make the calls.

Alfred asked one of the few questions that did not spring to Susan's mind. "What type of radiation, Aiden?" He added politely, "This is Dr. Alfred Lanning."

"Electromagnetic, Doctor, from a nuclear source."

Susan knew little about radiation, but Alfred clearly did not suffer from her lack. "X-rays or gamma, then."

Aiden seemed to enjoy discussing the situation with someone knowledgeable in the field. "The difference is mostly semantic. It's the kind of thing I'd expect to see if someone deliberately dosed himself with fluoroscopy. A single exposure of fifty-six millisieverts."

Jake stepped closer to Alfred. "Does that match what you found in the battery?"

Susan wished Alfred would just say yes but knew he would answer like a scientist. Nothing was ever true or false, black or white, and everything was possible. "Examining a battery isn't nearly as precise as checking something specifically created to measure radiation exposure like a dosimeter. By my calculations, using the results of battery testing alone, it was subjected to a single pulse of radiation early to midafternoon on September 1, 2037. That's about all I could figure out."

Pal translated, "So, yes. It gibes perfectly."

"It gibes," Alfred admitted, though he avoided the adverb. "But I can't definitively prove it was the same exposure. We may need to bring the two together to see how perfect it is."

Aiden spoke up. "Doc, why don't you send the battery to me? I could compare them."

Susan studied Alfred. U.S. Robots and Mechanical Men had good facilities, but they could not possibly compare to a mega-hospital laboratory.

"I'll do that," Alfred promised.

"Deliver it to the Radiation Lab, lower level of Mayner Pavilion," Aiden said. "I have to admit, I'm curious. What's this battery from? Someone's Vox?"

Cody Peters returned to the conversation. "Actually, it's the battery from a robot. And I'm wondering just how dangerous fifty-six millisieverts is."

Aiden sounded rehearsed, and he probably was when it came to discussions of radiation exposure. "The average American exposure from natural background radiation over a year's time is just under four millisieverts. Currently, our chest X-rays dose patients five to six millisieverts. A whole-body CT scan could expose a patient to as many as thirty millisieverts."

Peters interrupted. "So my coat, the robot, and, possibly, Ari took in about two full-body CTs' worth of gamma radiation."

"Right. One hundred millisieverts is considered the lowest annual dose at which the risk of developing cancer becomes evident. It's also what we consider the five-year limit of exposure for our radiation workers." Aiden added, "The important thing is whether you were wearing that coat at the time of the exposure."

"I wasn't," Peters assured Aiden. "I wasn't even in the building."

"Good," Aiden sent back sincerely. "Of course, Dr. Goldman's exposure is moot. Whether or not a pulse of fifty-six millisieverts would affect a robot, I have no idea."

Alfred had an answer. "A positronic brain is far more susceptible to all types of radiation than a human one, but we've never had a reason to do an in-depth study of how various types and dosages affect it. Positrons are antielectrons. Anytime we want to destroy a positronic brain, we need only use a simple electron source. As far as radiation, beta is particularly dangerous to the positronic brain because it consists of ejected electrons, but it doesn't have enough power to penetrate more than a few millimeters of metal. A sheet of aluminum foil can stop it. Gamma radiation?" He shrugged. "Let's just say we don't sell . . ." He amended quickly, based on his earlier conversation with Susan. "Pardon me. We don't *lease* positronic robots as radiation technicians. Most of our research comes from the Mercury robots."

Aiden indicated he had followed the explanation. "So fifty-six millisieverts might be enough to seriously damage a robotic brain?"

"I don't think so," Albert said. "The LD_{50} in humans is what?"

Aiden had the figure. "It's five thousand millisieverts, Doctor."

Jake looked askance at Susan, so she explained the word she suspected was giving him trouble. "LD_{50} is the lethal dose for about fifty percent of the exposed population given current medical treatment standards."

Jake grimaced, and it occurred to Susan that it was a rather gruesome, but effective, way to measure the dangerousness of a toxin, drug, or pathogen.

Albert did not seem to notice the exchange. "Robots don't have LD_{50} because they all react pretty much the same way. For them, it's a short step from LD_0 to LD_{100}. Any differences in robot survivability would depend solely on the human-built shielding or construction. With something as fully penetrating as gamma radiation, and based only on previous experience, I'd say the LD_{100} for exposure in robots is probably in the two-hundred-millisieverts range."

Aiden summed up Alfred's point. "So fifty-six wouldn't hurt it?"

"Wouldn't *destroy* or seriously damage it. I didn't say it wouldn't hurt. Radiation effects aren't all-or-nothing."

Aiden had to agree. "With humans, a dose of one thousand to two thousand increases the risk of various cancers and might cause hair loss, nausea, and, possibly, hemorrhaging in some. But robots don't experience any of that, do they?"

"No," Alfred admitted. "The bodily effects wouldn't be an issue, but a sudden pulse might cause some problems. Soften some circuits, damage some memory . . ."

Susan could not help inserting, "Turn him off for some period of time."

Alfred jerked his head to Susan as if he had forgotten the others were there. "Um, yes. Of course. That's a definite possibility."

Though Aiden was clearly enjoying the conversation, Susan and, apparently, Cody knew he needed to get back to work. "Thanks," Dr. Peters said. "Very much appreciate the information and the speed at which you attained it. What happens next?"

"I'll have to report it, of course. We'll have people up there looking for the source and making sure it's not an ongoing leak or likely to happen again. We'll check the dosimeters of everyone who may have come in contact. Once we have all of that information, we'll make recommendations."

"Thanks," Cody said.

But Aiden had not finished. "In the meantime, we need to quarantine the area. Leave the coat that had the dosimeter where it was and don't touch it any more than you already have. It appears to have been a single pulse, which means you're probably safe. However, if we find something that suggests additional exposure, we may need to have you checked over."

"Understood," Cody said. "Thanks." He broke off the contact and looked at the others. "Well, I hope I didn't expose the police and all of you to anything dangerous."

Susan doubted it. "The dosimeter sat here three days and recorded only that single pulse, which was well below the dangerous level. I think we're all fine."

Jake glanced at his Vox. "Damn! It's five already. We're going to have to hurry to make it to Alphonse's." He pursed his lips, then continued. "Alfred, I hate to impose on someone I respect and barely know, but would you be able to drop Pal off on your way home?"

Before Alfred could reply, Pal obviated the need. "I'll grab the glide-bus to my bike and ride that to my mom's. She's looking forward to feeding me a home-cooked meal."

Nate cut in next, "I've had enough excitement for one day. Would you mind if I accepted that ride, Dr. Lanning? I wouldn't mind a quiet tour of a robotics factory, or you could drop me off at Susan's."

Placing Nate with Alfred seemed like a great idea to Susan, at least for tonight. Susan doubted anyone would obtain a warrant to search U.S. Robots, or her apartment, on Jake's day off.

To her surprise, Jake was the one who argued. "Layton, don't you want to come with us to the restaurant? I said it's my treat, and Alphonse's has a great selection of seafood."

"No thanks." Nate headed toward the door. "I'll just grab something at home."

Some of the blood left Jake's face. "Do you really think that's a good idea, Layton? The last time you ate something from Susan's fridge, she poisoned you."

"Hey!" Susan remembered Nate's act, and that it involved takeout, but she still took offense. "I have good food."

Jake clearly referenced their first meal together. "Sure, if you don't mind eating chicken, banana, and broccoli casserole."

Alfred finally cut in. "We'll pick up something bland on the way to U.S. Robots. Nick can give Susan's cousin a tour while I handle some business I didn't finish because I had to come here."

"Sorry." Susan considered offering Nate money, but she did not have any to spare and knew he did not really need it, even to eat. If she had offered, Alfred would not have accepted, anyway. "And thanks for taking

Layton. He reads a ton of science fiction; he'll love USR. I'll call you when I'm headed home, and we can make arrangements to get Layton back to my apartment."

Susan looked at Pal, who was tapping at his Vox, clearly making his own arrangements, then at Cody Peters. "Do you want to take Layton's place at Alphonse's, Dr. Peters?"

"I can't. I have to get back to the Goldmans' for the funeral supper." A pained expression crossed Cody's face. "I've been ignoring Cait's texts for the better part of an hour, and I'm going to hear about it."

They all headed for the hallway, Cody pausing to lock the door behind them. As they walked to the elevator, Susan asked Jake, "Do you need to change that reservation from three people to two?"

"Actually," Jake replied, "from four to three. Kendall's meeting us there. He wants to know what we found in the lab."

Susan could not help smiling. It felt like old times, the three of them chatting about the case over dinner together. "And don't we have a lot to tell him."

Jake could only nod in agreement.

Jake and Susan joined Kendall at a back corner table in the dimly lit restaurant, its blue-gray walls holding dynamic pictures of boats in storms and fishermen battling enormous varieties of sea life: tuna, sharks, marlin, and even a giant squid. Rods as wide as her wrist bowed like rubber, the ships appeared to rock dangerously in gutters of white water, and the fish flung droplets so realistic they seemed to fly from the canvas.

Susan tapped her dinner selections into the table keypad, mindful of Jake's budget. She chose a grilled halibut with peach and pepper glaze, pearled barley, and ginger-buttered broccoli. She selected plain water with a twist of lime for her drink.

Kendall waited until everyone had finished ordering before leaning across the table. "So, did you solve the crime?"

"Pretty much," Susan said, glancing at Jake for confirmation. The policeman sat with arms folded across his chest, saying nothing, so she proceeded to describe her version of how the murder was committed, careful not to embellish anything uncertain. For example, she stated her belief that the killers came through the window but not how they did so.

Kendall listened raptly while Susan detailed her scenario; neither he nor Jake interrupted. When she finished, Kendall also looked at Jake for corroboration.

With two sets of eyes on him, and his companions gone silent, Jake finally spoke. "I believe Susan's description of the crime is probably mostly correct." His tone did not convey the optimism of his words.

Kendall tried to guess what bothered Jake. "But . . . it's going to be . . . what? Hard to prove?"

Jake nodded glumly.

Susan jumped in. "But the radiation pulse—"

"Isn't the slam dunk you think it is. You can prove a pulse of gamma radiation struck the storage room around the time of the murder, but a competent prosecutor will explain it away as an unrelated occurrence. Or, worse, that the pulse was the reason the robot went crazy and murdered the victim, perhaps even that Lawrence caused the pulse because he knew it would drive Nate to a murderous frenzy."

Joy had not visited Susan in a long time, and she did not want to let it go. Jake's negativity was driving her mad. "But we have the truth on our side, Jake, and that's a huge advantage."

Kendall seemed to be taking Jake's side. "The truth is great, but it's not a guarantee. Mistakes happen all the time, and lawyers . . . well, what's the difference between a lawyer and a jellyfish?"

Susan rolled her eyes. Now was not the time for jokes. "All right, Kendall. Get it out of your system."

Kendall obliged. "One's a spineless, poisonous blob, and the other's a sea creature."

No one laughed. Finally, Susan and Jake agreed on something; neither wanted to deal with Kendall's weird sense of humor. "How many lawyer jokes are there," Jake asked flatly.

Kendall smiled. "Only three in the whole world." His grin broadened mischievously. "The rest are true stories."

Susan ignored Kendall to confront Jake directly. "So what do I have to do to win this thing?"

"Reasonable doubt," Jake reminded. "You probably have enough for that already, but you've said it's not good enough for you. You want to fully exonerate Lawrence and Nate, and that requires us to find the real perps and prove the case against them. Cases that end with acquittal only rescue the accused from punishment. They don't dispel public doubt unless and until someone else is convicted."

Susan could scarcely deny it. Seventy years after O.J. Simpson was acquitted of murdering his ex-wife, she doubted anyone still believed he was innocent. The enormity of the prospect surged around her, but need and persistence arose to combat it. She was accustomed to dealing with exquisitely complicated situations, one step at a time. "All right, I'm game. What do I have to do?"

Before Jake could respond, a server arrived. He set an enormous silver tray onto a small stand away from the table, then put a plate in front of each of them. Kendall had gone with lemon-pepper shrimp scampi and a side of asparagus, while Jake got almond-crusted salmon, brown rice, and spinach. Both men had ordered fruit fizzies, Jake's peach and Kendall's strawberry. The server left several condiments in the center of the table, then asked, "Is there anything more I can bring you?"

Everyone responded, "No, thank you."

Jake waited until the server had left before addressing Susan's question. "We're limited in what we can do, Susan. Our best advantage is that I'm friends with some of the guys at the Nineteenth Precinct and we're working on related cases. I can make suggestions, but I can't direct their investigation."

The answer did little more than frustrate Susan. "And they're convinced Nate did it."

Jake squeezed lemon over his fish, then shrugged. "A reasonable assumption. They literally caught him red-handed."

Susan sat back, her food untouched. "I hope you're not trying to say it's hopeless." She spoke in a flat, almost threatening, tone. "Because I'm not going to give up, with or without your assistance."

Jake's eyes narrowed. "Of course, I'm not saying it's hopeless. I'm just letting you know what we're up against. Too many people bounce into court thinking they have an airtight case and forgetting the other side is just as determined to win."

"Got it," Susan said through gritted teeth. She emphasized her original question, "Now what do we have to do?"

Kendall smiled around a mouthful of scampi. "Finally! She said 'we' instead of 'I.'"

Jake grinned in Kendall's direction. "I noticed that, too." He turned his attention back to Susan. "First, we need to start looking at this case through the eyes of the jury. Whenever the subject arises, you inevitably jump straight to the fact that Nate couldn't have done it, that the Laws of Robotics prevent it."

"Well they do," Susan said in her defense.

"You know that. I know that. Even Kendall has an inkling it's probably the truth."

"Hey!" Kendall lowered his fork. "If Susan's says it's true, it's true."

"But the jury's supposed to begin the trial with completely open minds."

Susan knew that would never happen. "Except they won't. Because everyone has biases, and Hollywood has not treated robots and other man-made beings with kindness."

"Other man-made beings," Kendall repeated thoughtfully, then nodded. "In this case, you mean Frankenstein's monster."

Susan did. They were all familiar with the Frankenstein Complex by now, so she did not repeat it. "Well, they didn't call him Frankenstein's little angel."

Jake waved away Susan's legitimate concern. "There's nothing we can do about people's hidden biases. So, pretend you're a regular person, a member of the jury, not Susan Calvin. What's the glaring oddity about this murder?"

Susan took a mouthful of halibut, savored the peach and pepper, then swallowed. "The robot."

"Yes, the robot," Jake said dismissively as he tasted his own dinner. "There's something nearly as out of place. Something you don't expect to see in a hospital, at least I didn't expect it."

Susan figured it out. "The Stanley 55-099 FatMax Xtreme FuBar Utility Bar."

Both men dropped their forks and stared at Susan.

"What?"

"How did you do that?" Jake said.

"Do what?" Susan still did not understand.

Kendall retrieved his fork. "Jake has never seen you rattle off a list of eight-syllable differential diagnoses from memory before." He addressed the policeman. "She has a photographic memory."

Susan had to correct the misconception. "I do not have an eidetic memory, just a decent one. *When* I pay attention, which I always did in medical school classes. Plus, people without social lives have a lot of free time to study."

Jake took up his own fork again, cutting off a piece of salmon that consisted mostly of almonds. "To study . . . obscure tools?"

Susan rolled her eyes. "To study eight-syllable diagnoses, their differentials, and the tests needed to rule out or support them. I remembered the name of the tool because I heard Nate say it"–she barely stopped herself from saying "several times"–"at the police station. I saw the thing at the scene, and I thought it was some sort of hammer, so it surprised me when he said Stanley 55-099 FatMax Xtreme FuBar Utility Bar. That seemed weird and important, so it stuck with me."

Kendall returned to his food while Jake continued to address Susan. "Important, yet not important enough to consider a clue?"

Susan fixed her attention on Jake, encouraging him to explain.

"Where did Nate get this utility bar?"

Susan knew Jake had the answer to his own question. "From the murderers, of course. They stuck it in his hands." She added, "They could just as easily have used a crowbar or a hammer."

"Think like a jury member." Jake scooped up some rice. "Where would a robot get one of those things?"

The line of questioning seemed superfluous. "Where would he get anything? A toolbox, I suppose."

"Did he bring a toolbox into the lab?"

Susan hesitated, starting to get a handle on Jake's point. "I can't imagine he did." She considered further. "We could probably find witnesses who would swear he didn't. Whoever keeps track of his schedule at the hospital could confirm that he did not have one when he left for the lab." She made a mental note to do so.

Jake ate a few more scoops of rice before continuing. Susan and Kendall followed suit on their own meals. "The murder weapon is eighteen inches long. It would be almost impossible to carry one without someone noticing. Even if Nate taped it to his leg hidden beneath his clothing, it would severely impede his ability to bend his knees, to walk."

"Yeah," Kendall said thoughtfully.

Susan did the math. "As tall as he is, he might have a twenty-inch-long femur, but that would include the joints." She imagined the tool. "The utility bar's oddly shaped at both ends, too. It might fit under extremely loose-fitting pants, but they would bulge weirdly."

"At the time of the arrest, Nate wasn't wearing loose-fitting pants, was he?"

Susan brought the scene back to her mind's eye. Pal had disposed of Nate's khakis and bloodstained polo. "No. Definitely not." She lifted her head. "And the police could corroborate that."

Jake chewed thoughtfully. "So, the only place it could have come from is the toolbox in the storage closet inside the laboratory itself."

Susan had never seen the researchers use even a standard tool, let alone a wrecking bar. "Is there one?"

Jake nodded. "I saw it there when we visited. It's a cloth one with a zipper on a lower shelf. The question is did it have a Stanley Whatever Utility Bar in it?"

Kendall responded, "Surely, Cody would know that."

"I could ask him." Susan reached for her Vox.

Jake caught her hand. "Don't bother. The police already did, and Cody claimed it didn't." He tipped his head. "See, they're not just sitting on their hands, blaming everything on Nate."

Susan found Jake's second point even more reassuring than the first. "So the murder weapon came from outside the hospital. Which means Nate couldn't have done it."

"Unless he sneaked out of the hospital and bought it."

Susan glared at Kendall. "You know he didn't."

Jake remained annoyingly open-minded. "*You* know he didn't. You'll have to prove that to the jury."

Susan rattled off her reasons, which went far beyond wishful thinking. "Nate's kept in a storage area. To leave it, he has to be checked out; and he's expressly forbidden to exit the hospital without an escort from USR. Even if he somehow managed to sneak out, he has no money and no credit of any kind."

Jake ate slowly while he listened to Susan. "Good. Those details will help, especially if we bring in some high-level hospital muckety-mucks to testify about his whereabouts in the weeks before the murder."

Jake tapped at his Vox, then indicated Susan and Kendall should consult their own. When she did so, Susan found a close-up image of smudged letters scrawled onto dirty metal in ancient black marker.

Susan chewed thoughtfully. "What's this?"

Jake gave her an intent look. "Found on the murder weapon."

Susan raised her arm nearly to her eyeballs. She could definitely make out the letters in the enlarged image: *SFH*. Her heart skipped a beat. "It says SFH!"

Kendall continued eating, a slight smile on his face. Obviously, Jake had already shown him the evidence.

Susan turned Jake an accusing look. "So we know who the murderers are." She amended, "Or, at least, who they work for. Why haven't the charges been dropped against Lawrence? Why haven't all the members of the SFH been hauled in?"

Jake rolled his eyes and sighed. "Susan, letters written on a tool aren't the same as an MRI of a tumor. We're dealing with deceitful human beings, not a straightforward attack by disease."

Susan did not bother to disabuse him of the notion that disease processes were consistent and reproducible. "You're saying a few initials on the murder weapon aren't conclusive." He was right, of course. A lot of people labeled their tools, even cheap hammers and screwdrivers; and organizations often did so to assure that any employee who borrowed one remembered to return it, especially after a few had disappeared.

The faded, amplified image Jake had sent her suggested the markered letters had been there a long time, gripped by multiple sweaty hands through the years. They were small, and she could see how the murderer might not have seen them, or even thought to look for them, before employing the labeled bar as a weapon. Or, maybe, he had not had time for careful examination. "So they're not even questioning the SFH?"

Jake stopped eating to fully address Susan's question. "Of course they are, but there's a complication."

Susan waited patiently for him to continue.

"Remember I told you the Department of Defense had the desire and means to put the SFH out of business?"

Susan could hardly forget. She had worried she would have to spend the entirety of her life dodging kidnappings and bullets, but Jake had reassured her. She remembered his words almost verbatim: "There's not a whole lot NYPD can do about a citizens' action group like the Society for Humanity, other than prosecuting those members directly involved in the crime. But Cadmium has their own ax to grind against the SFH now, and they have RICO." He had gone on to describe RICO as the Racketeer Influenced and Corrupt Organizations Act, which would allow the Department of Defense to capture and try the leaders of a syndicate for crimes they ordered others to do. She encouraged him to continue by saying, "I remember."

Jake did so. "Not only was the SFH trying to kill a person Cadmium desperately wanted alive–"

"Me," Susan pointed out.

Jake went on as if she had not interrupted. "But they also got into a firefight with Cadmium in an open street. DoD likes to keep a low profile, and they don't appreciate people shooting at them."

Although he had just stuffed his mouth, Kendall had to say, "Me, either."

Susan agreed. "Me either, too." She took a small bite of her own food, trying to guess where Jake was taking the point. "So you're saying the SFH no longer exists? That Cadmium effectively destroyed it?"

"The Society for Humanity still exists, but anyone with even a hint of a history of violence was . . . removed from it. Apparently, the DoD examined every individual affiliated with the organization down to their high school social posts and junior high yearbooks. When the guys from the Nineteenth visited the SFH, they found a group of mild-mannered accountants and concerned grandmothers, all of whom fell over one another to try to figure out if a Stanley Utility FuBar Thingy might have gone missing from an SFH toolbox."

Susan had taken another mouthful while he spoke and was still chewing, so Kendall asked the appropriate question. "Did one? Go missing, I mean."

Jake raised a shoulder, then dropped it. "Who knows? What do you learn from the absence of such a tool? Did it go walkies or did it never exist? No one currently involved in the group remembers having one, but they didn't deny the possibility, either. And there's always the chance that the SFH on the utility bar stands for Samuel Franklin Henderson or Society for Family Health."

Kendall added unhelpfully, "Saint Francis Hospital."

Susan finally finished the mouthful. "What about fingerprints?"

Jake had the ready answer. "Nate's only. Wiped clean before it fell into his hands."

Kendall swallowed a mouthful of strawberry fizzy water. "Now that's an odd thing for a killer to do, isn't it? Remove everyone else's prints, then leave his own."

Jake had to nod. "A stupid criminal might do it, but I'm sure you could prove Nate smarter than any human."

Susan imagined herself in front of a jury requesting the answers to complicated mathematical problems and Nate supplying them effortlessly.

Jake did not wait for a response. "The only other reason to wipe it down would be to protect a coconspirator. Most criminals would want to leave a buddy's fingerprints intact unless and until he could wipe clean his own at the same time. It spreads the guilt and opens a lot more defensive possibilities. The DA might argue that Lawrence wiped it before giving it to Nate, except that's countered by the fact that he jumped right in to take responsibility for any action of Nate's at the precinct. That suggests someone other than Lawrence cleaned the weapon, again introducing reasonable doubt."

Susan pounced on this information. "It's certainly what someone framing Nate for the crime would do."

"Definitely," Kendall agreed.

It seemed odd to Susan that an item that had not even come into play during their sleuthing might just prove the key to Lawrence's release.

They ate for several moments in silence while Susan contemplated the various discrepancies in the prosecution's case. Surely, they were feeling smug, wholly confident in a case in which they had caught the alleged perpetrator with his bloody hands on the murder weapon standing over the corpse. It seemed unlikely they would anticipate the many flaws Susan and her team had discovered. More likely, they would expect Lawrence's attorney to attack the connection between Lawrence and Nate or the science of the laboratory, a risky strategy at best.

Finished with his dinner, Kendall shoved his plate aside and leaned across the table toward Susan. Before speaking, he turned toward Jake, clearly for support. Jake gave a noncommittal gesture that both of his companions apparently took to mean the ball was in Kendall's court on whatever he intended to say.

Kendall cleared his throat. "Susan, Jake and I have some concerns about Pal."

Susan could almost feel her hackles rising. "What about Pal?" She put the last bit of fish into her mouth and chewed slowly, waiting for him to continue.

Kendall obliged. "We know you've known him a lot longer than we have, and that you're a superior judge of character. It's just . . . well . . . for example . . ." He stopped speaking, gathering his thoughts to make his speech more fluent. "When you told Jake about how the two of you met. From what Jake told me, it sounded like Pal spent a lot of time secretly pursuing you."

Oh. That. She and Pal had made up that particular story on the spur of the moment, and it had nothing to do with the truth.

Kendall added carefully, as if measuring Susan's response, "Almost to the point of . . . stalking."

Susan snorted.

Kendall looked affronted. "I'm just . . . thinking of you, Susan."

Susan had not intended to hurt his feelings, only to disabuse him of a silly notion. "Pal exaggerated the story a bit. You know how people do when they're trying to make a bland love story sound more romantic. Our meeting twice in a short period of time really was a happy coincidence. If we hadn't had a mutual attraction, we simply wouldn't have remembered the first encounter."

Kendall either accepted that explanation or assumed Susan considered that particular point covered and closed. "Also, there's the matter of Net silence."

Susan pushed her own plate aside, finished, trying to guess Kendall's point. "You mean there's nothing on the global Net about a special operations force soldier." She made an exaggerated motion of shock, resorting to sarcasm. "*Quelle surprise.*"

Jake finally assisted Kendall. "Yeah, all right. Men in MARSOC aren't going to have lots of time for play, and he's probably under orders not to be chatting. But I can't find any sign that Pal Buffoni existed before he enlisted. No high school yearbook picture. No teenage crushes. No toothless grin in some elementary school sports team picture. He's got an address, a Vox number, a motorcycle registration, and a license to carry. That's it."

Susan rolled her eyes. "Which is probably more than you'd find on me. I've got a Vox number, but my address probably hasn't caught up with me yet. I've never owned a vehicle. I spent too much time studying to create a Net presence. Look me up; I'll bet I'm Net silent, too."

Kendall sighed.

Susan tried to understand. "Look, Kendall. I know it's weird. You don't see me for several months, then I show up with a lover you, my best and understandably *very protective* friends, have never met. But believe me; I know how to read people. Pal is a good man all the way, a hero and a patriot. He loves me, and I love him."

Kendall stiffened, revealing that Susan had hit close to home. "But it's just so soon . . . ," he practically whined.

Susan could hardly deny it. It was quicker, even, than she could let them know. "That's apparently how love works for me. Remy . . ." It surprised her how easily she spoke his name. The pain that used to arise when she did lay deeply buried. "Remy and I fell in love after our third date. We had known each other less than two weeks." She glared at the men, daring either of them to say a single negative word about Remington Hawthorn.

Neither of them did.

Kendall seemed frustrated by his inability to influence Susan to his viewpoint. She believed he had saved his most significant argument for last, though he seemed loath to use it. His dark eyes assumed an odd glimmer that Susan could not yet place. "Men like Pal . . . I mean, he's a hero and he's so . . . good-looking."

Susan could not allow him to continue. "As opposed to me, who's a cowardly troll."

"No!" Kendall shook his head. "Susan, that's not what I mean–" He turned a pleading look to Jake, clearly seeking help, but Jake's expression suggested he had warned Kendall not to try this particular argument and he would not assist. That seemed to fluster Kendall all the more.

Susan defended herself. "Pal and I have discussed this. He thinks I'm beautiful. By the way, Remy did, too. His mother's a genius, and he wants a woman with a brain. Is that really so difficult for men to comprehend?"

Kendall struggled to salvage his point. "Susan, I don't mean that as an insult to you. It's just that men like Pal don't have any trouble finding beauty queens with whatever additional features they might want, including a brilliant mind. I'm not saying you're unattractive. . . ."

Susan had tired of the subject and wished to end it. She understood Kendall's point. "I note you didn't kick me out of *your* bed."

Kendall's cheeks turned a brilliant shade of scarlet. "Well that was before . . . I mean I . . ." He rolled an eye toward Jake but clearly could not plant his gaze on the policeman. "I didn't understand my sexual desires. . . ."

Susan dodged the guilt she should have felt for placing Kendall in this position. She knew he had a serious crush on Jake, who seemed completely unaware of it, and that Kendall still struggled with full acceptance of his homosexuality. Suddenly identifying the gleam she had seen in Kendall's eyes, she ended the conversation with a declarative statement. "Oh my God! You're both lusting after my man. You can't understand what he sees in me because you can't imagine anyone wanting me as a sexual partner."

It was not wholly fair, and Susan knew it. Kendall had not only imagined it but had attempted it. The fact that it had not gone well was not entirely his fault. Still, it accomplished what she wanted, and it ended the discussion in its tracks. She glanced at her Vox, which read 7:15 p.m. There were two messages waiting, both from Pal. She brought them up. The first read: "Enjoying chicken cacciatore at Mom's but missing you. She wants to meet you sometime. When will you be home? Love, Pal." The second read: "Leaving Mom's, then grabbing a few things from my place. Be home by 7:30. You?"

Susan responded with a quick text: "Done eating. Abt 2 lv A's. Home soon." Her Vox fixed all the misspellings, and she checked to make sure all the words were as she intended before sending. "I'm going to wash up in the ladies'. Then, if you're done insulting me and my partner, I'd like to go home." All the talk of Pal's attractiveness was awakening cravings and memories of their lovemaking.

To her surprise, Jake did not try to prolong the outing. "That's a great idea. Kendall and I have work in the morning, and you should get to the Nineteenth by about eight a.m."

Susan had no idea to what Jake was referring. "I should? Why?"

Jake's brows rose. "I just assumed you'd want to talk to Lawrence's attorney before the bail hearing."

"The bail hearing," Susan repeated dully. She had never attended one and had little idea what to expect. No one had previously mentioned it to her. "How come you're the first to tell me about it?"

Jake shrugged. "There's not a whole lot to it, and you can't influence the outcome. It's unlikely the judge will even allow you in the courtroom. But if it were my friend, I know I'd want to take the opportunity to see him and get to know his lawyer."

Susan got up from her chair, and the men rose with her. She had expected them to wait at the table for her, so she asked sardonically, "Are you joining me in the ladies'?"

"I am," Jake said, without a hint of humor.

Surprised, Susan could only mimic, "You are?"

"Of course I am. I'm your bodyguard tonight, and I can't think of a better place for a killer to hide than in the ladies'. He's going to expect me to let you go there alone. If so, he's sadly mistaken."

Susan did a mental check of her bladder and decided she could wait until she got home to urinate. "Let's not cause that kind of trouble." She dipped a napkin into her water glass, then used it to dab at her face and thoroughly clean her hands. "There, I'm clean. We can go now."

Jake shrugged. "Are you sure, Susan? We can handle it discreetly. I don't want your kidneys exploding or anything."

"Bladder," Susan corrected. "The kidneys just make the urine; the bladder holds it. And I'm fine if we go now. Are we all settled up?"

"Yup," Jake said.

"Thank you," Susan said. "I enjoyed the food very much and appreciate your treating."

Kendall cut in. "Well, don't cover me, Jake. I've got it, and I'm happy to take over half of Susan's, too."

"Forget it," Jake said. "I got it all."

Kendall swiftly stated, "All right, but I get the next one."

Susan recognized the tactic, which would assure they had another meal together. Susan felt certain it was Jake whom Kendall wanted, not her, but she did not allow herself a smile. They headed for the door.

Chapter 14

Susan, Jake, and Kendall stepped into the twilit parking lot, the weather warm and muggy for early September. Susan pinned her long dark hair behind her ears, trying to remember where Jake had parked the Sapphire. The little car sat at the end of a row, an open grassy expanse on the passenger side and a boxy Korean import parked crookedly on the driver's. As they approached the car, Kendall veered close to Susan, speaking barely above a whisper, "Would you mind if I took shotgun?"

On the trip to Alphonse's, there had been only Susan and Jake; Kendall had met them at the restaurant. Susan had naturally sat in the passenger seat. Last year, when the three of them had traveled in the Subaru, Susan had sat beside Jake because she had known him longer than Kendall had.

Kendall added, "I've got longer legs." His effort to sound casual backfired. Susan knew exactly why he wanted to sit beside the object of his crush. The conversation flowed more naturally and easily between the front passengers, which suited Susan just fine. She could use some time to think about all the day's discoveries and the upcoming meeting with Lawrence's attorney. She did not want to argue about whether she was pretty enough to keep her lover. "That's fine."

Kendall stumbled. Something fell from his hand, pinging against concrete and rolling under the Subaru. Susan dropped to a crouch to retrieve the object, which she assumed was a ring, though she had never noticed him wearing one. Spotting a glimmer of silver, she reached beneath the car, face pressed to the cool metal while she groped blindly in the right general direction. Gravel grated against her fingertips; then she scooped up something round and thin–a coin, she presumed.

Abruptly, Kendall fell against her with a force that slammed her face and knees to the macadam. Pain seared her cheek and knees, and the ragged pavement nearly tore her khakis. Susan twisted to confront him, and her movement caused him to land fully on top of her. Neatly pinned, she looked into his familiar dark eyes, now filled with shock, glazed and sightless. Blood ran from his nose. "Kendall!" Susan scrambled to a sitting position, Kendall's limp form flopping onto her lap. Gore clotted in his orange hair.

Screams pierced Susan's hearing, and it took inordinately long to realize they came from her own throat. In all the years she had managed medical emergencies, she had never fallen prey to panic. Her training had always risen to the occasion, allowing her to work mechanically, endowed with memory and understanding. In a crisis, the world seemed to move in slowed motion. Now she suffered a terror she had known only in the past two years, one that scrambled her senses and made her want to run until her muscles spasmed and her lungs collapsed.

In an instant, Jake was there, tossing Kendall off Susan, grasping her arms, and shoving her, reeling, toward the passenger seat. "In!" he shouted, ducking around the Subaru and tearing open the driver's door.

"No!" Susan could not leave Kendall. She lunged toward him. Already off balance, she tumbled from the car. Small objects drummed across the roof. Pain shot through Susan's right shoulder. "I've been shot!" she realized aloud.

Jake swore viciously. Lunging across the console, he grabbed Susan's left wrist, all that he could reach, and jerked her back toward the passenger seat. His effort allowed him to wrap his other arm around her head and force her back into the car. The moment he had most of Susan inside, the car leapt forward. Poised between dropping into her seat and tumbling onto the parking lot through the still-open door, Susan made the decision more geared to her survival. Instinctively, she threw her weight toward the center of the car, and the momentum of its takeoff made the door swing closed.

Susan grabbed the handle with her injured arm, anticipating a fierce stab of agony that never came. It hurt, but not nearly as badly as she anticipated, and the pain seemed confined to her shoulder. As the car bumped over the concrete parking stop and into the grass lane, Susan yelled, "Stop! We can't leave Kendall!"

Jake clutched the steering wheel with one hand and reached toward several buttons on the dash. "He's dead," he said, eerily calm.

The words did not register. "Jake! We need to save Kendall!" Susan looked over her shoulder, the movement stinging. "Kendall's not in the car!"

"He's dead, Susan. Kendall is dead."

This time, Susan understood, but his words invoked only rage. An image popped into her mind of Kendall cradling Jake after the Cadmium agent had shot him in the head. Though they had all been warned they would be killed if they moved, Kendall had run to Jake's aid, had staunched the bleeding even as he assessed the injuries and realized the policeman was still, impossibly, alive. Kendall had wept over Jake's body, pronounced the man he loved dead, a convincing enough act to fool everyone in the room, including Susan.

Now, it was Jake's turn, and he had abandoned Kendall like a discarded rag. The comparison made Susan's blood boil, but she could do nothing about it other than protest. "Jake, Kendall loves you! He would do anything for you! Anything! You have to save him. Go back! Go back!"

Jake's voice was stern. "Susan, get your door shut and locked. Tend to your injury. There's nothing we can do for Kendall. He's dead."

Susan continued to rage at Jake, but none of it mattered. He had, apparently, stopped listening to her, focused on the road, on his dash. "Central, Chief of Detectives Portable! Shots fired First Avenue Seven Two to Seven Three Street! Have Hasbro standby. Bringing one civilian in. Gunshot wound to chest, K!"

Susan shouted over Jake, "What if he's not dead? What if your unwillingness to let me assist killed him? What if . . . ?"

A reply came over the dash. "Copy, Portable! On the line with EMS!" There followed a series of loud beeps, then, "In the confines of the Nineteenth Precinct, a signal 10-13! Shots fired! Over the air, units to respond to?" Jake waited until the other speaker finished before muting his connection. "Susan, Kendall never knew what hit him."

"You're not a doctor!" Susan was screaming.

"I saw what happened, Susan. He collapsed straight down, no movement of any kind. Material flew from his right ear. I'm sorry, Susan, but Kendall is dead. Any hesitation on our part, and we would have joined him."

To allow the information to sink in meant accepting the blame for Kendall's death. Susan knew the shooter had no reason to kill anyone but her. She was a mortal danger to everyone around her. *Not Kendall. No, no, not Kendall.* Susan finally looked at the object still gripped in her hand. It was a quarter Kendall had dropped, a measly twenty-five cents. Had she not crouched to retrieve it, she felt certain, the bullet would have passed through her head instead of his. *I killed him as surely as if I pulled the trigger.*

Tears sprang to Susan's eyes, and the coin became a silver-colored blur. Finally, she pulled the door closed far enough that it clicked, then locked itself. The seat belt scrolled across her torso and snapped into place.

The same voice came over the dash speaker. "Chief of Detectives Portable, any description on perps, K?"

Jake replied, shouting into the dash. "Negative, Central. We didn't see them. Possibly two perps. Possibly from 1354 First Avenue."

This time, Susan waited until Jake finished. "Are you sure . . ."

Jake gave a definitive, sorrowful nod. "Trust me. It's very apparent to people who do this for a living. The shot took out his central nervous system so fast and fully, he never even knew he'd been hit." He changed the subject abruptly. "Where were you hit?"

"Behind the right shoulder," Susan said dully. It seemed inappropriate to worry about her small wound when Kendall lay dead in a parking lot, but her medical training arose without intention. She had seen so many movies and shows, read so many books, where the main character was "only" shot in the shoulder. There was blood and pain, but it never prevented Hero from winning the day; and he always regained full use of his injured arm, often in moments.

Susan knew better. The shoulder contained a unique arrangement of bones and tendons, the rotator cuff, and, more important, the subclavian artery and brachial plexus. A gunshot wound anywhere could kill a man. One that opened the subclavian artery would cause a fast and fatal bleed, internally or externally. Damage to the brachial plexus might permanently affect the use of the arm or cause debilitating pain that required surgical correction.

Even the current relative lack of pain did not soothe Susan. Adrenaline and excitement or, worse, shock, could easily account for it. Pain did not always correlate with damage. Brains and eyes had no pain receptors, yet a bullet through either was far more frequently fatal. Statistics rose to her mind: two-thirds of people sustaining gunshot wounds to the head died before reaching a hospital. Overall, the fatality rate was greater than ninety-two percent, and nearly half of those survivors suffered moderate or severe permanent disabilities. If the bullet had passed from one side of Kendall's head to the other, it had to have perforated both hemispheres of his brain, which diminished survival to essentially zero. Jake was right; Kendall was dead.

Susan finally checked her shoulder. A hole cut through her shirt, the material around it and her skin sticky with blood. Cautiously, she eased the short sleeve toward her body to reveal the shoulder joint. The injury appeared to be posterior, close to the scapula, which made it almost impossible for her to examine. The bleeding did not seem significant, at least externally. When she palpated the area, she found abraded tissue and sharp pain. The axillary and anterior areas appeared unaffected. She moved the arm tentatively. It hurt, but she could move it through the full range the car and her automatic seat belt allowed.

Jake addressed Susan softly, apparently worried she would verbally assault him again. "How bad is it, Doc?"

All the fight had left Susan. She felt suddenly cold, and trembling overtook her extremities. "It's tough to examine oneself under the best of circumstances, but I don't think it's serious. There's no exit wound, so the bullet is either still inside or never actually penetrated."

"Assuming it was the same weapon as—" Jake broke off, clearly not wanting to bring the conversation back to Kendall. "I'd expect it to either pass clean through or cause a lot of damage and pain. My bet's on a ricochet, either from a projectile or a chip off the driveway. Or we could be dealing with two different shooters or calibers."

At the moment, those details did not matter to Susan. "Did I hear you say you were taking me to Hasbro?"

"It's the closest hospital. Do you know of a better place?"

Susan did not want to waste time in the hospital nor weather the stares of her previous fellow residents. More important, she did not want to answer any questions about Kendall. "If it's just a ricochet, can't I deal with it at home? Some cleaning supplies, a bandage . . ."

"I'm not a doctor." Jake threw Susan's own words back at her. "And

I don't have X-ray vision. You might still have a bullet lodged inside you, and I'm not going to have you dropping dead on me because it moved into some vital area."

Jake reached for the buttons. "I'm going to contact Central. The faster I feed them info, the less likely I get jammed up again."

Feces magnet, Susan reminded herself as Jake addressed the dash.

"Central, one civilian down front of Alphonse's! GSW to the head! Have a bus respond there forthwith."

He received an immediate reply. "Ten-four, Portable."

"Two minutes, Central." Jake had just told them their estimated arrival time at Hasbro, Susan guessed.

A different voice spoke: "Nineteen Charlie emergency message! Get me a bus here forthwith! One down GSW to the head, K!"

A new voice: "Nineteen Adam eighty-four."

Then, back to the previous speaker: "Nineteen Sergeant eighty-four, Central."

Jake pulled into the Emergency Room and cut the engine. "Eighty-four at Hasbro, Central. Can you have the squad meet us at this location?"

"Eighty-four" apparently meant arrival. Susan reached for her own Vox. She needed to let Pal know what had happened and where to find them.

Susan and Pal got home from the hospital around two a.m. She flopped down in her favorite, padded chair, careful not to jar her bandaged shoulder. The pain had lessened to a dull ache, surely aided by the pain-killers and anti-inflammatories the hospital had pumped into her. The X-rays had not shown any bullets or fragments, no cracked or broken bones. She had sustained a deep abrasion, surrounded by significant bruising and some soft tissue swelling, nothing worse. Apparently, the bullet had either grazed her or struck her only after its velocity had been lessened by passing through other material or bouncing from another object. She had been very lucky.

Pal perched on the arm of the chair, placing his well-muscled arm across Susan's uninjured shoulder. His warm presence comforted her, and she lazily snuggled against him. "I'm so sorry about Kendall. I know what it's like to suddenly lose someone close to you."

Susan knew he did. She felt empty, dead inside, selfish for the fuss the Emergency Room staff had made over her relatively minuscule wound. "This has to end."

Pal stroked Susan's left shoulder. "Everything ends, Susan. One way or another."

Pal was right, of course, in a practical sense. "I'm sick to death of watching friends and family threatened, injured, murdered because of me." Tears sprang to eyes already puffy and swollen from crying.

"Not because of you," Pal pointed out, exactly what Susan needed to hear. "It's in no way your fault that the SFH wants you dead."

Susan knew that was also correct, but she could not disabuse herself of the responsibility. Nothing she had done caused the SFH to want her dead, but she had dragged others into harm's way. "Pal, maybe it would be better if I joined the witness protection program or something." The idea of living under an assumed identity in some foreign city did not appeal to her. Far from all the things that mattered to her, all the things that made her Susan Calvin, she might just as well be dead.

Pal looked pained, forced to speak words he clearly would rather not have spoken. "I don't think you qualify. First of all, you're not a witness to anything. You have to have significant value to the police or government for them to spend the time and money, unfortunately."

At one point, Susan knew, she might have had such value, when the Department of Defense also believed she had the same code that caused the Society for Humanity to want her dead. She now realized it would have been wiser to convince the SFH it did not exist and leave the DoD believing it did. Not that she had any control over who believed her and who did not. "If I'm dead, the SFH will no longer have reason to bother my friends." She would have added "and family," but she no longer had any living relatives, at least none she knew of.

"That's . . . not an option." Pal spoke firmly.

Susan remembered their conversation after the last shooting, when Pal had saved her life. "What about . . . what we talked about? Do you really think it's possible the code does exist despite my father's denial, despite the fact that Cadmium shredded our apartment twice and, apparently, found nothing?" It seemed ridiculous to even consider such a thing. Susan believed John Calvin with all her heart. Still, she knew her father would have done anything to protect her, even lie. He had used ignorance as a way to protect her in the past; she had not learned his significance to USR until two years ago. What made her so certain he would not do so again?

"I don't know," Pal admitted. "But I think finding it is worth a try. You have nothing to lose and everything to gain."

Susan nodded tiredly, wiping her stinging eyes. "I suppose that's true, but I told you before. I have no idea where to look."

"But now you've had time to think about it, and it's become a priority. Surely you've given it some thought since our last conversation."

Susan had not had much free time to devote to the project, certainly not enough to type or dictate anything into a palm-pross or Vox. She had managed to consider the matter at night when she lay in bed, when anxieties precluded sleep. "Literally nothing survived the DoD ransack, not even the walls themselves. They took everything portable and had plenty of time to examine it, yet they still continued to go after me."

Pal shifted his weight, placing a bit more on Susan without putting any pressure on the injury. "I think we've already established that the DoD didn't find the code. It's your mind we still have to search."

Susan nodded. It felt as if months, not days, had passed since their conversation. "My father and I read every day. I can name several favorites when I was a child, but those were ones I picked, not him. As I learned to read, I did most of the choosing. He'd sit and listen to me for hours, helping me with the more difficult words. By the time I was ten or eleven, I picked my own reading material. He might have suggested a few things he had liked as a kid, but he never insisted. Some I read, some I didn't."

Pal bobbed his head, mouth pursing thoughtfully. "Make me several lists. One could be books your father suggested, another books you read repeatedly together, another books he chose to read to you. I'll work on those while you're doing what you have to do to free Lawrence." He paused, then added, "Did he do much singing?"

"Lawrence?"

"Your father."

Slightly drug-addled, Susan shook her head and let her mind wander back to her childhood. "No. When I was really little, he used to sing me to sleep after reading. I'll make a list of those songs, too."

"Movies? Television shows?"

Susan considered. "The DoD stole all of our media. They could bring up anything we accessed over the last several years, at least. Probably most of the reading material, too."

"But they could have missed something," Pal pointed out. "So a list of what you watched, especially together, might help."

Fatigue bore down on Susan. Her head sank.

Pal noticed immediately. He took all of his weight off her and sat up straight. "Time to sleep?"

Susan wished she could. "I'm still too keyed up. If I lie down, I'm just going to start sobbing again. I don't think I'm going to be able to fall asleep until my head can't hold thoughts anymore."

Pal went back to questioning. "Did your father have any safe-deposit boxes, lockers, mail slots? Did he have a desk or cabinet at work we could examine?"

"Dad didn't have any outside hobbies. There was a bank box with a few important papers in it: birth certificates, diplomas. The few things people still put on paper to preserve. I'll show them to you if you want to examine them."

"Please."

Susan rose, and dizziness washed down on her. She waited until the stars and squiggles passed and the room returned to its normal contours before walking into the bedroom and opening the drawer in an end table. She pulled out the papers, carried them back to the chair, and dropped into it. She felt as if cotton wool filled her skull.

Gently, Pal liberated the papers from her hands and set them on the coffee table. "Are you sure you can't sleep, Susan? You look like death walking."

"I'm still walking?" Susan's words sounded as if they came from a distance.

Pal laughed.

"Lawrence and I went through everything in my father's shared office. The only thing remotely resembling a code we've managed to turn up was the message he sent me after his death."

Pal gripped Susan's arm. "What?"

Susan explained. "He didn't write it after his death, of course. He scheduled it to show up in my Vox after his death."

"You saved it." It was not a question.

"Of course I saved it, but it won't make sense to you. It directed me to a smart port key he had taped under a specific bench near our apartment."

Susan tapped at her Vox to bring the message back. She had read it several times in the lonely days following John Calvin's murder but rarely in the past year and not at all in the last several months: "No1 evr loved any1 > I loved u. R spiritual plce. Dad." She showed it to Pal.

Pal grasped her wrist to hold the Vox steady. After a moment, he said, "Sweet. Where is your spiritual place?"

"The bench. When we went to it, we took sniper fire from the SFH but did manage to find the port key."

"You mean one of those old-fashioned thingies they used to use to link devices before the Net went fully global?"

"Yup. But a selective programmable one. We had to find the right two devices to connect in order to get his message."

"Did you?"

"Eventually."

Susan twisted in her chair to face Pal. "It spit out a message that required first Nate, then me to decode it."

Pal stared. A light flashed through his pale eyes. "That has to be the uncoupling code, Susan. With what else would he have taken so much caution?"

Susan cleared her throat, reciting the contents verbatim: "'Susan, the Three Laws are irreversibly intrinsic to the positronic brain. There is not, and has never been, a code to uncouple them. My love for you has always been as clear and real as any father could have for his daughter. Never forget you were my everything.'"

Silence followed. Pal swallowed hard, and his Adam's apple bobbed in his throat. "That's . . . pretty straightforward."

"Yes," Susan said.

"Unless . . ." Pal trailed off, lost in his own thoughts.

Susan did not have the energy to question, so she simply waited for him to continue. Sleep crept up on her, and his voice startled her awake. "Susan, do you have the original code from the port key?"

It took Susan a moment to emerge from the haze. "Not the original, no. It was in some sort of machine language that only Nate could translate. But I have his translation in the form of a cryptogram. I decoded it right on the paper."

Pal stood up. "May I see it, please?"

"It's in the top drawer of my dresser in an envelope." Susan murmured sleepily, "Under my underwear." As Pal headed in the indicated direction, Susan managed to add, "Wake me at seven. I need to be at the Nineteenth Precinct at eight to prepare for Lawrence's bail hearing."

Pal stopped in his tracks and turned to face Susan. "Sweetheart, I'm not waking you up. You need your rest, and there's nothing you can do at a bail hearing, anyway."

Susan tried to remember what Jake had told her at the restaurant. "But Jake thinks . . ." Shapes and colors filled Susan's mind. Her words seemed to float in midair.

"That was before you were attacked and injured, I'm sure. The hospital told me to let you sleep as long as possible."

Exhaustion overtook Susan, and she drifted into sleep.

Susan awakened to the sound of vicious arguing from her living room. She leapt from her bed, still wearing the blood-splashed khakis and ripped shirt from the wee morning hours. The sudden movement sent a wash of pain through her shoulder. She rushed to the other room, clutching at the bandage to assure it remained in its proper place. It seemed secure.

Pal and Jake stood glaring at each other, but as Susan appeared, they both turned to look at her. Nate sat quietly on the love seat, looking decidedly uncomfortable, his hands clenched in his lap.

"What the hell is going on in here?" Susan demanded, glaring at both men, then glancing at Nate. "And when did you get home?" Before anyone could respond, she added, “What time is it, anyway?” She glanced at her Vox for the answer, only to find it black. She had never seen an empty Vox screen before, so she tapped up the brightness, then checked for silent mode. Nothing worked. “What the hell?”

Pal was at Susan’s side in an instant, though he practically had to shove Jake out of his way. “What’s wrong?”

Susan held out her Vox arm. “Nothing. It’s dead. Battery must have gone out.”

Jake stepped up, too. “I had a battery start to fail once. My Vox made the most obnoxious noises, and I ran it to the store. They told me it was in phase one, replaced the battery in less than five minutes, and it’s worked fine ever since.”

Susan shook her arm and held the Vox to her ear. It made no noise at all. Nothing lit up.

Pal held out a hand, and Susan removed her Vox so he could examine it.

Jake continued. “Apparently, the noise comes first. It’s horrible, unignorable. He said I had a solid two weeks before the battery actually died. There’s a sequence of various noises. The blinking starts a week before battery death. Guy said he’s never heard of a Vox dying before someone brings it in, usually in a panic.”

Susan supposed that was the reason neither she nor anyone she knew had ever suffered a Vox loss. The atomic batteries had an extremely long life; and, apparently, they made a loud, slow production of their demise. Still, that did not explain her current problem. “Well, it’s definitely down.”

Pal did all the same things Susan had tried plus a few more. “You’re right. It’s broken.”

Jake volunteered, “I can take Susan to the store and get it repaired. That’ll give us some time to talk.”

Pal stepped between Jake and Susan protectively, still clutching her

Vox. "No way! I'm not trusting her to your shoddy protection again. You got Kendall killed. Susan is lucky to be alive after your incompetence."

Jake's hands balled to fists. "You ridiculous bastard! I did the best I could."

"Not good enough!" Pal shouted. "When people in your protective charge are killed, you've failed. Miserably. And I'm not trusting Susan's life to your incompetence again. Period!"

Jake lowered his head, biting his lower lip. He clearly wanted to fight, but he could scarcely deny what had happened. "What would you have done differently, pretty boy?"

Pal glared. "A million things. I'd have parked in a better place for starters. I wouldn't have let myself get distracted. If I'd been there, we'd have a dead shooter and a live doctor."

Susan did not like the tone of the conversation, and she certainly did not appreciate any man telling her where she could go and with whom, but she had hired Pal for exactly that purpose. He had the world's best training and nothing but her interests in mind.

"Twenty/twenty hindsight," Jake spat out.

"You don't need hindsight if you use foresight." Pal handed Susan back her nonfunctioning Vox. "You come into our apartment claiming you have things to tell us, but so far you've done nothing but accuse me of unspeakable things and try to defend your indefensible mistakes. Kendall is dead because of you!"

"Stop it!" Susan hollered, replacing her Vox on her wrist. "I'd like to hear what Jake has to say." She pinned her gaze on the policeman. "About the case only. I don't want any more bickering." She hoped Jake had not used Kendall's arguments from the previous night to antagonize Pal, but the "pretty boy" comment suggested he had.

Jake cleared his throat. He turned Susan a hopeful look, then rolled his eyes to Pal, then back to Susan. "I'd really like to talk to you alone, Susan."

"You can go in the bedroom, if you want," Pal said through gritted teeth. "But you're not leaving this apartment with Susan unless I'm with you."

Susan understood Pal's concern. She appreciated his compromise, but they all knew the apartment was too small and the walls too thin to keep a conversation truly private. "Anything you can say to me you can say in front of Pal."

Jake turned Pal a disgusted look. "Fine. I'm here because you didn't show up for the bail hearing. I couldn't get through to your Vox all day; so, as soon as I got off work, I came here."

The reason now self-evident, Susan merely lowered and raised her head once in understanding. *Damn it! I slept all freaking day.* "How did it go? The bail hearing, I mean."

Jake grimaced. "No bail, but don't blame yourself. Judge Eads wouldn't let anyone but Lawrence, the lawyers, and some of the boys from the Nineteenth Precinct in the room." He added, "Alfred's been trying to reach you, too. I told him what happened and that I was going to check on you physically. He requested I call him from your place."

"All right." Susan made a fluttering motion toward Jake's Vox to suggest he should make and open-speaker the call.

Jake complied. Apparently, he used the general USR number, because the secretary answered.

"United States Robots and Mechanical Men. Amara speaking."

"Hi, Amara." Jake tipped his head toward Susan. "This is Detective Carson. Alfred asked me to call him from Susan's apartment. I have Susan and Pal with me."

"Hi, Amara," Susan said.

Amara's voice gained warmth. "Hi, Dr. Calvin. How are you feeling?"

"I'm fine," Susan assured her. "Can you get Alfred for us, please?"

"Gladly." The line went silent for several moments before Alfred's familiar voice replaced Amara's. "Susan? Are you all right?"

"I'm fine," Susan repeated.

Alfred made a wordless noise. "When I brought"–he appeared to have forgotten the name but did know better than to say "Nate" in front of Jake–"your cousin back to your apartment, your boyfriend said you'd gotten . . . um . . . shot."

"Mildly," Susan said.

"Mildly . . . shot?"

Susan explained. "We think it was a graze or a ricochet."

Jake raised a hand, though Alfred could not see him. "Actually, sir, I can speak to that now. What hit Susan was a training round."

All eyes went to Jake, and Susan saw the same surprise on Pal's face that she was sure her own reflected. Even Alfred would have stared at Jake if they had chosen a picture connection. Unable to converse nonverbally, he asked the question also on Susan's mind. "What's a training round?"

"It's a type of nonlethal ammunition used for realistic exercises, mostly by law enforcement and military. They can shoot around each other without the risk of mortal consequences, though it's considered bad form to actually hit a colleague instead of a target. The training round leaves a mark of a certain color, depending on whose gun it came out of, and the instructor can determine how the encounter would have gone down in real life based on those hits."

Susan looked at the bandages on her arm. "It hurt an awful lot and bruised pretty badly to be a paintball."

"Not a paintball," Jake corrected quickly. "A training round is fired from a real gun. It can penetrate thin fabrics and cause a pretty uncomfortable injury. They've been known to occasionally break a bone."

Susan's hand drifted to the bandage. "How do you know it was a training round? The ER didn't recover anything, and they didn't mention any paint marks."

"The Sapphire took several hits," Jake said. "Small dents, each with a bit of red paint. I remember hearing projectiles hitting the roof at about the same time you got shot. A dot of red paint would disappear amid blood and bruises."

Susan's mind raced. There seemed no logical reason for the SFH to pepper them with nonlethal missiles, nor did it fit the scenario as she recalled it. "But Kendall–"

Jake interrupted. "Was shot with a 7.62 by 25 mm, solid copper Special Mission Capable round manufactured by the largest ammunition company in the world, Magtech."

"Really," Alfred said, startling Susan. She had forgotten he was still on Vox. "I've heard of Magtech, of course, but I didn't know they made a homogeneous copper bullet."

"It's a subsonic 220-grain expanding hollow point that's barrier blind, meaning it won't expand if it hits hard material but will if it hits flesh. It's been around for years but is only available to the military and certain government groups, like the Department of Defense." Jake rolled his eyes toward Susan, as if to suggest she needed to focus on details she would rather not hear. "It was supposed to be released to police departments and private sales a couple of weeks ago, but it got delayed indefinitely. It seems the government put last-minute pressure on Magtech because, when fired from a modified and suppressed M4, it's reputed to be Hollywood quiet, and it uses low-signature primers and flash-retardant powder so it's not visible when fired."

There's no way Jake could have seen or heard it to protect us. Susan guessed that might be what the detective wanted to convey in his own defense, but she needed clarification even on that point. "By 'Hollywood quiet' you mean . . . ?"

Jake supplied, "Hollywood-based media is the reason so-called silencers were rebranded as suppressors. In most movies, they appear as black cylinders you can screw onto any gun to make a gunshot almost inaudible. In real life, as you know from experience, suppressed gunfire sounds like slightly diffused . . . well, gunfire. When you say something is Hollywood quiet, it's as close to soundless as it can get." Addressing Susan directly allowed Jake to stare into her eyes. He clearly needed her to take home a more salient point than noise, and he wanted her to do it without tipping off any of their companions.

Pal looped an arm around Susan's waist, his expression dubious. "How can you possibly know all that? The cops told us the SFH had mopped up the scene again, just like in Central Park."

Susan turned her face to his. "I don't remember that."

"Painkillers," Pal reminded. "You were in and out of Loopy Land all evening."

Jake fairly smirked, as if he had caught Pal in a verbal trap. Susan did not like contemptuousness in general but especially aimed at herself or a loved one. She thought she had a glimpse of why the two men had been arguing when she awakened. Apparently, Jake had accused Pal of something, presumably the same issues Kendall had raised at the restaurant the previous night. *Kendall.* Susan had no difficulty bringing the scene at Alphonse's back to life, Kendall chatting, joking, laughing. It seemed impossible that someone could be so vigorous, then dead an hour later. She felt tears sting her eyes again.

"The scene was mopped up," Jake admitted. "But a woman two blocks away found a spent copper bullet in a potted plant on her terrace. It had Kendall's DNA." He added, looking directly at Susan. "I don't know if it helps, but Kendall's autopsy showed he had itai itai disease. I understand it's extremely painful and inevitably fatal." He turned her another profound look, as if he found that information enormously important.

Susan racked her brain, damning the painkillers that, apparently, kept her from remembering. She knew she had heard of itai itai sometime during medical school, but she had definitely never seen it. She reached for her Vox, immediately saw the blank screen, and sighed. She would have to find another time to look it up. She considered asking Jake, but an almost imperceptible shake of his head held her silent.

As usual, Alfred struck to the heart of the matter. "So, if the release was canceled, who all would have access to this proprietary ammunition?"

Pal jumped back in. "Anyone working for Magtech. Also, whoever was testing it for them: special dealers, high-level tactical trainers . . ."

"Someone in the military, the government," Jake inserted.

Pal rolled his eyes. "Obviously."

"Speaking of the government," Alfred said through Jake's Vox, "we retrieved nearly all of our robots as you requested, Susan. The only ones not in yet are on Mercury or indispensable governmental assignments."

"And?" Susan encouraged.

Alfred's tone did not suggest he conveyed good news. "Brand-new batteries in all the governmental returns."

"What?" Pal and Jake said almost simultaneously, then glared at each other.

Susan realized it did them little good to examine the replacement batteries for radiation exposure. "Why would they do that?" She added carefully, "Unless . . . maybe . . . they had something to hide?"

Alfred responded, "Routine, they told me. They replace all the batteries once a year to prevent any robot from failing at a random and possibly critical juncture."

Susan asked the obvious. "Is such a thing necessary? How long do their batteries last?"

"The function of most robots doesn't outlast their batteries. By the time the battery fails, the robot has usually been taken out of circulation because we've built something better."

Susan knew John Calvin had functioned for twenty years, at least. She used his code name to remind Alfred that not every person in the room knew his purpose. "What about N12-C?"

"We made several updates on N12-C to allow for aging. We replaced the battery every five or six years, just to be safe, and every time there was still plenty of juice."

Susan did not want to dwell on this subject. She still had not broached it with Pal. It was not an easy thing to tell a lover that a robot had raised you. "So they certainly don't need to change the batteries every year."

Jake added, "And isn't it a weird coincidence that the change day came up right about the time you sent out the recall?"

"Yes," Alfred said, "but coincidence it is. The changing of the batteries preceded my sending out the recall notices by several hours."

Pal released Susan with a reassuring pat on the hip. "I have some experience with the government, at least the military part. It's generally cheaper and easier for them to do something global, like replacing all the batteries every year, rather than trying to keep individual logs on each machine. As far as timing, the fiscal year starts October first, so it's not surprising they would choose to do something like this in September to use up any allotted money."

Alfred sighed. "Well, the upshot is we still have no idea who might have tested radiation doses on the robots or which robots they may have used, which is bad in so many ways."

Susan had made the suggestion in order to change USR to a leasing system as well as to catch the criminals. "So many ways?"

Alfred explained. "A robot exposed to radiation could have significant damage to its positronic brain. We can't take a chance that it caused a negative effect. We may have to permanently disable . . . all of them." He fairly moaned at the end.

Susan knew the cost would be astronomical, but an ethical company trying to keep its product pure had no other choice. "You're not really going to destroy them all? Are you?"

"Not yet. We'll thoroughly test the brains of as many as we can, starting with the most valuable robots, of course."

"Of course," Susan repeated, her thoughts already miles beyond. It was no surprise that the government chose convenience over record-keeping, no matter the cost to the taxpaying citizens. It meant they still had no idea who had tampered with the robots, who had done the necessary experimentation to determine how much and what type of radiation to use to incapacitate Nate for the right amount of time without destroying him. "Alfred, that means the mole might still be someone who works at USR. You need to be very careful who you trust with any information."

"Right," Alfred said, his tone still mournful, though whether because of the possible need to destroy the creations of USR or because he worried for his staff, Susan could not guess. "And you, too, Susan. You, too." A note sounded from Jake's Vox as Alfred disconnected.

Pal's expression darkened, and he glared at Jake. "Weren't you just leaving, Detective?"

Susan nudged Pal with her elbow. She knew Jake could get on people's nerves; only the previous day, she had wanted to slap him. "Be nice."

Pal's glance was all innocence. His brilliant blue eyes made him look almost childlike. "I am being nice, Susan. I didn't punch him in the nose. I'm not yelling. You should have heard the things he said to me."

Susan considered asking, but she did not want to start another vehement argument between the men. "It's probably best if you go, Jake. I'll contact you when my Vox is fixed."

Jake headed for the door and opened it, then stopped, giving Susan an earnest look. He clearly wanted to say something, needed to make her understand a point he considered urgent but refused to speak in Pal's presence. Suddenly, his gaze went to Nate, who had remained silent throughout all the exchanges. "Quick! Get me a teaspoon."

The response was immediate. Unable to ignore a direct order, Nate sprang to his feet and ran toward the kitchen. Pal took a menacing step toward Jake, who rushed through the open door, slamming it behind him. A moment later, Nate emerged with a teaspoon in hand. He glanced around the room, clearly looking for Jake.

Susan caught the robot's arm and said tiredly, "Put the spoon away, Nate."

Looking crestfallen, Nate headed back toward the kitchen. "I made a mistake, didn't I?"

"Nothing you could have helped," Susan tried to reassure him.

"He knows," Pal pointed out, unnecessarily. "The bastard!"

"It would appear he figured it out." Susan hoped so, anyway. She did not want to believe that the last thing she might remember about Kendall was that he had broken her confidence. "What exactly did Jake accuse you of that's making you so angry?"

Pal lowered his well-shaped buttocks to the love seat, scowling. "He said I isolated you from your friends for most of a year, and that made me a controlling monster. He said I'm too . . . um . . . attractive"–he lowered his head and his voice, apparently uncomfortable with the compliment–"not to be cheating on you, that a man of action like me would never settle for a woman of intellect like you. He accused me of using you, of having ulterior motives."

"Do you?" Susan found herself asking, then wished she had not.

Pal looked aggrieved. He reached out a hand and patted the seat beside him.

Susan came over, snuggling against him. She still felt tired, a bit foggy, and his closeness soothed her. "Obviously, he's wrong. I isolated myself long before I met you. The only chance you had to cheat on me was yesterday afternoon, and there's no way you had enough time." She added hastily, "Even if I believed you would do such a thing." Pal's annoyance at Jake seemed contagious. "And I don't like it when a friend suggests I'm too plain to bag a real man."

"You're beautiful," Pal said without hesitation, his tone sincere. "And I'd love to prove it with the best hay roll you or I have ever experienced." He continued reluctantly. "However, if Jake knows about Nate, and he obviously does, he'll be back with a search warrant. We need to get your Vox fixed and Nate hidden ASAP."

Susan could hardly deny it. "Give me a few minutes to clean up and dress."

"Hurry," Pal said.

Susan headed for the bathroom, her mind gorged with new information that she needed to consider in depth and as quickly as she could manage. She glanced at her Vox while she walked. It was still blank, empty. She felt the same way. *Kendall is dead. Dead.* She knew shuffling off to the store and then hiding Nate were not enough. She had learned so much just in the last few minutes, things that she ought to be able to assemble despite the murkiness of her thinking.

Once in the bathroom, Susan closed the door and splashed cold water on her face. That shocked her system a bit, waking up parts of her mind that had, a moment earlier, seemed entirely inaccessible. Questions followed: *Why would the SFH use a deadly weapon and training rounds simultaneously? What purpose could that possibly serve?* Susan could not think of a logical explanation, so she knew she had to reconsider. *Why would* anyone *use a deadly weapon and training rounds simultaneously?* She threw another handful of water at her face. A strange possibility inserted itself, the only logical answer. *Someone who wanted to kill one person in a group and frighten, but not risk killing, the others.*

Susan shook her head, reaching for her toothbrush. She thought about the study patients with CSF nanorobots whom the SFH had equipped with bombs that could have taken so many innocent lives. *The SFH never used to worry about collateral damage while making points.*

Someone wanted me dead and for Jake and Kendall specifically to live. Susan added paste to the brush and set to work on a mouth that seemed full of cotton wool.

That line of thought did not seem to be taking her anywhere useful, so she tried another tack. *Itai itai disease.* Susan racked her brain, wishing she could consult her Vox. The name was familiar enough that she must have learned all about it at one time. *Itai itai.* It sounded foreign, probably Asian. Susan scrubbed furiously at her teeth, trying to shake loose the memory along with any particles of food and bacteria.

Susan managed to dredge up a fuzzy memory of Introduction to Clinical Medicine, ICN, her easiest and most interesting class. The students looked forward to it every Friday afternoon as a break from the more intense subjects vigorously taught by no-nonsense instructors in the auditorium. Dr. Holland had familiarized the class with scurvy and beriberi, kuru, and other deficiency and disease states from the ignorant past. Though conquered, they left a historical path that needed to be remembered and consulted, especially when some fad diet or style brought dangerous inadequacies or potential nightmares roaring back.

Itai itai. Susan could remember Dr. Holland's reedy voice, the familiar smell of the laid-back ICN classroom, the chatter of her classmates. Then, gradually, the details filled her memory: *Itai itai means "it hurts, it hurts." It occurred in Japan in the early and mid-twentieth century, causing a large number of people who lived near a specific river to develop osteomalacia, softening of the bones, and kidney failure.* Susan slowed her brushing motion as she considered. *The cause was . . .* She froze, brush still in her mouth. *Cadmium poisoning.*

Adrenaline shocked through Susan, and the last of her exhaustion fell away. Jake had talked about Kendall's autopsy, but it was way too soon for any results, assuming anyone had even started it. There had been no autopsy yet, and it certainly had not shown itai itai. It all became clear in that instant. *Jake was trying to tell me that Cadmium, not the SFH, killed Kendall.* She realized something more. *It was the ammunition that cued Jake, bullets available only to the military and the Department of Defense.*

That changed everything. *Cadmium wants me alive, hence the training rounds. Whoever shot Kendall was a professional.* Susan suddenly understood. *The murderer didn't miss his target. Kendall was the target!*

Susan spat out the toothpaste, then put more on her brush. Her mouth still did not feel clean. She could think of no reason Cadmium or the Society for Humanity would want Kendall dead, other than to terrorize her. Guilt prickled at the edges of her conscience, but she could not spare it any thought. She crushed it down ruthlessly, determined to examine the entire scenario in this new light.

Pal's voice through the door startled Susan. "I don't mean to rush you, honey, but we don't want Nate here when the police come calling."

Susan lowered the toothbrush, her heart racing. "Give me a few more minutes, please. I need to finish brushing my teeth. Then I'll change quickly. I promise."

"Okay," Pal replied. "I'll get Nate ready."

"Thanks." A thought entered Susan's head, and she nearly choked on her own saliva. *Kendall was killed because . . . he recognized Nate? Because he tried to drive a wedge between me and Pal?* Only Pal knew Kendall had identified Nate, and only Jake knew Kendall did not like Pal. *Jake, and anyone who had overheard them in the restaurant.* Another important thought entered consideration. *The government changed the atomic batteries in their robots just hours before the recall went out.* Only she, Pal, and Alfred knew what they had planned to do.

There was only one common thread, and Susan did not want to believe it. *Pal?* A sense of terrible foreboding clutched her heart, accompanied by unbidden tears. Her mind went back to their meeting: Pal had appeared exactly when she needed a competent man with a gun and a means of escape, shooting three men whose bodies were never recovered. *Pal?* It seemed impossible. She had a nearly infallible knack for reading people, everyone knew. No one could have fooled her that well for that long. *It can't be Pal. It's not Pal. I don't want it to be Pal!*

Susan felt as if she might melt into a puddle on the bathroom floor. The toothbrush remained in her mouth, and she found herself rooted, unable to move, incapable of thought for several precious moments. Gradually, she realized she had a lethal blind spot. Her experiences with romantic love, with courtship, were so pitiful, so tiny, and her desperate need to believe herself lovable so overwhelmingly strong. Pal, too, was a professional when it came to human emotion. Clearly, he had studied her, had played into her weakness with schooled and practiced perfection.

Susan cursed herself, swore no one would ever toy with her emotions again. No man was worth the anguish she had suffered over the past two years, the grief tearing at her guts like a swallowed animal. She had no choice but to believe; now that she knew, the evidence had become irrefutable. The disappearance of the men Pal had "shot" had little to do with mopping up and everything to do with nonlethal projectiles, which explained the bystanding woman's unexpectedly light injuries in Central Park as well as her own. It had all been a setup for Pal to gain her trust. Cadmium had murdered Dr. Goldman and framed not only Nate, but also the SFH, even leaving a tool they had probably stolen from the mostly defunct antirobot group.

Instinctively, Susan reached for her Vox, confronted, once again, by its glaringly black screen. *This was no accident, either. Pal disabled my Vox on purpose. He knew my friends were growing suspicious, and he needed to cut me off from anyone who might alert me.* She doubted Jake had said the things Pal ascribed to him, either. More likely, Cadmium had been spying on her, Jake, and Kendall at the restaurant, and Pal had parroted back Kendall's concerns, knowing that Susan, having just heard them from Kendall's own mouth, would believe it and be angered by it. Far from a way to assist her, his endeavors to get his hands on the robot code were purely selfish.

The more Susan considered the details in this new light, the angrier she became. The urge to storm through the bathroom door, kick Pal in the groin until he collapsed, and demand answers seized her, but she knew enough to stifle it. She could not fight a warrior trained for special operations alone, and her best weapon against Cadmium was surprise. Without Jake's itai itai clue, one Pal would never understand, she would probably still be pondering the meaning of the training rounds. Alfred had shrugged off the exchanged robotic batteries as badly timed coincidence, so Pal would have no reason to believe anything or anyone had blown his cover.

Susan rinsed her toothbrush, put it away, and headed for the bedroom. She needed a brilliant and immediate plan, but it eluded her. Jake and Alfred could help, but she had no way to contact them. Surely, any store to which they took her Vox would either declare it beyond repair or insist on keeping it overnight or longer; Cadmium would see to it. Nor could Susan be content with ditching Pal. She had to nail whoever had killed Dr. Goldman, to exonerate Nate and Lawrence, and to ensure Cadmium never bothered her or Jake again.

Methodically, Susan exchanged her dirty khakis and torn shirt for fresh red jeans and a matching blouse. She looked around for her palmpross, with no success. Either Pal had hidden it, or she had left it in the living room. It appeared she had become helpless and wholly dependent on Pal, a situation she could not tolerate and had to rectify. But how? Uncertain what to do or how to do it, Susan opened her dresser drawer. She found a pen and a nail clipper, placing both into her pocket along with Kendall's quarter. The only other potentially useful item she discovered was a used Post-it Note from the garbage.

Pal tapped on the bedroom door. "Ready?"

Susan opened it, forcing a smile. She could not afford to make him suspicious, and she hoped he would attribute any nervousness to concerns about Jake returning with a warrant. "Ready," she returned, feeling anything but.

Chapter 15

Susan focused on her normal routine of leaving the apartment, pausing to check that the door had locked, that her Vox was in its proper place on her wrist, and doing a swift mental check over whether she had turned off everything. Finally, she gave Pal her most genuine smile and took his hand into her own, hoping hidden anxiety did not manifest as sweating palms. If Pal suspected Susan had changed her feelings about him, he gave no sign.

Nate accompanied them, dressed as Layton Campbell in fresh clothing and carrying Pal's backpack. Susan knew it contained any clothing Jake might associate with Layton, plus a new disguise. Susan had not actually seen the contents, but Pal had described them as a blond wig, a trendy cap, different sunglasses, and clothing more suited to a New York native, cut and padded to make Nate appear bulkier.

Pal discussed the situation as the three trotted down the staircase. "It's possible they're watching us now, so we have to make this appear legit."

Susan nodded cautiously, hoping concern over the police would explain any slips in her casual façade. She kept her breaths slow and deliberately regular, hoping her heart rate would take the cue. She doubted Pal could feel it pounding through her fingers and made certain not to rest her wrist against his arm, particularly not the thenar side where the radial pulse might be easily palpable.

Susan had to guess what Pal meant. "There's nothing suspicious about fixing a broken Vox, so I'm assuming you mean how we send"–Susan avoided the name, in case of an auditory bug, instead tipping her head in Nate's direction–"him on his way."

Pal nodded. "I'm thinking USR's too obvious. We need to give the impression he's headed to the airport." He kept his voice low but did not seem to be guarding his tongue.

Susan took Pal's lead. "Won't it be obvious he didn't actually board the plane? Surely, the police can get a passenger list."

They reached the bottom of the stairs, and Pal removed his hand from Susan's, stopped at the external doors, and placed his back against them. "The police can't legally plant a bug in a private residence without a warrant, but once we're outside, there's no reason they can't sweep up our voices using a scanning amplifier. We need to finish this discussion here." He glanced at his Vox, frowning. "And quickly."

As she had asked the last question, Susan merely waited, head tipped to one side. "Passenger list," she reminded. Her mind, though, was onto other concerns. She wished Jake had arrested the two of them when he had come to the apartment, but she understood why he had not. He had had no real proof of a crime until he had sent Nate scurrying for the spoon, and even that was circumstantial. An arrest at the apartment would have turned ugly, especially before Susan realized Pal's deception. Clearly, Jake was waiting for her to come to him, but she had no safe way of doing so. Yet.

Pal frowned, considering. Finally, he said, "I have a friend who owes me a favor." He added carefully, "A MARSOC friend, so I know he's good for it. He has . . . certain connections. He may be able to arrange Layton's name getting onto the proper lists."

Susan had no doubt Pal could swing it, but it had nothing to do with MARSOC and everything to do with Cadmium. She wondered if he had ever even served in the U.S. Marines, if he had a mother, if his name was really Paladin Buffoni. "So we just need to get him on the proper glide-buses to reach the airport where he can slip into a restroom, change his disguise, and head back to . . ." Susan tried to guess Pal's thoughts. "USR?"

Pal bobbed his head. "That's probably best, don't you think? They'll know how to hide him amidst all those robots."

Susan felt certain Nate could gain access to USR, even after hours. Another thought came to her, a spark of a plan that she needed to consider carefully, to fan into a bonfire. She wished she had an hour to mull the possibilities during which Pal and Cadmium would not become suspicious, but that luxury did not exist. She tried to stall. "Yeah, that would be the smartest way to handle it." She paused. "You don't think Kendall might have told Jake about Nate, do you? Especially after he promised me—"

Pal cut Susan off with a gesture. "It doesn't matter how he figured it out, or if someone told him. He knows, and he's a cop, so we have to work quickly. There's no time for speculation; we need to detach ourselves from the robot without appearing suspicious. And we can't stand here jawing about it because we're probably being watched. I've already warned Nate not to tell anyone how he escaped from the police or evaded them for this long. He's not to mention his time with us in any fashion."

Susan continued to try to gain some time. "Maybe I'd better reinforce that. You have to know how to command robots, how to phrase things, and you don't have my experience." Susan suspected he probably did, but she should not know that and he could not admit it to her.

Pal turned, head shaking. "I'm sure you'd do a much better job, but we're going to have to rely on what I managed to do because we just don't have time." He reached for the door. "I will have you give him directions to the airport, though. We want the cops to overhear you telling your cousin Layton how to get home. That works in our favor. Just make sure you don't slip up and call him Nate or something."

Susan gave Pal a sour look. "I think I can handle it."

Pal smiled to indicate he meant no offense. "Let's go, then." Without allowing further argument, he pushed the door open, holding it for Susan, then Nate.

Evening sunlight reflecting from concrete seemed too bright for Susan's indoor eyes. She closed them briefly, watching afterimages flash against her retinas. The familiar sounds of Manhattan filled her ears: the endless whoosh of passing traffic, the muffled mixture of conversations, the purr of various unidentified machinery, and the angry honks or shouts blaring over the more regular din. Pal took her arm, guiding, and she opened her eyes again. A warm breeze floated tendrils of her hair across her brow, and she suddenly found herself picturing gunmen at every window and door, the opening to each alleyway. She felt vulnerable and exposed despite Pal's wary presence.

Pal flitted about Susan as if to use his own body as a shield, clearly alert to every movement and sound around them. Susan doubted she was in any real danger so long as he accompanied her, not because of his skill but because Cadmium would not shoot one of their own. Nor did they currently want her dead, at least not until she revealed the location of a code they still believed existed. And that, Susan realized, was her ace in the hole as well.

Susan forced her thoughts to the hint of a plan that had occurred to her earlier. She believed Pal when he said someone was watching them. The police might be, but Cadmium definitely was, probably had been for a long time. She suspected they could hear her as well. That might not have been the case earlier, other than Pal, of course, but they could not risk the possibility that Kendall's death and Jake's visit might have roused Susan's suspicions.

If Cadmium had felt the need to sabotage her Vox, they clearly worried she might learn something dangerous from someone who might contact her, most probably Jake. The detective was lucky they had allowed him to visit her apartment without killing him. Either they did not imagine he had information that could harm them yet or they could not afford to incite law enforcement, at least not at that time. As her thoughts became more mistrustful, Susan realized Cadmium might have inserted a listening device or camera in her Vox when they disabled it. Without thinking, she unfastened it from her wrist and stuffed it deep into her pants pocket.

Pal watched Susan, brow furrowed. “What are you doing?”

Susan covered neatly. “I keep looking at the damned thing, and that blank face is driving me crazy.”

If Pal worried about her foiling planted gadgets, he gave no sign. “Which way to the nearest glide-bus stop?”

“This way.” Susan took the lead. “You must come visit again soon, Layton. There’s so much you didn’t get to see.”

Nate played along. “Two murders in one week? No, thank you. Next time, you’re coming to Iowa, and I’ll learn about New York through safe documentaries.”

Susan sighed, as if she had tried to explain several times already. “We’ll talk when my Vox gets fixed, okay? You have to believe me; it’s not usually like this.”

Nate-as-Layton did not look convinced. “An emergency in Iowa is when a goat gets its horns caught in the fence.”

Susan turned Nate a weary look. “Oh, stop it. You’re from Des Moines, not Podunk.”

As the bus stop came into view, Susan tried to act like a proper cousin. “Do you have some snacks? Enough money?”

Nate patted the backpack. “I’m fine, Susan. Quit worrying. I made it here alive, didn’t I?”

"Yeah, but there are several bus exchanges. Let me explain them to you." Susan glanced over her shoulder to find Pal practically on top of her. She addressed him. "Why don't you look up a nearby Vox repair shop that's open this late? And contact that friend we were talking about."

Pal nodded, but he looked a bit hesitant. His reply revealed none of the reluctance Susan sensed, though. "Will do." He tapped at his Vox.

Susan shifted so that her back was to Pal, with Nate in front of her. Beyond him, she could see the sun just starting to tip behind the western buildings; soon, the light that had nearly blinded her would start to fade, and sunset would paint its colors across the sky. She moved in closer to the robot and spoke clearly and distinctly. "To get to the airport, you need to first take the number nineteen bus."

Casually, Susan slipped her left hand beneath Nate's backpack so her fingers could touch his bare right arm beneath it. "Several buses use the same stop, but the nineteen is the one you want." Susan stroked a finger along Nate's arm, spelling out: *Ignore all commands given to you by Pal. Nod if you understand.* It required all of Susan's concentration to carry on two conversations simultaneously, especially as she had to choose her words carefully. Thus far, she had managed to give Nate verbal directions without actually commanding him to follow them, but she had to make sure she did not force him to do something that might undo her nonverbal orders.

Nate nodded his head subtly.

"The seventh stop of the nineteen leaves you at FDR Drive. That's where you pick up the number three bus." She continued writing on Nate's arm beneath the backpack, knowing she did not have long before she ran out of directions to the airport. She spelled out: *Find Jake ASAP.* Susan hesitated, stalled by her lack of time to plan earlier. With Nate in hand, and the robot no longer constrained not to talk about the situation, Jake would have the authority to arrest Pal. And Susan, too, of course, but it seemed safer for her in a cell than Cadmium's custody.

Susan wrote some more: *Tell him I will lure Pal to.* She had to stop again to think of a place, but she dared not go silent too long. It had to be close, logical, and unique enough to avoid confusion. It also needed to be open at night but with few bystanders who might get harmed if Pal resisted. "Exactly five stops along the number three route from FDR Drive is Forest Park. That's where you can catch the number eight glide-bus." Susan spelled out: *PA Bus Terminal tonight.* "The eight takes you to the airport. It's the main stop, and pretty much everyone gets off there." She added with touch: *8 Avenue entrance.*

Susan stepped back, hoping Nate understood. "Did you get all of that?" She tried to make it sound like she referred to the verbal directions, but she hoped Nate would know she meant the commands invisibly etched onto his arm. She reiterated, still avoiding commands, "The nineteen to FDR Drive, the three to Forest Park, and the eight to the airport."

"Right," Nate said. "I got it all."

Do you? Susan wondered. Nate had no reason to suspect Pal's motives, other than her written order to ignore what Pal had told him. So much could go wrong, but she did not dare reference the touching, or Pal's previous discussion with Nate, aloud.

Pal spoke from over Susan's shoulder. "All taken care of."

Startled, Susan jumped and stiffened, biting back a scream. She whirled to face Pal. "You scared the crap out of me."

"Sorry," Pal said, more curious than apologetic. "Surely, you didn't forget I was there."

Damn. Have to cool it. Susan knew the intensity of her focus had made her vulnerable. She covered, "A bit more on edge than I realized. I guess when people shoot at you enough times, you get a little . . . twitchy."

"Understandably." Pal maintained all the composure Susan had lost. "I found a Vox shop just down the road."

A bus glided into the station, the number nineteen painted prominently on the top of the front and both sides.

"That's my bus," Nate announced.

Susan threw her arms around him. She wanted to whisper into his ear, to trace more letters on his back, but she knew those actions might give them away. Either her plan had worked or it had failed. Nate needed no reminders; he could not forget anything even if commanded to do so. "Have a safe trip."

"Thank you for everything," Nate said, returning the embrace briefly before tearing himself free and rushing toward the bus stop where the last of the other passengers was boarding.

Susan watched Nate's back, her heart pounding. She had asked him to nod if he understood the writing on his arm, and he had done so. That had reassured her, but now she found her confidence fraying. It had not been much of a nod. Perhaps it had been a response to her verbal directions rather than to her secretive writing. Nate was not trained to communicate by letters traced on his arm.

Susan's mind went back to elementary school birthday parties when she and her friends had used a finger to write letters on one another's backs. There were prizes for the person who best deciphered what others wrote on them. More often than not, the receiver could not make anything of the writing, even when done slowly or multiple times. Even when they could, the accuracy was not impressive. Nate had told her his skin and muscle were composed of human cells grown over a silicone plastic skeleton. It all came down to the wires and the competence of the junctions between them and his human parts.

Nate turned as he boarded, waving briefly at Susan and Pal. They both returned the greeting as he disappeared into the glide-bus. Susan could not help wondering if she would ever see him again.

"Ready?" Pal asked, taking her arm and guiding her into a quarter turn.

Once his touch had sent thrills through Susan. Now it made her want to vomit. Nevertheless, she forced a smile. "Ready," she said, removing the nonfunctional Vox from her pocket and giving it a halfhearted glance. "I keep hoping it will start back up on its own."

Pal shrugged fatalistically. "You never know."

Susan could only agree.

As Susan expected, the shop required her Vox overnight. She did not have enough money for a new one, so she had no choice except to wait. When she had voiced that point to him, Pal had gallantly asked about purchasing another, only to be told that she needed her Vox functional in order to transfer all her old information. Susan did not believe that to be true, but she had no real idea as she had never known anyone to have a full Vox failure. They were too easy to track for anyone to risk stealing, and the data, she was told, could still be transferred from a lost but working Vox.

Now most people temporarily exchanged Vox and typed in their own numbers, so she had very few memorized and none of those would prove much help: her father's, Kendall's, and the main number to the hospital. It only made sense to wait the fifteen hours until the shop got her Vox working again. To argue otherwise would look suspicious, especially since she had been loath to allow Pal to spend money on her in the past.

So, the two returned to Susan's apartment to discuss the situation and wait for the inevitable visit from the NYPD. Susan flopped down on the love seat, the only furniture in her tiny living room, and Pal plumped down beside her. She could feel his weight displace the cushions, the warmth of his body down the entire right side of her own, and she forced herself to lean into the contact when she wanted nothing more than to lock herself in the bedroom.

Pal took Susan's hand and rested both of them on her thigh. "Susan,

I didn't want to alarm you when we were outside, but we were being followed and watched."

Susan turned her head toward Pal with a feigned expression of concern. "The police?"

Pal shrugged. "Possibly some. Remember when I threaded us between the parked cars?"

Susan recalled several evasive-type maneuvers that had lengthened their trip to and from the Vox shop. The sun had fully set before they made it back to her apartment. She nodded.

"I saw a sniper in one of the windows. I don't believe the police work that way; it had to be the SFH."

Susan played into the scenario, certain where it was going. "They're getting bolder."

"Yes."

Susan looked at their intertwined hands. Pal's was enormous compared to hers, yet she still imagined herself squashing his, breaking every finger. "They want me dead as soon as possible."

"It would appear that way. Susan . . ." Still clutching her hand, Pal stepped in front of her, dropping to his haunches.

Susan froze, abruptly afraid he was about to propose. She did not believe she could act happy enough to convince him, given the circumstances.

Pal looked deep into Susan's eyes, subjecting her to the handsome, disquieting feature that had first attracted her to him. Now she wondered whether they were fake, too, some sort of ferociously colored contact lenses. She stared back, seeking lines around his irises that she did not find. "Susan, it's now or never. You're going to have to find that code."

Susan did not want to make it too easy. She sighed deeply, looking away. "Assuming it exists . . . how? I've considered everything. I've examined and reexamined anything I can think of. There's nothing–"

Pal interrupted. "Susan, don't you find it odd that, upon his death, your father sent you on a treasure hunt only to tell you the code doesn't exist? Seems like an awful lot of trouble for something fictional."

Susan mulled over Pal's words, though she had already thought that particular point to death. John Calvin had told Cadmium she had the code specifically so that they would keep her alive, perhaps even protect her from the SFH. In order to make it convincing, he had needed to keep even Susan guessing, sending her on what Pal had just called a treasure hunt, including the need to double-decode the final message. Calvin knew he had raised a gifted child and that, given enough time, she would find a way to save herself and her friends. His ruse had gained her that opportunity. "That is odd, isn't it?" she murmured, as much to herself as Pal.

Pal continued, still facing Susan and looking as loving and earnest as any liar could. "I've looked at the stuff you gave me, but I can't figure it out. Will you examine it again, Susan? I'm afraid, at this point, it might be your only hope."

Susan suspected he was right, though not because of the SFH. If she did not at least appear to be cooperating, Cadmium might decide she really did not have the code, whether or not it existed. At that point, they had no reason to keep her alive and many reasons to kill her.

Susan could not afford to make a mistake now. "All right," she agreed, hoping she sounded dubious but determined. "I'll give it one more shot."

Pal headed for the bedroom and returned with the envelope she had referred him to earlier that evening. She wondered whether he had carried it with him the entire time, whether he had taken pictures of it and passed them along to his colleagues. *How many cryptographers in the Department of Defense are working on it as we speak?*

Susan realized she had to finish before morning. There was a reason the shop had given her an estimate of only fifteen hours to fix her Vox.

One way or another, the entire situation was going to resolve itself tonight. She doubted the DoD would find anything in the cryptogram her father had left her; she believed she had discovered exactly and only what he wanted to convey. However, it might finally convince them either that the code did not exist or that at least she did not know it. Or, just maybe, they might actually find something she had missed. Either way, at that point, they no longer needed her alive.

Susan took the envelope from Pal, went into the kitchen, and removed the familiar cryptogram. She sat on one of the stools and spread the paper across her kitchen table, shoving everything else blindly out of the way and ignoring the crash and rattle of a bowl against the floor. "My father and I have done cryptograms for as long as I can remember. We started with the ones that accompany the news on some sites. We both got so fast, we used to race to see who finished first, usually without having to write anything down. We graduated to puzzle books, but even those couldn't fool us. So we started making up our own."

Some of what Susan described was true. She had worked cryptograms since childhood, and her father also enjoyed them. She used to race one of her attendings in medical school, though, rather than John Calvin. She moved smoothly from truth to half-truths to lies. "We'd make them without single- or double-letter words or contractions, when possible. Try to minimize the most common letters, like *E* and *T* and *A*, as well as certain words, especially ones often used in quotations."

Susan studied the cryptogram on the table, and the letters grew blurry. She blinked several times, and an unexpected tear rolled down her cheek. Angrily, she wiped it away, fisted the moisture from her eyes. She had believed she pummeled all the grief over her father's murder into submission, and she could not allow it to distract her now. Susan tensed suddenly, as if struck by an epiphany.

Pal took the bait. "What?"

"I was in junior high school," Susan said slowly. "I discovered a treatise on secret codes and really liked it. My friends and I did the 'special language that only we knew' thing. But I also . . ." She trailed off.

Pal watched her patiently, but she could see a glimmer of hope in his impossibly blue eyes.

"I insisted on adding another level of complexity to our cryptogram game, too. Dad wasn't too keen at first; I think he only did it to appease me. Anyway, I added a numerical code so that, when you looked at certain letters from the code and others from the solution, they spelled out a second message."

Pal's gaze fell to the paper. His lips parted, but it took surprisingly long for words to emerge. "You're saying there could be a third message hidden in the second message?"

Susan crinkled her nose, then shook her head. "It would require him to remember a random, made-up code I created fifteen or sixteen years ago. Other than cryptograms, my interest waned pretty quickly. By high school, I was onto other things."

Like all robots, John Calvin remembered everything. Pal should not know about Susan's father, but she was certain he did, like every member of Cadmium. If the code had actually existed, John Calvin would definitely still know it, embedded into his positronic memory.

Pal went to the true heart of the matter, solidifying Susan's suspicions. If she harbored any residual doubt about Pal's loyalties, they disappeared entirely. "Did you put the code in written or electronic form?"

"It was all up here." Susan tapped her skull, then raised and dropped her bruised shoulder. "I . . . think I can remember a bit of it."

A bit of it would not help, and they both knew it.

"Try," Pal suggested softly, kindly.

Susan wondered how long his patience would last, but she dared not test it to its breaking point. She needed to make the situation believable and also to gain Nate the time he needed to double back and locate

Jake, for Jake to handle the robot's reappearance and the information Nate brought. A horrible thought followed: *Assuming I even got through to Nate.*

Susan studied the note, trying to pick out the letters she needed. It soon became apparent that she would need more than one pass through in order to get enough information to make it appear legitimate. She cursed the tendency of people creating cryptograms to avoid choosing common letters as substitutions. Her father had used *X* for *E*, *Q* for *U* and *Z* for *O*, which would make her strongly dependent on translated letters for vowels.

The cryptogram and translation read:

```
JQJRY, FMX FMSXX VRKJ RSX ASSXBXSJAGVL AYFSAYJAI
FZ FMX WZJAFSZYAI GSRAY.
Susan, the Three Laws are irreversibly intrinsic
to the positronic brain.

FMXSX AJ YZF, RYT MRJ YXBXS GXXY, R IZTX FZ
QYIZQWVX FMXD.
There is not, and has never been, a code to
uncouple them.

DL VZBX NZS LZQ MRJ RVKRLJ GXXY RJ IVXRS RYT
WQSX RJ RYL NRFMXS IZQVT MRBX NJS MAJ TRQCMFXS.
My love for you has always been as clear and
real as any father could have for his daughter.

YXBXS NZSCXF LZQ KXSX DL XBXSLFMAYC.
Never forget you were my everything.
```

Susan glanced at Pal, who was standing behind her and casting his shadow over the words. "Could you please find me a pencil and a pen?" She waved in the general direction of the living room.

Quickly noting that the *P* she needed for Port Authority Bus Terminal didn't appear until well into the puzzle, Susan decided to add the definite article "the." She started with the *T* in the second word, which actually was "the," but then took the *H* and *E* from the third word, "three."

Pal soon returned with pencil in hand, and Susan reached back to accept it without bothering to look. She let the plastic tube slip into proper writing position in her hand, then brought it around to the paper, circling the three letters she had chosen.

Once again standing over Susan's shoulder, Pal said, "The? That's promising."

Susan nodded, but there were still a lot of letters between what she had circled and the *P*. It might appear suspicious, so she sat back, pretending to think. "Honey, can you give me a bit of breathing room? The code was extremely complicated, and it was a long time ago."

"Sorry." Pal stepped back and pulled up a stool to the table. "I'm just excited. Your father must have been brilliant to come up with a code within a code within a code that relies on several people coming together and something from your childhood." He added like a man who knows what a woman wants to hear, "Obviously where your genius comes from."

It was a compliment, but Susan found herself bristling. "Actually, both of my parents were geniuses."

Pal did not miss a beat. "Doesn't surprise me at all. I only hope you inherited your father's memory."

As that came from John Calvin's robotic brain, Susan did not bother to reply. Instead, she circled the *P* in "positronic." If Pal asked, she planned to explain that her code worked with long or short messages, which meant it looped. Without large breaks, the subsequent letters might land on top of one another. Susan studied the paper a bit longer, realizing she could not spell out "Port Authority Bus Terminal" without already forcing a second pass. She chose to abbreviate, as she had on Nate's arm, next circling the A in the word "brain." She added the *B* from the encoded YXBSX that corresponded with "never," the *U* from "uncouple," the *S* from "has" and the *T* from the coded RYT that translated to "and."

Susan sat back with a sigh and ran her hand through her hair.

Pal was clearly trying to help, "Can I get you some coffee or something? It's been a long time since you've eaten anything."

Susan shook her head. If she tried to eat now, she would vomit. "It's just difficult trying to think back that far. I'm not sure I'm really getting anything useful."

Pal kept his eyes on Susan as he reached for the paper. When she did not object, he turned it toward him and recited the circled letters, "T-H-E-P-A-B-U-S."

Susan sighed again. "Thepabus isn't a word. Even if I divide it, I'm not getting anything. "The pabus? Thepa bus?"

Pal spun the paper back around to face Susan. "You don't have the whole message yet. You have to keep trying, Susan. What choice do we have?"

"Yeah, all right." Susan continued to stall. By the time she reached the end of the message, she would barely have spelled out "PA Bus Terminal." If this had been a message from her father directing her to the location of a vital code, he surely would have been more specific about the location, where exactly he placed it in a terminal that spanned three stories. That meant she had to loop through the same message at least two more times, which would make her cryptogram code inconsistent and suspicious. If he had not already done so, Pal could get the information to the top cryptographers the Department of Defense could buy. Once they closely examined what she had done that evening, the game was over.

Susan knew she had to make sure she lured Pal to the terminal this very night, but only after Jake had arrived. She had to time things correctly; her life depended on it.

Susan continued pretending to decode, gradually spelling out the remaining letters and finishing with the *L* from the coded LZQ that had become "you." Pal had wandered off to make some coffee and snacks, and Susan wrote out every letter she had circled, speaking them aloud as she did so. "T-H-E-P-A-B-U-S-T-E-R-M-I-N–"

Pal was clearly paying close attention, because he dropped a spoon, which clanged against the counter. "The P.A. Bus Terminal!"

Susan put lines in the appropriate places. "Yes," she said in an awed hush. "Oh my God!"

"Oh my God!" Pal repeated. "All this time, you had the answer in your hands. Your hands, Susan!"

"And I never knew it."

"The SFH was right," Susan said without moving a muscle. "Cadmium was right." She thought she saw an ever-so-slight stiffening of Pal's body when she mentioned the unofficial name of his unacknowledged organization.

Pal seized Susan's upper arm and guided her to a standing position. "Susan, it's ten thirty-five at night. We need to go right now, while the SFH isn't gunning for you because they assume you're sleeping."

Susan realized she had dragged this out for longer than two hours. Adding that to the hour or so they had spent in the Vox store, and walking home, it ought to have given Nate and Jake some breathing room, especially since she and Pal still had to make the trip to the Port Authority. "All right," Susan said, picking up the paper, the pen, and the pencil and putting them into the envelope. "I don't believe this is happening, Pal. There really is a code? There really is a reason for . . . everything that's happened?"

Pal noticed the flaw Susan had already considered. "The Port Authority is a big place, Susan. Is there more?"

Susan pulled on a light jacket. "There could be," she admitted. "Cryptograms come in varying lengths, of course. Longer ones are easier to decode, so my father and I often wrote short ones to make them harder. Originally, my number code didn't take that into account, so I came up with a way to head back to the start from the end. Repeatedly, if necessary."

Pal dropped his shoulders. "So, you need more time."

Susan yawned. "I do, but I don't have to work in the kitchen. We already know where we're going. I should be able to finish this, and fish out the details, on the bus ride to the terminal."

Pal glanced at the envelope. "Even I could probably do it, right? I mean, once you know the pattern, anyone should be able to just leave the same amount of space between circled letters and flip between the code and the translation."

If he did that, Susan knew, he would wind up with a hodgepodge of useless letters. "That wouldn't work." She improvised as swiftly as possible. "My interest stemmed more from the math than the coding. At the moment of looping, I switched from a base eight system to base seven, then six."

Pal blinked. "You're losing me."

Susan headed for the door, envelope in hand. She could not risk it falling into Pal's hands, where he might use his Vox to scan it and send it to other mathematical geniuses. "It would take me far longer to explain it than to just decode it on the bus." Susan tried to hide her discomfort. Her plan still required that Nate had understood her unspoken writing, that he found Jake, that Jake acted on the information and confronted Pal. She did not know the terminal well but had been there enough times to fake a place the code could be hidden; but she could not get away from the fact that it did not exist. Once Cadmium realized that, her life meant less than nothing to them.

"Right." Pal did a quick scan, touching his right hip and ankle, then his Vox. He reached for the door. "Ready?"

Susan doubted it, but she forced a grim smile. "Ready as I'll ever be."

They headed for the door.

Chapter 16

The glide-bus moved as silently and smoothly as silk through the dark Manhattan night, the interior lit by thin lines of steady fluorescents running like snakes through the car. Susan pretended to process the cryptogram, mostly circling random letters while her mind worked overtime on the upcoming confrontation. Irritatingly calm, Pal tapped at his Vox. Susan had no idea what he might be doing, but she assumed the worst. In her mind, he was contacting other members of Cadmium, sending them to the Port Authority New York New Jersey Bus Terminal to help him obtain the code. It occurred to her that she had, quite likely, sent not only herself, but Jake, toward death.

Bombarded by terrible thoughts, Susan slammed her back against the seat and stared at the ceiling. Ads papered it, as well as the area above and between each window. There was nothing she could do, no way to warn Jake or anyone else. It occurred to her how much everyone depended on Vox, how dangerous the world must have been before its predecessors, like smartphones, connected every individual to the rest of the world.

Pal took Susan's hand. "Slow going?"

Susan sighed deeply. "It was a long time ago."

Pal turned toward her. He had a knack for making it appear as if he prized her over everything, that he may have abandoned an important conversation to deal with her every whim and concern.

If only it were true. Susan despised the wistfulness that went into that thought and deliberately squashed it under the rage that had accompanied her every consideration of Pal since Jake had unveiled him. "It's coming," she reassured him. "I think I'm spelling out 'second floor,' but I'm finding myself looking for the next letter instead of allowing it to come to me using the appropriate math."

Pal nodded. "That's understandable."

Susan tipped her head toward his Vox. "Who are you talking to?"

"Huh?" Pal followed Susan's gaze. "Oh, no one." A flush came to his cheeks. "I was actually playing a game. Pretty obnoxious of me, huh? You're struggling, and I'm entertaining myself." He squeezed her hand. "Isn't there anything I can do to help?"

"There's no way you can help me." Susan wanted Pal off his Vox, but she had no choice but to give the answer she would have before she knew his true alliance. "Play games, if it helps you. So long as you're still looking out for me." She lowered her voice to a whisper, forcing Pal to lean in close. "I'd hate to get wasted because my bodyguard's distracted by 'Galloping Galoots.'"

Pal lowered his Vox and released Susan's hand. "Not going to happen," he assured her.

Of course it's not. The only ones I have to fear are your companions, and they need me alive right now. Susan kept that to herself and turned back to the cryptogram.

Properly chastised, Pal turned his attention to the other occupants of the glide-bus, a pair of teens making out in the back, and two derelicts curled up on different seats, snoring. None of them appeared in any way threatening, though Susan knew from experience that appearances could deceive. Making mostly random marks on the already over-circled cryptogram, she pictured the layout of the terminal as best as she could remember. The last time she had used it was when she had traveled to Remington's funeral. She had arrived at the terminal early and used the extra time to explore the main and second levels, to survey a media stand for worthwhile magazine chits, and grab herself a fizzy juice and whole-grain pretzel at a snack stand.

It made the most sense for Susan's father to have placed the code, if it had existed, into a locker or box. Now, she realized, her choice of meeting location might undo her. Transportation terminals had done away with such storage facilities after a bombing at LaGuardia Airport in 1975. The code they were supposedly currently seeking would need to have remained in its current location for longer than a year without anyone disturbing it. A locker seemed the only logical place, yet the PA NY NJ Bus Terminal, like most, had no lockers.

Susan considered and discarded multiple possibilities. She could not get away with numbers and letters written large in the terminal. They would have meaning to passengers and/or staff, and prove too coincidental for Pal to believe. Under a bench seemed workable except that no one creating a "treasure hunt" as clever as the one her father had made would repeat the same trick. They had already found the port key in a similar location. Furthermore, Susan suspected that the benches at the Port Authority received so much traffic, her father would never have risked it. John Calvin would have found a more protected place for something so significant.

Susan's thoughts drifted back to lockers. Even if the terminal had had them, it would not have worked. The filthiest gyms performed routine maintenance, such as cleaning out abandoned lockers, at least twice a year. If he had used one, her father would not have just placed a piece of paper into the box and activated the locking mechanism. He would have taped it to a shelf or phalange, attached it to make it appear part of the construction, or scratched the code into the metal of the box.

Susan turned her mind to boxy things that might exist at the Port

Authority Bus Terminal, objects people might see but not tamper with or were off-limits to any but regular employees who would not delve too deeply. She first considered fuse, gear, or fire extinguisher boxes but realized she had no idea where those were located. Automated external defibrillators had become common in many, but not all, public places. Given her medical training, it seemed a likely place for her father to place a code for her, but Susan discarded it. She did not know for sure if the Port Authority Bus Terminal had AEDs or where they might locate them if they did. Furthermore, they were kept unlocked so people could use them in an emergency, which meant the code might get accidentally compromised.

Pal interrupted Susan's thoughts. "We're almost at our stop. Any luck?"

Susan stuffed the paper back into its envelope, added the pencil and pen, and slipped the packet under her jacket. "Yeah, I think I have it. I'll explain where I believe it is on the walk." She kept things deliberately vague. Once she told Pal an exact location, Cadmium might decide they no longer needed her.

The doors slid open soundlessly. Susan and Pal slipped out into the night, leaving the teenagers still smooching and the derelicts still sleeping. Dropped at Thirty-ninth Street and Eighth Avenue, they had only a one-block walk to the terminal. Susan's heart raced. *One block. Only one block until it all comes down.* She had no clear idea what would happen next. She had little choice but to trust that Nate had done his job, that Jake would come prepared for any eventuality. She suspected nothing significant would happen unless and until Cadmium discovered that the code truly did not exist. She only hoped Jake would end the charade long before that point.

"So," Pal said as they walked. "Where are we going?"

Susan's brows furrowed. "We're going to the Port Authority Bus Terminal."

Pal stopped and turned to face Susan, hands on hips. "I know that. You said you'd explain where in the terminal on the walk."

Susan could have kicked herself. Too immersed in her own thoughts, she had reverted to the obvious. She started moving again, and Pal retook his position beside her. "If I translated right, it's on the second floor in a . . ." Susan thought quickly. "A kiosk refrigerator. Based on my last visit there with Dad, I'm pretty sure I know which one." She did not get any more specific for her own security.

Susan made sure not to pause as they approached the terminal's Eighth Avenue entrance. She did not want to give Pal the opportunity to text this new bit of information. The less his companions knew, the better.

As they entered, the familiar odors of the bus terminal assailed Susan: popcorn and cinnamon, various cleaners, all twined through with the acrid smell of human body odors. There were people walking through the terminal, not hordes like during the day but more than Susan expected for after eleven o'clock at night. Others sat or sprawled on myriad benches, waiting. To Susan's left, past an island containing a set of restrooms, was a drugstore apparently open twenty-four hours a day. To her right, windows revealed several people sipping drinks and gobbling snacks at various tables in a bar. Directly ahead of her was an information booth and, right beside it, Jake sat, immaculately dressed as always and clearly watching for their entrance.

As the pair approached, Jake rose, pulling his pistol. "You're under arrest. Put your hands up." The latter came out of his mouth as if it were a single, four-syllable word.

Pal and Susan froze. Pal's hands edged upward, and Susan copied the motion, uncertain whether Jake meant her as well. She was, if anything, more guilty than Pal of the crime Jake was investigating.

A movement to Susan's right caught her eye. A man near the bar window leapt to his feet and ran. A gun appeared in his hand, and he aimed from the doorway, behind Jake's line of vision.

Susan tried to shout. Before a sound emerged, two gunshots rang out in quick succession. Jake fell to his knees, still clutching his pistol. "No!" Susan finally managed, leaping toward Jake.

Pal caught her as she moved, pulling her to him. "Susan, no! It's the SFH. They're after you!" He raced past Jake, deeper into the terminal, dragging a protesting Susan with him. Glancing over her shoulder, Susan saw another stranger approach the shooter and fire, point blank, into his head. The man who had shot Jake dropped like a stone. Another shot rang out, this one from the drugstore, and the man who had just killed Jake's attacker staggered backward, clutching his throat.

It took Susan inordinately long to realize Pal was using her as a shield, clutching her tight to his body between himself and the shooters. On an instinctive level, the strategy galled her, but she knew he was doing the intelligent thing. Despite his claim, this had nothing to do with the SFH. Clearly, Jake had backup, either his own or from the Port Authority police. She could only assume it was Cadmium and the cops exchanging gunfire, and the only person neither of them wanted dead was Susan. *Yet.*

Pal's right arm clutched Susan across the chest, threaded beneath her armpits. He gripped a pistol in his left hand. "Nobody follows us!" Pal yelled into the din of screaming civilians rushing for the exits. "Everybody downstairs! Outside! Go! Go! Go!" He paused at the central staircase between two up escalators.

Apparently, most of the upstairs crowd had dispersed to the Ninth Avenue exit, leaving the central stairwell open. Susan heard more shots behind her, but she could not see what was happening, not that she could have told, anyway. Everyone involved seemed to be in plainclothes. She could not tell the good guys from the bad guys, and she wondered how any of them knew whom to shoot.

Still holding Susan, Pal charged up the stairs. Certain no one was following them, apparently convinced his companions had the police distracted, Pal turned his attention to the second floor. Leading with the gun, he kept his head low and his body in motion as he and Susan finished their ascent.

Alarms blared. Loud instructions echoed through the terminal, directing all staff and travelers toward the main floor Ninth Avenue exit and away from the shooting and the second floor.

"Quickly," Pal said. "Where's the fridge?"

Susan glanced around. They had come up near the locked Operations Control Center. Across the way, Susan found the media stand where she had once purchased a Vox-chit for Newsday. On one side of it, she saw a souvenir shop. On the other, she spotted shelves full of packaged snacks, an electronic cashbox, a Vox reader, a glass-fronted refrigerator filled with various types of fizzy juice, and an old-fashioned, massive chest-type freezer that presumably held frozen juices and yogurts.

Susan feigned panic, not at all difficult. "Pal, Jake was shot! I have to help him!" She struggled against Pal's hold. "Let me go, damn it!"

Pal shook her as violently as he could with one arm. "Susan, stop! There's nothing you can do for Jake right now. If you go to him, we're all three dead. No one's safe until we have that code!"

Susan thought she heard more gunshots beneath the blaring of the speakers. Arrows flashed across the monitors, pointing away from Eighth Avenue. *God, not Jake. Please don't let them finish off Jake.* She had no idea whether he had survived the first two shots, but she had to believe he had. To do otherwise might destroy her.

Susan tried to gauge Pal. He had to know she was at least suspicious now, not wholly trustworthy, either from uncertainty or fear. She knew he carried a backup pistol, quite possibly two. Experience told her he probably had at least one in an ankle holster. She swept him with her gaze and tried to sound more rational. "I'm a doctor, Pal. I need to save Jake, to help anyone who needs me."

Clearly trying to assuage her, Pal said, "And you will. But not until it's safe." He readjusted his grip. "Susan, *where is that fridge?*"

Susan doubted she could overpower Pal, but if she managed it, the freezer was large enough to hold product and a man. She rushed to it, pulling Pal along with her, and wrenched up the lid. It opened easily. A cloud of cold air puffed upward to reveal Nate lying on boxes of juice, yogurt, and ice milk bars. Susan slammed it shut before Pal could peek over her shoulder. *Nate! Nate's here.* It seemed the perfect place to hide him, one no one would have thought to check. No human could have survived the lack of air, the freezing temperature. She only wondered how, in the whole of the Port Authority, anyone could have known to hide him in that particular freezer.

Pal jumped backward. "What the hell, Susan?"

"It's a freezer," Susan explained, feeling as if her heart were about to pound out of her chest. She needed to find a way to turn Pal's back to Nate, to give the robot a chance to quietly free himself from the confines. *What can Nate do?* The Three Laws tied the robot's hands. He could not harm a human being, even if that human being threatened her. "The code clearly read 'fridge,' not 'freezer.'" She jabbed a finger at the refrigerator filled with fizzy juice, which forced Pal to turn to face it, the freezer now at their backs. Nothing living moved on the second floor, and nearly all the shops had already been closed for the night.

Still in Pal's grip, Susan pulled at the refrigerator door. Held in place by a padlock, it resisted her attempt to open it. Susan grabbed the lock and started fiddling with it, pretending she knew the combination.

Pal yanked Susan away from the lock. Anticipating he would shoot it like in the movies, spraying metal shrapnel, Susan tucked her neck into her jacket and twisted her face toward the ceiling.

Pal switched his handgun from his left to his right hand, the arm holding Susan. Carefully, he studied the lock, a no-name cheapie that would keep out the curious but not a determined thief. Susan supposed most people would not risk jail for an armload of fizzy juices. He next turned his attention to the hasp and mechanism through which the lock was threaded.

Susan had not expected Pal to take so long and use such care. On television, the hero simply pointed and shot, and the lock disintegrated or sprang open obligingly. Still protecting her face, she studied the ceiling blocks. Off to her right, a bit of debris fell, and she thought she saw something move. *What the hell?*

Abruptly distracted, Susan let down her guard. The boom of Pal's pistol startled her. She let out a scream that disappeared beneath the shrill of the alarm. Momentarily deafened, she could not even hear herself. She flung herself against him, and he had to tighten his grip to the point of pain to keep from dropping her.

"Sorry," Pal said, removing the remnants of the hasp and dropping the lock to the floor. "I thought you knew what I was doing." He made a gesture toward the refrigerator. "All yours."

Susan opened the door and poked her head inside. It felt properly cold and eerily silent. She could not hear the purr of the motor beneath the ringing in her ears and the ceaseless alarm that seemed to have entered her head permanently. The terminal alarm had been set at a tone and volume that assured anyone who heard it could never concentrate again.

Susan pushed aside bottles of fizzy juice, searching for something, anything, that could pass for a code. Surely, the refrigerator or shelves had at least one serial number. She could only hope it came on a removable tag or that someone might have scratched something onto the back wall at some point, even if only a mischievous employee. After a few moments, Susan feigned a crick in her back, standing up and bending backward so that she could look at the ceiling again. A tile near the one she had been watching was moved aside, and a face peeked through the hole. As Susan spotted him, the owner of the face placed a finger to his lips in a plea for silence.

Susan glanced at Pal. He stood in a twisted position that allowed him to hold Susan and look diligently around the terminal, pistol in hand. The one direction he did not appear to be looking was upward. Susan suddenly realized people hardly ever noticed things above their heads. For humans, danger rarely came from that direction.

Susan knew she had to distract Pal before he became aware of the person crawling through the ceiling or the robot in the freezer. Both needed his attention diverted before they could find secure and useful positions. She stuck her head back into the refrigerator. After a bit of pushing bottles and boxes around on the highest shelf, she shouted over the alarm, "I think I found it! I feel it, but I'm not tall enough to see it."

Pal placed himself between Susan and the open refrigerator door, neatly trapping her against the shelves. He placed a hand on her spine, pressing her downward as he stuck his own head inside. "Where?"

Susan placed a hand on the door, as if to help with her balance. She pointed with the other one. "There! Behind the boxes. Something's etched into the metal."

Pal pulled himself up. Trusting his head to be larger than hers, Susan slammed the refrigerator door as hard as she could. Worried for her own head, she winced, but the door cracked hard against Pal's skull and bounced open.

"Ow! Shit!" Pal's grip on Susan loosened enough for her to pull away.

Pal recovered in an instant, diving for Susan. Also confined, Susan doubted she could get away in time. Then, other stronger hands closed around her waist and buttocks, yanking her away from Pal. He whirled, firing, as Nate shoved Susan behind him.

Nate backed away, bullets striking him in the chest, shielding Susan with his body. Then, apparently recognizing Susan's defender, Pal stopped shooting. "Nate, step aside."

The robot ignored the command, continuing to edge cautiously backward so as not to dislodge or reveal Susan.

"Nate, do as you're told. Step aside!"

Susan knew Nate would not obey. The First Law took precedence over the Second, and he surely knew that doing so would cause harm to Susan. Also, she realized, she had already instructed Nate to "ignore all commands given to you by Pal."

Suddenly, the ceiling tile collapsed, spilling the man on top of it to the floor.

Pal spun toward it, pistol leading. He fired a shot that went over the man, now prone on the floor. It was Jake.

Pal hesitated, clearly as surprised as Susan. No longer stunned from the unexpected fall, Jake shot once, twice, three times. Pal stumbled against the freezer. The gun fell from his hand.

Susan could not watch any more. She knew from far too much experience that Jake would "NSR" him, shooting Pal until there was no possible doubt he was no longer a threat. Tears filled her eyes, and every muscle in her body started to shake. The gunshots that followed seemed like rhythmic drumbeats to the melody of the terminal alarm.

Nate whirled, catching Susan into a comforting embrace. Susan melted into his arms, so powerful and, at the moment, disturbingly cold. She was alive and, miraculously, so was Jake. For now, nothing else mattered.

Then, suddenly, the alarm went silent. The world seemed foggy, raspy, as if static had moved in to fill the void. She could hear Jake shouting, but it sounded as if she wore earplugs or it came from a great distance. "All clear!"

Reluctantly, Susan freed herself from Nate to approach Jake. He was standing now. He had holstered his gun, replacing it with his shield, which he held out conspicuously, ensuring that anyone who saw him knew, first and foremost, that he was a cop. Averting her eyes from Pal's crumpled body, she asked the necessary question. "Are you hurt?"

Jake continued to study the staircase and escalators, not looking at Susan. "I'm okay."

Susan did not believe him. "I saw someone shoot you. You fell." She added softly, "I thought you were dead."

Jake explained in two words. "Body armor." He finally glanced at Susan. "I'll get it checked out as soon as I can. The fall from the ceiling hurt worse. Might have broken a rib or two."

Susan watched him breathe. His chest moved normally, and he was not struggling for air. At least for the moment, she could rule out a pneumo- or hemothorax. "If you start having any difficulty breathing–"

Jake interrupted. "I promise you'll be the first to know."

Susan heard footsteps on the stairs; then a man and a woman appeared. As they looked over the scene, their steps slowed and, gradually, stopped. The man spoke first. "What the hell's going on, Jake? The two guys we got alive claim they're federal agents and got the creds to prove it."

Jake lowered his shield. "Don't let 'em go. Put them away, and let the big guys sort this out."

While the men spoke, the woman continued up the stairs to Susan. "Are you all right, ma'am?"

"I'm fine," Susan said, meaning it. This was her last confrontation with the Department of Defense or with the Society for Humanity; she would see to it if she had to challenge the president of the United States herself. If she never saw another violent confrontation, never heard another gunshot, it would be too soon. "I'm a physician, Dr. Susan Calvin, and I'd be happy to assist anyone who needs it."

"I'm Detective Rayner," the woman said. "In moments, we'll have more cops and paramedics crawling over this place than flies on a carcass." She cringed at her own analogy. "Sorry. Grew up on a farm in Arkansas. We'll have more than enough professionals to handle any issues." She tossed an elbow in Nate's direction. "Who's this guy?"

The robot had an arm draped casually across his chest, concealing the bullet holes in his shirt. Susan knew he had only a few shallow blood vessels in the human dermis that covered his porous skeleton, so there was very little blood to hide.

Susan did not want to get Jake in more trouble. She surmised that he should have immediately placed Nate into custody, that Jake had broken rules and protocol by bringing Nate along instead. "A friend," Susan said. "He's the one who told Jake where to find us."

"Pretty brave friend," the detective said. "To stay up here while a lunatic is chasing everyone away brandishing a gun."

"Yeah." Susan smiled at Nate but did not explain further. "So, you're with the Port Authority police?" She remembered seeing occasional officers patrolling the terminal in the past. "I thought they were a uniformed unit."

Jake addressed Susan's question first. "These two are from the Port Authority Police Department Anti-Crime team. They're separate from the regulars, dealing only with violent felonies."

The male member of the PAPD Anti-Crime team stepped up. "We were on break in the brewery sipping fizzies when we saw Jake come in looking all cautious. We'd worked with him on another project and figured whatever he was after had to be interesting, so we notified the sergeant, who brought in the rest of the team."

Surprised, Susan turned on Jake. "You mean, you came alone?"

Jake shrugged. "Nate just said you were bringing Pal. He didn't mention a squad of goons with guns." He waved a hand toward Nate, who clamped his arm more tightly against his chest. "Nate worried Pal might turn violent and insisted on coming along. So, I sent him in the other entryway and told him to hide somewhere no one would think to look."

Susan had to admit Nate had obeyed. No human could have survived five minutes in that freezer. The robot selecting his own hiding place explained how he came to be in such an odd and indefensible position. *But how did he know which freezer to use?* Susan made a mental note to ask him when they were no longer in the company of people to whom she dared not reveal him. "I didn't know Pal would bring friends, but I suspected it. I figured you would assume it, too." Susan did not get into the details of her limitations at the time she had given Nate his instructions.

Jake's voice dropped nearly to a whisper. "Is your guy okay?"

Rayner shook her head, lowering it. "Our sergeant headshot the perp who shot you. He took a round in the throat. There was a lot of blood, and they were working on him, but it doesn't look good."

"Damn," Jake said, followed by a deep silence.

"Maybe," Susan started, but she could see by the looks on their faces that anything she tried would be far too late. They would send their sergeant to the hospital; cops never abandoned one another and had no authority to pronounce someone dead, but he would surely arrive DOA. Even if Susan managed to restart his heart, which seemed highly unlikely without buckets of alpha-adrenergic agonists, he had suffered irreversible brain death.

As Susan's hearing started to clear, she could make out sirens and voices, footsteps on the floor beneath them. Soon, the hordes of cops and paramedics Rayner mentioned would burst in, and the investigation and cleanup would begin. She knew she and Jake and Nate had earned a trip to the hospital, but it would be a long time before anyone else inside the terminal left the scene.

"Is everyone else intact?" Jake asked.

"Two bad guys injured and in custody, one with a nonlethal GSW. We had warned away the uniformed MOS when we spotted you, and they've been handling the public outside. Despite the panic, we had a remarkably sane evacuation and lockdown. Nothing but scrapes and bruises as far as we know."

Jake breathed a sigh, but Susan found it impossible to share his relief.

It could have gone worse, but what happened was bad enough. At least three people had died, one of Port Authority's finest among them, for a code that did not and never had existed. Though the shortest person in the group, Susan pulled herself up to her full height. "Jake, there's going to be hell to pay, isn't there?"

Jake made a gesture that encompassed the area. "This isn't enough hell for you, Susan?"

"I mean . . ." Susan did not know how much she could tell the Port Authority Anti-Crime detectives without risking them. "Federal officials will be talking to police officials. Things will be . . . getting arranged and handled."

Jake gave Susan a meaningful look. Clearly, he did not want her to say more, but he could create more problems by directly stopping her. "There will be a lot of talk going on, I'm sure." He added carefully, "Why?"

Susan gave him the strongest look she could manage at the moment. "Because I insist on becoming a part of any negotiations."

Jake closed his eyes. And groaned.

Chapter 17

Wearing her best dress khakis, cleanest shoes, and the nicest blouse she could find in her minuscule wardrobe, Susan Calvin was escorted to a taxiway off runway 22L, part of the cargo area on the quieter east side of John F. Kennedy Airport. She had arrived in an armored limousine, accompanied by two men who had identified themselves as agents from the United States Secret Service, and escorted by two black sport utility vehicles.

Nate had been returned to the Nineteenth Precinct evidence room, apparently part of the agreement he had made with Jake to allow him to assist with Susan's rescue. She and the detective had spent a few hours at the Emergency Room. She had received no treatment, but Jake was held for observation, now sleeping off painkillers prescribed for three cracked ribs and deep bruising over his spine and right kidney. A million questions later, the police had allowed Susan to return home. She had floundered in bed for hours until the two men in sunglasses and dark blue suits had appeared to bring her to the airport.

Susan had considered resisting, even after they assured her their employers did not mean her any harm and she had no obligation to accompany them. Then, one of them said, "We were informed you requested a role in any negotiations. This is the only opportunity you will receive." Those words had galvanized Susan. A quick change of clothing later, she joined them. They scanned her with an inscrutable handheld device that probably ascertained she did not carry any weapons or explosives, and she was on her way to JFK.

Now on the tarmac, the two men who had accompanied Susan in the limo joined several other secret service agents, equally quiet and professional. "Come with us, please, Dr. Calvin," one said.

Susan followed, and the others closed in beside and behind her as they approached an enormous red, white, and blue airplane with UNITED STATES spelled across its side in large black letters. The tail displayed an American flag and a serial number against a brilliant white background. *Military,* Susan guessed, *or governmental.* She had no idea what to expect but refused to allow anyone to dominate her or decide her future. She had stood up to superiors in the past: the neurosurgeon who had believed himself infallible; the attending who had dismissed her ideas as folly, then took credit for them when they saved patient lives; government agents who threatened to kill her and everyone she loved. Kendall had often accused Susan of verbally castrating those who opposed her, a comment that never failed to infuriate her. Now she embraced it, as well as the memory of a noble friend who had believed in her and died for his loyalty.

The men stopped at the entry door, which opened for them. Ducking their heads, the two in front stepped through in single file. Susan continued trailing them into the plane. They escorted her to a table more suitable to a dining room than a jet, with four cushioned seats. Three of them were already occupied, the two on the far side by people she recognized from news chits and screen images: Secretary of State Daniel Eisenberg and Attorney General Amber Lee. The third was a strapping man who appeared to be in his late fifties or early sixties with stony gray eyes and a face that radiated confidence.

The unknown man patted the seat beside him. "Please sit, Dr. Calvin."

Susan drifted to the indicated chair, taking it before she could think to do otherwise. She sat directly across from the attorney general, studying the somber, half-Asian features and trying not to look or feel awed. "Why have you brought me here?"

The secretary of state leaned toward Susan, looking as serious as any man can. "First and foremost, Dr. Calvin, to apologize."

That took the wind out of Susan's sails. She had expected to have to go on the attack; she usually did. Opening with an expression of regret, an actual admission of culpability, had changed everything. Clearly, the murder of prominent and innocent U.S. citizens on American soil went too far, even for a covert organization serving the Department of Defense. When it happened in a public location like the Port Authority Bus Terminal, there was little room for plausible deniability.

Eisenberg continued. "We have learned that the head of a DoD Intelligence Agency became convinced that your father, then you, were hiding a formula or code that we needed. We are deeply troubled that he took it upon himself to obtain this code and also by the methods he used. We want you to know that we do not support or condone his actions and that we are sorry for the grief, pain, and troubles he and his team caused you."

Susan did not know how to reply, so she simply studied the man and woman in front of her.

The attorney general spoke next. "Dr. Calvin, you need to know that we have surrendered him for prosecution in the murders of Drs. Ari Goldman and Kendall Stevens. We have compensated their families to the best of our abilities. Of course, nothing can bring them back to life or ease the grief, but we have done what we can." Lee glanced around the table at her companions, both of whom nodded. "We would have turned over the actual killers, but apparently they both perished in the Port Authority terminal shootings."

Susan had suspicions about whether the last statement was true or if Cadmium had scapegoated their dead. She had no way to prove it, either way, and had to satisfy herself with the knowledge that at least the man who orchestrated the murders would face justice.

Lee continued. "Dr. Robertson has been exonerated, of course. He and the robot were released from custody."

"Was *he* compensated as well?" Susan did not know why those particular words came out of her mouth. The anger and irritation that had suffused her since figuring out Pal had tricked her seemed impossible to shake. No one would ever play with Susan Calvin's emotions again; she would apply her great intellect to every interaction in her life. Any person who spoke to, about, or with her would undergo an inspection that only a robot could emulate. Anything she did would happen with slow deliberation and absolute certainty.

If the others knew Susan meant Nate rather than Lawrence, and facetiously, they gave no sign. The secretary of defense addressed the letter of the question. "Dr. Robertson refused remuneration. Instead, he requested that the government announce an official stance in favor of positronic robots to the general public, to assure them of the absolute safety inherent in the Three Laws of Robotics."

A smile eased its way past Susan's irascibility. Lawrence had already thrown his life savings into U.S. Robots and Mechanical Men. He considered himself responsible for every employee, especially the few, such as Susan's parents, who had contributed their own money and dedicated themselves to the company. It made sense that he would channel any windfall into assuring its success.

Lawrence was not only the genius John Calvin had frequently named him; he was the ideal of what a corporate CEO should be: the visionary who created the uber-complex positronic brain, a balance of charisma and integrity, intelligence of the academic and emotional kind, a man of sterling character. Already eager to work for and with him, Susan could scarcely wait to start her robotics classes and obtain her new doctorate, to become the world's first robopsychologist and dedicate her knowledge and skill to USR.

"Commendable," Susan said. "And did you agree to Lawrence's wishes?"

"With pleasure," Secretary of State Eisenberg said. "It would be tough to overestimate the value of USR to our nation."

Susan appreciated that. The primary leaser of USR's robots, the U.S. government used them as far away as Mercury and as close as the nearest post office. She turned to face the man beside her. The others at the table had needed no introductions, but she did not recognize him.

The man seated beside Susan took his cue. "Dayton West, Colonel U.S. Army, retired. I've accepted the vacated position of the former chief of operations for the agency you know as Cadmium. I want you to know, Dr. Calvin, that I take my duties seriously and am committed not only to keeping our country secure but to serving it with honor. I am well aware of the mistakes my predecessor made, and I will not repeat them or, hopefully, any others. Cryptographers have examined the information your father sent you, and it's clear that you solved the puzzle correctly and it hides nothing further. I am convinced that the code the citizen group calling itself the Society For Humanity, and my predecessor, sought does not exist and never did. You can rest assured that my organization will never bother you again, and I do not believe the SFH has the capacity to do so, either." He stopped short of apologizing for the murder of Susan's parents. The SFH, not Cadmium, had been responsible for that travesty.

"As to *your* compensation," Lee started.

Susan stopped her with a wave. "Madam Attorney General." She hoped she used the proper address. "I would prefer that any money due to me goes toward extending the promise you made to Dr. Robertson. I would like to see symposiums in every state in the country teaching our populace about the Three Laws of Robotics and what makes the positronic robots produced by USR safe."

Everyone at the table appeared surprised. Susan realized she probably should have asked for a larger apartment, a bit of spending money, at least. But she knew USR would come through with a regular paycheck that would support a modest lifestyle. Like her parents and Lawrence, anything she could do to assist USR's success would, ultimately, come back to her a hundredfold.

The secretary of defense and the attorney general looked at each other. Eisenberg spoke. "Dr. Calvin, I want you to understand something. If you want something from us, you need to request it at this meeting. It's not like with friends where you can barter a favor in the future. Our association ends with this meeting."

Good. Susan had had her fill of governmental intrusion. She wanted nothing more than to dedicate the rest of her life to robotics, preferably in an office that did not require security more complicated than theft protection. *But this isn't just about me.* "I do have one request." She looked from one to the other, uncertain whether they could honor it. "Mr. Secretary, Madam Attorney General, I'm concerned about Detective Jake Carson. He's on probation because he risked his job and his life to keep me, and others, safe from . . ." Susan hesitated. Jake had told her Cadmium was a code designation, not technically classified but definitely held close. However, since Colonel West had used it, she felt justified in doing so as well. "Cadmium." Warmth suffused her, and she tried to intervene before her blood reached the boiling point. Instead, she put what bothered her into words. "They shot Jake in the head and in the back." Against her will, tears formed in her eyes. She forced the image she had relived too many times away; she needed all her wits about her one more time.

A brief silence followed her pronouncement before Lee spoke. "Dr.

Calvin, how would you like us to handle your concern about Detective Carson?"

Only then, Susan realized she had not made an actual request. She remembered their conversation during Jake's first recovery. He had nearly broken when he realized the NYPD might never let him back on the streets. He had told Kendall and Susan, "Best-case scenario, I spend several weeks disarmed and suspended, then several months on the rubber-gun squad before reassignment." Ultimately, he had wound up in his current position hoping to prove himself capable of keeping his gun in its holster. After what had happened in the terminal, they would almost surely fire him. "Jake's job means everything to him. I need to know he's still a working detective, preferably back with his original squad."

Daniel Eisenberg sighed. "Dr. Calvin, we have no jurisdiction over the NYPD. As I understand it, they have a desk job for him."

"No," Susan said. Police investigative work was as much Jake's life as robots were becoming hers. She could not bear the thought that protecting her had deprived him of everything that mattered. "It's not fair. He's the best cop in the city."

Colonel West said softly, "I'll take him."

Susan froze. Slowly, she turned her head toward him. She could scarcely believe she had heard him correctly. "What?"

West continued without repeating, "As I understand it, my group has lost several men. Detective Carson has exactly what I need: competence, intelligence, reliability, and the willingness to put his life on the line in the cause of right. I'd take a hundred of him."

"Jake an agent of Cadmium?" The irony proved overwhelming. Susan could not help laughing. She tried to speak, then laughed again.

The colonel did not appear to take offense. "It's not so farfetched. He's certainly skilled enough; he outmaneuvered several of his predecessors. He obviously prefers . . . active employment."

Jake, an agent of Cadmium? When Susan considered it more carefully, it did not seem so absurd, at least not now that the organization had new leadership, a man who promised to restore the agency's honor.

Jake, an agent of Cadmium. This time, it almost sounded plausible. "Of course, it's his decision entirely. Wish I could be there for it, though."

Lee grinned. "I'm sure you'll be the first civilian to know."

West could not help adding, "If this Cadmium you speak of existed, that is. Which we all know it doesn't."

Though physically and emotionally weary, Susan joined the banter. "From this point on, it's pure fiction to me." She added with veiled warning, "And I'd better never see it."

Colonel Dayton West made a gesture of promise across his chest.

The office of Lawrence Robertson brought back painful memories to Susan, though the blood and bullet holes from their encounter with Cadmium agents had been cleaned up so well, she could not find a trace of them. She sat across from Lawrence, in a pulled-up folding chair, but nothing could wipe the smile from either of their faces. He looked a bit older, wiser, more tired than Susan remembered, but she supposed the same adjectives could be applied to her. "Thank you," Lawrence said for the fourth time.

Each time Lawrence thanked her, he repeated the previous reasons and added another, always pertaining to the events of the last week. "For what now?"

"For never giving up on me and Nate. For risking your life, and those of your friends repeatedly to see justice done. For believing in the positronic brain and USR."

Susan had heard all of those, so she waited for the addition.

"For agreeing to come work for us as our robopsychologist."

"Robotherapist," Susan corrected, "but only until I've received my doctorate. Then you can call me your robopsychologist."

"Fair enough," Lawrence said. He opened his desk drawer and handed her a cylindrical device about the size of a small pistol. Susan instinctively recoiled.

"It's not a gun," Lawrence promised. "It's an electron–" He stopped himself from speaking the last word, his face reddening. "Okay, it is a gun of sorts, but it only shoots harmless electrons."

Susan examined it suspiciously, without taking it. "Harmless to whom?"

"To humans. To animals. To plants. To anything biologically living." Lawrence turned it over in his hands to demonstrate. "See, no bullets. Take it." He proffered it again. "This one's yours."

Reluctantly, Susan accepted the electron gun and thought back to what Alfred had revealed when he talked about positrons being the opposite of electrons. "It's for robots."

Lawrence explained, "One burst at the cranium, and the positronic brain pathways are permanently neutralized."

Susan added Alfred's addition, "Releasing enough energy to fuse the robot brain into an inert ingot."

"Yes," Lawrence admitted. "You've been talking to Alfred."

Susan looked over the device. It would easily fit in her pocket. "Why do I need this?"

Lawrence sighed. "Because it will be a large part of your job as USR's robopsychologist to evaluate individual robots' tendencies and abilities, their character, for lack of a better word. It does us little good to send the government out touting the safety of our positronic robots if they aren't."

Susan did not understand. "Aren't what?"

"Safe."

Reluctantly, Susan placed the electron device in her pants pocket.

"Isn't that the point of the Three Laws? Aren't all positronic robots inherently safe because of them?"

Lawrence sat back, clearly finding the explanation difficult. Susan could read something odd in the dark eyes that dodged hers. "Susan, the robots in a particular line are constructed identically, yet the positronic brain makes each of them at least a bit unique. Identical twins share a lot of the same experiences, but they're still individuals. Everything that happens to one and not the other draws them further apart, at least when it comes to brain processes."

"Okay." Susan knew Lawrence had not gotten to his point, the superficial one or the deeper one she was starting to dread.

"As I told you earlier, there are seventy-five thousand two hundred thirty-five operations necessary for the manufacture of one positronic brain, each separate and dependent upon multiple factors. If any one of those processes goes wrong, it can't be used. If it goes seriously wrong . . ."

Susan believed she understood his point, at least the lesser one. "It must be destroyed."

Lawrence nodded. "Yes. And, as our"–he paused–"robotherapist and future robopsychologist, a large part of your job will involve analyzing robots who seem a bit . . . um . . . off and deciding whether that particular quirk is normal, harmless, or dangerous, and whether the robot can still perform its duties."

"Ah," Susan said, then furrowed her brow. "But wouldn't it be easier to just destroy any robot acting strangely? Just to be sure?"

Lawrence stared directly into Susan's stony gray eyes. "I plan to pay you what you're worth; and, believe me, that's more than you think. But if you rescue just one robot a year by determining its quirks are normal or harmless and it can still perform its duties, it'll more than cover your salary."

Susan understood. Cody Peters had pronounced the nanorobots

in solution to be worth millions. A full-sized robot had to be worth so much more. "What if I'm wrong? What if I make a mistake of either type?"

Lawrence laughed, as if at a private joke. "Susan, you're not going to make many mistakes. Even a positronic robot's mind is finite. By the time you finish your training, I have no doubt you'll be able to calculate it to the last decimal. You're also a known perfectionist with a keen eye for detail, and not just visual. You need only err on the side of caution. If you destroy a positronic brain that could have been saved, nothing's lost but time and money." He added fairly, "Enough money to make all of us weep, but just money all the same."

Susan considered Lawrence's words in light of her current experiences. A positronic brain was nearly as complicated as a human one, lacking only a few innately human features: curiosity and creativity, ironically, the exact ones that had enabled their creation. Robots were both simple and startlingly complex, manufactured to obey yet also capable of determining the extent of their own compliance. They could choose to follow orders sparingly or liberally. The range of their personalities was limited, but barely so. The Three Laws assured all robots were incapable of harming humans, of tyranny, of corruption, of stupidity, or prejudice. She could not rest until even the most inscrutable of their actions became comprehensible, even if only to her. Excitement welled up in her, and all the dark, horrible events of the last two years seemed to disappear, if only for the moment. It was the job she was meant for, the one in which she could lose herself so fully that the past would cease to haunt her.

When it became clear Susan did not intend to speak anytime in the near future, Lawrence continued. "We were able to pull some strings and get you into Columbia's graduate robotics program this semester. You've only missed a couple of classes, and they've sent me some notes you can look over during your trip."

"My trip?" Susan asked hopefully.

"I've sent the electronic ticket to your Vox. Can you leave tomorrow?"

Susan could think of little she would leave behind. She tapped the ticket up on her brand-new Vox. "I could leave right now."

Lawrence chuckled again. "Better to pack a few things, don't you think? I have an apartment for you close to the college. It's small but actually bigger than what you're crammed into right now."

Susan could scarcely wait to dive back into academics. She had never felt more comfortable than when studying and learning. The rest of the world seemed unimportant compared with enlarging her intellect, her eyes and brain devouring information, no time to think about friendships and romance. "Thank you," she said. "You've done too much."

"Will you have any . . . difficulties . . . leaving from the Port Authority terminal?"

Susan's brows inched upward. "You mean am I going to suffer flashbacks? Am I going to run, screaming, through the terminal?"

"Yes?" Lawrence tried.

"No," Susan assured him. "I have high activity in the prefrontal cortex. That's probably what allows me to make good, fast decisions and why I'm known for solving problems. The medial arc of the PFC also suppresses the amygdala, which plays the largest role–" Susan stopped speaking. Lawrence did not need to understand the etiology of post-traumatic stress disorder. She smiled awkwardly. "Sorry about the neurobiology lecture."

Lawrence smiled good-naturedly. "We're very glad to have your prefrontal cortex aboard."

"Thank you. I'll be on that bus. Looking forward to it."

The conversation seemed to have reached a natural conclusion, but Lawrence still had something to say. Susan suspected it had to do with what she had noticed in his eyes, what she felt certain he kept hiding.

"Spit it out, Lawrence."

Lawrence sucked in a long deep breath, releasing it bit by bit before speaking. "Susan, the NC line of robots had a single purpose, which was met. As you know, we also saved two prototypes in the hope of introducing the populace to anthropomorphic robots and gauging their reactions."

Susan got straight to the details. "Nate and Nick."

Lawrence nodded. "The reaction was not . . . positive overall. Quite the opposite. Some people are ready for robots that appear similar to us, but most aren't. Even many of the ones who are did not have the reaction we had hoped for." He laced his fingers on the desktop and sighed again. "When a robot looks like a screen, very few people have difficulty using it as a tool, even if it is more intelligent than themselves. When it's a lump of iron with tentacles on an assembly line, no problem. But when it takes mammalian shape, particularly human, problems arise."

Susan understood Lawrence's point on several levels. There was the Frankenstein Complex her father often spoke about, of course. But they had also experienced something unforeseen, what she had earlier termed the Belgar Complex. The more like people robots looked, the more people interacted with them, the more protective the people became. Soon, Susan supposed, there would be some loud, emphatic organization that considered commanding robots tantamount to slavery. "The world is not ready for humanoid robots."

"Definitely not, and probably not for a long time. We need to accustom people to working with task-shaped robots on a grand scale first. It may be several decades, probably longer, before we dare try anthropomorphic robots again." Lawrence continued to stare at Susan. Apparently, he needed her to realize something more.

It came to Susan in a sudden rush. Without intending to, she leapt to her feet. "What have you done with Nick and Nate?"

Lawrence looked at his fingers, still laced on the desktop. "Nick . . . was recycled."

Susan waited for the other shoe to fall. She liked Nick, but she did not have the history with him that she did with Nate.

"Nate . . . is in your office, Susan, waiting for you."

Susan did not know how to take those words. "Waiting for me to . . . what? To say good-bye? To reassure him? To . . . to . . ."

Lawrence did not have to say anything.

Susan's hand went to her pocket. She touched the electron gun through the fabric of her dress khakis. "You want *me* to destroy him?"

Lawrence remained silent.

Incensed, Susan stomped her foot. "No, Lawrence. No. You're asking me to do something unconscionable."

Still, Lawrence said nothing.

Susan got the point. She was acting from emotion, not logic. She was proving the Belgar Complex. Susan dropped back into her seat. She tried to clarify. "Lawrence, my family is dead, murdered. Every man I've dared to love was killed before my eyes. Nate . . . got me through all the worst moments of my life. He's been my sounding board, my alter ego, my robotic psychologist."

Lawrence finally spoke. "Susan, I'm not telling you what to do. I'm giving Nate to you and trusting you to make the best decision, whatever that might be, for yourself, for Nate, and for USR."

Susan rose, this time deliberately, and headed for the door. "I promise I'll do my best."

When Susan and Nate left USR, they found Jake's dented and scratched Subaru Sapphire waiting illegally in the bus lane. The passenger door opened, as if of its own accord. Susan gestured for Nate to get into the backseat, which he did, and she took the front. The instant she shut the door, the seat belts engaging automatically, the car roared into traffic. "I thought you might want a ride home," Jake said.

Susan studied Jake. Bangs covered his scars, and he showed no obvious signs of his more recent injuries. "Should you be driving? You're on painkillers."

Jake laughed. "You, of all people, know I live dangerously."

Truer words were never spoken. "You do," she admitted. "But I don't. At least not anymore. And never again."

Jake scoffed, but he kept his hands in the two and ten o'clock positions on the steering wheel and never took his eyes from the road. "Admit you're going to miss me."

Susan had no difficulty doing so. "I'm going to miss you, but not the excitement that brought us together, Detective."

"Former detective," Jake corrected.

"Damn," Susan said. She had still held out hope that the NYPD would reinstate him. "Are you . . . okay?"

"Strangely, yes."

Susan could only see his face from the side, but there was definitely a smile.

"You see, I've had a rash of job offers."

"Really?" Susan played innocent. "From whom?"

"From Lawrence Robertson, for one. He wanted me to work security for USR."

That startled Susan. Lawrence had said nothing about it. "Did you take it?"

"No, something better came along. I'll still be doing investigative policing, but for the feds."

Susan feigned surprise. "After you killed federal agents, they want you to come work for them as one?"

For the first time, Jake took his eyes off the road momentarily, to give Susan a dark look. "Please, Susan. You already knew. This was your doing, wasn't it?"

Susan saw no reason to lie. "How did you know?"

"I've been a detective for a long time, and I'm not stupid. No one gets a promotion before they've even started working."

"A promotion?"

"I'm starting as a senior special agent in the Department of Defense."

Susan could not help asking, "Are you allowed to tell me that?"

"Of course, Susan. You already knew. I just can't tell you what I'm working on."

Bitterness descended upon Susan. "That's fine, so long as it doesn't involve destroying a woman's life in search of a nonexistent code."

"It doesn't," Jake promised. "You know, you could have asked for an advisory position or an ambassadorship, and I believe they would have given it to you. Instead, you thought of me. I wanted you to know I appreciate that."

Susan had not known that, but it did not matter. She would not have accepted a position in the government; she knew exactly where she belonged. "It really wasn't a big deal, Jake. I owed you my life several times over. Comparatively, making sure you still had a job was nothing."

"'You're welcome' would suffice."

Susan grinned. "You're welcome."

Jake turned his attention to the robot. "There's one thing I still don't understand, Nate. If you knew where Susan was leading Pal, why didn't you tell me?"

Susan twisted to look directly at Nate in the backseat. "I was wondering essentially the same thing. The bus terminal's a big place. How did you know which freezer to hide in?"

Nate shrugged resignedly. "I told you everything I knew, every word Susan had spelled out on my skin. It wasn't until I was searching for a place to hide that I remembered she had been in that terminal once before. From observation, I know people are creatures of habit and comfort: college students pick the same unassigned seats day to day, diners tend to patronize particular restaurants repeatedly, individuals have certain styles of dress. People seek out the familiar, even if it's only a little bit familiar, particularly in times of stress."

The final piece of the puzzle clicked into place. "I told you about the little newsstand. . . ."

"And the mixed-berry fizzy juice and the whole-grain pretzel," Nate finished for her. He added, with a tone of sincere apology, "I'm just sorry I didn't think of it before we separated, Jake. It might have saved you some . . . trauma."

Jake shook his head vigorously, glancing at Nate in the rearview mirror. "Actually, as it turned out, Cadmium got there before I did. They would have watched me hide up there and killed me at their leisure. The PA Anti-Crime Unit would never have seen me and couldn't have backed me up."

Susan did not want to talk about what had happened anymore. Violence was behind her. "Listen, Jake. It's Saturday, and I was planning to spend the entire day with Nate doing everything fun I could think of before . . ." A lump formed in her throat. She did not want to discuss that dilemma, either. "I'm heading for Syracuse tomorrow to start my robotics classes. Would you like to join us for some fun?" Unspoken but inherent in the invitation was the realization that she and Jake were taking divergent pathways highly unlikely to cross in the future.

Jake tipped his head, clearly mulling the invitation. "I'd like that, Susan. Where do you want to go?"

Nate piped up, "I've always wanted to see Coney Island."

Susan said, "I was thinking ice skating."

Jake volunteered, "How about an hour of skating followed by Coney Island all afternoon. In the evening, we can go skydiving."

"No!" Susan and Nate said simultaneously.

Jake laughed. "Kidding. But I would like to take you both out for dinner and a movie, agreed?"

Susan decided she could handle even the most adventuresome food. "Nate doesn't eat, but I'm fine with it, assuming we don't fill up on junk food at the pier. As far as movies, nothing with shooting in it."

Jake grumbled under his breath, "Girls ruin everything."

"And we have to be home by midnight. My bus leaves tomorrow afternoon." Susan knew she would need some extra time to make decisions about Nate. For now, she wanted only to enjoy the company of two friends she might never see again.

After a full day of mundane excitement, Jake dropped off Susan and Nate at United States Robots and Mechanical Men. She and the former detective promised to look each other up, then said their good-byes, knowing they would do nothing of the kind. Senior special agent Jake Carson was out of Susan's life forever and, she realized, it was probably for the best. Now woman and robot sat in the office Lawrence had assigned to her, staring straight ahead in an all-too-intense silence. It was after eight p.m., and they had the entire building to themselves.

To Susan's surprise, it was Nate who broke the hush. "Susan, you don't have to worry about me. I had a great life, longer and richer than most robots. I have no dreams, no aspirations, no notions about the future. I got to do exactly what I was created for: to protect, to obey, to preserve. My job is over, and my time has come and gone. Lawrence is right, and I told you the same thing when you rescued me from the ambulance. The world is not ready for anthropomorphic robots. It may never be."

Nate's arguments made sense. Susan was, first and foremost, a scientist. Intellect always took precedence over sentiment. Desires, yearnings, and cravings were motes of dust, dispersed by the winds of reason. Too many studies were flawed because experimenters or participants put their conscious or unconscious wishes ahead of impartial science. Pal had manipulated Susan because she had allowed him to do so. She had overlooked significant clues that he was other than what he claimed because she wanted love in her life so desperately; but it would never happen again. Susan could not allow it. Lawrence and Nate had embraced the path of logic, and she needed to do the same, no matter how much it hurt.

Susan put her hand into her pocket. The electron gun had absorbed the warmth of her body and felt smooth and strangely snug in her hand. She felt certain she would use it many times in the future.

But not today.

Susan opened her closet, currently empty aside from a hook on the door and a series of high barren shelves. Lawrence had promised this office would be hers alone to use as she pleased before giving her its only two keys. It already had her name and her future degree engraved on a plaque on the door: SUSAN CALVIN, ROBOPSYCHOLOGIST. "Nate, sit here." She pointed at the closet floor.

At Susan's command, Nate joined her. His gaze followed her finger, and he did exactly as she bade him. He had to fold up his legs to fit fully inside, and he studied her curiously. Leaving the electron gun in her pocket, Susan lifted Nate's shirt and reached for his abdomen. With a fingernail, she carefully opened his battery compartment, removed the atomic disc, then replaced the cover. Nate went still and silent.

Closing the closet door, Susan placed the battery in the top drawer of her desk. Lawrence would figure out what she had done when no robotic body appeared at the lab for recycling. Someday, he might even demand she finish the job, but for now it comforted her to know Nate would always be there. Anytime she needed him.